Jack Blank
AND THE IMAGINE NATION

Jack B

AND THE

IMAGINE

Aladdin / NEW YORK   LONDON   TORONTO   SYDNEY

lank
NATION

by
matt myklusch

ALADDIN

An imprint of Simon & Schuster Children's Publishing Division
1230 Avenue of the Americas, New York, NY 10020
First Aladdin hardcover edition August 2010
Copyright © 2010 by Matt Myklusch

For information about special discounts for bulk purchases, please contact
Simon & Schuster Special Sales at 1-866-506-1949 or business@simonandschuster.com.
The Simon & Schuster Speakers Bureau can bring authors to your live event.
For more information or to book an event contact the Simon & Schuster Speakers
Bureau at 1-866-248-3049 or visit our website at www.simonspeakers.com.
Designed by Karin Paprocki
The text of this book was set in Goudy Old Style Regular.
Manufactured in the United States of America
0610 FFG
2 4 6 8 10 9 7 5 3 1
Library of Congress Cataloging-in-Publication Data
Myklusch, Matt.
Jack Blank and the Imagine Nation / Matt Myklusch. — 1st Aladdin hardcover ed.
p. cm.
Summary: Twelve-year-old Jack, freed from a dismal orphanage,
makes his way to the elusive and impossible Imagine Nation, where a mentor
saves him from dissection and trains him to use his superpower,
despite the virus he carries that makes him a threat.
ISBN 978-1-4169-9561-6 (hardcover)
[1. Superheroes—Fiction. 2. Identity—Fiction. 3. Robots—Fiction. 4. Giants—Fiction.
5. Orphans—Fiction. 6. Virus diseases—Fiction. 7. Science fiction.] I. Title.
PZ7.M994Jac 2010
[Fic]—dc22
2009023533
ISBN 978-1-4169-9563-0 (eBook)

FOR REBECCA,

WHO SAID,

"MAYBE YOU'RE A NOVELIST."

Contents

A Boy Named Jack

The sign in front of St. Barnaby's Home for the Hopeless, Abandoned, Forgotten, and Lost read CRUSHING THE SPIRIT OF CHILDHOOD SINCE 1898. Appropriately, the words were carved in stone because it wasn't ever going to change. The faculty at St. Barnaby's turned bright-eyed children into boring adults, and they did it quickly. Usually before the children finished kindergarten. Some of the kids managed to hold out a bit longer, but it was not a fun place to grow up. Not at any speed.

St. Barnaby's was planted not so firmly on a stretch of swampland near the New Jersey Turnpike. Every year like clockwork, the building sank a few feet deeper into the muck. The foundation couldn't be fixed, but new floors and taller towers were constantly being added onto the roof to make sure the place stayed above swamp level. For an orphan growing up at St. Barnaby's, staying above swamp level was about as much as you could hope for in life.

From a window on what was currently the building's top floor, a boy named Jack stared out at another icy, gray morning. It was that time of year again when Christmas was already gone, the new year was already here, and there was nothing left but winter. Any holiday spirit still lingering around the orphanage was being stuffed into cardboard boxes for storage in the basement, and the drab hallways of St. Barnaby's seemed more bare than ever, now that their decorations were gone. With every box that disappeared down the cellar stairs, Jack wondered just how he was going to make it through another year in this place.

It wasn't Christmas presents that Jack was going to miss about the holiday season. St. Barnaby's offered nothing beyond what little was donated, and bullies like Rex Staples always stole the good stuff from kids like Jack, anyway. No, what Jack would miss about the holidays was the way people acted during the month of December. The way everyone smiled more. People were nicer everywhere, even to him. It was like having friends for a couple of weeks every year. That was important because it was the only friendship that Jack ever really got to know. In every school there's always one kid who gets picked on more than anyone else. At St. Barnaby's that one kid was Jack. The teachers did nothing to stop this behavior. They even encouraged it, seeing it as payback for all the trouble Jack caused them on a regular basis. He wasn't very good at doing what he was told and following the rules. Jack's teachers often told him that was probably why his parents had abandoned him in the first place.

Jack never knew his parents. He had been left on the steps of St. Barnaby's twelve years ago and found in a cradle with the name "Jack" written on the handle. Nothing was known about him beyond his first name, and no one ever cared to ask too many questions either. Whenever Jack had to write his name on a test or homework assignment, he just wrote "Jack" and left the rest blank. Jack Blank. After a while the name simply stuck.

Jack actually felt like he had a great deal less going for him than the other orphans at St. Barnaby's did. None of them had any family, but Jack didn't even have a name. He had no sense of who he was, even on the most basic level. He was a blank slate. The boy with the made-up name that didn't mean anything.

The other orphans at St. Barnaby's had a few ideas about where Jack had come from. The latest theory was that Jack's parents were sewer mutants who threw him away because he was too ugly, even for them. Jack wasn't really ugly at all, but that didn't stop the other children from calling him names like "Sewer Slime," "Ugg-Boy," and Rex's personal favorite, "Weirdo Face." No one ever accused Rex of being terribly creative or clever. Even so, the names didn't have to be clever to hurt Jack's feelings. Jack hated not knowing who he was or where he came from. He hated the stories the other kids would make up about him all the time. He never once suspected that the truth was something that would make even their wildest stories seem boring and tired.

The truth about Jack was nothing short of extraordinary. The truth was a beacon calling out to things both terrible and wonderful on the far side of the world. The truth was the reason why that icy, gray morning was the last one Jack would ever spend at St. Barnaby's Home for the Hopeless, Abandoned, Forgotten, and Lost.

CHAPTER

1

Unreal Tales #42

"Jack Blank, I know you're in there!"

Mrs. Theedwheck's shrill voice pierced the air, hitting Jack's eardrums like a siren. She stood at the library door, holding her yardstick.

Mrs. Theedwheck was a tall, spindly old lady with horn-rimmed glasses and a wound-up knot of frizzy gray hair. As usual, her face was scrunched up like she'd smelled something funny and didn't like it one bit. Jack could not imagine a Mr. Theedwheck existing anywhere in her past, present, or future.

Mrs. Theedwheck never went anywhere without her trusty yardstick. Ever. It was pretty much part of her hand. With it, she was ready to strike out at any and all knuckles and backsides within a three-foot radius, whether they deserved it or not. Mrs. Theedwheck had carried a ruler for years—*years!*—before a fellow teacher at St. Barnaby's finally suggested the yardstick. She tried it out once and knew right away that there was no going back. The yardstick was her weapon of choice, and she wielded it like a ninja master.

Jack ducked farther down behind the bookcase. Mrs. Theedwheck was bluffing. No way she knew where he was. No way.

"Don't *make* me come in there, Jack," she warned. "I want you out here by the count of three. Front and center, young man! One!"

Jack held his breath as Mrs. Theedwheck tapped her yardstick against the open door. She *was* bluffing, right?

"Two . . . ," Mrs. Theedwheck continued.

Jack cringed as she stepped through the library door and reached for the lights.

"Three," she said flatly.

Fluorescent lightbulbs flickered on, and Mrs. Theedwheck started searching the library. She reached out with her yardstick, banging on tables, bookshelves, and countertops. She was like a hunter flushing out her prey. Jack braced himself for the inevitable yardstick thwacking.

Jack heard Mrs. Theedwheck tap her yardstick on different surfaces. The tapping got closer and closer until Mrs. Theedwheck slapped the yardstick down on a bookcase right next to Jack. Jack was certain he was caught, but Mrs. Theedwheck let out a frustrated "Hrrmmph!" and turned, storming out of the library, shutting the lights off behind her. She hadn't seen him. He was safe . . . for now.

"Whew!" Jack said to no one in particular as his entire body unclenched.

Jack was hiding because it was the day of a big field trip. Ordinarily, children Jack's age looked forward to field trips. Jack would have looked forward to them too if he'd been allowed to go. Every time he got on the school bus, however, it broke down. Or it went too fast. Or the radio would mysteriously switch stations from the news channel to rock stations, hip-hop stations, and baseball games without anybody touching the dial. The teachers didn't know what these strange things were all about, but they knew they only seemed to happen when Jack was around. So whenever there was a class trip, Jack was sentenced to stay home doing chores until the other students got back. Mrs. Theedwheck had prepared an endless list of tasks to give Jack, but she had to find him first.

All things considered, it wasn't the worst thing in the world to miss a St. Barnaby's field trip. It wasn't like the students ever went to cool places like planetariums or museums with dinosaur bones or anything like that. As Jack hid in the library stacks, the other orphans were heading to the Mount Dismoor Maximum Security Prison. H. Ross Calhoun, the head disciplinarian at St. Barnaby's, always planned trips like this to scare the children into behaving and to show them where they'd end up if they didn't straighten up and fly right. Jack was glad to be missing this one. He was pretty sure that if he did go to the prison, Mrs. Theedwheck would have chores for him to do there, too. She'd volunteer him for everything from scrubbing iron bars on jail cells to helping train the guard dogs by giving them something to chase down and chew on.

Mrs. Theedwheck was also planning to get a look at the prison's new electric fence and bring the old one back with her. The electric fence that currently lined the perimeter of St. Barnaby's was practically an antique that shot sparks out when it rained. All the teachers agreed it was time for an upgrade, and even a hand-me-down prison fence was an improvement on the current state of affairs. Jack suspected that if Mrs. Theedwheck got him out to Mount Dismoor, she'd put him to work carrying sections of fence out to the bus in the pouring rain. That is, unless Rex and his buddies managed to stick him in a jail cell first. Either way, it would have been a pretty bad day, so he was quite happy to be right where he was, stowed away in the St. Barnaby's library with a stack of old comic books.

A few years back, the comics had been left in the orphanage donations box along with some old toys and secondhand clothes. Comic books were pretty high on the list of banned items at St. Barnaby's and were meant to be thrown out immediately. That's what would have happened if Mrs. Theedwheck had taken care of it her-self, but she hadn't. She had told Jack to do it.

Jack remembered that day and how excited he'd been. The comics were like no books or magazines he'd ever seen. They were old issues with faded, torn pages, but to Jack they were bright, colorful, and crackling with energy. They had superpowered heroes, laser beams, and explo-sions. They had action-packed words like WHACK, KAPOW, and ARRRGHHH!!! Jack couldn't bring himself to throw them away. He just couldn't. Instead, he hid them in the stacks on the second floor of the St. Barnaby's library, where hardly anyone ever went.

Almost all of the comics were missing covers, and quite a few were missing pages at the end. That didn't bother Jack. He was a creative kid, perfectly happy to make up whatever endings suited him. Jack figured out his own ways for Captain Courage to defeat Doctor Destructo, or for Laser Girl to escape the Warrior Women of Planet 13. He drew them on notebook paper and stapled them into the comics. He came up with all kinds of wild ideas like Dimensional Doorways, Time Traps, Freeze Ray Reversers, and more.

Jack loved the comic book world. He felt at home there. He could imagine himself standing shoulder to shoulder with heroes and believe that there was something spectacular out there in the world, that amazing things could really happen. Jack would hide out up in the library with a stack of comics and a flashlight for hours at a time, completely forgetting the grim lessons of his teachers at St. Barnaby's. Alone in that library, Jack learned new lessons. Lessons about justice, honor, and courage, about standing up for the little guy and doing what's right. These were the hallmarks of a hero. These comics were Jack's true teachers, and they never told him to grow up or stop dreaming.

Once Jack was absolutely sure that Mrs. Theedwheck was gone, he took the comics out of their hiding place. What was he going to read today? Jack had already read each comic at least a dozen times or more. It was all a matter of finding the right comic for his mood. He skimmed through the options. Chi, the supersensei ninja master, was taking on the evil Ronin assassins in the pages of *ZenClan Warriors*. Jack set that one aside—a definite possibility. The medieval adventures of barbarian kings were waiting for Jack in the pages of *The Mighty Hovarth*. Hovarth wasn't really one of Jack's favorites. Eventually, Jack settled on *Unreal Tales #42* and the escapades of the space-faring hero called Prime. It was one of the rare comics in Jack's collection with the cover still intact. The words ALONE AGAINST THE ROBO-ZOMBIES OF ASTEROID R! lit up the front page, right over a picture of Prime hopelessly outnumbered by an army of scrap-metal cyborg monsters. Jack settled himself into a comfortable position. He hadn't read this one in a while.

Jack was halfway through the comic when he thought he heard someone in the library. He almost got up to take a look around, but he was at his favorite part of the story. Prime was in mortal peril, surrounded by Robo-Zombies and blasted with a direct hit from a Robo-Rust ray gun. The black eye of the Robo-Zombies started appearing on Prime's face. Every Robo-Zombie had a dark line running around their right eye, with another line running down across their right cheek. Prime was turning into a Robo-Zombie himself! Would he be able to fight off the transformation? Would he become an evil Robo-Zombie bent on world domination?

Jack read on as Prime took a Robo-Zombie prisoner and blasted away from Asteroid R in a stolen starship. Over the next few pages, Prime pressed the zombie for a cure, but to no avail. The Robo-Zombie just laughed as a timer on its chest counted down. Jack turned the page to see a full-page picture of Prime's ship exploding in space. Did Prime get out in time? There was no way to know. The final pages were missing, ripped out long ago.

Jack got out his notebook paper and started thinking about how the comic should end. Really, he should have been putting it away because of the noise he had heard. Someone might have been out there, maybe even a teacher, but Jack wasn't thinking about that. He wasn't thinking about the fact that he never actually heard the last school bus pull away for Mount Dismoor. He wasn't thinking about the footsteps on the library's second floor, inching ever closer. He wasn't thinking about any of it until he was face-to-face with Rex Staples.

"Found him, Mrs. Theeeeedwheck!" Rex shouted back in the other direction.

"*Ha!*" the old bat shouted back.

Jack's face fell. "Oh, great," he groaned.

"Whoa," Rex said, looking at all the comic books. "You're in trouble now, Weirdo Face."

"Don't call me that," Jack said, standing up.

"Who's gonna stop me?" Rex asked, shoving Jack back down to the ground.

Rex stood over Jack and snickered. He had a pudgy face with freckles, spiky hair, and big teeth. He was the same age as Jack, but he was twice the size. At times like this, Jack really wished he had superpowers like the characters in his comics. Rex picked on him all the time. Calling him names, pushing him around, spilling coffee on his drawings . . . that's right, Rex drank coffee. A twelve-year-old who drank coffee! He was a classic bully, but no matter what Rex did, somehow Jack was always the one who wound up in trouble.

"Good work, Rex!" Mrs. Theedwheck declared as she made her way through the stacks of books toward the two boys. "I knew you were up here, Jack, I just kn—*oh my good-ness!* Are those comic books?"

"Yes, ma'am," Jack replied in a sullen voice. What else could he say? He was caught red-handed.

"The comic books I told you to throw away?!" Mrs.

Theedwheck let out a horrified gasp. "That was years ago!"

Jack just stood there looking guilty while Rex smiled on.

"This explains everything," Mrs. Theedwheck said, still in shock. "Why you won't behave, why you never listen . . . it's these! These ridiculous magazines poisoning your brain with nonsense! Childish nonsense! This is why you're always such a problem!"

"It's why he's always such a weirdo," Rex added.

"At least I'm not a snitch," Jack said to Rex, who immediately punched him in the shoulder. "Ow!" Jack yelled. "Mrs. Theedwheck, are you just going to let him hit me?"

"You deserved that," Mrs. Theedwheck scolded. "Calling Rex names when he's only being responsible," she added, shaking her head. "Young man, when are you going to grow up?"

"Grow up?" Jack said. "I'm only twelve years old."

"Well! When I was your age, I was much older than that!" Mrs. Theedwheck fired back. "Mr. Calhoun is going to hear about this, Jack. You can count on that. And as for all of these absurd comical books, this time we *are* going to throw them out. Rex, before you get back on the bus, I want you to put every one of these childish publications in the incinerator."

"No!" Jack yelled, and the lights in the room suddenly grew brighter, before fading down to their regular levels.

"What in the world?" Mrs. Theedwheck wondered aloud.

"It's Jack," Rex said. "He's messing with the lights!"

"What are you talking about?" Jack said. "I am not!" The lights grew incredibly bright again, then slowly returned to normal.

Mrs. Theedwheck went to the window and saw sparks coming off the electric fence. "Calm down, Rex, it's just the rain shorting out our fence. It drains the power from the school's generator. This won't happen when we get the new one."

"I'm telling you, it's him, Mrs. Theedwheck. This kind of crazy stuff always happens with him," Rex said. "Like with the bus breaking down, or that time Jack broke my calculator in the middle of a math test."

"That was my calculator!" Jack replied. "You stole it from me! And I didn't break it!" The lights intensified to their brightest setting yet.

"It's him, Mrs. Theedwheck! He's doing it! Make him stop!"

"I'm not doing anything!" Jack said, raising his voice for the last time, as the lightbulb above them surged with power until it blew out with a crash.

"*Oh!*" Mrs. Theedwheck screamed as broken glass rained down. "Jack, that's enough! Whatever it is that you're doing, stop it!"

"But I didn't do anything! Mrs. Theedwheck, please don't burn up my comics," Jack pleaded. "I'll do whatever you want. I'll do chores all day. All week, even!"

"Oh, I know you will, but the comics are getting burned either way. Rex, gather up every last one and then get on the bus. Jack, you have chores to do, but first things first." Mrs. Theedwheck took out her yardstick. Jack knew what would come next.

When Mrs. Theedwheck was through with him, Jack was pretty sure he wouldn't be able to sit down for at least a week. That wasn't the worst part of his punishment either. The worst was that there were so many comics that Rex couldn't carry them all, and Jack had to help him take them down to the incinerator. He had to help burn up his own comic book collection in the furnace. Watching those books go into the fire was the absolute worst.

With the other kids finally off on their class trip, Jack was left alone in the basement, or what was currently the basement, bailing out water to stem the tide of the swamp. When he was younger, there used to be classrooms down there. Now the basement was surrendering to the marshlands, slowly sinking a little more each year.

Jack hated the creepy, slanted basement, with its floor tilted on an angle. The basement was nothing more than a long, thin, warped hallway. The high end of the tilt was dry and the low end was wet. Jack thought of the low end as the "deep end," because all the way down at that end of the hall was a pool of water around a stairwell leading to the floor below, a floor completely submerged in swamp water.

The basement smelled of moisture, mold, and mildew. It was dark, too, since it wasn't safe to use electricity on a floor that was almost halfway below swamp level. The only sunlight that crept through the windows was a combination of dim rays that either climbed above or dove below the swamp water outside. On a gray morning like this, there was almost no light at all, making the whole place look like a ghost school with empty desks scattered about each room, unsolved equations left on the chalkboard, and lonely art projects still taped to the walls.

Jack navigated the puddle-ridden basement in squishy shoes. *Splish, splash. Splish, splash.* He had a bucket to carry water from the deep end of the floor up to the shallow end. Back and forth, he made his way across the basement, up the tilted floor to the dry side, where he would climb a rickety wooden staircase that led to a window by the ceiling. Once he got there, he'd dump a bucket of green water outside and go back to do it again. He was supposed to keep going until the floor was dry. *Splish, splash. Splish, splash.* It was no use. Swamp water seeped in everywhere. It was a never-ending job.

One way or the other, Jack always ended up doing jobs like this as punishment for something. These days, it was usually punishment for something he did, in fact, do. There was a time when he used to keep his head down and try to follow the rules, but he found out that didn't work at a place like St. Barnaby's. Not for him, anyway. Even when he did what he was told and played the part of the model student, he always managed to get in trouble with the teachers for some new rule he had broken or was suspected of breaking. It was no wonder he started side-stepping the rules whenever he could, like hiding from Mrs. Theedwheck to dodge chores or stashing the comic books in the library. Sometimes it worked out and sometimes it didn't. This time, it didn't.

While he worked, Jack thought about what had happened with the lights in the library. He had to admit, weird stuff like that did happen a lot—like the calculator incident Rex was talking about. Jack remembered it well. It was the day of a big math test and Rex had forgotten his calculator, so he stole Jack's. Jack was so mad, and then the calculator fried itself two minutes later. The look on Rex's face at that moment was almost worth losing the calculator, but Jack didn't have anything to do with it breaking. How could he have?

Jack's ponderings were cut short just as he was emptying a pail of water out the window. He heard something behind him. Something way back on the deep side of the floor. A sound almost like bubbles. A sound like something was coming up from the water.

"Hello?" Jack called back from the window.

There was no answer.

Jack waited a minute, then tried to shake it off. "Probably just some air bubbles," he told himself as he started back down the stairs. No big deal.

Then he heard the dripping. Heavy dripping, like water running off a person's body onto the floor. Like a large person stepping out of a bathtub. Or a swamp.

"Hello?" Jack called out again, a little more scared this time. "Is anyone down there?"

The reply was footsteps—watery footsteps from all the way down on the dark side of the basement. . . .

Splish, splash. Splish, splash. Splish, splash.

There was no question about it. Somebody was definitely down there.

Jack walked with his pail to the flooded side of the basement. He stood at the doorway of a waterlogged classroom. "Who's down here?" Jack called out with all the courage he could muster.

Again, he heard footsteps. *Splish, splash. Splish, splash.* The sound was coming from another room down the hall. Jack's first thought was that Rex and his cronies were messing with him, but everyone was supposed to be out on the field trip. So, who was down there? Slowly and carefully, Jack walked after the footsteps, following the sound.

He was sure the noise was coming from a classroom down near the deep end of the hall. He followed the noise to another warped doorway and looked inside to find dead quiet and an empty room. He checked a few more rooms but found nothing each time. The footsteps were gone. Jack decided it was just his imagination. He filled his bucket with water and started back toward the rickety wooden staircase on the dry side of the floor.

A door shut behind him. Jack turned around with a jump and dropped his bucket. An old, creaky door dragging several inches of water with it had just closed itself at the end of the hall. This was *not* his imagination.

Most of the classrooms were connected by interior doorways, so Jack had no way of knowing which door had just mysteriously shut. He stared down the hall, looking for a clue. The dim light from the windows flickered ever so slightly off the surface of swirling water at the very end of the hallway. Something was down there. Jack picked up his bucket and started inching down the corridor into ankle-deep water. The closer he got, the better he could see the water churning about, like someone had just slipped beneath its surface. He reached the stairwell, the very place where the swamp was flooding in from below. A lone banister was all that remained to mark the location of the staircase. It reached out from the murky depths in a futile gesture to escape the swamp.

Jack sloshed through smelly water to the open doorway at the stairwell. It was a doorway to both the staircase below and the depths of the swamp.

Jack was scared enough to keep his distance but curious enough that he had to find out what was down there. If Jack had known what was lurking below the surface, he would have run the other way as fast as his feet would take him. That wouldn't have mattered, though. It had followed him this far already. It had followed him across the swamp, up through the lower levels of St. Barnaby's, and right up to the basement stairwell, where it could feel Jack's presence. It was so close. Just on the other side of the water.

The time had come.

Jack was staring into his own blurry reflection in the

murky water when the image was dispelled by a grabbing hand reaching to clutch at his wrist.

"AGGHH!" Jack yelped, backing away so fast that he tripped on his own feet. He hit the ground with a splash. The hand that had grabbed at him disappeared back below the water's edge. What *was* that?

From the ground, Jack watched, trembling, as the rest of the thing emerged from the deep. It looked like a heap of scrap metal. It smelled of mildew and rust, a random collection of corroded metal plates. But it wasn't random. Not really. Wires, nuts, and bolts were sticking out everywhere, and the rising pile of waste looked like garbage left over from the construction work that was always being done around St. Barnaby's. That garbage was routinely dumped in the swamp, but this garbage was forming the shape of something.

The shifting mass lurched forward, out of the pool of water in the stairwell. Jack got a good look, and what he saw was impossible. The mass was dark gray everywhere except for a shining red light in the center of what was apparently becoming a person's chest. A newly formed neck raised a newly formed head, and on that head an eye blinked open.

An eye with a black mark running all the way around it and a dark line running down from its inside corner.

The creature was *exactly* like one of the aliens Jack had just read about in his comic books. He was looking at a Robo-Zombie. Jack shivered in place, letting out a stuttering burble of shock. Frozen with fear, his mind tried to tell him he was seeing things, that none of this was possible.

The Robo-Zombie opened its mouth to speak, and a mechanical noise poured out, screeching through the air like choppy analog ringtones and static:

"KSSCHHHHHHH-ANG-ANNG-ANNNG!!!!"

Jack screamed and threw his bucket at the mechanical beast. It was all he could think to do. The robot caught the bucket and crushed it in its left hand. It tossed the bucket away and slowly advanced on Jack.

Frantic, Jack scooted himself backward, still on the ground. The lights in the basement were coming on. Just like before, they were starting out low and gradually growing brighter. This was impossible, Jack thought. Then again, he was staring at a seven-foot robot that had just climbed out of the swamp, so what did impossible really mean? The light intensified. The Robo-Zombie noticed the lights as they reached their height of brightness and sparks shot out of the sockets. The power to the lights was supposed to be off because it wasn't safe. As Jack cleared the pool of water by the stairwell, electric bolts shot up through the water, striking the robot. It cried out in pain.

Jack ran.

Sprinting down the long hallway to the staircase on the dry side, Jack was scared beyond belief. Behind him, he could see the robot down on one knee, looking up at him. Smoke rose off its frame. It looked angry. Getting up quickly, it charged at the doorway. Too wide to fit through the door, it broke through the wall on either side. It was coming for Jack, and it was picking up speed.

Jack had always wished he'd had superpowers. He'd go to bed hoping that he'd wake up with the ability to fly, turn into steel, or shoot ice rays from his hands. While flying was Jack's first choice, anything would have been fine as the Robo-Zombie was coming after him. You don't get picky when you have a monster robot chasing you down the hall. Jack reached the wooden staircase that led up to the window. He scampered up the rickety steps, tripping halfway to the top. He caught himself and turned to see the robot powering up in his run. It left the ground and flew right at him.

Jack just barely managed to squeeze himself out through the window at the ceiling, and took off running across the marsh. The robot barreled through the window behind him, taking chunks of the wall off as it charged out of the basement. The damaged section of the building's foundation sludged into the swamp and the robot shot high into the air.

The Robo-Zombie circled around in the sky, looking for Jack. There was no real cover to be found in the marsh. It was an endless stretch of tall, colorless grass and weeds surrounding vast pools of cold, still water. The drab landscape was interrupted by a few trees and rocks planted here and there, with long, half-barren hedgerows winding in between. Everything was beige and tan. Everything looked dead.

With the robot up in the air, Jack knew he would be easily spotted running through the grass. In fact, any movement at all was sure to give away his position. Jack was scared to death but somehow managed to keep thinking straight. He stayed perfectly still and ducked down below the reeds.

A hundred or so feet away, the tall grass fluttered. The robot zeroed in on it immediately and swooped down from the sky. Diving like a torpedo, the robot hit the earth with a slam. Jack shook in his hiding place as a gaggle of ducks scattered off in a dozen directions, quacking up a storm.

The Robo-Zombie remained on the ground, swatting at the ducks. Jack ran. He ran hard with all the energy he had. All of it. Pure supercharged adrenaline and fear powered his legs as he ran blindly through the thin stalks of grass. The freezing water was past his ankles, but he ran as fast as he could and didn't dare look back. He plowed ahead through the marsh, and then suddenly he slammed right into the electric fence.

Jack bounced back with a shock. The robot heard him. Jack looked across the marsh and locked eyes with the iron brute. It was coming for him.

Unable to climb the fence, Jack just kept running. It was still raining outside, and sparks flew off the electric fence as he ran alongside it. From behind him he heard two zaps from the electric fence and then a third, louder noise.

"Whoa!" Jack yelped as he ducked behind a tree. That last zap was no spark from the fence. Some kind of laser blast had just missed him! The robot was fast approaching. It was taking shots at him as it came. The first two blasts disappeared in the murky water to Jack's left and right, and the third one struck the trunk of his tree, splintering it in two.

Jack kept running through bushes and weeds, trying to get away, but it was no use. The robot was closing in, screaming its static-filled battle cry and firing shot after shot from its wrist cannons.

Eventually, Jack cleared the swamp, exhausted and with no energy left to keep going. He reached a dead end, penned in by the electric fence at the edge of St. Barnaby's property. There was nothing there but the orphanage's power generator out back by an old shed. Jack hid in the shed, hoping to escape. It wasn't happening. No sooner did he get into a good hiding place than the shed's roof and walls were ripped off the ground. The robot threw them away and hovered menacingly over Jack. It trained its arm, ready to blast him into oblivion. Jack sat there shivering, wondering what he'd done to make a monster from his comic books come to life and try to kill him.

"What do you want?" Jack screamed at the monster. "Why are you after me?"

There was no answer, but the monster paused.

It was almost as if the iron beast that chased him all this way was now struggling with the thought of killing him. This came as no comfort to Jack. He was still terrified, and his heart bounced around in his chest like a racquetball. What he didn't realize was that the faster his heart beat and the more scared he became, the faster the power generator across from him seemed to run. The generator was big enough to light the entire orphanage and power the electric fence. The robot was hovering right over it.

Jack stared up at the monster that was still deciding whether or not to finish him off. Knowing there was nowhere left to run, Jack could only hope that the monster had some kind of a conscience. As the robot primed its wrist cannons, Jack could see that the evil thing intended to complete its mission.

Meanwhile, the power generator below the robot was redlining. A mechanical whirr grew louder and louder, faster and faster, until first one bolt popped and then another and another. By the time the monster finally noticed that the machine below him was bursting at the seams, it was too late.

The explosion was incredible. It rose up in a ball of orange and black flames, a vigorous blast that engulfed the robot in a blazing conflagration. Within that blast thundered a second explosion that knocked Jack off his feet. It was like something out of an action movie that Jack wasn't allowed to watch, or the comic books he wasn't allowed to read. The heat from the flames blew into Jack with a draft of sizzling air. The smoke set Jack into a coughing fit, but he didn't mind. He was actually pretty darn happy. The warm gust of air that hit his freezing body couldn't have been more welcome if it had come from an oven filled with freshly baked chocolate-chip cookies.

When the smoke cleared, Jack still had no idea what had happened, but he could see the destruction was total. A huge, smoldering hole in the ground and some burned-out chunks of metal were all that remained of the power generator. It was a good thing St. Barnaby's was getting a new electric fence for free, because the new generator they were going to need wouldn't be cheap. And there were no identifiable pieces left of the robot that caused all this mess. The generator had blown up and taken all of the robot with it. Jack sat down in shock and waited in the rain for someone to come and yell at him.

He knew no one was going to believe this.

CHAPTER

2

The Emissary

H. Ross Calhoun was far too angry to even look at Jack. The head disciplinarian stood facing away from him, staring out his office window with his hands clasped behind his back. Jack could still see the smoke from the explosion on the horizon.

"Let me get this straight," Calhoun began. "You didn't destroy the power generator and cause thousands of dollars worth of damage . . . an evil robot that came out of the swamp in the basement did it. Do I have that right? That's your story?"

Jack was sitting on the other side of an enormous oak desk. "It was a Robo-*Zombie*," he replied meekly. "From Asteroid R."

Calhoun sunk into his desk chair with a heavy sigh. He was a grim older man with a serious face, a crooked nose, and fiery black eyes. It was a known fact that he had only smiled four times in his entire life. This was not one of those times. Calhoun's intense eyes were closed and he rubbed his temples. The whole ordeal gave him a headache.

"The situation is worse than I thought," he said at last.

Jack didn't want to know what Calhoun was planning to do with him. This was a man who had once petitioned the Board of Trustees to change the name of the orphanage to "St. Barnaby's *Ward* for the Hopeless, Abandoned, Forgotten, and Lost," simply because he thought the word "home" sounded too soft.

"Basically, what you're telling me is that either you are a liar or you are, in fact, mentally ill," Calhoun stated.

"Or I'm telling the truth," Jack offered as an alternative.

"Mmm-hmm," Calhoun said. "Criminally insane would be another option, I suppose. I can't say I'm surprised. It's your own fault that you're delusional. Mrs. Theedwheck told me about the comic books."

"What have comic books got to do with anything?" Jack asked.

"This," Calhoun began, "is the exact reason I banned that type of subversive material in the first place. Robo-Zombies? Laser beams? Your brain has been bent by impertinent pulp. Clearly, you can no longer tell the difference between fantasy and reality."

"I *know* the difference between fantasy and reality," Jack replied a little too forcefully. He tried to dial it back to a more respectful tone. "Mr. Calhoun, please. That thing that came after me was real," he stressed. "If you don't believe me, you can look out in the swamp. It blasted a tree in two!"

Calhoun dismissed the idea with a wave of his hand. "Probably lightning."

"Lightning?" Jack thought about that for a moment. "So, how do you know the power generator wasn't blown up by lightning, then?" he asked.

"Don't be ridiculous, Jack. Lightning never strikes twice."

Jack thought that logic sounded even more illogical. "How do you know which bolt hit first?" he asked.

Calhoun frowned.

"Jack, I'm getting very tired of your constant need to point out things that don't make sense. And, if it *was* lightning, you wouldn't be here telling stories about flying robots," he said. "Now, you're going to tell me the truth about what happened out there, or I will have to assume you've suffered some kind of psychotic break."

Jack felt trapped. It seemed the truth wasn't getting him anywhere. He stuck to his story, adding, "You're not even listening to me. You never listen. That's the whole problem with this place." Jack knew he was just digging himself into a deeper hole with Calhoun, but in his mind, whatever punishment the head disciplinarian had in store was inevitable. Nothing ever changed at St. Barnaby's, but Jack at least felt a little bit better when he spoke up.

Calhoun issued a noise that was one part sigh, one part grumble. "Don't you get tired of being sent to this office?" Calhoun asked. "Honestly, Jack, why can't you just be more like the other children?"

Jack slumped down in his chair with a sad look. "I wish I knew," he said.

"Young man, you'd better start thinking about your future," Calhoun warned. He took out Jack's permanent record. "I know your test scores showed your potential to be fairly limited, but if you don't start living in the real world, you won't even live up to that!"

"Please don't bring up that P-MAP Test again," Jack complained. It was a bad move. Calhoun revered standardized tests. He was already angry, and disrespecting his precious tests only made it worse.

"Jack Blank! That test happens to be the standard by which children's futures are decided all over the world! Your contempt for this office and this institution are bad enough, but by God, you *will* respect the National Association of Tests and Limits!"

For Calhoun, standardized tests were beyond reproach. They made his life so much easier. They made it possible for him to discover everything worthwhile about a child without lifting a finger. When Calhoun put a Scantron sheet into a grading machine, he didn't get a test score back, he got truth. Absolute truth. How smart a person was, how far they could go, what their life would amount to . . . it was all there in little black dots made with a number two pencil.

The most important test of all was the Potential Mapping Test, or P-MAP. It outlined the ideal career choice for any test taker, covering everything from astronaut to toilet brush cleaner. Jack's test score didn't exactly put him on the fast track.

"I don't want to be a toilet brush cleaner!" Jack said with conviction.

"Nobody *wants* to be a toilet brush cleaner, Jack, but that's all the P-MAP said you could handle. I don't know what you want me to do about it."

"I've never even heard of a toilet brush cleaner," Jack argued. "Don't people just go buy new brushes when they need them?"

"And simply throw out the old ones?" Calhoun scoffed. "How wasteful! Don't you care about the environment?"

"Okay, then why can't people just clean their own toilet brushes?"

"Don't be disgusting," Calhoun replied. "That kind of activity is best left to professionals like yourself."

"But I don't want to do that," Jack protested. "Can't I just figure out what I want to be by myself?"

"Don't be ridiculous," Calhoun said, closing Jack's file. "The P-MAP Test has already assigned you a job. Your future is what it is, and that is that. The sooner you accept that, the better off you'll be. Like your friend Rex. He's a perfect example."

"Rex?" Jack asked. "Rex isn't my friend; he beats me up every day."

"Right, that's the boy." Calhoun smiled. "I believe his tests showed he would excel as hired muscle for some manner of criminal syndicate. Do you see him complaining? No, he's embraced that career path. He's taking to it like a duck to water."

"And you think that's a good thing?" Jack asked, baffled.

"I'll allow that it's not the proper way to make a living, but once a boy with Rex's temperament gets his foot in the door of an organization like that . . . Well, you just know that he's going to go straight to the top. That Rex is going to put St. Barnaby's on the map!" Calhoun stated with pride. "Unlike yourself, who seems determined to blow us off of it."

"I'm telling you, it was a—"

"A Robo-Zombie—yes, I know," Calhoun said, rolling his eyes. "Jack, you leave me no choice. Either you're lying or you're mentally unbalanced. In either case, you're a danger to everyone here, and I can't give you any more chances. I'm drawing up papers to have you committed."

"Committed?" Jack repeated. "Are you crazy?"

"This is what psychoanalysts refer to as transference. *You're* the one who's crazy. That's why I'm sending you away."

"I'm afraid I can't allow that," a voice called out from the door.

Calhoun looked up in surprise, and Jack spun around to see a man who had entered the office without knocking. But this was the type of man who didn't need to knock. He had an air of flashy confidence that opened doors all by itself. He was a tall, handsome young man with short black hair who somehow managed to look both official and cool at the same time. In his jet-black suit and shiny tie he looked like he was equal parts Hollywood and secret agent. Jack had never seen him around St. Barnaby's before.

"Who the devil are you?" Calhoun demanded.

"Agent Jason Knight," he said, flashing a badge and quickly putting it away. "I'm with the government. Department of Departmental Affairs."

"Who?" Calhoun replied. "The Department of what?"

"We heard about the incident here this morning," Agent Knight continued, ignoring the question. "It's a very serious matter. Very serious, indeed."

Calhoun was taken aback by the stranger's intrusion. "I'm aware of that," he shot back. "I don't know what you think you're doing barging in here, but I can assure you that I have the situation well in hand. Now, what do you mean that you can't allow—"

"I mean, I can't allow you to send this boy to the loony bin," Agent Knight interrupted. "He's going to have to come with me. Go pack your bags, son," he said to Jack.

"Don't you move!" Calhoun ordered Jack. He came around the desk to face Agent Knight. "How dare you? You can't just come in here unannounced and expect me to hand this boy over to . . . to the, ah . . . what agency did you say you were with?"

"Not an agency, a department," Agent Knight corrected. "The Department of Departmental Affairs. We're a Division of the Divisional Office."

"A division of the what?"

"I'm trying to help you, sir. To protect your way of life. We've been watching this boy for a while now, and he's been trouble for quite some time," Agent Knight said firmly. It was an assertion that Calhoun heartily agreed with, Jack knew. "Well, now he's causing explosions on American soil, and that means I have to deal with him before he threatens the security of our great nation."

"Me?" Jack asked.

"Quiet, Jack," Calhoun ordered. "That's all well and good, Agent Knight, but I've never heard of—"

"Oh, you've never heard of us?" Agent Knight cut him off. "I'm sorry, I thought you were in charge here," he continued in a patronizing tone. "My apologies, sir, you can go back to answering phones and processing forms. I don't deal with deputies and number twos. Your superiors would know who I am. I should probably be speaking directly with the Board of Trustees."

"No!" Calhoun said immediately. "No, I *am* in charge

here, and of course I've heard of the Office of Divisional . . .
Departments." He adjusted his tie nervously. "I remember
now, that's not the point. The point is, there are rules for
this kind of thing. Regulations! Paperwork! This boy's not
going anywhere until you tell me to what end, and for what
purpose!"

Agent Knight sighed. "He's being deported," he reluctantly revealed.

For the fifth time in his life, H. Ross Calhoun smiled.

"Jack," Calhoun said. "Go pack your bags."

When Jack was finished packing up all his worldly
possessions, a process that took less than ten minutes,
Agent Knight wanted to inspect the blast site where the
generator once stood. Calhoun insisted on coming along to
make sure Jack did no further damage to school property.

"I don't know what you're looking for," Calhoun said
as Agent Knight sifted through the wreckage. "Any fool
can plainly see that there's nothing salvageable."

"I'm sure *you* can plainly see that," Agent Knight
replied. "*I*, on the other hand, am looking for something
a bit more out of the ordinary."

"You mean, like a Robo-Zombie?" Jack asked.

"Hmmm . . . ," Agent Knight said, staring down at a curiously high-tech piece of debris. Before Jack had a chance to say anything, Agent Knight smashed it to bits with his bare hand.

"Good Lord, man! What are you doing?" Calhoun demanded. Agent Knight ignored him as he continued around the area, taking anything that looked even remotely like Jack's robot and pulverizing it completely.

"There we are!" Agent Knight finally announced, clapping the dust off his hands. "We're through here." He walked off without another word. A mortified Calhoun and a very confused Jack followed closely behind. They got back to the main gates just as the school bus was pulling in on its return from Mount Dismoor.

"That's it, then, Mr. Calhoun," Agent Knight said. "Thank you for your cooperation. With any luck, this boy will never see you again."

"Don't you mean, with any luck, *I'll* never see *him* again?" Calhoun said.

Agent Knight smirked. "Right, that's it. Sure."

Mrs. Theedwheck and Rex stepped off the bus in time

to see Jack getting into a very new, very expensive sports car with Agent Knight. "Hey! Where's Weirdo Face going?" Rex asked.

"Yes, Mr. Calhoun! Where *is* Weirdo Face, er . . . *Jack* going?" Mrs. Theedwheck asked her superior.

Agent Knight spun his tires in the mud, splattering Rex, Mrs. Theedwheck, and Calhoun from head to toe. "He's going somewhere far away from here," he said, leaning out the car window. And with that, they were off. Jack absolutely loved the sight of his mud-covered teachers and bully. He didn't know where he was headed, but he knew anywhere was better than St. Barnaby's. From the look on Rex's face, he knew it too.

"I'm not going to lie to you, Jack," the agent said as they pulled out of the main parking lot and onto the highway. "I really enjoyed that."

It didn't take a master detective to see that there was something funny about Agent Jason Knight. A few things, actually. For example, when Agent Knight had flashed his badge back in Calhoun's office, Jack had noticed that he'd spelled his name "Jazen." That was a little odd. Also, when the agent had been breaking up the wreckage out by

47

the power generator, he had seemed way stronger than any man his size had a right to be. But the strangest thing of all about Agent Jazen Knight was what he did when Jack told him about the comic book alien that had attacked him that morning.

The agent believed him.

Jazen listened to Jack's entire story and didn't question a thing. He didn't call him a liar and he didn't call him crazy. Instead, he told Jack that he'd showed courage. He said he was impressed with Jack. No one at St. Barnaby's had ever said anything like that to Jack before. He certainly didn't expect it from somebody who was supposedly there to kick him out of the country. As they drove away from St. Barnaby's, Agent Knight dropped another bomb.

"I should probably tell you," he began, "I'm not really an agent with the Department of Departmental Affairs. To be perfectly honest, there's no such thing. I haven't used that line in quite a while, but Mr. Calhoun back there seemed like the right type for it. Challenge his authority, and he'll do anything to show you he's the boss. People like that will buy any story. The more ridiculous it is, the fewer questions they ask."

"So, I'm not really getting deported, then?" Jack asked.

"You are and you aren't," Jazen replied. "Trust me, Jack, this is the best thing that ever happened to you."

When Jack had finished trying to process everything, he was still pretty much baffled. Finally, he asked the big questions: "What's going on here? Who are you? Where are we going?"

Agent Knight smiled. "My name is Jazen Knight. I'm an emissary of a secret country. The place you come from, actually. I'm taking you home."

"Home?" Jack asked. "You know where I'm from?"

"I'm pretty sure I do."

"I thought I was born here in Jersey."

Jazen shook his head. "I don't think so. There's only one place in the world where power like yours comes from. I'm taking you to the Imagine Nation."

Jack looked back at Jazen like he was a few scoops short of a sundae. "The *imagination?*"

"No," Jazen replied. "The Imagine . . . Nation. Let me guess, you've never heard of it." Jack shook his head and

Jazen shrugged. "I'm not surprised. It's only the biggest secret in the world. A secret country on a secret island, hidden out at sea. It's the most amazing place you can possibly imagine . . . a refuge for the extraordinary, filled with superpowered people, aliens, androids, medieval knights . . . "

"Wait a minute . . . superpowered people?" Jack repeated. "You mean, like in the comic books?"

"I mean, like in comic books, movies, TV shows, Saturday morning cartoons . . . you name it. It's all there. All the wild and fantastic things you can dream up are just reflections of the Imagine Nation," Jazen said. "Emissaries like me go all around the world, seeding it with little pieces of our home. We leave bread-crumb trails, hints, and clues about it in all kinds of places. Sometimes we do more than that, though. Every now and then, we bring somebody back with us."

Jack studied his strange driver for a moment. "Why? Why me?" he asked.

"Don't you know?" Jazen replied. "C'mon. I'm sure you can think of a reason or two why you might be at home in a place like the Imagine Nation."

"No, not really," Jack said. He was lying, though. He had something of an idea why. It was sitting way in the back of his mind, but it was there. Jack dismissed it. It was crazy. It wasn't a real possibility.

Jazen nodded. "Okay," he said. "That's fine. I guess that Robo-Zombie this morning blew up all by itself, then."

"That was the power generator," Jack corrected him. "I didn't have anything to do with that."

"Of course not," Jazen countered with a smirk. "What was I thinking?"

Jazen continued driving. Jack didn't know what to think of all this. This guy couldn't be saying what he thought he was saying. Could he? Everything was happening so fast. Jack spent so much of his life dreaming about leaving St. Barnaby's, but when he fantasized about his future it always seemed so far away. No one ever thinks their future is going to start today. Besides, those were just dreams, anyway. Jack had no shortage of crazy dreams, but regardless of what had happened that morning, he wasn't so sure he ever really thought they could come true.

"It's up to you, Jack, but I hope you can believe me,"

Jazen said. "If not, this is going to be a real short trip. If you want to go to the Imagine Nation, there's one very important rule. You have to believe in it first."

Jazen pulled the car off the highway, taking the exit toward the harbor. Down on the docks he parked right in front of a huge NO PARKING sign, next to a row of private yachts. A man in a red jacket watched Jazen as he stepped out of the car.

"You can't park your car there," the man said.

"Park it wherever you want," Jazen said, tossing the man his keys. "It's your car now." Jazen scooted Jack off in the direction of a sixty-four-foot yacht at the end of the pier. They walked through a metal detector that rang out alarms as Jazen walked through, but the man in the red jacket paid it no mind. He just stood there looking back and forth between the car and the keys.

"Did you really just give that guy your car?" Jack asked.

"No car's going to take us where we're going," Jazen said. "That's what this baby's for."

Jack looked up at Jazen's boat. It was christened the *Vision*, and it more than lived up to its name. The *Vision* was a pristine white ship with a sleek frame that sloped forward into an aerodynamic point. Despite its massive size, it looked fast—the kind of ship that could slice through waves like scissors through paper. It was gorgeous.

"That's incredible," Jack marveled.

"Ha! Wait until we get where we're going—then you'll see incredible. But I'm serious when I say you have to believe in it first."

"I don't understand. Why?"

Jazen knelt down in front of Jack and adopted a solemn tone. "Because, Jack, all the fantastic, unbelievable things in this world start in the Imagine Nation. It's a real place, but you can't get there if you try to keep one foot in the real world when you go. Only people who believe in the unbelievable are able to see the island. To find it, you have to believe that there's a place out there where the impossible is possible. You have to believe it deep in your heart. If you can't do that, you won't recognize it when you see it. Even if it's staring you right in the face."

Jazen stood up and put one foot in the boat. He reached out a hand to Jack.

"You think you can do that?" he asked.

"I guess so," Jack answered.

"You *guess* so?" Jazen grimaced. "I gotta tell you, I was kinda hoping for an absolute one hundred percent yes here."

Before Jack could say anything, Jazen snapped his fingers.

"I've got it!" he said. "My partner. He'll convince you I'm not crazy." Jazen turned around and stuck his head below deck. "Blue!" he shouted. "Get up here! Time to get this show on the road!"

"About time!" a deep, booming voice called back. "I was getting ready to leave without ya."

"Who's that?" Jack asked.

"That's my partner, Blue," Jazen replied. "He's a cop."

As the owner of the voice made his way upstairs, Jack saw that he was nothing less than a giant. The entire boat rocked from side to side as Blue walked up the steps. When he opened the door to exit onto the deck, he could barely fit through it. He was a ten-foot-tall hulking mass of muscle who looked like he could pick up every boat on the pier and juggle them if he wanted to. He wasn't called Blue because he was a cop, but rather because his skin was a clear, bright shade of royal blue.

"What's goin' on, little man?" Blue asked Jack. "You comin' with us or what?"

Blue put out a fist for Jack to bump. The only bump Jack returned was the one where his head hit the floor. One look at Blue and he fainted straightaway.

CHAPTER

3

Shadow of the Rüstov

Jack woke up to the sound of rolling waves. He was confused at first, as people generally are when they wake up in strange places without warning. As he sat up in bed it all came flooding back: the Robo-Zombie, the emissary, the blue giant . . . and the boat!

This was no dream. He was really on the boat. This was really happening.

Jack could feel the ship moving as he looked around the bedroom, or stateroom, as it was called on a sea vessel. Jack's vocabulary was filled with nautical terms he had learned from his Pirate Adventure and Star Fleet comics. The stateroom was nicer than any room he had ever slept in, but Jack was too excited to stay in bed. He got up to explore the ship.

Jack walked upstairs, wobbling a little as he went. He had never been on a boat before and needed some time to get his sea legs underneath him. He stumbled into the upper deck.

The main room was empty. Worn burgundy leather couches and club chairs rested on honey-colored hardwood floors, and a classic globe turned slowly with the tides in an oak stand. Jack saw countless charts and maps spread out on tables next to various artifacts, or rolled up and tucked away into cubbyholes. There was a TV in the room, but it wasn't like any TV Jack had ever seen. It was a razor-thin holographic projection floating in midair, just off the wall. Jack reached up to touch it. The screen rippled like a pool of water as his hand passed right through the light image.

Sunlight poured in from sweeping windows that lined the walls and looked out on the open sea. There was no land on the horizon in any direction.

Jack stepped forward through a full kitchen (or galley, as he knew it to be called) and onto the bridge of the ship. The captain's chair sat empty before him. The golden floorboards at the helm were contrasted by dark wood that encased a high-tech computerized control panel. In front of that panel was an ornate wooden wheel that looked like it had been taken from an old pirate ship. Jack felt like he was looking at the future and the past at the same time. The readout on the control panel flashed the message AUTO PILOT ENGAGED over and over. Jack wondered where everyone was, before hearing voices outside the cabin. Voices talking about him, coming from upstairs. Behind him, a stairway wound up to the open-air top deck. Jack crept up slowly and silently, listening closely as he climbed the steps.

"I can't believe you," Jack heard Blue say to Jazen.

"Why would I lie?"

Jack crouched at the top of the stairs, just out of sight, to listen in.

"I don't think you're lying," Blue replied. "But you said we were going to check him out, not bring him back. I can't believe you'd make a decision like this based on some random letter someone wrote you."

"That letter was real," Jazen replied. "It came from—"

"You don't know if he wrote it or not," Blue said. "No one's seen him since the invasion. It could be a trick. I mean, isn't he dead?"

"Don't say that," Jazen said. "You don't know that for sure."

"I know you're stirring up a storm," Blue said. "And you know what you're starting too. Smart's not going to be happy when he finds out that you're bringing in somebody new. You of all people."

"Smart's never been happy his whole life," Jazen replied, "and he's not going to be happy until he makes the entire Imagine Nation a police state. People are finally starting to talk about it, you know."

"I know," Blue said. "Someone has to stand up—I'm with you there. I just hope you're not using this poor kid to do it."

Jack raised an eyebrow. He didn't like the sound of that.

Jazen scowled at Blue. "Do I tell you how to do your job?" he asked. "The proper way to punch somebody in the face, or how to put your head through a brick wall? The kid has a right to go home, Blue. No matter what anyone says, he deserves that much."

Blue put a hand on Jazen's shoulder. "I always back your play, partner, you know that. But what's right and what's popular aren't always the same thing. Even in the Imagine Nation, people get awful funny where the Rüstov are concerned."

"The Rüstov just tried to kill him," Jazen said.

"And when was the last time you heard of that happening?" Blue asked. "Rüstov Para-Soldiers operating in the outside world? You'd have to go back to the invasion for that. The question is, what's next? Ten Rüstov? A hundred? People back home haven't had to deal with those kinds of numbers in quite a while, and the fact is, they like it that way. If more of those things follow this kid back, it's going to be bad for him *and* you."

"What things?" Jack asked, stepping out of the stairwell. "Is that what you call the thing that came after me today? A Rüstov?"

Jazen and Blue looked up, taken totally by surprise. They traded embarrassed looks after being caught red-handed talking about Jack.

"All right, Jack," Jazen said. "You're going to find out soon enough, anyway. Have a seat up here, and we'll tell you everything."

Jack did as he was told, taking a seat across from Jazen and Blue.

"I'm sure you have a million questions," Jazen said. "The fact is, so do we. Even by our standards, this has been a pretty unusual day. This morning you faced off against one of the baddest bad guys in the whole universe."

"What was that thing?" Jack asked.

"A Rüstov Para-Soldier," Blue answered. "Alien invaders. Nasty ones too."

"I read about them today in a comic book," Jack said. "Only they were called Robo-Zombies. They were fighting a hero called Prime."

"You know about Prime?" Blue asked.

Jack looked at Blue. "He's real too?" he asked.

"As real as the Rüstov," Blue replied. "I can see why you call 'em Robo-Zombies. Infected people usually end up looking like zombies by the time the Rüstov are done with them."

"They're cybernetic parasites," Jazen explained. "Most

61

people in the Imagine Nation are still pretty scared of them. They infect other living organisms and use them as hosts, taking over their bodies and stealing their life energy. They can only survive on the backs of other life forms, and their victims turn into Rüstov soldiers just like them."

Jack thought it was all remarkably similar to what he had read about in the pages of *Unreal Tales #42*. "In my comic book Prime was turning into one of them too," he told Jazen and Blue. "He started getting that mark on his eye, like the one they all have."

"You'll be glad to know that Prime is just fine," Blue said. "But that's how it starts. That mark on the eye, that's the first sign of infection."

"The one that came after me . . . it didn't try to infect me," Jack said. "It tried to kill me."

"I know," Jazen said. "It's strange, I can't explain that."

"What does all this have to do with me going to the Imagine Nation?" Jack wanted to know.

"I told you about my job as an emissary," Jazen began. "How we go around the world planting clues about the Imagine Nation, and looking for people who are developing superpowers. Well, twelve years ago the Rüstov invaded

Earth. Ever since then, we've been discouraged from actually bringing any superpowered people back to our island. People are still very suspicious of outsiders back home."

"Hang on," Jack said. "Superpowers? You really think I have superpowers?"

"I know you do," Jazen said without blinking.

Blue agreed with Jazen. "You don't survive a Rüstov ambush without a few superpowers," Blue said.

Jack could hardly believe his ears. Even with everything that had already happened that day, he still couldn't quite accept he was a part of all this. He kept waiting for Jazen and Blue to realize it was some big mistake.

"I didn't do anything this morning," Jack said. "I didn't even try, I just ran. Where would I get superpowers, anyway?"

"Look," Jazen said, "not everyone has an obvious superpower origin. For every person who gets their powers from a lab accident or some magic amulet, there's another ten people who just happen to be born with powers. People don't always know which category they fall into; they just know they have superhuman abilities."

"But I don't know that," Jack said. "Yeah, weird stuff

happens around me, but not because I'm doing anything. There isn't anything special I can do. Anyway, why bring me to the Imagine Nation if we're just going to get in trouble for it? I don't need to go someplace where everyone is going to give me a hard time. I could have stayed at St. Barnaby's for that."

"I'm bringing you there because I have a feeling about you," Jazen said. "You're special, Jack, you have to trust me on this. Standing right here, I can gauge your power level, and it's off the charts. You have incredible potential. I felt it all the way from the Imagine Nation."

"Really?" Jack asked. "Mr. Calhoun said my potential topped out at toilet brush cleaner."

"A toilet brush cleaner?!" Blue repeated, flabbergasted. "What?"

"That guy was a real piece of work," Jazen said, shaking his head. "You know I used the Department of Departmental Affairs line on him?" he asked Blue.

"You did not," Blue said.

"I did! Jack, am I lying?"

Jack shook his head and smirked, and Blue busted out laughing. Jazen followed suit, and eventually Jack did too. One thing about laughter, it's contagious.

When Jazen caught his breath, he turned to Jack with a smile.

"Don't worry, Jack. I've got a feeling the Imagine Nation is ready for you whether they know it or not. You've got a big future, a real big future. And it starts today."

"No doubt," Blue agreed. "Anyone says otherwise, and I'll bring the pain. Right, partner?" Blue added, tapping Jazen with a little punch on the shoulder.

"Right," Jazen said, wincing and rubbing his shoulder.

"We're partners now too," Blue said to Jack. He put his fist back out for Jack to bump. "Don't leave me hangin', little man. C'mon."

Jack smiled. "All right," he said, and gave Blue's fist a pound.

"That's what I'm talkin' about!" Blue said with a laugh, and he gave Jack a small pat on the back that nearly knocked him over the side of the boat.

That evening, Jack watched the sunset from the bow of the *Vision*'s forward deck. Out there on the ocean, the view was like nothing he had ever seen before. The whole sky was filled with an orange and red glow that lit the clouds from behind and made the colors spread out like finger paint. The sun was a golden coin, sinking into an invisible piggy bank somewhere far beyond the horizon. The warm breeze on his face and the soothing sound of gulls squawking in the distance was quite a change from the icy, gray weather he had observed from his window that morning. "Shouldn't it be colder out here this time of year?" he asked Jazen.

"This boat travels faster than you think—we've made some minor modifications to her," Jazen said with a wink as the *Vision*'s powerful motor hummed along smoothly. "Blue can't stand the cold, so he sped us out to warm waters while you were sleeping. We're somewhere in the Caribbean now."

"Is that where the Imagine Nation is?" Jack asked.

"It is right now," Jazen answered. "It's hard to say where the Imagine Nation is, though, because it never stays in one place for too long. It's what we call a roaming island."

"It moves?" Jack asked.

"The whole island," Jazen said, nodding. "All around the world, constantly. It never stays in one place long enough for people to simply stumble upon it. If you want to find the Imagine Nation, you have to really go looking. And people do. Or at least they did." Jazen gave a disappointed look. "People used to come from all over the world, each bringing along their own culture, their own style. When the island was close to China, when it was close to England, when it was close to Guadalajara, people from those places would seek out the Imagine Nation."

"But you said you have to believe in it to get there," Jack said. "How did they even know to look for it?"

"It wasn't always such a big secret," Jazen explained. "Before our time, the legend of the Imagine Nation used to be a lot more widespread. Emissaries did their jobs back then just like we do now, but back then, a lot more people took notice. In the Age of Exploration? During the Enlightenment? Back then, people had ambition. They had a sense of adventure."

"And today?" Jack asked.

"Today it's different," Jazen said, staring out at the setting sun. He looked sad, like he was watching the sun go down on something he cared for very deeply, something nearly gone. "It doesn't help when emissaries only do their jobs halfway, either," Jazen finally added. "We haven't closed the borders yet, though. By law, anyone who finds the Imagine Nation on their own is welcome on our shores, and people still do find the island. They find the clues, they hear the stories, and they come. It's not like it was before, though. Somewhere along the line, people just stopped believing."

"That's a shame," Jack said.

"It is," Jazen agreed. "But there's always tomorrow. We may not get as many visitors as we used to, but the people who come still go on to do amazing things. I'm not just talking about people with superpowers, either. I'm talking about writers, musicians, philosophers . . . people you've probably heard of. People who changed the world."

"But if there are really superheroes and other stuff out there, how come I've never seen them or read about them?"

"*Haven't* you read about them?" Jazen asked.

"Yeah, in comic books, but not in the news. Wouldn't that change things? Wouldn't more people believe?"

"We have people who make sure we stay out of the

news," Jazen said. "Don't get me wrong, I absolutely dream of a day when every man, woman, and child believes in the Imagine Nation, but we can't serve up proof on a silver platter. The world isn't ready for that. People have to discover it for themselves. We seed the world with the fantastic and new to change it little by little. Day by day."

Jack leaned forward on the railing and watched the waves roll by.

"Do I have family in the Imagine Nation?" he asked. "Do they know about me? Are they superheroes?"

"I don't want to get your hopes up, Jack," Jazen replied. "Your parents might be there and they might not. There's a lot of different ways you could be tied to the Imagine Nation."

"Like what?" Jack asked.

"Could be, your parents were normal people from New Jersey with distant relatives who come from the Imagine Nation," Blue called out from over at the wheel of the ship.

"Or you might have one parent who's a superhero and another one from the outside world," Jazen added.

"Then again, maybe they're both superheroes and

they're flying around Empire City right now," Blue said. "Of course, if that's the case, I gotta wonder how you ended up in New Jersey with the Rüstov chasing after you."

Jazen put his hands up. "We could do this all day. You're a mystery, Jack, but that's all about to change. First priority when we get to the Imagine Nation is to run a DNA scan and find out everything we can about you, starting with your name."

"My name?" Jack asked. "Can we really do that?"

"As soon as we get there," Jazen said. "That's a promise. Assuming, of course, you still want to go."

"Are you kidding? Yes, I want to go!"

"I can't guarantee it's going to be easy all the time," Jazen warned Jack. "Are you sure you're ready to deal with it? With all of it?"

Jack thought about what Jazen had said about the Imagine Nation not being very welcoming to new visitors at the moment. That meant Jack's future was every bit as uncertain as his past, but he thought about the past he *did* know. About life at St. Barnaby's with the likes of Mr. Calhoun, Mrs. Theedwheck, and Rex. A chance at something better had to be worth the risk. It had to be.

"Going back isn't an option," Jack told Jazen. "I'm ready. I'm in."

"Then what are we waiting for? It's time for you to take the wheel."

Jack's eyes became saucers. "You want me to drive?" he asked.

"You have to drive! You think I trust that big blue knucklehead to get us there?"

"I heard that!" Blue shouted.

Jazen laughed a little. "Besides," he added, "how can I make sure you believe if you're not the one driving us in?"

"I don't know," Jack said, a little nervous. "Machines and I don't usually work well together."

"Oh, I think you're doing okay," Blue said, giving Jazen a wink.

"We haven't sunk yet, have we?" Jazen asked.

Jack followed Jazen to the captain's wheel where Blue was steering the ship. Blue stepped aside, but he kept one hand on the wheel. "You believe, little man?" he asked Jack before letting go.

Jack thought about it. Just the idea alone made him smile. "I do," he said. "I believe in the Imagine Nation."

"Then take us home," Blue said, bowing in deference to the ship's new commander.

Jack grabbed the wheel, and the ship lurched to the port side as he took the helm.

"Whoa!" Jack said as he pulled the *Vision* back, righting the ship. She was a big boat. "Which way?" he asked.

"You tell us, Captain," Jazen replied.

"Captain," Jack repeated with a smile. "This morning I wasn't even allowed on a school bus!" This was by far the coolest thing Jack had ever done. Jack looked out at the ocean before him. They wanted him to find his own way to the Imagine Nation, and he had no idea where to start.

"Just follow your feelings," Jazen said. "We trust you. Trust yourself."

Jack closed his eyes and let his heart tell him which way to turn. It wasn't long before he had a heading that felt good. When he opened his eyes and looked around, something felt different. The water seemed cleaner. The air seemed fresher, even happier, if that was possible. The

Vision was surging over the waves, and Jack knew it was time to kick things up to the next level.

"How do you make this thing go faster?" he asked.

Jazen sat down and buckled up as Blue pointed toward a lever. "That one, but—"

Jack threw the lever to go full speed ahead, hurling the *Vision* toward the horizon and sending Blue straight into the back wall. Jazen laughed from the safety of his chair.

"—But you might want to take it easy at first," Blue grumbled as he got up.

Jack had never been happier. The boat was going so fast, it was almost flying, and it wasn't breaking down! What's more, he seemed to be on the right track. After a little while, Jack started to see all kinds of clues that they were nearing the edge of the normal, ordinary world.

"Thar she blows!" Jazen yelled, pointing off the starboard bow at one such clue.

Jack turned to see a giant blue-green dragon surface next to the *Vision* and soar through the air. It was a long, winding sea serpent with scales, fins, and a beautiful woman riding it. She had aquamarine skin and a glittering, bright gold dress. She kept pace with Jack's ship for a time, then waved good-bye and dove her mount back down below the waves.

As they sailed on, they passed pirates, mermaids, and talking fish. Jack felt like he had crossed a line drawn between the normal world and the imaginary. Everywhere he looked, his own eyes confirmed that even if something *was* imaginary, that didn't mean it wasn't real. The walls between the possible and the impossible were breaking down, but the weather turned uglier the farther Jack sailed.

Storm clouds started rolling in like angry spirits blocking out the sun. Jack could see them in the waters ahead, but he didn't turn away. Emboldened by his success thus far, he headed straight for the storm. Neither Jazen nor Blue questioned him. Jack reached the squall, and within minutes the sun was gone. Despite the hour, the sky turned black as night. Between the heavy rains and even heavier fog, Jack couldn't see anything. Still, he followed his heart. It had taken him this far. He just hoped it wouldn't take him to the bottom of the sea.

The fog was thick like smoke from a fire. After sailing completely blind for a few minutes, Jack spun the wheel to his left on instinct alone and just barely dodged a series of huge rocks jutting out from the ocean floor, large enough to scuttle the ship in an instant. Before he could even appreciate how close he had just come to death, something told him to jerk the wheel in the opposite direction, and he did. He followed that impulse, just missing a shipwrecked boat that was dashed upon more jagged rocks. There was danger all around as Jack weaved through countless near-misses in the fog, fighting the storm with nothing more than gut feelings and intuition.

If Jazen and Blue were scared, they weren't showing it. Their faces betrayed neither fear nor encouragement. This was all on Jack, and he steeled himself for what lay ahead. Throwing common sense out the window, he refused to change course. He was close. He could feel it. The storm raged against the *Vision* as lightning crashed and waves rained down upon the deck. Hurricane winds rocked the boat as Jack sailed on blindly through the mist. *Forward!* he thought. *To the heart of the storm! To the edge of the impossible! To the shores of the Imagine Nation!*

To clear skies?

Without warning, Jack cleared the mist, leaving the storm completely behind. The water turned dead calm.

With the setting sun nearly gone from the sky, the Imagine Nation came into view.

It was an astonishing, impossible sight.

The island floated in midair over the center of a ring of waterfalls, a thousand feet in diameter, opening up like a giant hole in the ocean. The falls ran to the bottom of the sea, and the roar of the rushing water was tremendous. Cities, towns, and villages were scattered across the island's lush green face. Countless airships bustled about in the skies overhead as well as on the rocky bottom below. A giant, translucent mountain with a razor-sharp peak and a wide base hovered behind the island like a crystal shard dangling in the sky.

As the last rays of the setting sun shone through, the crystal mountain became a prism that bent the sun's light in every direction, casting an image more beautiful than any rainbow Jack had ever seen. The massive, unstoppable waterfalls that surrounded the island roared with all the sound and fury of the seven seas. They called out to Jack, telling him that from this day forward, his life would be an extraordinary adventure.

Jack had found his way. He belonged. It was every

orphan's dream. All the answers to his questions, everything he ever hoped for, was waiting on the island. Twelve years after he was born, his life was finally beginning. He didn't have the words to express what he was feeling. Jazen had only two, but they were the right ones:

"Welcome home," he said.

CHAPTER

4

Empire City

Once Jack had had a moment or two to fully appreciate the mind-boggling view that was the Imagine Nation, it sunk in very quickly that he was headed straight for the world's biggest waterfalls. Unless someone plotted a new course in the next few minutes, it wouldn't be the only thing to sink very quickly.

"Permission to take the helm, Captain?" Blue asked.

"Permission granted!" Jack said, immensely relieved.

Blue stepped into Jack's place at the wheel of the

ship, and Jazen reached out his hand. "Fine work, Jack!" Jazen said, giving Jack a vigorous handshake. "That was impressive. Very impressive!"

"You mean it?" Jack asked.

"Are you kidding? You went straight through the heart of a white squall! Are you sure you've never captained a ship before?"

"I'm sure," Jack said.

"Okay, I'll take your word for it," Jazen replied. "Blue, how we doing?"

"All back full," Blue said, reversing the ship's engines. "Activating tangital control panel now."

Blue flipped a switch, and Jack heard a series of beeps as several keyboards and display screens started appearing all around him. They were all semitransparent images projected in luminous reds, blues, and greens. Jack thought they were more holograms like the TV inside the ship, but when Blue started hitting their buttons, the images didn't ripple—they clicked. They were solid.

"Cool, huh?" Blue said, noticing Jack's fascination. "These are tangitals. Tangible digital images. They've got all the computing power of your basic tech, but they take up less space because they're holograms. We call 'em Hard-Light Holos for short."

Jack reached out to touch the controls. "Can I?" he asked.

"Be my guest," Blue replied. "Hit that one."

Jack hit the button that Blue had indicated, and a woman's voice announced, "HOVER MODE ENGAGED." On the main display screen a schematic of the *Vision* appeared with sections of the ship's hull extending outward. Jack watched in wonder as hatches on the ship's extended panels slid open to light up with a blue glow, and the ship began to rise above the water. Once the ship was a good foot and a half clear of the relentless current, the holo-computer issued an alert beep and the woman's voice declared, "HOVER MODULES FULLY DEPLOYED."

Jack marveled at the futuristic technology all around him. "Minor modifications, you said?" he asked.

Jazen shrugged. "More or less."

"Is this how we're going to get across the falls?"

Jazen shook his head. "The HoverPanels can only lift us about two feet off the ground. They have to be close to the surface or they won't work. We're going to need help to get across."

"FriendShips at ten o'clock," Blue said.

Jack looked across the water and saw two small ships flying toward them. They were pod-shaped one-wing aircrafts, each with only enough room for one pilot. As they got closer, Jack could see a powerful mechanical arm below each wing.

The glow of the tangital communication display grew brighter than the other controls, and an official-sounding voice crackled over the radio.

"FriendShips *Beta* and *Zulu*, hailing crew of the *Vision*. Welcome home, Emissary Knight. Do you require an escort?"

Jazen tapped a holographic button to address the incoming pilots. "Thank you, gentlemen, that would be fantastic. We're ready whenever you are."

"Very good, sir," the voice replied, and the FriendShips swooped in and lined up next to the *Vision*, one on each side. The robot arms under their wings latched on to the ship and locked down tightly.

"Here we go," Jazen said as the FriendShips fired up

their engines and lifted the *Vision* high into the sky. Within seconds they were flying the boat through the air like birds gliding on a breeze.

"We call them FriendShips because they carry you wherever you need to go," Jazen explained as they soared through the sky. "There it is up ahead. Empire City, capital of the Imagine Nation. That's where we're headed."

Twilight was setting in, and Jack got a good look. It was the most unusual city Jack had ever seen or even imagined. It was built on a hill that ran right up to the cliffside edge of the floating island, and Jack could see what Jazen had meant when he said that people brought their own cultures and styles with them when they came here. Looking at Empire City was like looking at six cities crammed into one. Jazen called out the different boroughs of Empire City, describing them for Jack as they made their approach.

There was Galaxis, the futuristic spaceport, home to aliens from across the cosmos and beyond. Directly above that was Karateka, a singular fusion of modern and ancient China, where kung fu masters trained in martial arts disciplines long forgotten by the outside world. On the opposite side of the city the walls of Varagog guarded gothic castles, medieval villages, and ancient magic. Behind that stood the mysterious and ever-changing borough of Cognito, where the streets had no names and the residents answered no questions. Higher still were the smooth-lined towers of Machina, shimmering with data bytes and binary code messages that only the androids who lived there could read. And in the center of Empire City, towering over the wide expanse of SeasonStill Park and the majestic monuments of Hero Square, were the mighty skyscrapers of Hightown, the tallest buildings in the world. As the evening sky took on a shade that was equal parts purple, red, and pink, the shining towers of Hightown responded with an opalescent reflection that was so beautiful, it seemed to be singing the next verse in the sky's favorite song.

This was Empire City, capital of the Imagine Nation, and Jack's new home.

Below the edge of the city, built into the rocky underside of the island, was a hangar bay large enough for a thousand ships to land. The FriendShips pulled the *Vision* in safely, and Jack was finally there. It was an exhilarating moment. The FriendShip escorts disengaged and waved good-bye as a team of men in blue and gray jumpsuits rushed out to load the *Vision* into HoverStorage. Jack jumped down from the deck of the ship as the flight crew carted the *Vision* off for safekeeping. He couldn't stay inside the ship a second longer. He was too excited to stay inside of anything now that he had one foot in a whole new world.

"Holy cow," Jack said, looking around in wonder.

The flight deck was filled with all manner of space-age shuttles, ultramodern fighter jets, and flying saucers. Everywhere Jack looked, there were men and women wearing skintight supersuits and other brightly colored costumes complete with capes and masks. They were flying off into the sky and landing under their own power, and that was just the beginning.

There were people wearing jet packs. There was a boy creating discs of light out of thin air and then throwing them like Frisbees at his little brother until his mother told him to stop. There was a man made out of electricity talking to a woman made out of solid rock. There was a ninja warrior arguing with a futuristic robot about a parking space. The myriad powers of everyone on the crowded flight deck were impossible to discover in a single glance around. Jack stopped dead in his tracks, hypnotized by the sight of it all. Jazen snapped his fingers to get his attention and keep him moving.

"Jack. Jack, you okay?"

Jack snapped out of his daze. "I don't believe it."

"If that were true, you wouldn't be here," Jazen replied.

"Is everyone here a superhero?" Jack asked.

"Not everyone," Jazen replied, leading the way through the hangar. "Remember, you don't need superpowers to find the island, you just need to believe. But you name it, we've got it. Ninjas, sorcerers, aliens . . . even a few so-called 'regular' people. Emissaries like me are supposed to bring the gifted here to the Imagine Nation, but not every gift is a superpower, Jack. Not every superpowered person decides to become a superhero, either."

"They become supervillains?" Jack guessed.

"I try not to use that term," Jazen said. "There are some real villains out there, sure—people who use their powers to do whatever they want, no matter who gets hurt. But some people who get labeled as supervillains are just misunderstood. Not everyone's looking to take over the world."

"Some people just don't want to be heroes, either," Blue added. "That's okay; it's a lot of pressure being a hero. Some people would rather just go on about their lives, like Gramps here." Blue gestured toward an old man carrying around a two-ton jet, looking for a parking space.

"Coming through!" the old man grumbled as he pushed past them.

As Jack, Blue, and Jazen walked to the other end of the flight deck, glowing letters that took the place of signs started scrolling through the air around them. They flashed out the words HALL OF RECORDS in an endless loop. Jack followed the signs through the cavernous hall. As he neared the other end, Jack noticed several flying surveillance cameras skittering about in the air. Eventually, they scurried over to him. Each one was about the size of a winged football, with "SmartCorp" written on the side in shiny blue lettering.

"Blue. SmartCams," Jazen said, pointing to the flying cameras.

"I see 'em," Blue said, reaching out to shove one away. "Go bother somebody else," he muttered as the SmartCam skidded through the air and bumped into one of its compatriots.

"Sorry, Jack, these things are everywhere lately," Jazen explained. "They're really annoying." The SmartCam whirred around them with a series of angry, offended beeps, but kept its distance as they rode a turbolift up to the records room.

The Hall of Records was carved deep into the rocky interior of the island's base, and was even more crowded than the flight deck. It was a customs and security checkpoint just like in an airport, except instead of bustling tourists and passengers, it was jam-packed with superhumans, robots, and aliens. There were giants who were bigger than Blue waiting in line next to monsters and people with four arms. The ceiling must have been at least a hundred feet high, and Jack looked up to see superpowered fliers waiting in midair lines. Words continued to flow through the air, blinking out directions like RESIDENT ALIENS, RETURNING CITIZENS, and SECURITY CHECKPOINT. Everyone was producing paperwork and going through security checks. There were big, transparent X-ray panels at the head of each line for people to step behind, and

Jack could see right through to people's skeletons.

Jack and the others navigated the crowd past winding lines of people, as well as advertisements that flashed off the walls like pop-up banners from the Internet, calling out SMARTCORP: BRINGING YOU TOMORROW . . . TODAY! and SMARTCORP: THE FUTURE IS NOW! Jazen led the way through the great room with a swagger, and Blue swatted away SmartCams that buzzed around like gnats. They made their way to a completely empty line next to the words NEW VISITORS.

The podium at the head of the line stood empty. Jazen hit a signal light, requesting service. "You see how many new visitors we get these days, Jack? We don't even staff the line anymore," he said, shaking his head. "Let's get started on the paperwork while we wait." Jazen gestured to a row of glowing forms floating next to the line and snatched one from the air. When his hand touched it, it turned into a solid piece of paper with a blinking cursor flashing on the page.

"What's that?" Jack asked.

"SmartPaper," Jazen said. He showed Jack an immigration form with blank spaces for Name, Code Name,

Age, Date of Birth, and other similar information. "It's like a computerized sheet of paper. It's just as thin as regular paper, but you can edit it like it's still on a computer screen. You can highlight stuff, delete things, change fonts, whatever you want. It's another tangital. Smile!" Jazen said, holding the page up like a camera in front of Jack's face. A light flashed and Jack's headshot was inserted directly into the top-right corner of the form.

"This is awesome!" Jack said, grabbing the paper to check it out. The back of the page read "Another Smart-Corp innovation."

"What's SmartCorp?" Jack asked.

"The biggest company in the world," Jazen answered. "They do business all around the globe, but under a lot of different fake names. You'd be amazed at who some of their front companies are. Tangitals and Hard-Light Holos were invented by the owner of the company, a man named Jonas Smart."

"He also invented HoverPads, SmartCams, MagLev roads, and a ton of other things," Blue added. "In addition to being the senior member of Empire City's Inner

Circle, he also runs SmartCorp. These days, that means he pretty much runs Empire City."

"He must be a genius," Jack said. "Do you think I'll get to meet him?"

"Probably sooner than you think," Blue said, looking at Jazen. The expression that Jazen returned silenced the giant.

Jazen tried to fill out the form for Jack but couldn't put in much. He didn't know Jack's real last name, birthday, or any family information. However, there was one section that they could try to figure out on their own: the description of superpowers.

"I don't know," Jack said, still somewhat skeptical. "Trust me, I've spent a lot of time reading comic books and thinking about superpowers. A *lot* of time. If I had any powers myself, I think I'd know about it."

"Not necessarily," Jazen explained. "Especially at your age. Depending on the power, you probably wouldn't even be deliberately controlling it. But in times of stress, excitement, or fear . . . there are flare-ups."

Jack thought about it for a minute. He had to admit, that did sound like him.

"You said weird stuff happens around you," Blue said. "Weird like what? Weird like this morning with the Rüstov?"

"No, nothing like that," Jack said. "Machines act funny around me—that's it. Maybe I make them break and stuff?"

"I don't know," Jazen said, stepping behind an X-ray screen at the head of the line. The X-ray panel revealed Jazen's insides to be a mechanized system filled with millions of flashing lights and wires hiding underneath his skin. "Something tells me that's not it."

Jack nearly fell over when presented with the sight of Jazen's electronic insides. "You're a robot?" Jack exclaimed.

"I'm an *android*," Jazen replied. "A bioengineered Mecha with a human appearance. Here, check it out."

Jazen rolled up his sleeve and double-tapped his inner forearm. Jack watched as short bursts of compressed air escaped Jazen's arm and a panel of skin dropped down and slid away. Inside, a complex circuit board lit up like a slot machine. Jack latched on to Jazen's arm and peered inside for a closer look. Jazen's skin felt soft and natural, but there was no denying the hard steel frame and circuitry underneath.

"That's why you set off the alarms back at the harbor," Jack said, fascinated by Jazen's inner workings. "This is so cool! I can't believe you're a robot!" he exclaimed.

"Android," Blue corrected again. "Jazen's an android. We call 'em Mechas here in Empire City."

"And look at that," Jazen said, pointing to a digital display near his wrist. It read that all systems were operating at 100 percent capacity. "I feel fine around you, so your powers have got to be something else."

"Yeah," Blue added, "besides, you steered the *Vision* like you'd done it a million times before. That's a pretty big machine."

"That was weird," Jack admitted. "It was like the ship just knew what I wanted to do. I was surprised that it came so easy, but I was too psyched to even think about it."

"Interesting . . . ," Jazen said, thinking.

"Why didn't you tell me about being a ro—I mean, android, earlier?" Jack asked.

"I didn't want to blow your mind," Jazen said. "You passed out when you saw Blue; I didn't know what you'd do when you saw this."

"This is the coolest thing ever," Jack said again, sticking his hand behind the X-ray panel to get a look at his own bones, then sticking Jazen's hand in next to compare. Meanwhile, someone finally appeared behind the podium. It was time to get down to business.

The customs clerk was a space alien whose skin had a gray and black quality that emitted a white glow. He looked like a black-and-white film negative. "Can I help you?" he asked in an annoyed tone. His voice had an echo-like reverberation that gave Jack the chills.

"You can try," Jazen replied. "Emissary Jazen Knight." He flashed his badge. "I'm here to process this boy for entry into the Imagine Nation."

The clerk paused a moment, as if he didn't quite hear Jazen correctly. "A new visitor?" he asked.

"That's right."

"This line is not open, sir," said the clerk. He started to walk away, but Jazen grabbed his wrist.

"Then I suggest you open it," Jazen said. "As far as I know, the borders of the Imagine Nation aren't closed."

The clerk locked eyes with Jazen for a moment, but quickly lost the staring contest with the emissary. He could see that Jazen wasn't backing down. "No, sir, the borders are not officially *closed*," the clerk said, pausing to look up at a SmartCam that was trained directly on him. He then leaned in toward Jazen and spoke softly. "But it is our understanding that in these trying times, with the Rüstov threat to our planet still lingering, that all emissaries have been discouraged from bringing new visitors to the Imagine Nation."

"Interesting," Jazen replied. "I guess I didn't get the memo. I've actually been *encouraged* to bring this boy here." Jazen held up Jack's forms in front of the clerk. "Let's get started." The clerk still hesitated.

"I'd do what he says if I were you," Blue said, bearing down on the clerk. "You see, I'm here with them, and I *really* don't have a lot of patience for waiting in lines."

The clerk's lips quivered as he stared up at Blue. He reluctantly took the form and fed it into the screen of his holo-computer, grumbling about how he better not get in trouble for this. The page broke up into a million data bytes, then reassembled in the proper order, projected in the air next to the podium with most of the information still missing.

"Relax," Jazen said to the clerk. "For all we know, this

boy's a returning citizen. We don't have any info on his background. You're going to need to run a scan to find out who he is."

"Put your finger there, please," the clerk said, indicating a red dot on the podium. Jack did as he was told, and a needle pricked his finger.

"Ow!" he said, pulling back his hand.

"It's just a little pinprick," the clerk said in a curt tone. "We need a drop of blood for the DNA scan. See? It's searching the database now."

Jack looked up at the screen that displayed a single drop of his blood. It read SEARCHING.

"I can't believe this," Jack said. "Am I seriously going to find out my real name right now? I mean, what if I still have family here? I might have relatives, a home . . ." Jack held his tongue, forcing himself to say no more, but he couldn't help thinking about what else might be waiting for him in Empire City. There might even be a mom and dad.

A ding sounded and a light on the screen flashed green.

"We have a match," the clerk said, a little surprised.

Jack's heart leaped. "You do?" he exclaimed. "Really?"

"Looks like you *have* been here before." The clerk nodded. "We'll just pull up your birth certificate, and . . . wait a minute." Before the clerk could finish, the screen froze and started flashing red. The screen zoomed in on Jack's blood drop to reveal millions of tiny microchips floating inside of it. Jazen and Blue leaned in toward the screen with confused looks on their faces. "Nanites in the blood?" the clerk exclaimed as he watched the screen in disbelief.

"What the?" Jazen said. "No, that can't be right."

"What can't be right?" Jack asked. "What's going on? Where's my file?"

"Legend's ghost!" the clerk gasped, clapping a hand over his mouth. He looked at Jack and his white glow intensified greatly. Jack got a real bad feeling in the pit of his stomach as the fear rose up in the clerk's face.

"Hang on a second," Jazen began. "Don't-zzzt-don't-zzzt-don't . . ."

Jazen stopped in place like a frozen computer as the clerk slammed his hand down on an alarm and screamed, "RÜSTOV!!!"

Heads spun around from every direction as the alarm

sounded. People shrieked in terror. Shock and confusion took over the crowd as the sirens wailed in the background.

The orderly crowd in the Hall of Records devolved into a frenzied mob running for the exits. The room turned to chaos, and hundreds of people ran, flew, and teleported out every available door. SmartCams zoomed in and started buzzing around Jack with flashing lights as an alarm blared over and over:

"INFECTION! ALARM! QUARANTINE! INFECTION! ALARM! QUARANTINE!"

"I don't get it," Jazen said, regaining his movement. "I had a glitch. I never glitch!" He looked at Jack.

"How can he be infected?" Blue asked. "Look at him, he's fine!"

"What do you mean, infected?" Jack asked. "What's happening? What about my file?"

Jazen looked around and pulled Jack in close to protect him. "I think we might have to wait on that," he said just before something blew a hole in the wall behind them. It wasn't an explosion. It was a man. When the smoke cleared, they were surrounded by a group of tough-looking superheroes and a legion of soldiers with laser rifles.

"I hate to say I told you so," Blue said to Jazen. "But I told you so."

Jack, Jazen, and Blue were taken to a secure room somewhere above the Hall of Records. It wasn't the worst room to be stuck in, since it had a majestic view of the waterfalls that surrounded the island. Still, the team of supers that escorted Jack in there had no intention of letting him leave. They were called the Peacemakers.

The Peacemakers all wore the same black supersuits, complete with the SmartCorp logo and different colors specific to each team member. While waiting, Jazen and Blue explained to Jack that the Peacemakers were a private security force, not real police. They were founded as a result of some ill-advised laws passed shortly after the Rüstov invasion to ensure the security of the Imagine Nation. There were several Peacemaker teams like this one, each with just enough authority to be truly dangerous. They were empowered to act as judge, jury, and executioner when it came to the Rüstov. For obvious reasons, that didn't sit well with Jack.

"What are we doing here?" Jack wanted to know. "What's going to happen to me?"

"Don't worry about it, Jack," Blue said. "We just have to hang here until Jazen sorts this out. This is all a big mistake. It's gotta be."

"The only mistake was you thinking you could sneak a Rüstov into the Imagine Nation," said Surge, the Peacemaker team leader who was a human power cell. Instead of blood, he had pure energy coursing through his veins. He was so filled with power, it leaked out his eyes and mouth if he didn't release it. The red lines on his suit glowed brightly as his charge built up to full capacity. Harrier, the woman next to him, was a walking arsenal: a bionic commando with golden body armor, a winged jet pack, and more guns than any one person could possibly need. Finally, there was Speedrazor, a thin but superfast Peacemaker with pale white skin and straight black hair that went down to his shoulders. His skintight black suit cut off at the forearms, revealing shiny silver hands with fingers sharp as knives. Jack decided he didn't like these Peacemakers one bit.

"What are we waiting for?" Speedrazor railed from

across the room. "The child is infected. Once the Rüstov takes root, the host is already dead." Jack blinked and the man crossed the room and placed his knifelike fingers to Jack's throat. "We have to put him out of his misery. For his sake as well as ours! This is exactly what the Peacemaker teams were created for!"

"He's not infected!" Jazen said, grabbing Speedrazor's shoulder. "You touch one hair on that boy's head and Blue is going to make sure you get a real close look at those waterfalls out there."

Blue glared at Speedrazor. "You think you're fast enough?" Blue asked. Speedrazor scowled and dropped his hand away from Jack's neck.

"Too bad," Harrier observed. She fine-tuned the laser sights on an oversized gun. "It would be a mercy."

"Says you," Blue replied. "Don't pay 'em no mind, Jack. These Peacemakers are just glorified rent-a-cops, if you ask me. Corporate mercenaries."

Speedrazor smirked mockingly. "Sticks and stones may break my bones . . ."

"That sounds like a good idea to me," Blue cut in. "You threaten Jack again and I just might."

"You're not going to do anything," Surge said. "This is a Rüstov matter. We outrank you here."

"You don't outrank *me*," Jazen cut in. "Jack is a charge in my custody. He can't be touched and you know it. As an emissary of the Imagine Nation, I can only be overruled by the Inner Circle on this."

"We've called the Inner Circle," Surge said, his eyes gleaming with power.

"So, we'll wait until the Circleman gets here," Jazen said. "Until then? Stay on your side of the room. We'll stay on ours."

Jack rubbed his neck where Speedrazor's bladelike fingers had scraped his skin. He was lucky to have Jazen and Blue there to defend him. Jack was used to standing up for himself, but these bullies were a lot tougher than Rex Staples and his coffee breath.

"Jazen, what's the Inner Circle?" Jack asked under his breath.

"A group of very powerful beings," Jazen answered. "They're elected from each borough of Empire City to govern and defend the Imagine Nation. I think one of them might have wanted me to bring you here. With any luck, he'll get here before their boss does."

"Jazen, what if they're right?" Jack asked. "What if the Rüstov from this morning infected me somehow? Can that happen?"

The door swung open and a SmartCam flew into the room. Jazen frowned.

"PRESENTING CIRCLEMAN JONAS SMART!" the SmartCam announced, introducing a tall, gaunt man with a grim face, sunken cheeks, and dark circles under his eyes. He had unusually long fingers and black hair that was graying at the temples. His black one-piece suit made him look like a walking shadow, and his mood was no brighter. Jack wasn't so excited about meeting this man anymore.

"Hello, Jonas," Jazen said, nodding a cold greeting to the Circleman.

"Emissary Knight," Smart replied with the same lack of warmth.

Smart took in the room slowly, rolling his eyes from left to right, and eventually settled on Jack. The look on his face sent shivers down Jack's spine. Smart leaned down to Jack's eye level and studied him with narrow, penetrating eyes, scrutinizing his face from several different angles.

"This is quite alarming, Emissary Knight," Smart began. His voice rang with a deep, rich resonance, like the sound of a purring cat. "I always assumed that sooner or later you would attempt to challenge our informal border control policy, but I never once imagined that you would attempt to smuggle in a Rüstov spy."

Jack took offense at that. "I'm not a Rüstov spelughh—"

Smart interrupted Jack by sticking a tongue depressor into his mouth. He held it open and shined a penlight inside to look around. Jack fidgeted as Smart moved on to his eyes, holding the lids open and shining the light into each pupil.

"He's not a spy," Jazen said, taking away Smart's penlight and pulling Jack free of his clutches.

"But he *is* infected," Smart countered.

"Not a chance," Blue said.

"See for yourself," Smart said. He took out a pocket holo-computer and projected a lab report on Jack's blood into the air. "The blood tests are quite conclusive."

Jack watched with his heart in his throat as Jazen

crossed the room toward the holographic report and studied it for what felt like forever. Finally, Jazen turned to him with a defeated look on his face.

"I'm sorry, Jack" was all Jazen could muster.

"You're infected with a Rüstov parasite," Smart added without feeling. "I'm afraid there's no cure."

All the color drained from Jack's face. His stomach went cold, like he had just swallowed a freezer full of ice. His mind reeled, and somewhere in the back of his brain, he started wondering just what ended up happening to Prime in the missing pages of *Unreal Tales #42*.

"What does that mean, no cure?" Jack asked, frantic. "Am I going to die? Am I going to turn into a Rüstov? How much time do I have?"

"Very little, if I can help it," Smart replied. "Speedrazor, if you don't mind?" Speedrazor smiled, bared his claws, and started toward Jack.

"Whoa, whoa, whoa . . . not so fast, psycho," Jazen said to Speedrazor, stepping in front of Jack. "What do you think you're doing?"

Smart looked surprised at Jazen's challenge, but he didn't miss a beat in responding to it. "The law is very clear on dealing with the Rüstov. Distasteful though it may be, the infected branch must be cut away before it endangers the tree. I don't know why you think this boy should receive special consideration."

"Open your eyes!" Jazen shouted. "It's obvious Jack is a special case. Infected or not, he doesn't even have the mark of the Rüstov on his eye. You know that whenever the Rüstov infect a new host body, that mark is the first thing to appear. Jack doesn't show any signs of decay at all!"

"The boy is quite a find, I can't argue with you there," Smart admitted. "His infection almost appears to be in complete remission."

"He might even hold the key to a cure!" Jazen said. "He could be the answer to defeating the Rüstov!"

"Yes, the boy promises to be extremely valuable to my work," Smart agreed. "There's no denying that."

Jack breathed a sigh of relief.

"After he is executed, I'm going to want him brought immediately to my lab. He needs to be dissected and studied extensively."

Jack's relief quickly evaporated.

"Executed?" Jazen asked.

"Dissected?" Jack added, his eyes bulging out of their sockets.

"Extensively?" Blue said.

"You can't have him executed!" Jazen told Smart.

Smart sighed. "Emissary Knight. Where there is one Rüstov today, there will be a hundred tomorrow," he replied coldly. "When the parasite is done with him, others will be next. It's elementary. Perhaps I should have said 'put to sleep'? Would that have been more sensitive? I'm afraid I'm not very good at emotional expressions."

"It doesn't matter how you say it!" Jack shouted. "What are you, crazy?"

Smart rolled his eyes. "What I am is the smartest living person on planet Earth. If my decisions confuse you, it is simply because you aren't smart enough to understand them. Now please, adults are talking."

"I won't let you do this, Jonas," Jazen said. "This is a child under my protection."

"Yeah, I have rights!" Jack said. He paused to look at Jazen. "I do have rights, don't I?"

"No," Smart scoffed. "As far as the law is concerned,

you died the second the infection took hold. You're an enemy combatant. You have no rights."

"He's a citizen of the Imagine Nation!" Jazen said. "Check his record."

"I have—it's worthless," Smart replied. He used his pocket computer to project Jack's birth certificate into the air. Sure enough, the form appeared, but it was just scrambled letters and meaningless gibberish. "It's your fault, you know. When you ran his DNA scan, the nanites in his blood corrupted the file with the Rüstov techno-virus. It's frozen. Useless. We had to sever the infected file from the system so the virus didn't spread to the entire SmartCorp database. This child has neither a past nor a future."

Jack grabbed the tangital image from the air to get a closer look. Smart was right—the file was ruined.

"You're a heartless jerk," Jazen said.

"I'm quite comfortable with who I am, Emissary Knight. The Imagine Nation is at war," Smart declared. "We must remain ever vigilant against our foe. I'd execute a thousand children like him if I thought it would keep us safe."

"The Imagine Nation is a democracy," Jazen countered.

"The entire Inner Circle has to vote on this, not just you."

Smart scowled. "Have a care, Emissary," he told Jazen. "It isn't prudent for a Mecha to side with a Rüstov. There's a little too much history there, I should think."

"I'll take my chances. And so will Jack."

"Have it your way." The Circleman snorted. "It won't change anything. The law is very clear on this, and I haven't lost a vote at the Inner Circle since being elected nearly twelve years ago."

"You mean, you haven't lost a vote since Stendeval disappeared twelve years ago," Jazen said. "I'm calling for a full circle vote. As an official in the Empire City Police Department, Blue here is a witness to that. The entire Circle will be here tomorrow for Dedication Day. You're going to have to wait at least that long."

Smart grinned a sickening grin. "Fine—we'll finish this in the sphere," he said, then turned to Jack. "This is a stay of execution, nothing more," he said in a frigid tone. "Until tomorrow. I'll be waiting." He angled a long finger up to the floating SmartCam. "And I'll be watching."

Smart left the room without another word. The Peacemakers followed him out.

"Wow," Blue said. "That went well."

Jazen looked away, embarrassed. Jack looked up at the SmartCam that was hovering over him, recording and broadcasting his every move. "I guess I'd better get used to these things," he said.

It turned out Jack was right. The SmartCam followed Jack and the others out to Blue's HoverCar and up through the ritzy streets of Hightown. It trailed them past energy trains that ran up the sides of buildings, and over highway bridges that crossed between soaring skyscrapers.

Blue kicked the HoverCar into flight mode and blew the car by NewsNets that were broadcasting footage from the SmartCam on floating billboards. The headlines declared: RÜSTOV SUPERVILLAIN ALLOWED TO STAY IN EMPIRE CITY! NO ONE IS SAFE! Impromptu interviews with Smart and his Peacemakers condemning Jack as a Rüstov threat played on giant floating screens. Everywhere random superpeople flying through the skies, or fighting one another in the streets over who knows what, stopped what they were doing to read and watch the breaking story. Within minutes the entire city knew about Jack's arrival. He was news. Big news.

Rocketing away from the SmartCam, Blue pulled the HoverCar up to the 437th floor of the Ivory Tower, an immaculate white building in the center of Hightown. The curved window of Jazen's apartment slid open outside the car door. Jazen keyed in a sequence on the dashboard, and a holo-platform appeared below the car so they could safely get out. Jack said good night to Blue, who promised to see him in the morning. He told Jack to remember that he and Jazen had his back. Jack thanked him and followed Jazen into the apartment.

"All right, Jack, this is your new place," Jazen said. "What's mine is yours."

"Yeah," Jack said as he trudged into the building and into a posh living room. "For one night at least." He plopped down on a couch.

The emissary exhaled with a sympathetic air. It was amazing how well his android systems reproduced every human function and emotion. "It's been a long day," Jazen admitted. "I know you haven't exactly received the warmest welcome, but it's going to be okay. It really is."

Jack wasn't so sure.

"You know, back at St. Barnaby's, I always thought about

what it would be like to be a superhero when I grew up," he said to Jazen. "I didn't dare say that to Mr. Calhoun, but I did think about it. Then when you told me about this place, and about my superpowers, I started to think about it for real." Jack shook his head. "I haven't even been here a full day, and already I'm a supervillain instead."

"Hero and villain are *both* overused words, if you ask me," Jazen said. "Not all heroes wear capes and masks, Jack. A real hero just wants to make a difference in the world. He gets out of bed in the morning and tries to make the world a better place, that's all. That's the kind of hero I try to bring back to the Imagine Nation. That's why you're here."

"You think I could be that kind of hero?" Jack asked. "Even with the whole Rüstov thing?"

"I think you could be anything you want," Jazen said. "Now try to get some sleep. I promise you, we'll take care of all this tomorrow."

Jack agreed that he was exhausted and it was time to call it a day. He was soon off to bed in the guest room that Jazen kept ready for visitors to the Imagine Nation. It was a sparsely furnished room, nothing too extravagant, but far nicer than anything Jack had ever known. He pulled the covers over himself, hoping things really would look better in the morning.

As the SmartCam bumped up against the window trying futilely to get inside, Jack had mixed feelings about this new home. He was free of St. Barnaby's. He had his own room in an apartment overlooking a wondrous city of superheroes, aliens, and magic. He should've been on top of the world. Sadly, even in a place like this, where nobody in the entire city could be considered remotely normal, Jack still couldn't fit in. He stared at the picture in his infected history file, quite certain that he'd never find out who he was.

Jack lay in bed, his energy fading fast, and the lights in the room faded with him. He was so incredibly tired after such a long day, he almost didn't notice the lights shutting off by themselves. But he did notice, and when he realized what was happening, it got him thinking about the lights in the library that morning. He thought about how he had been feeling when the lights had flared up and blown out. Next, he thought about that day when Rex had stolen his calculator, and how he had been feeling when it had broken. Finally, he thought about how he was feeling right there in that room.

He was tired, and the lights were going out. . . .

A completely different kind of lightbulb switched on in Jack's head. He had it. His mind raced back through the rest of the day's events and more. Suddenly, it all made sense to him. He felt a burst of excitement, and the lights responded in kind. Just like Jazen had told him. Flare-ups. Jack couldn't help but smile a little as he drifted off to sleep. It seemed he recognized his superpowers after all.

CHAPTER

Dedication Day

The next morning, Jack awoke to find a man sitting outside his window.

As if seeing a man sitting outside of a window on the 437th floor wasn't strange enough, this man appeared to be sitting on the air itself. He had an orange-white glow emanating from his body, and a ring of red energy particles swirling around him. He appeared to be an Indian man and had a clean-shaven head that was decorated with five or six lines of red henna paint on his dark brown skin. The stripes were drawn from the back of his head to the front, running toward a single red dot in the center of his forehead.

Jack moved over to the window and opened it. The man's eyes were closed and he was humming gently with his arms outstretched. "Hello?" Jack said. "Can I help you?"

The man didn't hear Jack at first. He sat there with his legs folded, humming away. He was barefoot, dressed in loose-fitting bright orange clothing, with a crimson silk belt tied around his waist and a matching red sash slung over his shoulder. He opened his eyes to find Jack staring at him.

"Oh, hello," he said, eyeing Jack's messed-up, mangled morning hair. He had a deep, rich voice. The accent was a mixture of English and Indian, sounding both comforting and wise. "Did my meditations rouse you from your slumber? Forgive me, young friend. That was not my intention."

Jack was a bit surprised to receive such a neighborly reaction, but he certainly wasn't complaining. It was a nice way to start the day after getting off to such a rocky start the night before.

"It's okay," Jack said. He rubbed his head, trying in

vain to get a cowlick to lie down. "It was about time for me to get up, anyway. Besides, I've never seen anyone meditate four hundred floors up before. That's kind of cool."

"It's how I welcome each new day," the man said, looking out on a glorious city morning. "A day such as this should never be wasted, not even for a minute. I trust this morning finds you well?"

"We'll see," Jack said, still slightly wary of each new person he met in Empire City. "You're not going to start screaming and run away or try to dissect me or anything, are you?"

The man's back straightened. "Dissect you? What an odd thing to say," he replied, somewhat confused. "That also is not my intention."

Jack pointed to a billboard that was puttering by with his face stretched across a high-definition screen. The scrolling headlines questioned whether Jack was an evil spy, a supervillain, or both. "Sounds about right to me," Jack said. "I'm not exactly normal. Even for this place."

"Why would you ever want to be normal?" the floating man asked with a laugh. "To try and be normal in Empire City would be abnormal. Normal is boring. Differences inspire. Every now and then, there comes a person so incredibly different that everyone normal wishes they were different in the same exact way."

Jack nodded. "I never thought of it like that."

"You should try," the man said, returning to his meditations.

"Jack? Who are you talking to?"

Jack turned around to see Jazen standing at the threshold of his door. Before Jack could answer him, there was a flash of light behind him, and he spun back around to find the man in orange was gone. In his place there was only a spinning mass of energy particles shrinking into an ever-tightening spiral until they vanished from sight. Jack shrugged. It was probably nothing out of the ordinary for this place. Just another day in the city.

"I don't know," Jack said. "No one, I guess."

Jazen nodded. "We've got a big day ahead of us, Jack. Better get started. How do you feel about breakfast? I've got 2.7 million recipes in my memory bank, you know."

Jack's stomach growled. "Breakfast sounds great."

Jazen led Jack downstairs to the kitchen, where appliances were already springing to life and preparing an exotic breakfast filled with foods Jack had never seen or even heard of. In the morning light Jack got his first good look at Jazen's apartment, a spectacular open-air loft space. Throughout the loft, steps were suspended in midair, leading up and down to Anti-Gravity platforms that supported a kitchen, living room, and multiple game rooms on separate floating stages. Everything had a sleek futuristic design—light on the furniture and heavy on glass and steel.

"This is some place," Jack told Jazen, ogling the apartment.

"Perks of the job," Jazen replied. "Loft space in the Ivory Tower gets rented out at five thousand credits a month, but emissaries get to stay here free of charge. Not bad, huh?" Jazen took a moment to admire the view from the curving windows that lined the walls of the lavish apartment. "Like I said, this is your place too now, so make yourself at home."

"I will," Jack said. "At least until they dissect me, anyway."

"Hey," Jazen said. He walked over to Jack and put his hand on the boy's shoulder. "That isn't going to happen. Everything's going to be all right, I promise."

"You're probably programmed to say that."

Jazen pulled his hand back. "I happen to be self-programmed, just like every other Mecha in this city. I'm a sentient android with free will. I make up my own mind about things, same as you."

Jack could tell he'd hit on a sensitive subject. "I'm sorry, Jazen, I didn't mean anything by that. I'm just really messed up by this whole Rüstov infection thing."

"Don't be," Jazen said. "You're going to beat it."

"How do you know that?"

"Listen to me, Jack, because this is important," Jazen began. "No one's ever survived a Rüstov infection. Ever. When a person gets infected, circuits weave their way through bones and tissue, transforming every inch of what was once a person into a Rüstov soldier. The body starts to rust and decay, and it takes less than a minute to start happening. No one's ever lasted longer than that." Jazen smiled. "But look at you! You don't even have the Rüstov mark on your eye. Your parasite doesn't control you; you control it. You have to trust me on this, Jack: You're special."

"You're the only one who seems to think so," Jack

said. "Mr. Smart and that guy with the sharp fingers really freaked me out yesterday. My face is all over the news. I'm a little worried about what else is going to be out there today."

"I'm not going to lie to you," Jazen said. "There are people in the Imagine Nation who are going to be suspicious of you. They might wonder if you're safe to be around, or if you're a Rüstov spy. Some people are going to wonder if you beat the parasite, or if it's just a matter of time before you turn into one of them."

"How many people?" Jack asked.

"Almost everyone," Jazen answered.

Jack slumped into a chair. "Fantastic."

"Jack," Jazen said, "nothing is going to happen until you go before the Inner Circle. And you're with me," he added. "You should know my systems are equipped to handle seventy-two percent of all superhuman attacks we may encounter in the city today."

"Really? Seventy-two percent?" Jack asked. "Why didn't you say so? In that case, I've got nothing to worry about!"

Jazen raised an eyebrow, allowing a slight smile to cross his lips. "Seventy-two percent covers more than you might expect," he said. "I'm also one hundred percent fluent in sarcasm, in case you were wondering. Now finish your breakfast. We're going to be late."

After breakfast Jack and Jazen rode a lightning-fast elevator 437 floors down to the lobby, where the Smart-Cams were anxiously waiting to begin their broadcast day. They didn't get much footage for their trouble. Jazen had a HoverCar ready and waiting. He ushered Jack quickly inside and followed him in, careful not to step on the road.

"The HoverCars in Empire City don't run on gasoline," Jazen explained. "They have powerful electromagnets that propel them along MagLev roads that are charged with the same magnetic currents. If any metal, including what makes up my interior frame, gets too close to the road, it gets magnetically locked down to it until someone comes and cuts the power to the street."

Jazen tinted the windows to give Jack a break from the SmartCams and staring onlookers as they drove through Hightown. To Jack, it looked like the New York City he had seen in his comic books, only fast-forwarded about a thousand years into the future. There were buildings stacked on top of other buildings, with streets, bridges, and trains running endlessly through the gaps in between. HoverCars, AirSpeeders, and countless superpeople criss-crossed paths on their way through jam-packed highways and skyways. Men and women swung through the air, flew across the sky, and jumped off rooftops. A whole family of superspeedsters ran alongside Jack's car before veering off in another direction, and Jazen drove past three separate superhuman battles along the way to Hero Square.

Jack and Jazen were just gliding down the street when something thumped on their roof. Jazen didn't bat an eye, but Jack certainly did when he looked out the windshield and saw a ninja crawling onto the hood of their car. Jack recognized the colors the ninja wore from his comics. "That's a ZenClan ninja," he said, somewhat surprised to hear the words coming out of his mouth.

"It certainly is," Jazen replied. The ninja asked Jazen to speed up, and he was happy to help out. He was chasing two other ninjas wearing white masks with no holes for the nose or mouth. Their form-fitting white suits were as tight as a second skin stretched over their long, stringy bodies and thin, chiseled muscles. Jack recognized them, too.

"Are those . . . Ronin assassins?" Jack asked Jazen.

"Yup," Jazen said. "Let me guess, you read about these guys in *Dragonfist Comics*? Or was it *Kung-Fu Killers*?"

"*ZenClan Warriors*, actually," Jack said.

Jack rolled up his window and locked his door. The Ronin always creeped him out whenever they showed up in a story—undead, soulless ninjas who worked for the evil ShadowClan Shogun. If Jack had to see them in real life, he was glad that it was in broad daylight with a ZenClan ninja hot on their tail. Based on what he'd read about them, these ShadowClan ninjas were not creatures he ever wanted to meet in a dark alley.

The Ronin were flipping back and forth between speeding cars as they swiped at the ninja on Jazen's hood with sai blades and dodged punches and kicks. Not every driver dealt with the distraction as well as Jazen seemed to. Up ahead, a HoverCar swerved to avoid a Ronin's leap, crashing into a truck right in front of Jack and Jazen.

"Buckle up, Jack!" Jazen called out. Without slowing the car down, he banked a hard right onto a street that literally ran straight down. Jack's stomach jumped up to his throat as the car made a ninety-degree turn and raced down a hundred-foot vertical drop. Jack buckled up just in time and screamed like he was on a roller coaster. This was not a steep hill they were driving down; they were driving down the side of a skyscraper. When they reached the bottom, Jazen just kept driving like it was no big deal.

"All right, excitement's over," Jazen said. "Just a random superfight. No big thing. Are you okay?"

"Yeah," Jack replied. He paused for a moment. "Can we do that again?"

"Maybe later," Jazen replied. "Look out your window, I want you to see something." Jazen turned into a fenced-off area. "Remember when we were flying in and I mentioned SeasonStill Park?" Jack nodded and Jazen continued, "This is it. Each corner of this park is permanently fixed with the weather of one of the four seasons, so kids can play in whatever weather they want. You'll definitely want to come back here later when we have more time."

Jazen drove through the snow flurries blowing in Winterwind Way, past the swimming holes and tire swings in Spring Falls, the bright autumn leaves dropping around the lakes of Fall Springs, and finally past the boardwalks and beaches of the Summershore Stretch. Jack decided that this was the best park in the world, a playground for all seasons. He wanted to see more, but Jazen said he had to get him to the Dedication Day festival by noon.

"What's Dedication Day?" Jack asked Jazen with his face pressed up against the car window.

"It's where we relight the Legendary Flame Monument and dedicate the city to the memory of the man who saved it during the invasion. The history books of the Imagine Nation simultaneously remember it as both our greatest victory and worst defeat."

"The Legendary Flame?"

"It's in Hero Square, where the festival is held each year. That's where we're going."

"Tell me about the invasion," Jack said. "What happened?"

"The Rüstov happened," Jazen replied. "It was twelve years ago today. It was terrible. Without any warning the entire Rüstov Armada appeared one morning and launched a full-scale invasion on the Imagine Nation. Thousands died. It . . ." Jazen paused, as if lost in the memory. "It was the first day of a war some people say might never really end."

"I thought you said we won that battle," Jack said. "The superheroes fought back, right?"

"Everyone fought back," Jazen said. "Even the so-called villains. But there were so many Rüstov, and every infected super became another soldier in their army. The battle for Empire City went on for an entire day, and there was one of them . . . There was one of the invaders who just could not be beaten . . . Revile." When Jazen said Revile's name, he scowled. The loathing and dread in his voice was palpable, synthesized android speech or not. "Revile was a Rüstov supersoldier who simply could not be killed. No matter how many times our side blew him up, he regenerated. He rebuilt himself from scrap, again and again and again. In the end, it was only Legend, the strongest of all our heroes, who could fight him."

"I never heard of Legend," Jack said. "He was the strongest hero?" Jazen nodded. "Tougher than Captain Courage?" Jack pressed.

"Captain Courage?" Jazen laughed. "C'mon, Jack," he added, shaking his head. "Captain Courage is just a comic book character. Legend was real."

Jack didn't quite understand why a real-life Captain

Courage was any crazier than real-life Ronin assassins, but he didn't interrupt Jazen.

"When all the other supers fell, Legend fought Revile by himself," Jazen continued. "He never gave up. Even when he knew he couldn't defeat Revile, he just kept going."

"How did he win?"

"The Legendary Sacrifice," Jazen said in a reverent voice. "Revile engaged a self-destruct mechanism, what the Rüstov call the 'Omega Protocol.' He was going to detonate his nuclear power source and blow up the entire city. A cheap and cowardly way to end the battle, but it would have worked. It would have worked if not for Legend, that is. He grabbed Revile and flew him straight into the Rüstov mothership, right into the Infinite Warp Core engine. The explosion filled the sky, destroying the mothership, Revile, and any hope the Rüstov had of winning the Battle of Empire City."

"And destroying Legend, too?" Jack guessed.

Jazen nodded. "We won the battle, but it cost us the greatest hero the world has ever known. Today we dedicate the city to his memory, and celebrate lasting another year in our war against the Rüstov."

Jack leaned back in his seat and exhaled deeply. It was quite a story, but as he turned it over in his head, something about it didn't quite fit. "I don't get it," Jack said. "How did the Rüstov find the Imagine Nation? Did someone take them here like you took me?"

"Yes," Jazen said bitterly. "A traitor. The Great Collaborator."

"A traitor? Did they ever catch him?"

Jazen thought about it for a moment. "That all depends on who you ask," the emissary said as he pulled the car up to the edge of Hero Square. "We're here." Jazen got out of the car, and Jack hopped out after him. Jack's curiosity about the Great Collaborator was quickly sidetracked by the spectacle of Hero Square.

The square was gigantic: a gargantuan plaza built from granite and marble, at least a thousand feet wide and packed with people—humans, aliens, superhumans, and nonsupers—as if all of Empire City had turned out for the Dedication Day festival. There were food vendors, candy stands, and street performers scattered everywhere, combining to create a dizzying array of scrumptious smells and flying acrobatics. Jack and Jazen passed beneath a colossal arch and out onto the animated plaza.

An immense, classic stone building lined the perimeter of the square with arches, pillars, and a museum-like stateliness. Floating over a pedestal in the center of it all was a giant iron sphere with several large rings swinging around it like a gyroscope. Jazen explained that this was the heart of Empire City. The boroughs of the diverse metropolis surrounded the square like members of a dysfunctional but happy family.

To Jack's right the ancient walls of Varagog stood strong like a fortress against the modern era. Jack spotted chivalrous knights, fair maidens, and noble monarchs gathered behind gothic castle windows. Hundreds of provincial townsfolk lined the tops of the stone walls, standing on every ledge and peeking through every nook and cranny. It was like a place that time forgot.

On Jack's left was the exact opposite, the space-age borough of Galaxis. Alien families from across the universe were huddled together on the roofs of orb-shaped buildings and on the decks of glistening starships. Jack looked up past the boroughs of Karateka, Cognito, and Machina. He looked on to the towering spires of Hightown. The skyscrapers were all built into the hills of the island. From Hero Square, Jack could see the entire city.

Behind Jack a stone bridge ran through the square, past the edge of the island and out over the bottomless waterfalls. At the end of the bridge stood the statue of a noble hero, reaching out to the city with a tiny blue flame burning in his palm.

"Is that—"

"Legend," Jazen finished. "The man who saved the Imagine Nation from the invaders."

Invaders like the one hiding inside of me, Jack thought. The very idea made his skin crawl. An alien parasite, somewhere inside his body, living off him. That wasn't even the worst of it either. The worst was that it might one day take him over. It was exactly what everyone in Hero Square was worried about.

As Jazen led Jack through the crowd, the reaction that Jack got was pretty much the one he expected. His face was already famous all over Empire City, and not in a good way. Music grinded to a halt, and the crowd parted like the Red Sea. People were shrinking back, mumbling to one another about "the infected boy" and giving Jack dirty looks. Even more were shouting angrily at Jack, calling him "Rusty." The SmartCams caught up to Jack and broadcasted live coverage on the NewsNets like reality TV. Jack could tell that nobody wanted him there. They were afraid of him and what he represented. Part of him had to wonder if they were right to feel that way—if it really was only a matter of time before he turned into a Rüstov. He shut the thought out of his mind. He had more immediate concerns, like the Inner Circle and the mob of people outside the sphere. The crowd's fear made it dangerous, and Jazen's assurance that he could fend off 72 percent of any trouble was not very reassuring. To make matters worse, Jack recognized the uniforms of several more Peacemaker superteams working security, scaring people back behind dotted lines. If the crowd decided to go after Jack, the Peacemakers were more likely to join the mob than stop it. Jack grew more nervous until he saw a familiar blue face in the crowd.

Blue walked out to meet Jack and Jazen, flanked by several large members of his police unit. They were all part of the Brute Force, a squad of Empire City's toughest supercops. They escorted Jack safely through the mob and deposited him at a special VIP area directly under the black iron sphere.

Standing in the VIP area were two other children Jack's age. The first, a girl with liquid metal skin, shrieked when she saw Jack and turned into something resembling a puddle of mercury. A boy, dressed in the garb of a young squire from Varagog, actually drew two swords on Jack before Jazen stepped in to stay his hand.

"Easy, Skerren, we're all friends here," Jazen said to the boy. The young swordsman muttered something decidedly unfriendly and skulked off on his own. "What'd I tell you?" Jazen said to Jack. "No worries."

"Yeah, we're doing great," Jack replied, pointing up at a NewsNet screen that read RÜSTOV SPAWN TERRORIZES HERO SQUARE!

Jazen grumbled at the headline and led Jack to the marble pedestal. They walked up a staircase that was carved into the sides and stood directly beneath the sphere. "Here we go," Jazen said. A moment later, the platform began to rise up toward the iron globe above them. The sphere's swirling rings whizzed by over their heads, and Jack thought about just how much it would hurt to get hit with them. He also took note of the solid iron frame of the fast-approaching orb. "Shouldn't that thing have a door?" Jack asked.

A ring swung by, inches from the top of Jack and Jazen's heads. Jack ducked, missing whatever Jazen said in reply as they continued rising toward the sphere. There was no door opening up that Jack could see. They were going to slam right into the bottom.

Another ring flew by, but closer and faster this time. Jack and Jazen were almost at the sphere, and just as Jack was sure they were going to be crushed against the bottom, they passed right through it. The iron surface gave way and became soft metal that ran over Jack's skin like melted chocolate, only without the stickiness. Jack passed through the sphere unharmed and emerged inside the sanctum sanctorum of the Inner Circle. As the metal exterior of the sphere slid off his skin, Jack looked around. This was the place where his fate would be decided. The rest of his life, however long or short it might be, would hinge on the next few minutes in this great, round room.

CHAPTER

6

The Inner Circle

On the outside, the sphere of the Inner Circle was only about ten or fifteen feet across. On the inside, the sphere was bigger than a football stadium. There was enough room to fit fifty thousand people or more, and the only thing more striking than the vast space hidden inside the sphere was its complete and utter emptiness. Jack and Jazen were alone, standing in a pit, and looking up at a table that ran around them in a circle. The pit wasn't very deep, but it was still an intimidating spot to be in. Jack was scared, though he trusted that Jazen knew what he was doing. He was pretty sure he did, anyway.

Six separate tunnel openings lined the walls of the sphere. Each one had the name of an Empire City borough inscribed above it and a path leading to a seat at the tribunal. Jazen explained that this was where the Inner Circle met, although it was more like the Half Circle these days. There were supposed to be six Circlemen, one person elected from each borough. When all six were there, they were said to be at "Full Circle," and could choose a seventh member to join them. "Right now there are two empty seats," Jazen explained, pointing up toward the empty chairs. "That seventh seat once belonged to Legend. The seat next to it, the one from Cognito, belonged to Stendeval."

There was that name again. Jack remembered Jazen mentioning Stendeval's name back when Jonas Smart was talking about executions and dissections.

Jack's reaction to the name must have struck Jazen as odd. "You don't know Stendeval," Jazen probed, "do you, Jack?"

Jack's eyebrows tied themselves up into knots. "Know him?" he asked. "I just got here. I don't know anyone but you and Blue."

"Right, right, of course," Jazen said, clearly disappointed. "It's just that no one's seen him in twelve years, and I thought maybe . . . never mind."

"Who was he?" Jack asked.

"He was the Circleman from Cognito. That's what we call them," he added, gesturing up toward the seats. "He held his seat for almost five hundred years. He was a real hero, like Legend. And he was a good friend."

"Five hundred years?" Jack asked. "How'd he live so long?"

"It had something to do with his powers, but I'm not exactly sure."

"Why hasn't anyone replaced him?" Jack asked.

"He was there so long," Jazen said. "After five hundred years he was more than just a man. He was an institution. No one could replace him. No one wanted to try to fill his shoes. Also, you have to understand, Cognito is an odd part of town. The whole place is one big hideout. People go there to disappear, not run for elections. If they wanted to be in the public eye, they wouldn't be in Cognito."

Jack thought Cognito sounded like a good place for

someone like him to live. "What's it like there?" he asked Jazen.

"I don't really know. Without Stendeval, Cognito's more mysterious than ever, and the Inner Circle . . . well, it just isn't the same. I can tell you this: If Stendeval were here, we wouldn't even be talking about anyone dissecting you."

Jazen had a concerned look about him that he couldn't quite hide entirely. He didn't come right out and say it, but Jack got the feeling that with Stendeval gone, anything could happen.

Jack gulped as the clock struck noon. It was time. Jack heard footsteps in the tunnels, and the members of the Inner Circle began to enter the sphere. The first to arrive was a giant man dressed like a medieval swordsman, with a thick, bushy beard and a fur cloak. Jazen whispered that the brute was the warrior king of Varagog Village. Jack recognized him instantly as Hovarth, the barbarian warrior from his comic books. "Holy cow, that's Hovarth!" Jack said. Hovarth looked down on him with a suspicious eye and rested a giant sword and battle-ax on the table. Next, a man with silver skin and a bright blue supersuit flew into the room. He took his seat at the Galaxis chair. Jack knew who he was too.

"That's Prime!" Jack exclaimed.

"Right again," Jazen said.

"I don't believe this," Jack said. "He's one of my favorite heroes!"

"One of ours, too," Jazen said. "He's the Circleman of Galaxis. He's also one of the last Valorians in the galaxy, which is something you may or may not have read in your comic books."

After Prime, a mechanical orb about the size of a grapefruit whizzed into the room. The orb settled by an empty chair and then projected a beam of golden light that formed the shimmering image of the most beautiful woman Jack had ever seen. She looked like a backup character from a sci-fi comic book Jack liked. "Is that . . . Virtua?" he asked.

Jazen looked at Jack, a little surprised. "Just how many comic books have you read, Jack?" he asked.

"A *lot*," Jack answered.

Jazen told Jack he was correct, and that Virtua was the new Circlewoman of Machina. Like Jazen, she was a sentient program, a Hard-Light Holo projection of a gorgeous artificial intelligence. She was followed by another familiar face: Chi, the Circleman of Karateka and leader of the ZenClan ninjas. Chi walked slowly toward his seat and then flipped through the air to land in it without making the slightest sound. He looked just like he had in Jack's comics. He was an Asian man with snow-white skin, wearing a sleeveless blue karate robe over a black supersuit. He carried himself with a quiet, dignified authority—a dangerous ninja wrapped in a cloak of tranquility.

Finally, the Circle was joined by Jonas Smart, who also required no introduction. The Inner Circle was filled with heroes from Jack's comic books. He hoped that would work in his favor, but had no idea how accurate the portrayal of these heroes in his comic books really was. Jack looked from face to face. Virtua showed signs of pity, Hovarth eyed him with contempt, and Smart's expression conveyed outright disgust. Prime looked on Jack with a stern military gaze, and Chi's face was impossible to read. "Call me crazy, but I don't think any of *these* guys wanted you to bring me here," Jack said to Jazen.

Jazen stared at Stendeval's empty seat. He opened his

mouth to say something, but stopped when Jonas Smart knocked on the table, calling the meeting to order.

"Shall we begin?" Smart asked the rest of the Circle, leaving Jack to wonder what Jazen had started to say. "The reason I called this meeting is standing before you now," Smart said, walking around the Circle like a lecturing professor. "Throughout the ages the people of the Imagine Nation have been blessed to live in the best of all possible worlds. As we in the Inner Circle all know, that is no accident. We have fought to keep things this way, and paid for our perfection with the blood of heroes. That fight continues today. Our world is under siege." His face turned sour. "Twelve years ago we were invaded by an enemy who has targeted us as the next stop on an intergalactic feast. Invaders who go from planet to planet, eating up all life and natural resources before moving on to the next target. One needs only to look upon the once-green planet of Mars to understand the full scope of the devastation that the Rüstov leave in their wake."

"Jonas," Prime interrupted, "we were all there. The whole of this Circle fought in the battles. What is the point of this history lesson?"

140

Hovarth answered for Smart, speaking in a thick English accent. "I think the point, Prime, is that if we're not careful, history might repeat itself."

"Thank you, Hovarth," Smart said. "That is exactly right. The Rüstov attacked us here first, knowing full well that if the Imagine Nation were to fall, there would be no one on this planet strong enough to stop them. These are dangerous times. The idealist traditions of our great nation notwithstanding, we do not need to be tempting fate by bringing new people into our lands, people we do not know or trust beyond the shadow of a doubt." Smart pointed to Jack. "Emissary Knight has crossed the line by bringing this creature, this infected child, here. Knight will tell you this boy is somehow resisting the Rüstov technovirus. What I see is a Rüstov sleeper agent, brought here by a Mecha, no less! Emissary Knight expects us to stand by idly while he sneaks an infiltrator in to infect our perfect world! Impossible. I want this boy terminated and sent to my lab immediately, and Emissary Knight dismantled pending a full investigation."

"You can't do that!" Jack yelled.

Smart shot down a fierce look. "Emissary Knight, you will instruct your charge to be silent or—"

"The boy has a right to defend himself," Jazen cut in. "And so do I, for that matter."

"Jonas, please!" Virtua agreed. "Emissary Knight's loyalties are well-known. Let the boy speak. I for one would like to hear what he has to say." Chi and Prime agreed, and Smart sat down and sulked.

"What should I say?" Jack whispered to Jazen.

"Just tell them the truth," Jazen said. "Tell them who you are. You've got nothing to hide."

Jack swallowed hard and looked up at the Inner Circle. Smart's words had cut him pretty deep, but Jack could at least take comfort in the knowledge that he wasn't a Rüstov sleeper agent. He also thought about what Jazen had said earlier. It didn't matter that no one else had ever survived the Rüstov infection. He could beat it. He was special. He had to be to make it this far, didn't he? Jack wasn't so sure. He didn't feel very special. His stomach felt hollow like an old, dead tree. He could barely breathe, let alone speak.

"Hi. My name is Jack Blank?" he squeaked out, sounding more like a question than a statement. "I'm uh . . . twelve years old, and I, umm . . ." Jack paused, unsure what to say next. "I wasn't really ready for all this," he admitted. "I don't know anything about invasions, I don't know anything about Rüstov spies . . . I don't even know my real name. I just know that I'm not a Rüstov." Jack was finding his voice. "I know it's only my word against Mr. Smart's, and you don't have any reason to trust me. You don't know me. But I know you. I read about all of you back where I came from. You're my heroes. Heroes wouldn't go through with something like this. The heroes I read about would give me a chance. Because I'm not a Rüstov. I'm just me. I'm just a kid who would really love to not be dissected."

Jazen patted Jack on the back. "Well said," he muttered. The panel stared back at Jack with curious eyes.

"What do you mean, you don't know your name, boy?" Hovarth asked.

Jack shrugged. "I don't know anything about who I am," he said. "I only found out yesterday that I was born here. I have this birth certificate. We were hoping to find out more, but my file was ruined." Jack took out his infected file and placed it on the table above him. "I'm not looking to make any trouble for anyone. Really, I'm not." The members passed Jack's file around the table, examining it. Hovarth held it with only two fingers, keeping it as far away from himself as possible, before passing it to Prime.

Prime squinted at the file but didn't seem to make sense of it. "Jonas, is there no other way to get any information about this boy's past?" he asked. "No other way to find out who he really is? He may be telling the truth."

"That information is immaterial—he is infected," Smart replied. "As for his records," he continued with a patronizing tenor, "I'll spare you the history lesson and simply remind you that countless records were lost in the invasion along with a great many lives. His family is most likely dead."

"Jonas!" Virtua scolded. "Don't say such things!"

"We can hardly assume otherwise," Smart replied. "The SmartCams have been constantly broadcasting his image since he arrived and no one has claimed him."

"That's hardly surprising given your coverage of his arrival," Virtua countered. "'Rüstov spawn terrorizes Hero Square?' A bit sensational, I think."

"It's the truth," Smart said. "This boy is a danger to us all. I refuse to take any chances with him. Lives are at stake."

"Including *his* life!" Jazen said. "He's one of us. He has powers and he's immune to the Rüstov infection. They tried to kill him because of it. When I found Jack, he had just destroyed a Rüstov Para-Soldier."

A surprised murmur ran through the panel. Prime tilted his head, clearly impressed. "Is this true?" he asked. When Jack nodded, Prime seemed pleased. "Just what are your powers, young man?"

"He doesn't know what—," Jazen began.

"I control machines," Jack interrupted.

"You what?" Jazen asked.

"I figured it out last night," Jack quickly whispered to Jazen. "I was going to tell you, but I didn't want to freak you out. You know, seeing as how you're technically a—"

"Don't worry about me, tell them!" Jazen exclaimed.

"I control machines!" Jack repeated, turning back to Prime and the rest of the Circle. "I don't mean to do it, it just happens. It doesn't happen all the time, but that's got to be it. It's the only thing that makes sense.

Machines react to my feelings. My mood. Yesterday I was really excited and drove a huge boat through a crazy storm to get here. I'd never even been on a boat before, but it worked with no problem. In the Hall of Records I had all this nervous energy and suddenly Jazen had a glitch. And before that . . ." Jack paused and thought about the events of the previous day in a new light. "Before that I was really scared and yeah, I'm pretty sure I used a power generator to blow up a Rüstov Para-Soldier."

The Inner Circle whispered excitedly among themselves.

"Destroying a Rüstov Para-Soldier . . . ," Prime repeated. "Impressive for a boy your age. More than impressive."

"It's simply unheard of," Virtua added. "Your powers must be mighty, indeed."

"It makes sense," Jazen said, seizing the moment. "It makes perfect sense. Let's say Jack controls machines. The Rüstov are living machines! If his power is automatic, that has to be how he survived infection this long. His natural instinct to survive is keeping the Rüstov in check. That's how he controls the Rüstov inside him!"

"But he doesn't control his power," Hovarth argued. "It changes with his moods. What if the Rüstov adapts when he relaxes? Gains the upper hand?"

"That's why Jack belongs here, where we can teach him to control his abilities," Jazen argued.

"It's why Jack is dangerous," Smart countered. "For all you know, this boy is controlling you right now. He could be using you to slip past our defenses so he can call back the Rüstov Armada!" Smart turned to his fellow Circlemen. "This is all the more reason why Emissary Knight has to be dismantled, if only temporarily. I want to run a full diagnostic on him. He's not himself! I'm not questioning his loyalty, it's this . . . *child*. He needs to be exec—" Smart stopped himself. "He needs to be *put to sleep* so that we can end this threat. Then I can dissect his body and examine both his biological organs and any technological tissue. It's the only way to harvest his power so that we can all resist the Rüstov infection. That way, everyone can benefit!"

"Everyone except me!" Jack said. "They're not actually going to do this, are they?" he asked Jazen.

Jazen looked over the Inner Circle's faces one by one, trying to guess their feelings on the matter. "This is the

Imagine Nation!" Jazen pleaded. "Here, of all places, we should be able to find an alternative to this. I know what I'm doing. I'm not being controlled by Jack."

"So *you* say," Hovarth interjected. "Surely it is better to err on the side of caution, no?"

"Not if it means dismantling me and killing this boy," Jazen said. "We've already sacrificed so much to the Rüstov. We've all but closed our borders. Now we're going to kill the people who come here?"

"You're the one who brought him here, Emissary Knight," Smart noted. "His blood is on your hands."

"Harming this boy won't serve this city," Jazen replied. "It will betray everything the Imagine Nation stands for. If you do this, the Rüstov have already won."

"On the contrary," Smart reasoned. "Legend's sacrifice against the Rüstov proves that the suffering of one individual can, in fact, serve the greater good. The logical conclusion is that the more suffering we see, the better things are actually getting."

"That makes no sense!" Jack objected.

"Child, don't tax your feeble mind trying to understand why I'm right—just accept that I am," Smart said. No one else argued with him. Jack was suddenly worried. Coming into the sphere, Jazen had made it seem like Smart's whole plan to dissect him was too crazy to take seriously. Now it looked like a real possibility. "Enough of this," Smart continued. "I move that we vote on this matter now, and then proceed to the festival outside."

"I have a question first," Chi said softly, speaking up for the first time.

Smart blew a sharp snort of air out his nostrils and frowned. "How nice of you to join us, Chi," he quipped.

Chi opted not to dignify Smart's barb with a response. He directed his attention to Jack and Jazen. "How exactly did you find this boy, Emissary Knight? What led you to him?"

"It's part of my job to seek out gifted ones, Circleman Chi," Jazen replied. "Generally, when dealing with power levels like Jack's, they're impossible to miss."

"Yes, but that wasn't the case here, was it?" Chi guessed. "I reviewed the SmartCam footage from the Hall of Records. You told the customs clerk that you were encouraged to bring this boy back. What did you mean by that?"

Jazen hesitated but was compelled to speak. "Two

nights ago I received a letter . . . a letter that told me about Jack. It was from somebody important, somebody we all trust. He told me where to look for Jack. I followed the directions, and there Jack was."

"Who was this letter from?" Chi pressed, digging deeper.

Jazen pulled an orange envelope from his jacket pocket and held it in the air. "It was from Stendeval," he said.

The entire Circle let out a collective gasp, but no one was more shocked than Jack. A letter from Stendeval, the man who had been missing since the Battle of Empire City, written about him?

Smart wasted no time in casting further suspicion on the matter. "I can see why Emissary Knight didn't bring this up himself. That letter was probably sent by the Rüstov!"

The letter was passed around the table, and the Circle erupted with arguments debating its legitimacy. All of the Circlemen were up in arms, quarreling. All except for Chi, who somehow maintained his Zen-like calm. "Thank you, Emissary Knight," Chi said peacefully. "Jonas, I agree. We are ready for a vote. I invite you to begin."

"I intend to," Smart said. He stood up, clearly upset by the Stendeval business. He cleared his throat, then straightened his jacket and hair, composing himself like a lawyer readying his closing statements.

"Even if you don't believe this child is a Rüstov conspirator," Smart began, "no one can argue that he is not infected. Our laws demand that we terminate him before he becomes one of the Rüstov himself. It is unfortunate, but there is no other possible future for him. Any attempt to forcibly remove a Rüstov parasite has resulted in the death of the host, in every case! On the motion to have my Peacemakers execute the infected child and donate his body to science, I vote yes," Smart said, unflinchingly certain of his own infallibility.

As Jack listened to Smart pontificate before the Circle, he was floored by the man's ice-blooded nature, as well as the absolute pride he seemed to take in that nature. Jonas Smart wore his lack of a heart on his sleeve.

"I might add that I resent Emissary Knight's tactics," Smart added. "Invoking the name of Stendeval in the hopes that it might sway this panel's ruling. You dishonor his memory, sir." Smart pointed an accusing finger in Jazen's direction. "But perhaps that is part of the enemy's plan. A mysterious letter written in the hand of an old friend. Someone whom we all miss. Whom we all trust. But a letter telling you to bring an infected child into the Imagine Nation . . . It troubles me that you did not find this suspicious, Emissary Knight. I further move that the emissary should be dismantled immediately for a full system scan by SmartCorp engineers. Circleman Prime, you are next."

All eyes turned to Prime, who was pondering the issue with a very serious look on his face. "As you all know, the Rüstov destroyed my home world and killed nearly everyone I ever loved," Prime said, rising to his feet. "And despite everything they have done to me, I still say they will find no more ardent foe than you, Jonas Smart. You are willing to kill children to defeat them." He shook his head. "I will not vote to kill this boy because we are afraid of what he might become. If he turns or corrupts the emissary, I will be ready. I am a Valorian soldier, and the sons of Valor know no fear. I vote no. On both counts."

Jack breathed a sigh of relief as Prime returned to his seat.

The vote moved on to Hovarth of Varagog. Hovarth picked up his sword and stared down the blade, examining it. "I'm sorry, lad," he said with a distant look. "I mourn the loss of all who fall prey to the Rüstov, I truly do. But in Varagog we trust no machines, and it's only a matter of time before you become one." Jack's face fell. "Take heart, young fellow!" Hovarth urged. "If what they say is true, if we can discover a cure to the Rüstov virus by studying your body, why, you'll be remembered as a hero!" he promised with great enthusiasm. "In Varagog we ask nothing more from life. On both counts, I vote yes."

Hovarth's vote made the score now 2-1 in favor of executing Jack and dismantling Jazen. Jack's heart pounded in his chest and his mind raced. What would he do if he lost the vote? There was no way for him to escape the sphere. He was trapped, and one more vote against him would seal his fate.

Chi stood at his seat, his expressionless face hiding any emotion. Jack fought the urge to hyperventilate. He was just about ready to really freak out.

"I vote no," Chi said firmly. "Jack is an innocent child. Emissary Knight has done nothing wrong. No other explanation is required."

Jack exhaled deeply and smiled up at Chi, mouthing

the words "Thank you." He wasn't out of the woods yet, though; it was time for the tiebreaker. He held his breath for the final vote.

"It seems that it is up to you now, Virtua," Smart said fiendishly. "A word of advice before you decide this matter. Do not forget it was your predecessor, the android Silico, who was revealed to be the traitor to this Circle—the Great Collaborator responsible for the Rüstov invasion."

Virtua looked daggers back at Smart. "I haven't forgotten," she said. "I haven't ever forgotten! What exactly do you mean, bringing this up to me now?"

Smart put up a finger. "Think for a moment. A vote for this child could be interpreted by some as the behavior of a Rüstov conspirator. A vote to protect the infected? To protect the Mecha that brought him here? It all reeks of more traitors in Machina. Tread carefully, or I might be forced to send Peacemaker teams in to sweep your borough for Rüstov agents all over again."

Virtua's holo-image flickered as she let out a startled gasp. Prime pounded the table, his fist crackling with radiant energy. "You go too far, Jonas Smart!" the Valorian bellowed.

"The public would demand it!" Smart retorted. "Don't subject your people to that over this boy," he told Virtua. "Who knows who might get caught in the cross fire?"

"That's not fair!" Jack yelled. "He's bullying her! You can't bully her like that!"

"This is blackmail!" Jazen agreed.

"I'm merely offering my opinion," Smart said, waving his hands. "By all means, Virtua, vote your conscience. We are all equals in the Inner Circle," he added with a smug grin.

Virtua looked trapped, and Jack could tell she was conflicted. The look on Jazen's face didn't do anything to put him at ease either. Jack could see that Virtua wanted to vote in their favor, but the looming shadow of doubt cast by talk of the Great Collaborator worried her, and that worried Jack. If one more vote went the wrong way, he would be as good as dead and Jazen would be spare parts.

"There is no cause for concern," Chi announced. "I am sure your counsel is appreciated, Jonas, but the final decision will not fall to Virtua's shoulders alone. You see, it is not yet her turn to vote."

Chi motioned to an empty chair between himself and Virtua—the chair that had once belonged to Stendeval.

"You're not serious," Smart said, incredulous.

The Circleman of Varagog roared with laughter. "Chi, Stendeval has been missing for years! Do you think he's going to come here today simply because the emissary got a mysterious letter? Jonas is right; surely the letter was sent by the Rüstov."

"No, it wasn't, actually," Chi stated, his voice cool and even.

"You know this for truth? How?"

Chi reached into his robe. "Because twelve years ago Stendeval sent me a letter too. He wrote to tell me that on this day he was going to be fifteen minutes late for a meeting concerning one Jack Blank."

The room fell silent as Chi dropped another, much older orange envelope onto the table.

"Imagine that," he added with a smile.

Jonas Smart picked up the letter and read it silently to himself. The clock on the wall struck 12:15 p.m., and Jack saw all the color drain from Smart's face.

A gust of wind blew through the room. Above Jack's

head, tiny red energy particles swirled in the air, spinning outward from a teeny-tiny dot into a large ring. A humming sound grew and the room shook.

A radiant orange-white light flashed out, blinding Jack. When Jack's sight returned a moment later, a man was floating in the center of the room with his legs folded beneath him. He had dark brown skin and red lines painted on his smooth, bald head. The entire Inner Circle, whom Jack imagined saw the impossible happen every day, fell speechless.

"Hello again, young friend," the man in orange said to Jack.

"Am I glad to see you," Jazen said.

"Yeah," Jack agreed. "It's good to see you again . . . Stendeval."

CHAPTER

7

The School of Thought

"Og's blood!" Hovarth exclaimed. The feeling was shared by everyone in the room, even if they didn't put it the exact same way.

It took a minute for the group to get over the initial shock of Stendeval's return and also for Stendeval to give everyone a proper hello. He first greeted Chi, whom he had written to about this moment so many years ago. Stendeval lowered his head in a formal bow to the ninja master, who returned the swift motion with his arms at his sides. Facing Prime, Stendeval raised a fist to his heart, in what looked to Jack like some kind of Valorian salute. Prime snapped to attention and returned the gesture without a word. Next, Stendeval greeted Virtua and congratulated her on her election to the Inner Circle. He also offered his condolences about Silico, the reason her seat was open in the first place. On the other side of the table, Stendeval gave Hovarth's hand a hearty shake. Hovarth leaned in to look him closely in the eye, perhaps to see if it was really him. Whatever he saw satisfied his curiosity, and he told Stendeval it was good to have him back. He appeared to genuinely mean it. The same could not be said for Jonas Smart. He reached out to Stendeval, offering his hand with all the strength and enthusiasm of a dead fish. "Welcome back," he said drily.

Once the formal greetings were complete, Stendeval nodded to Jazen and Jack with a thin smile and drifted through the air to his seat at the table.

"I must apologize for my lateness to this meeting," he announced. "And also for the fact that I will be unable to answer any questions regarding my whereabouts for the last twelve years." Stendeval settled into his chair like an old pair of comfy slippers. "I hope I have not missed the vote."

"You have not," Chi told him.

"Excellent."

Smart cleared his throat. "Ahem!" he grunted. "Surely you don't expect to cast a vote here today," he said in protest. "You don't even know what we're voting on."

"I've been watching your NewsNets," Stendeval replied. "I can deduce." He looked to his fellow Circlemen. "The entire city is terrified of an infected child who just happens to be standing right in front of us. Obviously, you are all here to decide what is to become of him." Stendeval raised up his hands with the palms out. "Elementary."

Smart frowned. "But the motion itself," he pressed. "You haven't heard any of the arguments."

"That, too, is not overly difficult," Stendeval said. "Based on how well you have done for yourself in the wake of the Rüstov invasion, I expect that you are taking a hard stance against this child, favoring execution and dissection. Hopefully in that order, but knowing you, perhaps not."

Smart raised a crooked eyebrow and leaned over the table, glaring at Stendeval. "How well I've done for myself?"

"Indeed," Stendeval replied. "Since my return this morning, I don't believe I've seen an inch of Empire City without your thumbprint on it."

"What exactly are you implying?"

"At the moment?" Stendeval asked. "Nothing. I am merely remarking that your dogged pursuit of the Rüstov has made you quite a powerful man. I expect that you realize this better than anyone, and will continue on that path by calling for this boy's head. And perhaps the head of Emissary Knight as well, am I right?"

The other members quickly agreed that Stendeval was as wise as ever, and that he fully understood the matter at hand. They all affirmed his right to vote, even Hovarth, whom Jack sensed had a grudging respect for Stendeval. Hovarth could likely guess how Stendeval's return would affect the outcome of the vote, but he appeared resigned to it. Smart was a different story.

"I seek only to protect our people from the Rüstov," Smart stated. "We must never forget the lessons we learned the day that Legend died. If I must remind the people, so be it. Too often, it seems I must remind this very Circle."

"You make a strong case, I am sure," Stendeval replied. "Fear is a very effective political tool, and I know that you can be very . . . persuasive." The way Stendeval said the word "persuasive" reminded Jack of the way Smart had tried to "persuade" Virtua before Stendeval had arrived. "I cannot endorse your motion," Stendeval continued. "I went through too much trouble to help bring this child here. Jack must live. He must be trained in the proper use of his powers. He must be trained in the School of Thought."

"Og's blood!" Hovarth cried again. "You mean for us to *train* this Rüstov?!"

"I do, mighty Hovarth," Stendeval said. "I do, indeed."

"The School of Thought?" Smart asked. "Have you gone mad?"

"What's the School of Thought?" Jack asked Jazen.

It took Jazen a second to form an answer. He was still reeling from Stendeval's proposal. "It's the most prestigious . . . it's a big honor, Jack—only the most powerful students get a chance to go." Jazen stopped himself, realizing he wasn't answering the question. "It's a school run by the Inner Circle. If we get through this, you're going to be taught how to use your powers by the champions of the Imagine Nation."

Jack's eyes grew to the size of silver dollars. "They want me?" he asked.

Before Smart or Hovarth could argue further, Chi and Prime reasserted their votes, each of them seconding Stendeval's amendment. Jack should not only live but have his chance at admission to the School of Thought. Suddenly, a 3-2 majority was voting in Jack's favor! The vote moved on to Virtua. As she was no longer the swing vote, Smart's threat now rang hollow.

"It seems the matter is all but decided, Jonas," Virtua said. "Your advice notwithstanding, no one can fault me for standing alongside Stendeval the Wise. I shall vote with the majority. Emissary Knight will not be disassembled, and Jack shall be allowed to live, on the condition that he be trained in the use of his powers. To that end, he will be considered by this Circle to be an official candidate for the School of Thought!"

"Bah!" Hovarth tossed his ax out on the table.

"Yes!" Jack shouted, jumping up and down and hugging Jazen.

Jazen put his arm around Jack and messed up his hair. "I told you everything was going to be fine, didn't I?"

"Yeah, no worries," Jack said.

Smart looked down on the happy little scene with disgust. "This is outrageous!" he asserted. "Worse, it is irrational. Virtua, I order you to change your—"

Stendeval started laughing softly to himself. Smart stopped talking and flashed a *How dare you?* look. "I'm sorry, Jonas," Stendeval told him. "I was just thinking of something an old English king once told me. 'It is only a great fool that tries to sit at the head of a round table.'" The other Circlemen chuckled a small bit as well.

"Who do you think you are?" Smart asked Stendeval. It was clear he couldn't stand the man. Despite his earlier proclamation, it seemed Smart regarded Stendeval as "greatly missed" only when he was missing. "We have rules and protocols for dealing with the Rüstov! While you've been off on vacation, my policies have kept this city safe! I've personally forced this Circle to keep the Rüstov at bay! Now we are supposed to just follow you, without a word to where you have been all these years? You can't just waltz back into this sphere after twelve years and change the way we do things."

"In my humble opinion, change should be the only constant in the Imagine Nation," Stendeval replied. "As for where I've been, I do not mean to be cryptic—that is just my nature. I do apologize. Trust that the information you seek will be revealed in time."

"I will not allow this child to enter the School of Thought."

"Time will tell, Jonas. Time will tell." Stendeval looked to the rest of the Circle. "I move that we adjourn," he announced.

"I second that," Virtua said, giving off a warm, happy glow.

"And I," Chi added. "You must open the festival. The people outside will be most glad to hear of your return."

Stendeval looked down into the pit where Jack was standing. "Jack Blank, Emissary Knight . . . you are excused with the thanks of this Circle. Be well."

Stendeval raised a single finger and the floor beneath Jack's feet once again turned into thick metallic syrup. Jack and Jazen passed through to the platform outside.

Jack squinted as he cleared the orb, jolted by the bright

light outside the sphere. When his vision adjusted, he looked out on Hero Square with new eyes. This was officially his home now. He was going to stay with Jazen in his übercool apartment. He was going to Hero School! Jack's heart was still beating superfast, but it was a good kind of superfast. The best kind.

Blue was waiting for them at the base of the pedestal, anxious to find out how things went. "Well?" he asked.

"It went good," Jack told him. "Real good."

Jazen stepped up behind Jack. "Remember that letter I told you about?" he asked.

"No way," Blue said.

There was an orange-white flash, and the crowed oohed and ahhed as the Inner Circle materialized on the square. Seconds later, there was another flash and Stendeval appeared, floating in a ring of red energy.

"No way!" Blue said again.

The crowd went absolutely bananas when they saw him. They cheered loud enough to shake the walls of Varagog. It was the loudest sound Jack ever heard, a noise you might expect to hear if the local Empire City sports teams won the World Series, Super Bowl, and

World Cup all at the same time. Stendeval was back and the SmartCams buzzed over to him, automatically shifting to record and broadcast the most newsworthy story. STENDEVAL RETURNS! instantly appeared on all of Smart's NewsNets, and soon the entire city was cheering. People who were watching in their homes, people at work, and people everywhere else.

Stendeval tried to quiet the crowd. "Please! Please, I thank you, but that is not necessary," he said with a booming voice that carried over the crowd. He had no microphone or megaphone, but his voice was still so amplified that he could have been heard all the way up on the 437th floor of the Ivory Tower. "It feels good to be home!" Stendeval continued. "I can't tell you how much I've missed this place, and all of you. I promise you I won't be disappearing like that again."

The crowd roared. They loved him. Jack asked Jazen about the strong reaction, and Jazen reminded him of Stendeval's age. He had been a guardian of Empire City for as long as anyone in the crowd could remember. They had grown up with him. Their parents had told stories about him. Stendeval's effect on the people was visible on every face in the crowd. He made them feel safe. He was a comforting presence, like an old grandfather: noble, wise, and caring.

"So much has changed since I've been away," Stendeval said. He turned to look on the monument of Legend, the Legendary Flame ever burning in the statue's hand. "They tell me that today is Dedication Day. That is good! It is good that we should honor those heroes who fought in the Battle of Empire City, and of course Legend, who gave his life to save us from Revile the Undying."

As Stendeval spoke, Smart pulled out his pocket holo-computer and rerouted the SmartCams to focus on Jack, filming, bumping, and generally annoying him. New headlines began to scroll on the NewsNets: INNER CIRCLE BUNGLES RULING ON RÜSTOV INFILTRATOR. DEDICATION DAY FESTIVAL MARRED BY INSULT TO LEGEND'S MEMORY. The screen went on to display how each of the individual members of the Inner Circle had voted.

Stendeval grimaced. "Legend was my good friend," he declared. "I miss him more than words can say. Still, it is my hope, my great hope, that the shadows of the invasion do not ever loom too large in this place. It is one thing to

remember our past, but quite another to become mired in it. Paralyzed by it. Paralyzed by fear. That we can never do without losing sight of who we are, for imagination is never static, never the same. Imagination is change. Many years ago in India, I met a man who told people, 'Be the change you want to see in the world.' I would urge all of you to do the same."

Jack felt like Stendeval was speaking directly to him. He could hardly fathom that this man had had a hand in bringing him back to Empire City. Stendeval had written to Chi about it twelve years ago, apparently planning Jack's return since the day Jack had left. What did it all mean? What did he know about Jack's past?

"Imagination looks forward!" Stendeval told the assembled masses. "Imagination creates. Imagination dares. Here we look forward to a future filled with promise, not fear. Here we look to a world where anything is possible. That is the world Legend died to save!"

Thousands upon thousands of people in Hero Square raised their voices in agreement.

"That is the world we wish to live in, yes?" Stendeval asked.

The whole of Empire City answered with a resounding "YES!"

Stendeval nodded. "Then with your permission, I humbly submit that from this day forward, Dedication Day be known as Rededication Day! Here we do not merely dedicate this city to memories of our fallen comrades, but we rededicate ourselves! To everything they stood for! To the impossible! To the future! To the unbound wonder of the Imagine Nation!"

The Inner Circle applauded vigorously except for Smart, who looked like someone had just told him the stock market had crashed. The crowd, however, roared a deafening approval.

"I'll take that as a yes," Stendeval said to his fellow Circlemen. "Chi? Will you do the honors?"

Chi nodded. "With pleasure," he said.

Chi broke ranks with the Circle and leaped into the air, landing a few feet before the stone bridge leading out to the Legendary Flame. At the threshold of the bridge stood a marble headstone. Jack could see the words DEDICATED JANUARY 25, 1998 engraved on the face of it. The words were glowing with a brilliant blue light.

As Chi's feet hit the bridge, he rolled his landing toward the headstone and sprung up to punch it. The headstone exploded with a furious blast of energy. A million tiny pieces of marble flew into the air, then froze in place as Stendeval raised a fist, stopping each stone from continuing along its trajectory.

There was a glowing ball of blue energy at the center of the debris. Chi reached out and took some of the blue energy into his hand. He channeled it into a fireball and threw it at the statue of Legend, showing the tiniest sign of strain on his face.

The fireball landed in the palm of the statue's hand, raising the flicker of blue flame into a mighty bonfire. The cheering grew louder. Stendeval opened his own hand and the pieces of the headstone were all sucked back toward the center, joining together once again, reforming with a new message: REDEDICATED JANUARY 25, 2010.

The crowd rejoiced. A new tradition was born. They could all feel it. It was a tradition that would honor the past as well as the future—where the people of Empire City had come from, as well as where they were going.

Stendeval smiled down at Jack, who was blown away by

what he'd just seen. From his robes, Stendeval withdrew a small orange envelope. He turned it over in his hand and it vanished. No flashing lights, no fanfare about it. It was a magician's sleight of hand, nothing more. Or was it?

Jack felt something in his pocket, and reached inside to find the very same envelope. Jack looked back up and Stendeval was gone. He tore into the envelope and read the note.

SCHOOL OF THOUGHT
Orientation

WHERE:
The Cloud Cliffs of Mount Nevertop

WHEN:
Right now

Before he had time to wonder what it meant, Jack was blinded by a flash of orange light and transported away from Hero Square.

Jack's first day of school was about to begin.

Jack found himself planted firmly in a tunnel that was carved into the side of a mountain that he guessed was Mount Nevertop. He felt woozy. His vision was fuzzy, the room spun around him, and he could hardly stand. Jack stumbled forward and collapsed to all fours like his legs were made of rubber.

"Teleportation," Chi explained, patting his shoulder. "Most people throw up the first time." Jack shook his head, grateful for once that he wasn't like "most people."

Mount Nevertop was the name given to the crystal mountain that floated behind the Imagine Nation. Jack decided the mountain had the perfect name—it had such a sharp peak that to try and stand on the summit would have been like trying to stand on the tip of a knife. Up close, Jack saw that the mountain had a cloudy, semiclear coloring. It looked like it was made out of quartz or some other mineral. Jack saw that he was in a great hall, at the bottom of a grand staircase that had been carved into the crystal with steady, professional hands. Excavating this tunnel either took years and years or some pretty impressive superpowers.

The Inner Circle was there, as were two children Jack recognized from the VIP area at Hero Square. Realizing that he was the only one still on the ground, Jack scurried to his feet. The silver girl shied away from him, stepping back behind a crystalline pillar. At least she managed to keep herself in one piece this time. The young boy, Skerren, drew his swords again, planning to see that Jack did not.

"You again! What's this Rüstov doing here?" Skerren demanded.

"Sheathe your swords, Skerren," Stendeval commanded. "Jack is a candidate for our program, just as you are. Allegra, come out from there," Stendeval told the girl in soothing tones.

"Is he the infected boy?" the girl asked.

"It's perfectly safe, I assure you."

The silver girl peeked out from behind the pillar. "Do you promise?" Her shiny silver skin was just like Prime's. Jack wondered if she was a Valorian too.

"Everything I say is a promise—always," Stendeval replied. "Please, come."

"What is this?" Skerren asked. "How can he be a candidate for the School of Thought? He just got here, and he's a Rüstov to boot!" He seemed appalled at the notion. "Is this really true?" he asked Hovarth.

"Aye lad, I'm afraid so," Hovarth answered.

"Don't worry," Jack said to Skerren, trying to put him at ease. "I'm stronger than the Rüstov. My powers beat the infection." He reached out to shake Skerren's hand. "My name's Jack. Jack Blank."

"I don't care what your name is, Rusty," Skerren said. He looked at Jack's hand like it was covered with the plague. "And I don't shake hands with the enemy either." Skerren scraped his twin blades together. "Back up now and you can keep your hand. Linger too long and I'll chop it off."

Skerren spun his swords in front of Jack's face before sinking each weapon into the scabbards on his back. Jack recoiled. If someone had called him "Rusty" yesterday he wouldn't have given it a second thought. Today the word hit him like a racial slur. Jack's lips turned downward with an offended grimace as Skerren turned away. Jack had to admit the kid was a phenom with those swords. Too bad his personality was every bit as pointed as his blades.

"Nice guy, huh?" Jack said to Allegra, who was tiptoeing her way out into the open.

"Eeep!" she yelped, and liquefied into a puddle again. She spilled across the floor and reformulated behind Prime, who tried and failed to repress an embarrassed sigh.

"Oh-kaay . . . ," Jack said. It was clear he was going to have trouble making friends at school. What else was new?

"Children!" Stendeval called out from the steps. "Come. We have a great many stairs to climb before we reach the Cloud Cliffs."

That was the understatement of the year. Jack looked up the full length of the staircase, which seemed to rise all the way up to the top of the mountain. It was going to be a long climb.

As Jack ascended the stairway with the others, they passed countless sculptures of battles between the Imagine Nation's most renowned heroes and their infamous arch-enemies. These epic clashes between good and evil were so well known that no one bothered to put plaques on them to identify the combatants. Despite his vast comic collection, Jack had no idea who many of them were, so Stendeval and the others rattled off the names of each one they passed.

There were so many that Jack couldn't keep track of them all. He did remember the carving of Veritas, one of Hovarth's ancestors, fighting Loki, the evil Norse god of mischief. There was also Iditarod Kane, the dauntless arctic adventurer, who was depicted rescuing a winter princess from the Ice Trolls of Siberia, and even Prime, sculpted in mortal combat with the dreaded Draconian emperor. Prime modestly downplayed the incident as no big deal. Jack found that hard to believe.

While the history of heroes and villains was all very interesting, Jack's ears really perked up when his future teachers started talking about the School of Thought.

The School of Thought didn't meet in a single building; instead, the world was its classroom. Jack's classes could be held anywhere: the Great Wall of China, Mount Everest, Atlantis, and even outer space.

"You are not students in the School of Thought yet," Smart told the children. "First, you all have to survive the time of testing."

Smart and the others went on to explain that over the next two weeks, Jack, Skerren, and Allegra would all be tested and observed by each member of the Inner Circle during the School of Thought's version of an entrance exam. Before going out into the world to learn, each of the candidates would have to earn the vote of each Circleman in a series of tests to be conducted within Empire City. Smart made a special point of noting that if even one Circleman failed Jack, he'd be out of the program.

Jack groaned. Just when he thought things were looking up. How the heck was he going to get Smart not to fail him . . . or worse? The Inner Circle said the testing would be dangerous. Hovarth stated that if they were to live, they would prove themselves worthy as the mightiest of their age. That was the whole point. In the School of Thought the most powerful supers of the last generation teach the most powerful children of the next.

The Inner Circle took an interest in Jack and the others because they were the future. As Prime put it, these children might find themselves occupying a seat in the Inner Circle one day, and there was more to being a hero than learning how to fly straight. Hovarth agreed heartily, and spoke with passion about dedication, resolve, and strength. Chi emphasized philosophy and a strict moral code. Virtua stressed ways of thinking about the world that are accepting and compassionate to all, while Prime preached confidence and courage. Smart offered no words of wisdom, but Stendeval summed things up nicely. "Heroes view the future as full of possibility and opportunity," he said. "They see the good in the world. They believe that nothing is impossible and every day is a chance to change the world for the better. 'Never underestimate the power you have over what happens today. And never forget the power today has over tomorrow.' A great hero once told me that."

Jack and the others reached the top of the stairs. There Stendeval led the group through a hall so filled with clouds, Jack could barely see the floor. He walked toward a ledge that opened out into the sky, where crystal fragments from the mountain floated among puffy white billows.

"Change begins with the individual," Stendeval stated. "For all the power you have—and you three do have great power—what you need to find first is the power to believe in yourself. It's one thing to say it. It is another to live it."

Stendeval walked out onto the crystal shard cliffs that were suspended in the sky outside. "Who among you will join me here on the Cloud Cliffs?" he asked. No one moved. Jack and the others were perfectly happy to stay right where they were.

Stendeval laughed. "This is what I am talking about. You must remove the word 'can't' from your vocabulary. You'll find that you are more powerful than you realize."

With a wave of Stendeval's hands, the clouds in the hall cleared to reveal that Jack and the others were already standing on floating cliffs. What they thought was a solid floor was just more crystal fragments over a tremendous chasm! Jack's eyes bugged out from their sockets, and he staggered as he looked down into the heart of the mountain. He'd been stepping from stone to stone without a care, never guessing there was a five-thousand-foot drop below him. Allegra screamed, just barely stopping herself from liquefying. If she had, she would have run off the edge and straight through to the bottom. Skerren stabbed a sword into the center of the shard he was standing on, just so he'd have something to hold on to.

"You think you cannot do this, but I say you have

already done it!" Stendeval called out. "I ask you, if you had known the road ahead, would you have walked the same path?"

The answer from everyone involved was, of course, no.

Stendeval smiled. "But now you know you can. You can do more than you know. You are here to learn about the world, to gain new perspectives. Testing will be dangerous, but I believe in you. You are already stronger than you think, and you will become stronger still if you open your minds to all possibilities before you. I only ask that you always remember that the path you choose to follow is your own."

Stendeval's words hit Jack like beams of sunlight. After a lifetime of people telling him that they knew what was best for him and what his future was going to be, it was wonderful to hear someone say that it was really all up to him. He didn't have to be a toilet brush cleaner if he didn't want to be. It was almost enough to make him walk out there and join Stendeval on the Cloud Cliffs. Almost.

Luckily, Stendeval was as good as his word, allowing everyone to choose the path they wanted to walk. Prime flew, Virtua hovered, and Chi flipped from stone to stone. Stendeval used his powers, which Jack still didn't quite understand, to levitate everyone else, including Hovarth and Smart, back to the staircase. Stendeval didn't fail anyone for refusing to walk in the clouds. This was just a lesson, not a test. True testing wouldn't begin until tomorrow.

They were about halfway down when Jack paused to take in one of the sculptures he hadn't noticed on the way up. "Hey . . . hey, I know that one!" Jack said.

Skerren, who wasn't getting any friendlier, rolled his eyes and blew a sharp hiss through his teeth. "That's Legend," he said. "Everybody knows that one."

Jack frowned. He was already sick of this kid. "I know it's Legend," he said. "I'm talking about the Rüstov he's fighting. That's the one who came after me."

The entire group stopped short. "What?" Smart asked. "What did you just say?"

"Impossible," Hovarth said, not even waiting for Jack to answer. "It's impossible!"

"Look again, Jack," Virtua said, suddenly very concerned. "Perhaps you're mistaken?"

"No," Jack said, confused. "That's the one who came after me. I'm sure."

"He's lying," Skerren said. "He's just trying to scare us."

"Scare you? What are you talking about? I'm telling the truth." Jack was surprised at the disbelief everyone seemed to share. He expected that back at St. Barnaby's but not here. "What's wrong?" Jack asked. "I'm telling you, this thing came after me and I blew it up. I recognize the red light in its chest."

Another gasp.

"There was only one Rüstov with that mark," Prime said with a concerned look.

"Impossible!" Hovarth said again, louder this time.

"Didn't you all just say nothing was impossible?" Jack asked.

"A fair point, young Jack," Stendeval agreed. "The only thing I find impossible is the concept of impossibility."

"Yes, but this . . . ," Smart said, "this is impossible."

"Why?" Jack asked. "Why is that so crazy?! That's the robot who came after me yesterday. He tried to kill me. Why is everybody acting so weird about it?"

Stendeval knelt down and looked at Jack. "The figure

that Legend is fighting in that sculpture is quite famous. He's the most deadly Rüstov ever encountered, and one that everyone here hoped never to see again."

Stendeval put a hand on Jack's shoulder.

"His name is Revile."

CHAPTER

8

Powers

The next morning, the story was all over the *Empirical*, Hightown's local paper: BOY RÜSTOV THREATENS INNER CIRCLE: "REVILE IS BACK FROM THE DEAD!" The editorial slant didn't surprise Jack too much. In small letters below the *Empirical*'s masthead were the words POWERED BY SMARTCORP.

Jack wanted to tear the *Empirical* in two, but it was printed on SmartPaper. You couldn't tear up SmartPaper, you could only delete it, and that wasn't anywhere near as satisfying. Jack found that reading a tangital newspaper was like holding the home page of a news website. There were no pages to turn—it was just one sheet of digital paper programmed to run the news all day. Jack could touch the section tabs to jump to any part of the paper he wanted, or tap specific headlines to load the stories he wished to read in the paper's main window. It cost half a credit to read each day's stories, which Jazen generously charged to his own account. Articles updated themselves automatically as news broke, video footage ran in a media player, and the lead story's headline literally jumped off the page.

As Jazen prepared another extravagant breakfast, he read the paper over Jack's shoulder. "I didn't really say that," Jack told Jazen. "I didn't threaten anyone. They're twisting it."

Jack had told Jazen how he'd found out that the Rüstov that had attacked him at St. Barnaby's was Revile. Smart was spinning the facts to his advantage, making it sound like Jack and Revile were on the same side.

"He never misses an opportunity, does he?" Jazen said, trailing off with a grumble. "Still, I wouldn't say any more about this Revile business if I were you. It's only going to scare people, and the city is afraid of you enough as it is."

Jack couldn't argue with that. He was already short on

friends, and it was plain to see that the situation would not improve with him telling everyone that Revile, the worst Rüstov ever, was back. But while Jack was willing to leave the Revile question alone, he would've been lying if he had said it didn't worry him. If that really had been Revile back at St. Barnaby's, he could be out there right now. He could attack at any moment. Who would stop him this time?

"You believe me that it was Revile, right, Jazen?"

"I believe that you believe it," Jazen replied. Jack could see Jazen hoped he was wrong about this. *Jack hoped he was wrong about this too.* Trouble was, Jack was pretty darn sure he was right.

Jazen turned the conversation to Jack's training while he whipped a bowl of blue eggs into a scrambled frenzy. This morning Jazen was serving butter-battered Flopflips with special Kazellian Floovberries. The Flopflips were something very much like light, airy blue pancakes, but the flavor of the Floovberries, found only off-planet deep in the heart of the Kazellian Nebula, was literally out of this world. They were as delicious as they were rare.

"So! The School of Thought," Jazen said. "Quite an

honor there, Jack. They only pick a few students every year. Never more than one per Circleman, and sometimes not even that many. This year it's just the three of you."

"There are other kids in the program already?" Jack asked.

"Older kids from other years," Jazen said. "You'll meet them when you get in."

"If I get in," Jack corrected. "I have to get everyone in the Inner Circle to vote for me first." He held up his copy of the *Empirical*. "There's no way the guy who writes *these* headlines is going to give me his vote."

"All you can do is try," Jazen said. "Just put your best foot forward every day. At least you don't have to worry about being dissected anymore."

Jack agreed that was a definite improvement, and promised to do everything in his power to get into the good graces of his teachers. However, while Jack certainly wanted to get into the School of Thought and learn how to use his powers, finding out the answers about his past was still first and foremost on his mind.

When he was done eating, Jack offered to clean up the dishes if Jazen would go get the letter Stendeval had sent him. Jazen said there wasn't anything in the letter except where to find Jack, but he agreed to get it. When Jazen left the room, Jack busied himself trying to figure out how to work a strange contraption called the SmartWater-CleanWindow, which was like no dishwasher Jack had ever seen. Jack tried to figure it out, but after pushing a few buttons that didn't seem to do anything other than get him wet, he ended up just washing the dishes with plain old soap and water, and drying them with a rag. When Jack finished, Jazen came back without the letter.

"Jack, I'm sorry," he began, "I can't find it. Which is weird, because I know I left it in my room."

"Isn't this it right here?" Jack asked, eyeing an orange envelope on the counter. Jazen looked confused as Jack picked up the envelope that was definitely not there a few moments earlier. "No," Jack said after reading the letter. "This isn't it. It's just directions to Cognito."

"Let me see that," Jazen said, taking back the letter and looking it over. "He changed it," he said.

"Who did?"

"Stendeval," Jazen replied. "Hmm . . . almost ten

o'clock, too. C'mon, Jack, we've gotta go. We can't be late, not in Cognito."

"Late? Late for what?" Jack asked while Jazen pulled him toward the door.

"For your first School of Thought test," Jazen replied.

Jack and Jazen rushed off to Stendeval's corner of Empire City, the mysterious borough where everything was a secret or a riddle, just like him. Getting there was tricky. Directions in Cognito had to be followed exactly as they were written, straight down to the exact time a person had to be at a certain place. Jazen and Jack hurried through town with the SmartCams following close behind. Everyone else kept their distance, but no one shrieked and ran or tried to kill Jack, which was a vast improvement on his short but eventful stay in Empire City thus far. Apparently, word had spread pretty fast that Jack was a candidate for the School of Thought and protected by the Inner Circle. More importantly, he was personally vouched for by Stendeval, whose word carried considerable weight throughout the Imagine Nation. That said, Jack still got his fair share of dirty looks from some of the city's more stubborn residents, and overheard the occasional person call him "Rusty" as well.

Soon the sleek ultramodern skyscrapers of Hightown gave way to rocky terrain at the border of Cognito. Futuristic MagLev roads were replaced by low-tech, brick-laid streets and red rock. Everywhere Jack looked, he saw identical white stone buildings. They had no markings, no molding, no gargoyles—nothing that would allow someone to distinguish one building from another. The buildings all had simple rectangular windows peppered about in odd places on their exterior. The only notable difference between any of the structures was their shape. Some were in L shapes, some in T shapes, and some were designed with random staircaselike patterns. The white buildings jutted out of the red rock and turned at right angles, some connecting to each other with bridges and steps, some not. When Jack looked at the skyline of Cognito, it was like looking at one giant interconnected puzzle. Cognito was a labyrinth.

After following Jack less than a block into the mysterious borough, the SmartCams started to weave and sink in the air. They flew in erratic patterns and bumped into each other. One of them even crashed into a wall. Eventually, it looked like the SmartCams had decided enough was enough, and they zipped back across the border into Hightown. Jack was happy to see them go.

"SmartCams don't work in Cognito," Jazen explained. "In fact, no cameras work here. It's one of the reasons why it's such a good place for a person to disappear. Most superpowered beings have their secret lairs and hideouts right here. It's tough to keep a secret identity these days, so people set up their hideouts in Cognito. Or they rent them from the Secreteers."

"Rent them? Don't their landlords know where the hideouts are, then?" Jack asked.

"Well, as you might expect, Secreteers are very good at keeping secrets. People trust them with all kinds of information, but you'd never hear it from them. They keep things quiet. They're also the ones who make sure all the 'superheroing' that goes on in the world doesn't spill over onto the front pages of your newspapers. They're not the only things in Cognito that work to keep hideouts hidden, though."

"What else is there?"

"You'll see." Jazen held up the directions Stendeval had sent, and looked around. "There," he said, pointing.

"That street corner. Twenty paces north and ten paces east." Jack and Jazen walked to the appropriate corner and stood there waiting. "Ten thirty-two a.m.," Jazen said. "Right on time."

"For what?" Jack said. "There's nothing here."

Jazen put his hand to his lips. "Listen," he whispered.

At first Jack didn't hear anything. But soon he heard a rumbling noise, followed by tremors. The city started shaking like it was being hit with an earthquake, but it wasn't the whole city. It was just Cognito.

Jack watched in wonder as the streets around him began to turn over in place like blocks in a Rubik's Cube. Encrypted street signs changed their code names. Dead ends became intersections. Buildings transformed, separating and attaching themselves to other buildings, sinking into the ground and rising up out of it.

Jack was speechless as the city blocks before him turned like cogs in a mighty machine, then finally settled and came to rest in their new layout. In less than a minute the landscape had completely changed.

"What just happened?" Jack asked.

"That's the other way things stay hidden here," Jazen

said, leading Jack back the way they came, which was now a different path than it had been when they had first walked it.

Jazen went on to explain that every day the streets of Cognito rearranged like puzzle pieces being scrambled, and nothing looked the same twice in ten years. Jack remarked that this was where he ought to be living. No one would bother him there. Jazen laughed and asked him how he would ever find his way around. "Only the locals know the way, and it's not like you can ask for directions. Everything in Cognito is *supposed* to be hard to find," Jazen told Jack. "Streets have no names that you can understand, doors don't always lead to the same place twice, everyone uses aliases, and no one will tell you anything. We'd never reach our destination without Stendeval's directions, and after today they're useless."

As Jack walked down the street, he saw people in supersuit costumes flying away, and people in civilian clothes who didn't want to be seen without their masks. Everyone in the borough crossed the street, ducked into open doorways, and even scaled building walls to get away from Jack. They avoided everyone, though, not just him. As a general rule, people in Cognito kept to themselves. Eventually, Jack and Jazen reached Stendeval's building. It was a large rectangular tower with a crooked shape. With the exception of an orange handprint slapped above the front door, Stendeval's home looked no different from any other building in Cognito.

"This is it," Jazen said. "I'll be right here waiting for you after class."

"Let's just hope that the building hasn't moved by then," Jack replied. Jazen wished Jack luck as he went into the building alone.

Stendeval's home may have been simple and clean on the outside, but the inside looked like the attic of a great museum, or the prop room of a long-running theater company. Jack entered into a single cluttered chamber that took up the whole of the building. The perimeter of the room was jam-packed with a random collection of old furniture pieces stacked on top of one another, plus sculptures, busts, and other antiques, some of them under tarps, some not. It seemed like every available space upon which something could be set down and still keep its balance was taken up by some manner of artifact. In short, it was a mess, but a mess made up of some very cool and interesting stuff. The only clear space in the room was in the center of the floor, where Skerren and Allegra waited.

Jack walked toward his classmates. Looking up, Jack saw more of the same clutter. The walls were lined with books and filled with massive paintings, portraits, and pictures that were all housed in oversize, ornate frames. All the way up to the ceiling, wooden scaffolding ran rings around the four walls, each level with a ladder leading up to the next level, like a fire escape. These "fire escapes" were, of course, all crammed with a hodgepodge of Stendeval's curios.

As Jack approached the center of the room, he found Skerren practicing his swordplay, shadowboxing against a stationary suit of armor. Skerren glanced at Jack but continued with his training without saying anything. Thrust. Parry. Ignore. Allegra was standing by herself, waiting for class to begin.

"You think he ever puts those swords down?" Jack asked Allegra, hoping to make conversation.

"I think he must sleep with them under his pillow," Allegra replied. "He's been practicing since I got here. He didn't even stop to say hello."

"Sounds about right," Jack replied. "Hey! You didn't turn into a puddle!"

"Oh?" Allegra asked, perhaps just realizing that herself. "Oh, right," she added with a bashful chuckle. "I'm Allegra," she said with a smile.

"I know," Jack said. "I remember. It's a really nice name. I'm Jack." He reached out his hand. As Allegra shook Jack's hand with a shy smile, Skerren's eyes cut over toward the pair for an instant. He frowned and resumed sparring.

"Sorry I always liquefy around you," Allegra said.

"It's okay. That's no big deal."

"It's kind of embarrassing. It's not about you, though. It's more about the Rüstov."

Jack sighed. "You don't have to be afraid of me," he said. "I'm not a Rüstov."

One of Skerren's swords shrieked its way through the torso of the suit of armor. Jack and Allegra looked over to see him thrust it through with an angry stab.

"I'm not a Rüstov," Skerren mimicked Jack. "Isn't that just what a Rüstov spy would say?"

"What's your problem, Skerren?" Jack asked.

"I don't know," Skerren replied. "Maybe I just don't

like the idea of letting the enemy into a school for heroes."
Skerren walked right up to Jack. "Know this, Rusty," he
began. "I've been training my whole life to get into the
School of Thought. Whatever you're up to, you're not
going to get away with it."

Jack stared back at Skerren. "Know this, Skerren. You're
a huge jerk."

Somewhere in the jumble of bric-a-brac on the wall,
several cuckoo clocks struck eleven and began to cluck.
When the children turned toward the noise, they saw
Stendeval hovering above them, his legs folded. "Amazing," he said. "It never ceases to astound me how often
friends begin their relationship as enemies."

"Friends?" Skerren repeated, incredulous. "I'll never
be friends with *that*," he said, pointing to Jack.

"Works for me," Jack replied.

"So certain of the future, are we?" Stendeval asked.
"Beware that impulse, boys. It has led many a man to draw
sad conclusions and take unfortunate actions. But that is
a lesson for another day." Stendeval lowered himself down
to hover around the children's eye level. "Today's lesson
is about confidence," Stendeval announced. "Confidence

in yourselves. Confidence in your powers. This is always an exciting lesson. Some of you may even be introduced to new facets of your powers today."

"I already know about my powers," Skerren declared in a brash tone.

"Life is an education, young one," Stendeval told Skerren with a patient smile. "Now. The first step is to take the lid off how you view your powers. To remove limits from your minds. To help you do this, I must first see how you all think of your powers. What limits you are unconsciously placing on yourselves but may not be aware of."

Stendeval could see that Skerren was dying to go first and show his skills. "Skerren, I suppose we can begin with you." He paused. "If you're ready?"

Skerren blew a sharp snort of air through his nostrils. "Of course."

Stendeval nodded. "Excellent." He waved his hand and red energy flowed forth as he craned his neck to look skyward, up into the tower. Jack heard a rumbling, high in the upper regions of the building, far out of sight. All the way up in the top, Jack could hear something making its way down, tumbling through the tower. Jack saw it was a series of cannonballs flying down toward the group, being waved along by Stendeval. He directed the cannonballs to swoop in with a light glide and form a pyramid in the center of the room. He dove straight into his lesson.

"Skerren . . . do you think your blades can cut through these cannonballs?" Stendeval asked.

As always, Skerren was bold. "My blades can cut through anything."

"Confidence!" Stendeval said. "Very good." With no further warning he sent a swarm of cannonballs hurling at Skerren. They came whirling at him from all directions, with a life of their own. Skerren quite effortlessly sliced them all in half like cantaloupes. Each one fell to the ground with a clank. He was good—there was no denying it.

"Impressive," Stendeval said. "Most impressive."

Next, Stendeval raised the stakes, moving a marble column with a tarp over it into the center of the room. "I want you to cleave this column in half, straight down the middle," he told Skerren.

"Heh. And I thought the School of Thought would be able to present me with a challenge," Skerren said.

Stendeval pulled the tarp off the column to reveal a bust of the mighty Hovarth sitting on top.

"What is this?" Skerren asked.

"It's only marble," said Stendeval. "Are you not up to the task?"

Skerren grumbled under his breath. He was uncomfortable with it, but he wasn't going to back down. He sheathed one sword and raised the other high in the air. He brought it down hard on the stone homage to Hovarth. With a great clang the sword rebounded in the opposite direction, driving Skerren back. He cried out, dropped his sword, and shook out his wrist. The bust of Hovarth was undamaged.

"No!" Skerren said, dropping to his knees.

Stendeval lowered himself to the ground and paced slowly around Skerren. "So. You slice through iron cannonballs like butter, but when you face off against a marble bust of Hovarth, whom you grew up idolizing in Varagog Village, you can't even chip it."

Skerren looked up, mortified. "I don't understand," he said. "I've never . . . I thought I could cut through anything."

Stendeval just smiled and reached out his hand. "It would appear that your only limit is your conscience," he said, helping Skerren to his feet. "You *can* cut anything, but only if your heart is in it. This is a good start. It pleases me that you could not break your mentor's image. Your confidence in your swordsmanship is well placed, but to what end will you use those swords? That is the question. Your power is amplified by belief in yourself. A true hero must believe in much more than that."

Skerren nodded. It seemed to Jack that his arrogance was replaced with genuine respect. Stendeval moved on to Allegra.

Allegra started to tell Stendeval about her powers, but he stopped her. He wanted Allegra to show everyone what her powers were. "Our actions tend to speak louder than our words," he said to her. "Allow me to help you."

Stendeval thought for a moment, then with a wave of his hand, he drew an ornate glass sculpture out from a random corner of the room. It was a crystal globe the size of a bowling ball, filled with a million different designs and colors. It danced through the air at Stendeval's whim, illuminating the room with color like a reflective disco ball.

"This glass comes from Murano, an island in the Venetian lagoon. I purchased it from a master glassmaker there in the year 1565. It has extraordinary value, to be sure, but greater still is its sentimental value to me." Stendeval placed the sculpture on a stand some ten feet away from Allegra. "Allegra. Please hand me the globe."

Allegra started walking toward the stand, but again Stendeval stopped her. "Ah, ah, ah . . . from where you are currently standing, please."

Reluctantly, Allegra reached for the globe. Jack watched in wonder as her arms extended across the room, her silver limbs stretching like pulled taffy. Her fingers wrapped around the globe and she picked it up. She was about to hand it to Stendeval, when he levitated up to the next level of the tower. "Please hand it to me up here," he said.

"It's too far," Allegra protested.

Stendeval looked down kindly. "Try."

Jack could tell Allegra needed more encouragement. "You can do it," he told her. "It's not that much farther."

Allegra nodded, steeling herself for the attempt. She reached up, extending her arms even farther. She was doing it, but she looked nervous and unsure.

"I don't like this," Allegra said. "It's too valuable, I can't . . ."

As she spoke, her hands first began to shake, then turned to fluid. The crystal globe passed through her fingers like water and shattered on the floor.

"Oh!" Allegra cried out. When she looked at the countless crystal shards on the ground, Allegra's face bunched up like she was about to cry.

Stendeval lowered himself down. "It's quite all right," he assured her.

A twirl of Stendeval's fingers and the fragments of the globe zipped back together into crystalline perfection. Allegra was immensely relieved.

"I can see you are blessed with all the power of a Valorian woman," Stendeval told her. "Unlike Valorian men, who can fly and fire plasma blasts from their hands, you can shape-shift and extend your form into any solid object. You do, however, have your limits. The farther you stretch, the less solid you become. That is also a defense mechanism." Stendeval winked, and a suit of armor lunged for Allegra. She melted into a puddle. "When frightened or unsure of yourself, your instinctual reaction is to shift to a liquid state," he told Allegra as she pulled herself back together. "Perhaps the opposite is true as well? If you could banish fear from your mind, perhaps you could become solid. Indestructible. The first step is not being afraid to try."

Stendeval patted Allegra on the shoulder and put the globe away. Now it was Jack's turn to be nervous. He was next.

"I don't know how much I can do here today," he blurted out as Stendeval hovered over him. "I can't turn on my powers like these guys. My powers just kind of show up."

"Yes, when you're angry or scared," Stendeval agreed. "Still, they are there waiting for you to command them. Your power over machines has helped you beat your Rüstov parasite thus far. If you can learn to truly control your powers, the Rüstov may find they committed a grievous error by infecting you." Again, Stendeval looked around the messy room. "Let's start with . . . this," he said, drawing an appliance out from the heap. Jack recognized it right away as a SmartWater-CleanWindow. Stendeval set it down on the stand. "Jack Blank, the floor is yours."

Jack shook his head. "I couldn't make this thing work this morning *without* my powers," he said. "I didn't even know what it was."

"Please try, Jack."

Jack breathed deep. Stendeval was right. He at least had to try. His powers were the only thing keeping him alive, and he'd basically gotten by on luck and instinct so far. There was no guarantee that was always going to be enough. If he wanted to make sure that his powers were always there to counteract the Rüstov, he was going to have to master them. The tough part was, he didn't really know where to begin.

Jack looked at the machine. He thought hard about making it go, about turning it on with his mind, but he didn't know what he was doing. He wasn't sure if his powers really even worked like this. His powers always just happened, and right now they weren't.

"I can't do this," Jack said at last. "I told you I don't even know what this Smart-thing is supposed to do."

"Fair enough," Stendeval said. "I shall explain. It's really a very clever invention." Stendeval moved to the machine and turned it on. "It's one of Jonas's older ideas, from before the invasion. As you can see, it produces a high-powered, ultrathin stream of water in a rectangular frame, resembling a window. The water is infused with nanotechnology—little microscopic, intelligent computer chips that seek out any form of dirt or refuse, then clean it away. You simply pass a dish through the Clean-Window, and let the water do the rest." Jack watched Stendeval pass an old, tarnished silver platter through the CleanWindow. He set it down on the table and the water continued to scrub the platter until it was shinier than Allegra's silver skin.

Stendeval urged Jack to try again, this time with the knowledge of what he wanted the machine to do. Jack did so, but he was still nervous: nervous that nothing would happen, that he couldn't do it, that he didn't belong.

"Here goes," Jack said.

Again, Jack thought really hard, reaching out with his mind to try to make the machine work. This time, it was different. This time, his eyes looked deep into the machine. At first, Jack wasn't sure, but after a minute he could swear he saw the gears turning inside and the circuit boards firing information back and forth. A dribble of water began to fill the CleanWindow and then stopped.

"Something happened!" Jack said. "It was . . . I could almost see inside of it for a minute. Something happened!"

"Why did you stop?"

"It was too complex. I felt like I could see the little microchips in the water and . . . it was too much. I couldn't wrap my head around it."

Stendeval nodded and started digging through his collection of artifacts for something for Jack to try his hand with next. Eventually, he whisked a tricycle down from the upper levels of his tower. "I have another idea," he said, setting the small bike down before Jack. "Make this one work," he challenged.

"A tricycle?" Jack asked.

"It's a machine," Stendeval replied. "A simple machine but a machine nonetheless. All you have to do is make it go."

Jack thought about it. It seemed pretty silly, but he did understand how this particular machine worked. In his head he saw the pedals rotating. They were connected to the axle on the front wheel, which, when turned, would move his bike forward. He saw it all happening in his head, and before he knew it, the tricycle was riding around the room in a circle with no one on it. It was completely under Jack's control.

"You're doing it!" Allegra said to Jack. Stendeval applauded.

"I can't believe this," Jack said. "It's working!"

"You see, Jack?" Stendeval asked. "You *can* control machines. But in order to do it on command, it would appear you have to know how the machine works. I suggest you study science and engineering. The more you learn, the more you'll be able to do. Knowledge is power, young friend. Knowledge is power."

Skerren clapped a slow, sarcastic clap, and Jack's concentration broke. The tricycle slowed and then halted.

"And what a power it is," Skerren said. "Rust-boy can make tricycles move. The enemies of the Imagine Nation must be quivering with fear."

Stendeval gave Skerren a disapproving look. "A journey of a thousand miles begins with a single step, young Skerren. A Chinese philosopher who visited this island long ago once told me that. You would do well to remember it, for you have a ways to go yourself." He looked at the class. "You all do."

Skerren quieted himself. "Does that mean we didn't pass?" he asked.

"Pass?" Stendeval repeated. "No. There is nothing to pass here today. In fact, I will not be testing you at all," he revealed. "Some of the Circlemen will test you. Others will simply observe you in your daily life and make their decision based on your actions. It is my firm belief that life will test each of you better than I ever could. I will simply evaluate how you react to life's trials when I make my decision about each of you. In the meantime, I hope you have all learned something here this morning. Something you will think about even after you leave my class. The rest of the day is yours."

With that, Stendeval's lessons were over and class was dismissed. On his way out, Skerren purposely bumped into Jack, knocking him to the floor. Looking up from the ground, Jack saw Allegra looking back, nibbling at her lower lip. Jack could tell she felt bad for him, but she didn't stop to help him up. No doubt, she was afraid of getting on Skerren's bad side.

Jack picked himself up. "I'm used to people giving me a hard time, but this is too much," Jack said to Stendeval as the others left. "Everyone here either hates me or is afraid of me."

"Things will not always be as they are today," Stendeval said, drifting down to Jack's level. "I am more than five hundred years old. I have seen much change in my lifetime. Change begins with the individual, especially individuals with power like ours."

"What are your powers, Stendeval?" Jack asked.

"My powers," Stendeval began, "are whatever I decide to devote my power to. Each day I have a certain amount of energy I can use to do almost anything, and I use those energies to whatever ends I decide," he added, using his powers to send the cannonballs back where they belonged, and the suit of armor back into place.

"So, you can do anything?"

"Well. Some things take a lot of power, some take a little, and some are beyond my reach. At the end of the day when the power well is dry, I am just like anyone else."

"I wish my powers were that easy," Jack said. "It's going to be hard to make my powers work, because I don't really know anything about machines. I certainly don't understand the ones you have here. They're too complex."

"So, what do you understand in machines?" Stendeval asked. "Start with that. Start small. Sometimes you have to think small to think big."

"What do you mean?"

"Look at me," Stendeval replied. "Am I immortal? No, that is beyond my power as well. But the first thing I do each morning is reverse my body's age by one day. Just one day. I do this every day, so technically, my body is the same exact age as that first day I thought to do it, nearly five hundred years ago. If I looked at that whole task at once, if I tried to reverse five hundred years in a day? That is too much to ask. But to deal with one day—today—I can do that. In a way, so can you."

Jack looked over at the SmartWater-CleanWindow with a new idea in his head. He asked Stendeval not to put it away just yet. He looked at the on/off switch at the top of the machine. He focused on it. He focused hard. In his head Jack saw the switch moving. It was part of the machine, a lever with a simple mechanical motion. Jack thought small to think big and managed to flip the switch, a simple part of a complex machine. SmartWater filled the CleanWindow, humming away with cleansing power.

Jack smiled.

"Impressive," Stendeval told him. "Most impressive. You control that which you *can* control. The rest will come in time. You're a quick study, young Jack. Some people never learn that lesson."

"But I still have so many questions," Jack said. "Did you really write Chi about me twelve years ago? How did you even know about me? Do you know who my family is, or *where* my family is? Why am I here now?"

"Many questions, indeed," Stendeval said. "Patience, Jack. The answers will come in time. All in good time."

"But I just want to know who I am."

"That is not for me to say—that is for you to say," Stendeval replied. "I predict that you will tell *me* the answer to that question before you get into the School of Thought."

"Yeah, right," Jack said.

"You doubt my word?"

"More like I doubt I'm going to get into the School

of Thought," Jack said. "How am I supposed to get Mr. Smart's vote? Do you really trust him to be fair?"

"Fear not," Stendeval said. "I trust Jonas to be Jonas. Everything will work out in the end. With a little help from you, of course."

"I don't understand."

"You will," Stendeval replied. "In time."

CHAPTER

9

Jonas Smart: Man of the Future

The next day, Jonas Smart sent a few Peacemakers over to the Ivory Tower to collect Jack for his next test. His men were tall, imposing supers with humorless faces and military crew cuts. Jazen recognized them both. The first one, Stormfront, wore a black and gray super-suit and could control the weather with his powers. The other one, Battlecry, wore black and blue. Battlecry's supersonic voice was his weapon. One word from him could punch through a brick wall, and he was quick to let Jack know it.

"Just so you know, Rusty," Battlecry warned Jack on their way out the door, "I could pulverize your bones with a word."

"You can what?" Jack asked.

"That's right," Stormfront added. "All we do all day long is hunt down Rüstov, so don't think we're afraid of you."

Jack wasn't quite sure what to do with either comment.

"Give it a rest, you two," Jazen told the Peacemakers. "What are you doing here anyway, trying to play 'bad cop/bad cop'? SmartTower is just up the street. We don't need an escort."

"Circleman Smart says you do," Stormfront replied. "He wants every possible precaution taken, what with the increased Rüstov activity we're seeing."

"Increased activity?" Jazen asked. "What are you talking about? This boy's the closest thing to a Rüstov anyone's seen around here in years."

"Wrong again," Battlecry said. "A Left-Behind was spotted in Galaxis just this morning."

"It was on all the NewsNets," Stormfront added. "The entire city is talking."

"A Left-Behind?" Jack asked, looking up at Jazen for an explanation.

"A Rüstov Para-Soldier who got stuck here after the invasion," Jazen told Jack. "And spotted by whom?" he asked the Peacemakers. "Is this an actual, confirmed sighting or just another rumor you guys are passing off as fact?"

"We don't have any reason to doubt the NewsNets," Battlecry replied.

Jazen eyed the Peacemaker skeptically. "Of course you don't. SmartNews is *never* wrong," he said with obvious sarcasm. "Let's just get going—Jack's going to be late."

Jazen decided to accompany Jack and his escorts over to Smart's lab. He had no intention of leaving Jack alone with the Peacemakers. As the four of them made their way through the megametropolis of Hightown, Jack could tell he was in a section of town reserved for the wealthy, which made sense since it was Smart's neighborhood and he had more credits than anyone. Well-to-do people they passed along the way crossed the street and hid their babies when they spotted Jack. More than a few concerned citizens recognized Jack from the NewsNets and asked the Peacemakers why Jack wasn't in restraints.

"Ought to be a law against it!" a snooty old man snooted.

"They *do* have a law against it!" his crusty, ancient wife added. "Don't think you're fooling anyone," she told Jack. "We heard all about those Left-Behinds in the city this morning . . . whatever you all are up to, you won't get away with it!"

"Don't worry, ma'am," Stormfront assured the woman. "That's what we're here for."

"Bless your heart," the crotchety old woman replied.

On the short walk to SmartTower, Jack met several more people who felt the need to comment on the Left-Behind infiltrators and Jack's "obvious" connection to them. The number of Left-Behinds in the city seemed to go up with each new person they met. By the time Jack got across the street, it was a whole team of Left-Behinds led by Revile that was spotted in Galaxis that morning.

As Jack and the others continued onward, pampered Hightowners also complained about Jack living in their borough. Each time, the Peacemakers pointed to Jazen, who would flash his badge and tell them to get lost. Most Hightowners scoffed at Jazen, too. The idea of an android emissary didn't suit them any better than a freely roaming infected child. "Probably another Mecha Collaborator," one man noted as he passed.

The one person who was nice to Jack was a kid his own age—a boy with red hair who waved and said hello while they waited at the corner for a light to change. The boy's mother scolded him for it and immediately pulled him off in another direction. Stormfront looked up at one of the SmartCams that was following Jack. "Let's put that redheaded kid on the watch list," he said to it.

"Possible Rüstov sympathizer," Battlecry added. The SmartCam acknowledged the order with a beep and then flew off after the child and his mother.

"Why do you live in Hightown instead of Machina?" Jack asked Jazen as they walked along. "The Ivory Tower is great and all, but these people are the worst."

"Tell me about it," Jazen said. "Machina isn't really built for bi-orgs, though. That's Mecha-speak for biological organisms like yourself. I have to be a good host to anyone I bring here, and even the nicest building in Machina wouldn't be too comfortable for you. No bathrooms, no kitchens . . . rechargeable docking stations instead of beds. You get the picture. Besides, if I live here, I get to vote against Smart every time he runs for Circleman. Of course, SmartCorp is the biggest employer in the borough, so he still wins every election in a landslide."

When the group arrived at Smart's corporate headquarters, Jack was not at all surprised to learn the building was the tallest in Empire City. Smart owned property in every borough, but SmartTower was the crown jewel of his collection. The building did not occupy the central position in the Empire City skyline, but it was the most prominent by far.

The tower was a vertigo-inducing six-hundred-floor structure capped with a spire that was every bit as sharp as the peak of Mount Nevertop. A curved incline sloped down from the pinnacle of the spire, jutting out over the side, then cutting back in to run straight down. The face of the building was half-bare, and half lined with cylindrical windows that began at the bottom floor and ran all the way up to a massive round window at the top. Smart's office was on the very top floor, behind that massive round window. Much like the man himself, Smart's office was positioned high above the rest of the city, with a view that overlooked everything.

Jack ran an exhausting gauntlet of security checks on his way up to the office. The Peacemakers took Jack's fingerprints, scanned his retinas, and recorded his voice-print. The entire building was riddled with cameras, micro-phones, and special sensor walls. Once the tower system had Jack's bio-data, the Peacemakers told him, it would be impossible for him to hide inside the building or disguise himself in any way while there. The sound of his voice would be picked up by hidden audio sensors that would recognize his specific vocal patterns. Anything Jack touched would register his fingerprints. SmartCams and other secu-rity cameras were constantly "ret-scanning" the building and would easily identify Jack's unique eyeballs.

Having taken the necessary precautions, it was finally time to bring Jack before Jonas Smart. The Peacemakers took Jack up to the top floor in an elevator that made the one in the Ivory Tower feel slow. Smart's lesson was being taught in his laboratory. Battlecry checked in at a ret-scanner to open the lab door, and Stormfront halted Jazen at the entrance.

"School of Thought only," Stormfront told Jazen smugly, holding up his hand.

Jazen didn't argue. He simply pointed out that if he couldn't go with Jack into Smart's lab, then the Peacemakers couldn't follow him in there either. Stormfront immediately lost his haughty grin, realizing that separating Jack from the Peacemakers was probably all Jazen hoped to accomplish in the first place. Jack thanked Jazen for coming this far with him and entered the lab. The Peacemakers stayed outside and Jazen waited with them.

Smart's lab was built like an airplane hangar. It was an immense room, a vast, wide-open space. The smooth contours of the arched ceiling were bright white and backlit by intense lights, the kind you needed sunglasses to guard against. After Jack's eyes adjusted, he saw an incredibly clean and orderly laboratory with minirobots hard at work in every corner. The lab was a precision machine, illuminated with brilliant light and cast in an unblemished, perfect white hue. Jonas Smart had an experiment in progress for anything and everything you could think of. There were sparks flying and the smell of welding metal in the air. Mechanical assembly lines whirred and chemicals bubbled. Engines ran and turbines turned. The breadth and variety of machines in the room overwhelmed Jack, reminding him just how much he needed to learn if he was going to master his superpowers. Words scrolled through the air like the holo-signs Jack had seen back in the Hall of Records. Their message was less than inspiring:

THIS WAY, JACK BLANK . . . YOU ARE LATE . . . PENALTY POINTS WILL BE ASSESSED.

Jack soldiered on and found Smart in the back of the lab, standing in front of what looked like a tangital chalkboard he could write on with a laser pen. There were three desks before him. Skerren and Allegra were already seated.

"You are four minutes and twenty-seven seconds late," Smart said, pointing to a timer that was counting away on the holo-board. "In case you are wondering, this is not the way to earn my vote."

"I've been here for twenty minutes," Jack said. "The Peacemakers had me going through your security checks forever."

"I'm not interested in excuses," Smart replied. "Lateness is lateness, regardless of reason."

"It wasn't my fault, though. The SmartCams—"

"I'm not complaining, Jack, it was an enjoyable four minutes and twenty-seven seconds," Smart said. "Truth be told, you're only here because I am bound to abide by the ruling of my fellow Circlemen. Even so, a student must show respect for his teacher, and as such your conduct is unacceptable. Completely unacceptable." Jack put up his hands as if to say "I surrender" and sat down. He was off to a great start. Smart scowled at Jack as he took his seat, then resumed teaching.

Smart was supposed to be teaching, anyway, but he was apparently incapable of doing anything beyond bragging about his own intelligence. Five minutes into the lecture, it was plain to see that Smart's "class" would be little more than a pompous diatribe describing his many great accomplishments: SmartPaper, SmartWater-CleanWindow, SmartTrash-Disintegrators, and more.

"The greatest of all my inventions was the Time-Scope," Smart said, proudly pointing to an image that flashed on the holo-board. It looked like a giant telescope, except the end with the lens disappeared into some kind of hole torn in the sky. Smart explained that the TimeScope used a supersharp ion-blade attachment to cut a hole in the very fabric of reality and look deep into the time-space continuum. From there, an image-relayer inside the TimeScope beamed pictures back to the TimeScreen, where Smart could tune in static-filled snippets of the future like a TV with fuzzy reception. "The further into the future I look, the more static-filled the image becomes. I've tried to fix that, but so far, to no avail." Smart paused, smiling wistfully. "I know what you must be thinking. I create an amazing wonder like this, and still I'm not satisfied. Well, that is what it means to be Jonas Smart. In fact, I believe this device can do more than simply see into the future. My theory is that if someone were to dive through that hole in the fabric of reality, they could physically travel through time." Smart looked at his students. "Any volunteers?"

Skerren raised his hand. "I volunteer Jack," he said.

"You can't volunteer someone else," Allegra said. "That's not how it works."

"Yeah," Jack said to Skerren. "If you're so tough, why don't you volunteer your—"

"Enough," Smart said. "Your mindless prattle is both tiresome and misplaced. This class is not about you, it is about me. Now, let's all take a moment to reflect upon my brilliance, shall we?"

While the students observed the moment of silence, Smart rode around the lab on a floating platform, checking on his many ongoing experiments. He continued his lecture while going from project to project, preoccupied with his own interests as he spoke. He droned on about himself, showing little to no interest in his students.

"By the time I was your age, I had already written volumes and volumes of scientific texts," Smart boasted. "I redefined scientific theory and was responsible for several magnificent breakthroughs, including MagLev roads! I later tried to change the name to SmartRoads, but the term 'MagLev' had already caught on with the public. Something I find to be rather annoying," he grumbled.

Jack rolled his eyes. Smart had his name on half the buildings in Empire City, and here he was complaining about a lack of recognition. When Smart's back was turned, Jack looked at Allegra and silently mouthed "Blah, blah, blah . . ." as Smart blathered on.

Allegra giggled. Jack snickered too.

Smart spun around in a flash.

"Something amusing?" Smart asked pointedly. "Let's see what's so funny . . . Holo-board! Playback!"

Jack was mortified to learn the holo-board recorded everything that happened in the classroom. Moments later, the board replayed a high-definition video of Jack's antics, and Smart's temper hit volcanic levels.

"This is the second time you have disrespected me today . . . there will *not* be a third!" Smart bellowed. "In fact, I might just cast my vote on you right now."

Technically, it was only the first time Jack had disrespected Smart. His lateness wasn't his fault, but there was no point in trying to convince Jonas Smart of that. Jack said, "Sorry, sir. Really. It won't happen again."

Smart glared at Jack. "I should hope not."

There was a tap on Jack's shoulder as Smart returned to the holo-board. It was Skerren. "Just give up now, Rusty," he hissed. "You can't get on Smart's good side. There is no good side! He's heartless!"

Jack ignored Skerren's whispering. He figured his insufferable classmate was just trying to get him into more trouble by goading him to talk out of turn again. When

Smart was done showing off all his inventions, he asked if there were any questions. Jack tried to take the opportunity to show some interest and make back some points with the teacher.

"Could I read some of your science books?" Jack asked with his hand in the air.

Smart just looked at Jack. "Whatever for?"

"Well, we found out that I can only control machines if I know how they work," Jack explained. "I'm really impressed with all your inventions. If I could get a look at some of your books and the cool things you've done, maybe I could start to see what makes everything tick."

"Don't get ahead of yourself, boy," Smart said dismissively. "My work is all very complex. You wouldn't understand any of it."

Jack leaned forward, squinting at Smart. *Wouldn't understand it?* Of course he wouldn't understand it. That was the whole point of trying to learn it! Jack slumped in his chair.

"Something you should know," Smart told Jack. "I am not describing my inventions so that you can learn how to manipulate them. I'm not at all comfortable with training a future Rüstov soldier to better control powers that he will one day use against me. I am just gracing your brain with a brief history of the greatest and most innovative mind the world has ever known. My own. This lecture has little to do with your testing or my vote. In fact, all the information I need from you will come in the form of little light-dots made by your laser pens." He held up three sheets of SmartPaper. "Namely, your answers to this test."

With that, Smart handed out his very comprehensive Total Personality Test. It was a test designed to create a snapshot estimate of an individual's knowledge on every possible subject. As an added bonus, the TPT (as Smart was fond of calling it) could psychoanalyze a student's personality into one of several predetermined profiles. The Total Personality Test distilled every unique characteristic of an individual person into a single test score. Smart was immensely proud of it.

Each copy of the test was entirely contained on a single sheet of SmartPaper. Jack scrolled through his test. There were more than a thousand questions in all. The tangital sheet went on and on, covering every subject and question type he could imagine. There were math, linguistics, science, history, and grammar questions. There were logic puzzles, analogies, essays, and more. Jack scrolled down for what seemed like forever. It was a dizzying experience to feel so unprepared for a test of this magnitude. Jack hadn't studied a thing. Then again, what do you study when you're going to be tested on everything?

Smart announced that the four-hour examination period would begin immediately. A four-hour test! Jack held back a groan. Smart said there would be no break, since it would waste test time. The whole thing reminded Jack of Calhoun's P-MAP Test, except way longer.

As Smart left the room, Jack concentrated on trying his best on the exam. After the first two hours of questions about algebra, classic books, and thermodynamics, the questions all gelled together into a blur of multiple choices. The only standouts were the additional questions, specific to each test taker. They were automatically generated by the test and Jack found them especially annoying. Some of the questions the Total Personality Test posed to Jack were:

WHY DID THE RÜSTOV
SEND YOU HERE?

A. To attack humans

B. To spy on humans

C. To spy on humans now and
attack them later

HOW OFTEN DO YOU
DREAM ABOUT
CONQUERING EARTH?

A. Always

B. More often than not

C. Now and then

IF AND WHEN THE RÜSTOV
INVADE AGAIN,
WHAT WILL YOU DO?

A. Join in the fight against humanity

B. Help find another planet to attack
and systematically destroy

C. Both A and B

Whenever Jack didn't like answer choices A, B, or C, he decided to write his own responses in the margins. He wrote in that the Rüstov didn't send him here to do anything, that he never dreamed about world domination, and that if the Rüstov were to come back, he'd fight against them. Jack wondered what kind of questions Skerren and Allegra were getting. They didn't seem to be enjoying the test any more than he was.

When Jack was finally done, Smart collected the tests and took them to be scanned and graded. He was going to base 100 percent of his vote on these tests. The very idea made Jack's stomach turn. He had answered so many questions that he had no idea how he had done, or what any of it had to do with becoming a superhero. He just hoped that he would somehow pass.

Jack turned around in his chair after Smart left the room. "After this is over, do you want to go to SeasonStill Park or something?" he asked.

"I don't have time to play in the park," Skerren scoffed. "I have to train. Unlike you, *I'm* going to get into this school. When you fail, it's going to be because you didn't work like I did. Either that, or because you'll turn into a Rüstov Para-Soldier before we even get that far."

"Thanks for sharing, Skerren," Jack said. "I was talking to Allegra."

Allegra shied away as Jack and Skerren turned toward her. She didn't do well as the center of attention. "Um . . ." was all she could say.

She was still struggling to reply when Smart returned with the test scores. *That was fast,* thought Jack.

"Here comes your first F," Skerren said, tapping Jack's shoulder. "Time to hit the MagLev road, Jack." Jack felt queasy. Skerren was a jerk, but he was probably right. Jack braced himself for the inevitable as Smart approached.

Smart handed Skerren's test back first. Skerren passed easily with a 98, earning both Smart's vote and his praise. The test categorized Skerren's personality as an "Ultra-compulsive Overachiever." Apparently, that was Smart's personality type as well, and he was proud to say so. Next was Allegra. She scored an 85, which was also a passing grade. Smart told her it was tolerable, and that he would not vote against her. Her personality profile was a mixture of "Jittery Jitterbug" and "Late Bloomer." Jack had to admit Allegra was pretty jittery, but he didn't agree with the second part at all. He actually thought Allegra was kind of cute. Finally, it was his turn. He fully expected to be classified as "Evil Rüstov Spawn" and sent packing, but Smart just paused a moment and looked at Jack with an odd sort of look. Jack waited anxiously as the dreaded test sheet was laid before him on the desk.

There was no score.

The grading area read NEED MORE INPUT.

"What the—," Jack began.

"Yes," Smart said, unnerved and upset. "Your test was inconclusive. I assume you expect me to believe you had nothing to do with this?"

Jack stared at the test paper in front of him in disbelief. "I took the test, that's all I did," he said. "I don't understand."

Smart looked at Jack like he was trying to will his head to explode. "Don't you? I designed the Total Personality Test to be perfect. The TPT has never failed to categorize an individual, and yet it cannot evaluate you, the boy who knows how to control machines."

Jack looked up at Smart. "What are you saying?"

"SmartPaper is a machine. Obviously, you're using your powers to cheat on my test."

"My powers don't work like that," Jack said. "I don't have a clue how SmartPaper works—I couldn't mess with it if I tried."

Of course, Jack hadn't known how the power generator back at St. Barnaby's had worked either, and he had blown that up without any trouble, but he didn't feel the need to bring that up. He wondered if Smart was right. Was he so scared of failing that his powers had actually affected the test?

Smart didn't pick up on Jack doubting his own story. Smart was in his own world, pondering away and talking to himself. "This is intolerable," he muttered under his breath. "How can I be expected to make up my mind—to *vote!*—without the test telling me what to . . ." Smart grunted and went on pacing the room. After a few intense moments of rubbing his chin and pacing with a distressed look, Smart composed himself. He straightened his back and addressed the children with confidence.

"I have it," Smart announced. "I've decided to wait."

"What?" Jack and Skerren exclaimed at the same time, for very different reasons.

"I will wait to judge you, Jack Blank. I've thought long and hard on this. Forty-seven seconds, in fact. An eternity for someone with an intellect such as mine. I need more data," Smart explained. "You are an unfinished equation. It irks me. *You* irk me. I will delay my vote, but only on the condition that you voluntarily submit to a battery of additional medical tests and experiments. We'll get to the bottom of this mystery."

"Whoa," Jack said. "What kind of tests and experiments?" He had every right to be suspicious of a man who had very recently lobbied to execute and dissect him.

"Whatever kind I deem necessary," Smart replied. "Not to worry, you'll be quite safe. I can't dissect you without the Inner Circle's permission. My experiments will simply explore the nature of your infection and alleged ability to resist it. We will explore the full extent of your powers and find out just how you've confounded this test!"

"And if I pass your tests, you'll vote me into the School of Thought?" Jack proposed.

Smart paused before answering. "If you pass all my tests and I deem you safe?" he asked. His compulsive need for more data was in conflict with the absolute disgust he felt at the thought of voting for Jack. "Yes," he said finally. "If that *extremely* unlikely scenario comes to pass, I will give you my vote."

"Give him your vote?" Skerren protested. "But, but— he's a Rüstov!"

"And I expect I'll prove that. But I need to hear my tests say so."

"Why?" Skerren asked.

"I JUST DO!" Smart shouted back. "Now be silent! It's not your place to question me!" This was a very different Jonas Smart than the one Jack had seen up until now. He was harried. Agitated. Quite unlike himself. "Jack, you have heard my terms," he said. "The choice is yours. Take all the time you need to decide." He glanced at the clock on the wall. "You have four seconds."

"Uh . . . okay, deal," Jack said.

"Excellent," Smart said, taking a deep breath. "Excellent." He shut down the holo-board and leaned over a lab desk, facing away from the students. He exhaled deeply. "Tests will begin today," he said. "Now. Perhaps sooner. The rest of you can leave," he added with a wave of his hand. "Go. Play. Do whatever it is that children do, but be gone." Skerren and Allegra couldn't have left any quicker if Stendeval had teleported them away.

Jack didn't think it was possible, but Smart's additional tests soon had him longing for more sheets of SmartPaper filled with thousands of rude questions. True to his word, Smart didn't try to dissect Jack, but the tests he had in mind were no walk in SeasonStill Park. Jack had figured he'd be sleigh riding in Winterwind Way or swimming down at the Summershore Stretch by now. No such luck. Instead, he had to stay after school.

The whole experience did at least give Jack some insight into how Jonas Smart thought. The more Jack saw of Jonas Smart, the more Jack thought maybe he wasn't the smartest guy in town after all. Jack never had any problems with his infection or heard any Rüstov voices in his head. He never even knew about his infection. In a sense, he was the only one beating the Rüstov. If he were to get really good at using his powers, maybe he could help beat the whole bunch of Rüstov once and for all. It was pretty obvious to Jack. If Smart weren't so busy making everybody afraid of Jack, he'd see it too.

But Jack could tell that Smart saw the world differently. He saw the world as a disorganized, chaotic place in need of a hyperintelligent person like him to simplify it. He didn't think, *he knew* that everything had its place. A job to do. A role to fulfill. Smart knew that everything had a category it fit into neatly and never moved from. "There is an order that must be preserved," Smart told Jack while strapping him into a lab chair. "Think of the world like a mathematical equation. We don't ask mathematical truths to be something other than what they are, do we? No, there is only one correct answer to balance the scales of any given problem. Things must be how they must be. We cannot change that. We must accept that."

Smart lived his life by numbers. "Numbers don't change and numbers don't lie," he told Jack. Smart trusted only his experiments and inventions. His machines spit out answers based on hard data, and he did whatever they said, because he didn't make machines that made mistakes.

It amazed Jack that someone like Smart could be so closed-minded. How could an inventor, in this of all places, be so lacking in imagination? Smart claimed to love logic and reason, but he didn't even seem to think for himself. It appeared he was happy to let his machines to do that for him.

Jack could see that even without the Rüstov infection, Smart would have disliked him because of the effect he had on machines. Smart's Total Personality Test should have categorized him as a Rüstov and recommended immediate termination. Smart "proved" long ago that no biological organism could withstand a Rüstov parasite for longer than five minutes. Yet here Jack was, showing no adverse effects or symptoms of any kind. People like Jack upset the natural order of things. Jack was a set of numbers that didn't add up. He came along, and simple things that Smart knew to be true were suddenly false. Jack came along, and suddenly 2 + 2 equaled 458.

"We're going to find out if it was your powers or the parasite that affected my test," Smart said. "Are the Rüstov adapting to my methods of detection? I need to know."

Smart took a vial of Jack's blood to run some old-fashioned lab work. He couldn't run it through his high-tech machines, for fear that the blood might corrupt the system. Jack's blood had crashed his history file back at the Hall of Records pretty easily, and Smart was not about to put his precious mainframe at risk. As for the tests, Smart told Jack he wanted to observe his reaction to a number of different machines in stressful situations. He ordered Jack not to try and take control of the machines, no matter what was happening. "We're going to gauge the levels and limits of your powers by observing your reaction to negative stimuli."

"Negative stimuli?" Jack asked.

"Electroshocks," Smart explained.

"*Electroshocks?*" Jack cried out. "Are you serious?" Jack struggled to get free of his chair, but he was strapped down.

"Be still!" Smart ordered. "And don't question my methods. Impertinent youth," Smart muttered once Jack had stopped fighting.

Smart hooked electrodes up to Jack and began the experiment. If he had wanted to be honest with Jack, he could have called it what it really was—an interrogation. Smart asked Jack question after question, and whenever he didn't like the answer (which was quite often), he gave Jack a shock in the arm, belly, or neck.

Smart was relentless.

"Did you really battle Revile?" *BZZT!* "Where is he

now?" *BZZT!* "Are you leading him here to the Imagine Nation?" *BZZT!*

No matter what the question was, Jack got a shock. He even got a shock for telling Smart that his favorite color was blue. Eventually, he couldn't take anymore, and he shorted out the machine. He didn't mean to do it. It just happened.

"But did it really 'just happen'?" Smart asked. "Did your powers activate to protect you, or did the Rüstov act to protect its host?"

There was only one way to find out. Jack was ordered to report back the next day for more tests.

Jack was having second thoughts about the deal he had made with Smart. What exactly had he gotten himself into? He had to wonder if Smart was planning to *accidentally* kill him in a lab accident. *Whoops, I guess now we know we can't give Jack a hundred thousand volts of electricity. . . . Oh well! Might as well dissect him now.*

When Jack filled Jazen in on everything after they left the lab, Jazen said he was pretty sure that wasn't Smart's plan, if only because it would have required Smart to act like he had made a mistake. Jazen thought

Jack had made the right decision. Now he at least had an outside chance of getting Smart's vote.

Jack found it funny how things were working out. So far, Jack's School of Thought report card had two incompletes. He had gotten less than he expected from Stendeval, and more than he expected from Smart. Jack didn't see that coming. Nothing in the Imagine Nation was ever what you might expect.

By the time Jack got back to the Ivory Tower, he was fried. He wanted to go check out Seasonstill Park, but he was too tired. He collapsed onto a couch and opted to do some reading instead about the machines of the Imagine Nation. He managed to get one of Smart's books to help with that after all. The book was Smart's autobiography, called *Jonas Smart: Man of the Future*.

Jack didn't really expect to get much out of it, but was still curious to read what kind of stuff Smart put into his SmartPaper-powered book. Jack stared at the "start" button on the cover. After a minute or so of intense concentration, Jack managed to turn the book on with his powers. "Nice," Jack said to himself, and started scrolling through the pages by hand.

JONAS SMART:
MAN OF THE FUTURE

AS TOLD BY JONAS SMART

Dear reader,

You have made a wise decision by purchasing this book. What follows is a detailed description of the accounts of my life. Who I am, and how I came to be. In short, what makes me … me. If you are lucky and work extremely hard (reading this book more than once and purchasing several copies), you will find qualities to emulate and, in time, become more like me.

At the time of this writing I am honored to be the most senior member of the Inner Circle. The residents of Hightown voted me to this seat shortly after the Rüstov invasion, and I have been shaping Imagine Nation policy ever since that day. As you are almost certainly aware, my superior intellect helped divine the treacherous nature of the Rüstov attack and the identity of the Great Collaborator. At the time, I was known only as a rising young industrialist. I was a brilliant inventor and innovator with no combat training or battle-ready abilities, but my brain proved to be a super-power unto itself. My mind was my weapon. Even today, I am not a fighter. I am a thinker. More importantly for the people of Empire City, as my life story proves quite conclusively, I am a survivor.

Years ago, I was diagnosed with a terminal heart condition. Countless transplant attempts failed, each one condemning me to die. A lesser man would have turned to despair, but I did not sit around waiting for a fatal heart attack to end my life. Using my TimeScope, I uncovered a cure perfected many years in the future and acted upon that information: I had my heart surgically removed.

After my heart was cut out of my chest, its functions were duplicated by a series of magnetic implants placed throughout my body. I now ingest iron-rich supplements that magnetize my blood and circulate it through my veins. A radical solution, to be sure, but no one can argue with the results.

We must not be afraid of going to extremes in order to ensure the future of our great nation, because our secret war against the Rüstov still wages on. Who knows how many Rüstov Left-Behinds are still hiding on Wrekzaw Isle, waiting? Waiting and plotting! Luckily, I have been able to properly protect our borders from the Rüstov Armada so far.

The people of Empire City have me to thank for the Peacemaker security forces that keep us safe. Some say the Peacemakers are too violent and too reckless. The same critics argue that my SmartCam surveillance program is an infringement upon theoretical rights of freedom and privacy. I ask you: How can people expect privacy and freedom if we are to preserve safety and order? We must remain vigilant against our foes. To be anything less is to be Anti–Imagine Nation.

With Legend gone, killed by Revile, and with Stendeval missing, probably off hiding some-where . . . the people have turned to one man to make sure they live to see tomorrow. They have turned to me. I am Jonas Smart, the man of the future, and I will not let you down.

Next chapter: Is Jonas Smart always right? Turn the page and find out!
Hint: The answer is yes!

When Jack could stomach no more, he turned off the book. He could hardly believe it, but Skerren hadn't been kidding when he'd called Smart heartless. The man literally had no heart!

Jack thought that made Smart even scarier. There was no reasoning with Jonas Smart—he dealt only in abso-lutes. Smart considered Jack to be a Rüstov, and wanted him dead because of it. Meanwhile, Jack knew the Rüstov wanted him dead too, and if the NewsNets were to be believed, they'd followed him here to finish the job. Jack could only guess what their reasons were, and hoped that if there really were Left-Behinds in Empire City, that Revile wasn't with them.

Jack tossed Smart's book into a corner. "How'd I end up with the worst possible enemies on both sides of this war?" he wondered aloud.

Just lucky, I guess, Jack thought.

Jack shook his head and forced out a laugh. He didn't really find it funny, though. He knew the real answer was hidden in his own lost history, and he couldn't shake the feeling that someone—or something—out there knew exactly what it was.

CHAPTER

10

Virtua's Reality

The following day once again brought news of Rüstov activity. Reports of Left-Behind sightings were now coming in from all six boroughs of Empire City. Jazen broke the news to Jack over breakfast, stressing that he didn't necessarily believe all these reports were grounded in fact. Even so, Jack could tell the city's reaction to them was real enough. As Jack ate breakfast in the Ivory Tower loft, a SmartNews anchorman was droning on in the background about preparations for a second Rüstov invasion getting under way:

"This morning in Hightown, Circleman Jonas Smart launched a petition to return his Peacemaker security teams to post-invasion force levels. The Circleman promised to do whatever is necessary to protect this city, and urged all loyal citizens of the Imagine Nation to give the measure their full support." The newscaster turned to his cohost. "Seems like a no-brainer to me," he said.

"Absolutely," his perky female cohost agreed. "Maybe next we can do something about that infected boy who's causing all this trouble," she added brightly.

Jazen scowled at the holo-screen from his seat at the kitchen table. "Unbelievable," he said, shaking his head. "There's a couple of no-brainers for you right there behind the news desk," he added.

"I don't know," Jack replied. "Everyone I've met here seems to share their opinion. I'm actually starting to wonder about all this myself," he admitted.

Jazen looked at Jack. "*You* are? What are you talking about?"

Jack looked up from his cereal. "Let's be real for a minute, Jazen. You don't think it's possible that I have some connection to the Rüstov?" he asked. "They already came after me once. I *am* infected with their techno-virus . . . what if these things are here because of me?"

Jazen shook his head. "You've been watching too much SmartNews," he said. "You know they only report Jonas Smart's side of any story. No one that matters is going to take this seriously. Trust me." Jazen was about to change the channel when a videophone call came in, overtaking the holo-screen. It was Virtua. She wanted to talk to Jack about the recent spike in Rüstov activity. Immediately.

Jack gave Jazen an *I told you so* look. "You were saying?"

Jazen just frowned uncomfortably.

Not looking to keep the Circlewoman waiting, Jack and Jazen quickly struck off for Machina, home to robots, androids, and other artificial intelligence. Jack found the borough to be like one big machine. It was filled with gleaming, clean buildings, each one glowing with data flow. The buildings' pointed peaks were capped with flashing lights, and the tower shafts all had a smooth metallic sheen with minimal design and decoration. Jack thought the streets were so clean, he could eat off them—not that there was any food in the borough. There weren't any signs or advertising messages cluttering up the landscape either. Instead, coded messages flashed nonstop at lightning speed in ones and zeroes on the sides of Machina's buildings. Everything, everywhere—all the machines—were alive and talking, communicating with one another. Their words hit Jack's ears like an off-key orchestra blaring out noise that he could only partly understand.

One thing Jack understood right away was that he had a lot in common with the Mechas. The SmartCams that followed him everywhere he went were all over Machina, watching every inch of the borough.

"And I thought *I* had no privacy," Jack said to Jazen as they made their way through the borough. Jazen explained that the excessive SmartCams were holdovers from the Peacemaker occupation days that followed the Rüstov invasion, after the Great Collaborator was revealed to be a Mecha. As Jack and Jazen walked through the streets, Jack noticed several SmartCorp buildings and SmartCorp-owned businesses. He told Jazen that he was surprised to find Smart had such a strong presence in the other boroughs.

"Smart owns property everywhere," Jazen told him. "His business is especially strong here in Machina, though.

It's hard for people here to say no to the deals he puts together."

"Because he's the smartest man in the world?" Jack asked with a trace of sarcasm.

"No, because Mechas that don't agree to his terms generally find themselves being investigated as possible Rüstov conspirators," Jazen said grimly. "I guess you can relate to that, though," he added.

"You think that's what Virtua is worried about?" Jack asked, remembering the way Smart had threatened her during the vote in the sphere. "You think she's having second thoughts about siding with me on Dedication Day?"

"I can't imagine Circlewoman Virtua ever backing down against Smart," Jazen replied. "Then again, I never imagined you'd get summoned to her data center like this either, so who knows?"

As soon as Jazen said the word "data center," a street-light scanned him and Jack up and down. When the scan was complete, a computer chime sounded and a holo-image of a Mecha robot appeared before them.

"Hello. Welcome to Machina," the image said. "I am

Shortcut, your help agent. It appears you are trying to find port DCv26/27, data center of the Circlewoman Virtua. May I be of assistance?"

Jazen thanked Shortcut but declined his offer, saying he knew the way well enough. The help agent's image vanished from sight. For the moment. A few blocks later, Shortcut appeared again.

"Hello again," the image said. "I am Shortcut, your help agent. Are you sure you don't need me to—"

"No," Jazen said, cutting Shortcut off. "Thank you, we're fine. Really." Shortcut nodded and blinked away again with a smile on his face. Unable to take a hint, he reappeared one last time a few blocks down the road.

"I don't mean to be a bother, but perhaps I could just—"

"NO!" Jack and Jazen yelled, having run out of patience with the program's bothersome interruptions.

Shortcut straightened up, clearly offended. "Well! If that's your attitude, forget it," he said before vanishing for the third and final time. Jazen and Jack just shook their heads. They got along fine without Shortcut. It wasn't long before they were standing outside Virtua's physical home—the data center. Jack was nervous about going in.

He knew Virtua had stuck her neck out for him when she had voted against his execution and dissection. She couldn't be happy with the way that was coming back to bite her, with all these Rüstov sightings popping up in the news.

Jack entered Virtua's home and was overwhelmed by what he saw. All around, at least a hundred holo-screens floated about, circling the air like carousel horses. Lights, images, codes, and information flashed on the screens and servers at blinding speed, too fast to read unless you were a Mecha. For Jack, it was like staring at a strobe light. At least seven images of Virtua glided through the air. The many Virtuas were looking at the many screens at the same time, drawing videos out from the walls and expanding some screens, while minimizing others and sending them to the background. An additional projection of the Circlewoman generated at the door as Jack entered.

"Welcome, Jazen . . . Hello, Jack," she said. "You may wish to enter slowly and give your eyes a moment to adjust."

It was already too late for that. Jack's eyes spun like slot machine dials, and he leaned against Jazen for support. He struggled to find his balance as the data center assaulted his senses and a kaleidoscope of sound and color bombarded him with a merciless information overload. Flying tangital holo-screens launched a rapid-fire barrage of video clips. Free-flowing Wi-Fi data feeds ghosted through the air on their way to mechanical eyes and ears that could better see and hear them.

"Do not be alarmed by the multiple projections of my avatar," Virtua told Jack. "You aren't seeing double or octuple, as the case may be. I'm just running some additional programs in the background while we talk. I'm trying to finish upgrading the data center to version 27. I trust you don't mind."

Jack shook his head no as Jazen helped him inside. Jack could barely walk straight. He was blinded by the multimedia light show, and his equilibrium was completely thrown off with his right eye—which, by all rights, should have a Rüstov mark on it—somehow seeing the room better than his left did. It was a realization that did nothing to ease Jack's concerns about his Rüstov connection, but he forced himself not to think about that.

"I'm sorry to call you here on such short notice, Jack," Virtua said. "But with the recent unpleasantness so prevalent in the news, I decided it was time you and I had a little chat."

"Circlewoman Virtua," Jazen began, "surely you can't believe that Jack has anything to do with—"

"And I wanted us to talk sooner rather than later," Virtua continued, raising her voice to talk over Jazen. Jazen shut his mouth. He and Jack traded uneasy looks. The Circlewoman was not in a good mood this morning.

"No problem," Jack said to her. "What did you want to talk about?"

"Truth," Virtua replied instantly, turning to look Jack in the eye. "Truth, justice, and the Rüstov." Her image flickered with displeasure when she noticed a SmartCam that had followed Jack in from the street. "However, I would prefer a true face-to-face for this conversation, which is why we will have the discussion elsewhere. We will speak in my home."

Jack was confused. "Your home?" he asked. "You don't live here?"

Virtua shook her head. "The data center is just a hardware accessory plugged into the machine that is Machina. It's an access point to cyberspace. That is where I truly live."

"I'm going into cyberspace?" Jack asked.

"I need to see you with my own eyes," Virtua replied. "What you see of me here, this is just a hologram created by Projo, my image-caster." The Circlewoman gestured to the orb-shaped projector that followed her everywhere. "Projo helps carry my face and voice to the Unplugged World, but these are only images of the face I have chosen as my avatar. My core program, my 'self,' resides in C-Space. This way."

Virtua led Jack through the data center with her glowing image in constant flux. They weaved their way around mainframes and servers, and a new image of Virtua waited around every corner in a fresh color, sporting a new and different wardrobe. Eventually, Jack turned the last corner and was shocked to find several long tube-shaped aquariums filled with blue-green water. There were people floating inside all of them but one.

Jazen took note of Jack's increased heart rate (projected at an additional 35 beats per minute), heightened pulse (23 beats per minute), and, of course, his obvious increase in oxygen consumption (heavy breathing). "Don't worry, Jack," Jazen said, drawing attention to the diving suits with special breathers and the virtual reality headsets with cyberspace viewfinders worn by all the people floating in the water. "These are sensory deprivation tanks. Bi-orgs need them to enter cyberspace."

Jazen went on to explain that jacking into C-Space can be jarring, but the tanks help calm the traveler so the bi-org mind can communicate with the landscape of the Mecha mind. The sensory deprivation tank eliminated all sights, sounds, and smells in the physical world, so there was no confusion distinguishing between the Infoworld and the Unplugged World. "It's also safer in the water," Jazen pointed out. "Less chance of anyone coming to harm in the physical world through any sudden movements." Jack watched the people in the water jerk around like puppets on a string. He wondered what they were all seeing.

Jack put on his wet suit, which was also a cybersensor suit that would track his body's vital signs and display his highly elevated stress levels on a holo-screen. As Jack entered the tank, Projo beeped out a snarky comment about how nervous Jack was, and wondered if he had anything to hide. It didn't look good to have a suspected

Rüstov sleeper agent here in the data center, he said in a series of high-pitched squawks and squeaks.

"I'm right here, Projo," Jack said. "You don't have to talk about me like I'm not in the room." Jazen and Virtua turned toward Jack with surprised looks. "And I don't have anything to hide," Jack added. "I've just never done this before and I'm a little tense, that's all."

"Jack . . . did you understand Projo's beeping just now?" Jazen asked.

"Yeah, why?" Jack replied through his headset.

Jazen looked at Virtua. "It's just . . . unusual," he said.

"Very unusual," Virtua said, intrigued as well. "Please excuse Projo, he's merely reacting to the all-too-popular opinion that it is dangerous to train you in the use of your powers. And yet I'm beginning to wonder . . . I think we will try something different today, Jack. Normally, we would emit an ultrasonic frequency to put you into a half-sleep state and complete your dive into cyberspace, but I think today we will leave the rest to you."

"Leave it up to me?" Jack gulped. "What are you talking about?"

"Please join me anytime you are ready, Jack Blank,"

Virtua said. A wry smile formed on her lips. "But don't keep me waiting too long."

With that, the Circlewoman's avatar blinked out, along with all the holo-screens and data center lights. Jack was alone with his fellow submerged bi-orgs, Jazen, and Projo. The room was silent and dark other than the low hum of the computer servers and the glare of the SmartCam's spotlight. Now Jack's stress levels *really* started to climb.

Every stat on Jack's cybersensor suit's readout was redlining. "Jazen, what is she talking about? Join her anytime I'm ready? I don't know the first thing about cyberspace dives. I can't control these machines."

Before Jazen could reply, Jack heard Virtua's voice through his headset. "Have you ever thought of simply asking the machine for help?" she said.

Jack blinked. "Asking?"

"Try to make friends with it. See if it will trust you."

"Make friends with it? It's a machine."

"So am I," Virtua replied. "So is your friend Jazen."

Jack nodded. "Good point," he said, feeling a little foolish. "Sorry about that."

"You should be," Projo beeped out.

Jack rolled his eyes at Projo. He was doing his best to ignore the cranky image-caster. Still, hearing Projo's beeps in English again did get Jack thinking. If he could understand machines . . . then maybe they could understand him, too. Maybe he didn't have to *control* machines. Maybe if he just asked nicely, they would do what he wanted, whether he knew how they worked or not.

"Open your heart and mind to the machine," Virtua told him. "Believe me, Jack, every computer in Machina knows you. They know what the NewsNets say—that you are a Rüstov spy sent to infiltrate our city and that the Rüstov have returned because of you. We all have reason to fear the Rüstov here in Machina. After all our trouble with one Great Collaborator, we want no association with another traitor. But if you hold nothing back, these machines will know your heart. And if my fellow machines will trust you, perhaps I shall too."

Jack nodded and did as he was told. He stared into the viewfinder with an open mind and an open heart.

Hello, um . . . cyberspace? How are you doing?

Lights flickered in the data center, but nothing else happened.

*Oh-kaay . . . I hope everything is cool over there. My name's
Jack. It's . . . nice to meet you, I guess . . .*

The data center remained powered down.

*Listen, don't believe everything you read about me. I'm really
a nice guy. Really. Do you think you can let me in?*

Nothing happened.

. . . please?

Bubbles started flowing up in Jack's tank like a Jacuzzi.
Bright light filled the water, and an ever-so-faint high-
pitched tone cried out. Jack's vision blurred and 1.2 seconds later, he was cyberspace-bound.

Cyberspace was the exact opposite of the data center. In
C-Space, Jack found an infinite amount of data flowing
across a digital landscape like sweet music. It was a brilliant
masterpiece, a triumphant symphony of code drafted by a
million composers, each with their own vision and song
that somehow gelled perfectly with the collective work of
their peers. Every algorithm, soaring strings. Every info
packet, roaring horns. Every data byte, a note perfectly
placed, precisely on key, and in time with every other.
Cyberspace was poetry in motion.

Jack stood on a white sandy beach of glistening silicon that brushed up against crystal glowing water. Out at sea, programs surfed data waves into the shore. Behind Jack, an information superhighway with an endless stream of flowing info-light charged past him. Behind that, smooth colors filled the air, rolling out like ripples in a pond, and running through the entire spectrum with each new color blending softly into the next. Jack saw an aurora borealis of information and computer code that at its tiniest level was a digital mosaic of rapid-motion video and high-resolution still images. And Jack could see it all. He could appreciate the beauty of both the large and the small with equal measure. Everything was talking to Jack, and Jack understood every word.

Virtua was nowhere to be found.

A gentle breeze blew across the beach, and Jack saw all the micropixels that made up the cyberworld around him flip over like tiles. They moved in a steady wave, falling like dominoes, reformatting his surroundings. When the last one fell, Jack was standing in Virtua's home. Virtua's real home.

The wind was a command. Jack felt it run a program

that transformed the endless horizon of sandy shores into Virtua's gilded palace. Here Jack found all the comforts that were lacking in the data center. Jack stood in a cushion-filled parlor worthy of a sultan, surrounded by pillows on all sides. Big ones, the size of hippos, filled with feathery goodness. Little ones, speckled with tiny jewel designs and tied off with little tassels at the corners. Curtains were draped over the lounges like cabana covers, and old-fashioned lanterns with multicolored glass panes floated about the room giving off a soft, warm light. In the center of it all, on the biggest pillow Jack had ever seen, in front of a reflection pool filled with scattered rose petals and floating tea lights, was the Circlewoman Virtua. She was clapping.

"Bravo, Jack. Bravo. Welcome to cyberspace. Can I offer you an Energon beverage?

"Uh . . . sure," Jack replied, though he had no idea what an Energon beverage was. The drink came to him in a glass that crackled with energy. Jack was hesitant to put it to his lips, but not wanting to be rude, he tried it anyway. The voltage tingled Jack's insides on the way down, which he thought was kind of funny because his insides weren't really in cyberspace at all.

"What do you think?" Virtua asked him.

"It's like drinking electricity," Jack said. "In a good way, though. Thank you." Jack looked around Virtua's lavish parlor in awe. "This isn't what I expected at all," he told Virtua. "I thought your home would be more"—Jack searched for the right word—"technical."

"I prefer a soft pillow to computer hardware any day," Virtua told Jack. "You don't approve?"

"No, I approve," Jack said. "I like it *way* more than the data center."

Virtua laughed. "I'm not surprised. In the Unplugged World, human senses have a difficult time processing Mecha environments. Here in cyberspace, our minds are on equal footing. Here you can see things how we see them. Please. Have a seat."

Jack started toward the lounge that was closest to him, but stopped himself when the pillow started whispering something back to him. The voice was soft, low, and in another language, but somehow Jack understood. And somehow he knew that it was the pillow talking. It said he didn't physically need to go anywhere, reminding him that his body wasn't in cyberspace, only his mind was.

Jack didn't physically move from the beach to Virtua's home. Cyberspace moved for him.

"Can I . . . ," he started to ask Virtua.

Virtua raised a hand in the air, as if to say, "See for yourself." So, Jack asked the pillow to come to him, and come to him it did. As the cushion digitized, vanished, and reformulated beneath him, Jack learned something new about himself. He could talk to machines. Yes, he could impose his will on any machine that he understood the inner workings of, but he could actually talk to them too. He could ask them nicely for help and see what happened.

"I can see why Stendeval has taken such an interest in you," Virtua told Jack. "Your powers appear to be growing by the day."

Jack looked around, letting his mind reach out to the rest of the room. The voices of other programs started to fill his ears. "I think you're right," he said, trying to sort them all out. "Does that worry you?"

"Don't you think it should?" Virtua replied. "When you consider that most of this city believes you to be a Rüstov spy, something that is already associated directly with my people, I should say that any actions on my part to expand your power should certainly worry me."

"Right."

"That said, as long as you're talking to machines," Virtua advised Jack, "you might want to ask them how they work as well. With their help you'll learn much, much faster. You just have to ask nicely. As I've heard many bi-orgs say, you catch more flies with honey. Although I can't understand what bi-orgs want with *any* flies, let alone more of them."

Jack chuckled and thanked the Circlewoman for her advice. He couldn't quite figure out what this meeting was about. On the one hand, Virtua was worried about his powers. On the other, she was giving him tips on how he could learn more. It was confusing, but he did notice that the hard edge he had observed in Virtua's voice back in the data center was gone now that they were here in her home. "If you don't mind me saying so," he began, "you seem a bit more relaxed in here than you did out there."

"I have reason to be," Virtua replied. "It's getting ugly out there, don't you think? I've been through this before. Thankfully, we can still speak freely in C-Space."

Jack leaned back in his seat, enjoying the privacy that Virtua's cyberhome afforded them. "It *is* nice to get a break from all those stupid cameras Smart has everywhere," he agreed.

"Jonas's SmartCams are a nuisance, yes," Virtua admitted, "but we Mechas have endured worse. Much worse. The Peacemakers . . . they practically ran Machina for years after the invasion, and the Mechas who live there suffered greatly. Believe me, if you weren't under Emissary Knight's protection first, and the Inner Circle's protection later, you would have tasted the Peacemakers' brand of justice long before now."

Jack leaned forward in his chair. "Yesterday I thought the Peacemakers were going to arrest some kid just for saying hi to me on the street," he said.

Virtua shook her head. "Even today, with Rüstov sightings dwindling, they wield more power than free people should ever grant figures of authority. And now people want to return their numbers to post-invasion strength. It seems that rumors are all that is needed for Jonas to keep his private army strong as ever."

"You think all these Left-Behind sightings are just rumors?" Jack asked.

"It doesn't matter what I think," Virtua said. "Not really. When rumors are reported as fact for a long-enough period of time, people eventually lose the ability to tell the difference. But I do wonder . . . why is it that we never actually see any of these Left-Behind infiltrators on the NewsNets? Circleman Smart has cameras everywhere. If Revile and these others are all truly back in the city, why is there never video footage of anyone but you?"

It was a good question, Jack thought. It did seem odd that he should continue to take up so much news time, given everything that was supposedly going on in the city.

"As far as I am concerned," Virtua continued, "the only confirmed Rüstov sighting . . . is you. Now, tell me the truth, Jack, it's what we're here for. Are you a Rüstov spy?"

Jack grimaced. It was just as he feared. Virtua was questioning his loyalties like everyone else. It seemed he had lost her support now too.

"No," Jack told Virtua sternly. "I'm not."

Virtua studied Jack for a moment. "Fair enough," she

replied, surprising him. "I believe you. Congratulations, Jack, you will have my friendship and support, as well as my vote for a place in the School of Thought."

Jack looked at Virtua like she was speaking another language. He couldn't believe his ears. "Are you serious?" he asked. "You trust me? Just like that? No test?"

"On the contrary," Virtua began. "I've been testing you from the moment you arrived here. The Energon beverage you drank allows me to track your brain wave activity here in cyberspace. If you were lying, I would know."

Jack frowned. "So, you just tricked me, then," he said, pushing his glass away.

"Please understand, the proof is not for me," Virtua told Jack. "I am going to be attacked in the media for siding with you again. Of this I have no doubt. I was actually satisfied that my instincts about you were correct from the start. When I first met you, I saw a child standing up to the Rüstov, beating them in a way no one had ever done before. Even if I did feel otherwise, I trust Stendeval, and his belief in you is evidence enough for me. I believe that education is an inherently good thing. That teaching you will not empower a future enemy, but rather prevent you from realizing that fate. I *want* you in the School of Thought, but as a Mecha I cannot be too careful where the Rüstov are concerned. I need to be able to validate my opinion in the public eye for my safety and the safety of my people."

Jack's eyes brightened. "But now you have proof that I'm not a Rüstov spy? Will it be proof enough for Mr. Smart?"

Virtua shook her head. "Any proof of mine will have little use beyond political cover. Jonas won't trust my tests. He won't trust any machine he didn't build."

Jack held out hope. "Other people might trust your tests, though, right?" he asked.

Virtua shrugged and gave Jack a pained look. "Who knows? I'm a Mecha, Jack. Just like the Great Collaborator." Virtua gestured to a portrait on the wall. It was a digital image of herself standing in Hero Square alongside the Imagine Nation's most infamous Mecha traitor. Jack recognized his picture from Smart's book.

"You knew the Great Collaborator?" Jack asked, getting up to look at the portrait.

Virtua's glow dimmed. "I choose not to remember him

that way, but yes. I knew him. Silico was my very good friend. I can only hang this picture in cyberspace. People in the outside world wouldn't understand. But I keep it to honor the memory of my friend, regardless of what other people may think of him."

"Why did he do it?" Jack asked. "Why did he betray the Imagine Nation?"

"That is a good question," Virtua said. "I'm not sure I have an answer for you. To the Rüstov, Mechas are just scrap metal. They think of us as little more than spare parts, not equals, and certainly not allies." Virtua shook her head, frustrated. "Sadly, no one cared about that after the invasion. Jonas Smart killed Silico, the Great Mecha Collaborator. That was the only story people cared to hear, and the only one Jonas cared to tell."

Jack thought about the danger that Virtua put herself in by keeping this picture, even if it was just in cyberspace. "Why are you showing me this?" he asked her.

"Because I wanted you to see that I stand by my friends, come what may," Virtua told Jack. "No matter what others might say about people, I remain a free thinker. I make up my own mind. We came here to talk of truth, trust, and the Rüstov. Since the invasion, I have seen very little of each. But your presence here is changing things."

"I don't understand," Jack said. "What do you mean?"

"I think you are part of something we cannot yet completely comprehend," Virtua replied. "And I believe that the Rüstov threat is more real than it is rumor. But I don't believe you are conspiring with the enemy any more than I believe Silico was a traitor." Virtua paused to gaze upon the picture of her long lost friend. "Mark my words, Jack . . . the real Great Collaborator is still out there."

CHAPTER

11

Wrekzaw Isle

Jack stood at a window in the Ivory Tower watching another superfight going on outside. It was hard to say what surprised Jack more: seeing his comic book heroes in real life, or the fact that he was getting used to it. He barely even flinched when one of the fighters, a glowing woman, was thrown right into his window. A being made of pure light, she rebounded harmlessly off the reinforced glass. Before Jack could worry if she was okay, she zapped back into battle as Blue called Jack down for dinner, telling him that Jazen was almost finished cooking.

Jack hurried down. As usual, Jazen had made a sumptuous feast, cooked with spices that Jack's nose had never smelled before. "Pan-seared scissor shark steaks, fresh from the fish farms of Atlantis," Jazen announced as he set down the plates.

"Let's do this," Blue said, rubbing his hands together as he sat down at the table. He took a bite and melted into his chair. He was in heaven. "I tell ya, I'll never understand how someone with no taste buds can cook this good."

"Watch out, Jack," Jazen said as he sat down with Jack and Blue. "If you're not careful, Blue here will be digging into your plate for seconds before you even get started."

"You know, I don't need to come here to be abused," Blue said. "I've got supercriminals out there for that."

"Speaking of which, was that another superfight I heard hit our window?" Jazen asked.

"The tower shields took care of it," Jack said with his mouth full.

"Anyone you recognized, big guy?" Blue asked.

"Actually, yeah—it looked like Laser Girl," Jack guessed, recalling a heroine from his old comic book collection.

Jazen raised his head to look out the window. The fight

was moving farther away, but his robotic eyeballs made a whirring sound as they zoomed in, tracking the action across the city's skyline. "It *is* Laser Girl," Jazen confirmed. "Good eye, Jack."

"Who's that she's fighting?" Jack asked.

"I don't recognize him," Jazen said.

"Probably someone doing something they shouldn't," Blue said. "I swear, every time I turn around, someone's trying to take over *something*. Trouble is, every time we lock 'em up, they always end up breaking out sooner or later. Is it like that where you come from, Jack?"

Jack nodded. "It is in the comics," he said. It came as no surprise that Empire City's heroes and villains constantly tumbled through the sky in battle. It was exactly like that in Jack's comic books. Every day, heroes were hard at work trying to stop villains from extinguishing the sun, reversing the earth's magnetic poles, or conquering the surface world with an army of subterranean molemen. It was hard to keep track of it all.

"Don't get me wrong, Jack, I don't mind having to go catch a bad guy two or even three times," Blue said. "I just can't stand all the paperwork that goes with the job." Blue looked at his watch and grumbled. "Hate to eat and run, guys, but I'm going to be late," he said, forcing an entire scissor shark steak into his mouth at once.

Jack quickly wolfed down the rest of his dinner to try to keep up with Blue. He had places to go too, and Blue was dropping him and Jazen off on his way to the police station.

Jack had another School of Thought test scheduled for that evening, a test he was greatly looking forward to, because it was being taught by the hero of *Unreal Tales #42*. Jack's head spun like a top as Blue's HoverCar flew over the streets of Empire City's alien borough. Jack was getting used to the idea of seeing superheroes on every street corner, but Galaxis was something else entirely. Galaxis was *the* traveler's hub for the Milky Way galaxy, and nothing prepares you for the first time you see an intergalactic spaceport up close.

Galaxis was on the cliff side of Empire City, right next to Hero Square. Launch pads lined the edge of the floating island, and aliens of every shape, size, and color were hurrying back and forth between crowded stargates. Rocket ships and flying saucers took off and landed without

"Good evening and welcome, candidate Blank," Prime said. "It pleases me to see you advancing through our program. I was afraid I might not get the opportunity to test you here tonight."

"It's good to be here," Jack replied. "I don't know if we can really say I'm advancing through the program yet, though. I've only got one vote so far. The other two are still undecided."

"Better undecided than decidedly against you," Prime told Jack.

Jack agreed that was true, but at this point he wasn't even 100 percent sure what he was being tested on anymore. He told Prime about Smart's extra tests, including how he'd spent the entire morning in a high-powered centrifuge, rocketing around in a circle at five hundred miles per hour.

"My test will be much more straightforward," Prime assured him. "Here we test for one thing only, an indispensable quality shared by every hero, everywhere: courage."

Jack asked Prime if he knew anything about his comic book alter ego. Were his exploits in the pages of *Unreal Tales* true? Did he really fight the Rüstov out there in space? Did he ever fight off a Rüstov infection?

Prime smiled. "Many an artist and writer have come to this island over the years, son. When they come, they want to know everything. When they leave, they pretend that they do. They tell stories." Prime patted Jack's shoulder. "They embellish."

While they waited for Skerren to arrive, Prime told Jack that he and his men were once universal defenders of all planets who could not defend themselves. Earlier, when Jack had guessed that Prime seemed like a general, he wasn't far off. Prime was more than a superhero code name—it was his title as a commander of the Valorian Guard. He wore the same blue uniform as his men did, save for the addition of a white circle with black lines in the center of his chest, signifying his rank. The Valorians were a dignified, brave, and mighty people. They were also all but extinct.

Many years ago, Prime's home world of Valor had been destroyed by the Rüstov. Prime and his battalion had been off-world when it happened, answering the distress call of an allied space colony. The call had been a ruse perpetrated by the Rüstov to draw out Valor's defenses while the Rüstov Armada laid siege to the planet. By the time Prime's men had returned, there was nothing left to defend. Valor had been wiped out. Prime had organized the remaining Valorian forces and led them after the Rüstov. They had followed the Rüstov all the way to Earth, arriving just in time to fight in the Battle of Empire City.

"I want you to know that while I have every reason to hate the Rüstov, I don't group you in with them," Prime told Jack. "Infection or no, you had nothing to do with what happened to my planet. I won't hold their actions against you."

Jack was incredibly appreciative of Prime's fair-mindedness. It was very refreshing, and especially gracious given his tragic and bloody history with the Rüstov.

"Are you and your men the only Valorians left?" Jack asked.

"We used to think so, but then one day Allegra arrived here on a refugee ship. That is reason enough to hope that other sons and daughters of Valor are still out there. If fortune smiles upon us and we are reunited, my men and I will teach them of their Valorian culture and history, just as we are trying to do with Allegra."

Jazen asked Jack to go wait with Allegra while he spoke

privately with Prime. Jack walked over to where Allegra was standing and took in the view from the roof. Galaxis was futuristic in a different way from Hightown. It had more flavor. Alien architecture was very creative, and the buildings were multicolored and designed in irregular shapes. Orbs, pyramids, and other geometric figures lit up the skyline with a variety of bright metallic shades.

When Skerren arrived, Jack was surprised to see his king was with him. Hovarth lumbered onto the roof, letting out an unfriendly grunt as he passed by Jack. He was a grizzled mountain of a man, more than seven feet tall and at least three hundred pounds in weight, most of it muscle. He had a beard as thick as steel wool and a fur cloak that was even thicker. The iron battle-ax he carried was as tall as Jack.

Hovarth announced his intention to join his test with Prime's, as they were both looking to see the exact same thing from the candidates: courage, or as Hovarth liked to call it, heart. Jack was actually relieved to hear that, considering Hovarth had voted against him back in the sphere. Jack had figured that when the time came, he'd go into Hovarth's test with two strikes against him. If Hovarth and

Prime's test were going to be one and the same, he could trust it to be fair. Still, Jack was surprised Hovarth would agree to test the students in Prime's futuristic borough. Sure enough, the Circlemen soon revealed that the test would not take place in Galaxis at all.

"What do you mean?" Allegra asked. "Where are we going?"

"There," Prime said, pointing out across the waterfalls. "Wrekzaw Isle." Jack followed Prime's pointing finger. Floating in the air over the rushing water was a charred hunk of rusted metal and jagged rock.

"Wrekzaw Isle?" Skerren exclaimed, unable to hide his surprise.

"Not Wrekzaw Isle . . ." Allegra groaned.

"What's Wrekzaw Isle?" Jack asked.

"Get in," Prime said, motioning toward an Air-Speeder waiting on the roof, ready to fly. "We'll tell you on the way."

As the group raced over the chasm that separated the Imagine Nation from the open sea, Prime explained that Wrekzaw Isle was the spot where the Rüstov mothership had crashed twelve years ago, effectively ending the Battle of Empire City. After Legend had flown Revile into the ship's main engine, it had dropped like a stone and collided with a rocky outcropping on the cliffs at the city limits. The ship had exploded with enough force to break off an entire piece of the island, and burned with enough heat to melt its way around it permanently. The result was Wrekzaw Isle, an unusable, abandoned landmass that orbited the Imagine Nation like a ghost ship.

"If you three make it to the School of Thought, I will teach you everything I know about space travel and galactic warfare," Prime told the children. "About capital ships, starfighters, and infantry troop deployments. About alien science, starmaps, and wormholes."

"And I will make you strong," Hovarth added. "Other Circlemen will no doubt tell you that knowledge is power. I say power is power. You all have your own special abilities. They are not enough. You must train and learn combat. Hand-to-hand fighting! Tactical ability! Endurance! Those of you who pass this test . . . we'll find out just how powerful you can be." Hovarth poked Jack in the chest and Jack coughed. It felt like someone had jabbed him with the skinny end of a baseball bat.

"But first, you must show your courage and face the fear that everyone in the Imagine Nation seems content to live with, especially lately—fear of the Rüstov," Prime said. "You must spend the night here on Wrekzaw Isle."

"Spend the night?" Allegra cried. "Alone?"

Prime nodded, and Skerren stifled a laugh. "Just one night?" he asked. "That's all?"

Allegra's skin rippled. "Shut up," she told Skerren. "That's plenty!"

Jack was looking around quietly as Prime's men set the AirSpeeder down on a clearing in the middle of the floating wasteland. This place gave him the chills. Wrekzaw Isle was a fearsome mass of twisted metal fused with hard stone. Dirty orange rust covered the saw-toothed edges of shrapnel and debris that were literally everywhere. Old wires and tubing sprouted out of the ground like weeds, and the imprints of overloaded circuits were burned into the landscape. A massive crater in the ground told the story of the battlefield, marking the path that Legend had forced Revile down so many years ago.

"Is it true that Rüstov soldiers are still hanging around here?" Jack asked.

"Many Rüstov were rumored to be left behind after the invasion, hiding out right where you three are standing, tunneled deep in the heart of Wrekzaw Isle," Hovarth said. "Who can say for sure?"

Maybe it was true, maybe it wasn't. Either way, Allegra didn't like being there one bit. Jazen told her not to worry. "Revile's grave is the safest place on Wrekzaw Isle," he whispered. "Left-Behinds don't like to go anywhere near it. At least, not usually."

"We're at Revile's grave?" Jack asked, decidedly not reassured.

"That is correct," Prime replied. "And if you want to pass our test, this is where you will spend the entire night." Prime handed each of the children little remote controls to wear around their necks. "These are distress call beacons," he explained. "If at any point in the night this becomes too much for you, simply press that button and all of this will end." Prime looked each child in the eye. "All of it."

Jack tucked his beacon inside his shirt. Under no circumstances was he going to press that button. He understood that doing so would mean more than just the end of this field trip—it would mean the end of his chances at the School of Thought. He told himself that there were probably no Rüstov around, anyway. Jazen paced the landing area with two fingers pressed against his temple, scanning the area with those robotic eyes of his. When he was through, he nodded to Prime, which Jack hoped meant "all clear."

"Farewell, candidates," Hovarth said, stepping back onto the AirSpeeder with Prime. "I hope to see you all at first light and not a moment before."

Jack noticed that Jazen had a slight mechanical twitch as he boarded the AirSpeeder with the others. He looked over at Jack and Allegra. Likely Jack's nervous energy was giving him a minor glitch again. "Be strong for each other," Jazen told them. "You can do this."

Skerren rolled his eyes. "Please. It's going to take more than a creepy campsite to scare me. I'm actually hoping to see a few Rüstov here tonight."

As the AirSpeeder drove out of sight, Jack thought about the old saying "Be careful what you wish for—you just might get it."

* * *

Wrekzaw Isle would have been an eerie and haunting place even in broad daylight. When Jack and the others had arrived, it was already dark. After the adults left, taking with them the headlights from the AirSpeeder, there was no light at all.

The ever-roaming Imagine Nation was still passing through tropical waters, so the children weren't cold, but they weren't exactly comfortable, either. Since they hadn't planned on camping that night, they had no tents, sleeping bags, or flashlights. Skerren suggested building a fire.

"Maybe it's better if you don't," Allegra said.

"The moon is new and the stars aren't getting any brighter," Skerren said pointedly. "Unless you can see in the dark, I'm going to make a fire."

There was no wood on Wrekzaw Isle, but Skerren traced a mixture of oil, coolant, and fuel that was running around Revile's grave like a miniature moat. It filled grooves in the rock and lined the area like a little river with random tributaries splitting off and dead-ending in dried-out shallows, or pooling up in deep pockets of stone. Skerren produced a flint from a pouch on his belt and started a fire the old-fashioned way.

"Skerren, don't!" Allegra said as Skerren clapped a stone against the flint. Sparks flew into the oily channel and with a whoosh, flames ran around the perimeter like horses at the track. After the initial flare the flames calmed to a slow, even burn, lighting the area nicely.

"Let there be light," Skerren said as the rusted junkyard glowed in the light of the fire. Jack realized he was standing right at the mouth of the pit that led to the infinite warp core. He backed away from the edge.

"Perfect!" Allegra said, a bit on edge herself. "Now every Left-Behind for a hundred miles will see that fire and know we're here."

"So what if they do?" Skerren replied. "Activate your beacon if that bothers you." He threw his own beacon into the fire and jumped up onto the ridge to see if anything was out there. "Honestly, Allegra. You could at least try to put on a brave face. I can't believe Prime lets you call yourself a Valorian."

Allegra's face rippled, and for a second, Jack thought she was going to cry. Instead, she stormed off to the other side of the campsite. She went as far away from Skerren as she could safely go.

Jack looked at Skerren. "Why do you have to be such a jerk all the time?"

"Don't test me, Rusty," Skerren sneered at Jack. "It's not my fault if she can't handle the pressure."

"You don't have to make it any worse than it already is," Jack replied.

"Really? Look who's talking," Skerren countered. "I'm not the one who threatened everyone about Revile coming back to life."

"I never threatened anyone," Jack answered back. "Warned, maybe, but never threatened."

"Why did you even say you fought him? What's your game? Trying to psyche out the enemy? I bet that's it. I bet you just love how everyone in Empire City suddenly thinks they see the Rüstov every time they turn around."

"I'm just telling the truth," Jack maintained. "I don't know about these other Left-Behinds everyone's talking about, but I know I saw Revile."

Skerren scoffed at Jack. "Whatever you fought back before you came here—if you really fought anything at all— it wasn't Revile. If it was, you'd be dead. It took Legend flying him into this ship's engine to stop Revile. If that explosion didn't kill him, how could anything you have in your New Jersey do it?"

"It couldn't," Jack agreed. "That's exactly what worries me."

Jack walked off to check on Allegra. He found her sitting by a pocket of fire with her knees drawn up to her chest and her arms wrapped around her legs. Her shoulders bounced lightly up and down as she cried. Jack gave her a minute and then came up behind her slowly.

"Hey, forget about him," Jack said. "He thinks he's so tough, but nobody cares what he says."

"That's just it," Allegra said, wiping away tears that she didn't want anyone to see. "I care! I'm not supposed to be scared. But I am. I'm scared all the time and I hate it. I hate it."

"This is a scary place," Jack told Allegra. "Even the SmartCams wouldn't follow me here." That was the truth. When Prime had started talking about Wrekzaw Isle, the SmartCams had taken off in the other direction. "It's totally normal to get a little creeped out here. You're only—"

"Don't say *only human*," Allegra interrupted. "Because I'm not, you know. I'm Valorian. And a true daughter of

Valor knows no fear." She said the last part mimicking Prime's deep baritone.

"I was going to say you're only a kid," Jack replied. "Just like I'm only a kid, and even Skerren over there . . . even Skerren's only a kid. I wouldn't be surprised if deep down he's a little bit scared too. No matter what he says."

Allegra was barely listening. "I don't like being back in Rüstov territory," she said.

Jack blinked. "What do you mean *back* in Rüstov territory?"

"Back where I started." That's when Jack realized her tears were about more than just the general creepiness of Wrekzaw Isle.

Allegra told Jack that she had been born in a Rüstov "body farm," which, Allegra explained, was a place where the Rüstov kept future host bodies prisoner. "That was what they called it, a body farm. After the fall of Valor that's where they took the survivors."

Allegra's people always fought until victory or death, so Valorian prisoners of war were rare. Her pregnant mother had been one of the few survivors. She had had an unborn child to think of, so she had wanted to live, to fight another day. But while she had allowed her daughter to be born in captivity, she could never allow her to grow up there. When Allegra had been just a few weeks old, her mother had organized an escape with the other aliens in the farm, and had died getting Allegra out. She had died a prisoner so that her daughter could live free.

"I don't remember any of it," Allegra said. "I was too young. The others on the ship told me the stories. I grew up on a refugee ship, fleeing Rüstov space. It took years to get to safety. To really get all the way out. We always had to be quiet, we always had to stay hidden. . . ." Allegra shuddered, unable to go on.

"Fear of the Rüstov was all you ever knew," Jack said, finally understanding why Allegra turned into a puddle every time she saw him.

"I grew up thinking the Rüstov killed everyone who ever looked like me," Allegra added. "And then we came here, and I saw that there were others like me, but I was nothing like them. Prime and the others . . . they're fearless and strong. Not like me. I think Prime is embarrassed of me." Jack wanted to tell her that wasn't the case, but he thought she might be right. "I'm all alone," Allegra said.

"The cowardly Valorian. No matter where I go, there's no one like me."

"Yeah," Jack said. "I know exactly how you feel."

Allegra thought about that for a moment.

"Yeah, I guess you do," she agreed. Just like her, he'd been an outsider his whole life, and it only got worse when he got to Empire City.

"Stendeval says normal is boring, but I don't know," Jack said. "People here can have blue skin, three arms, and computerized brains and that's still normal. I'm the only one interesting enough to terrify an entire city." Jack gave a little laugh, like it was no big deal. Like he was used to it. In a way, he guessed he was. Allegra didn't laugh with him, though.

"Do you ever get scared about your infection?" she asked. "How do you know you're not going to turn into one of them?"

"I guess I *don't* know," Jack admitted. "I really don't."

It was the first time Jack had said anything like that out loud. Jack hoped he wasn't making a huge mistake. He checked to make sure that Skerren was out of earshot, but he honestly didn't know what had prompted him to admit the possibility of turning into a Rüstov. Maybe it was because he and Allegra had so much in common; he felt he could trust her. Maybe it was because she seemed genuinely concerned for him. Maybe it was just something he needed to get off his chest.

"Scary, right?" Jack said. "I get scared if I let myself think about it too much. I try not to let myself do that. Everything in my life has changed so fast, I just have to focus on this one thing to stay sane. I have to believe I can beat this . . . I have to. I mean, what's the alternative?" Jack shook his head. "I can't think like that. I have to learn how to use my powers and beat this thing. It's the only chance I've got."

Allegra marveled at Jack. "I can see why Prime is so impressed with you. You have the courage of a Valorian."

Jack looked at Allegra. The courage of a Valorian? "I don't know if it has anything to do with being brave," he said, trying to downplay the compliment. "It's more like I don't have any other choice."

"My people say that we always have a choice. It's only the brave who choose not to surrender where there's no reason left to hope."

297

Jack looked at Allegra. "There's nothing hopeless about either of us. And nothing bad is going to happen here. I don't even think there's any Rüstov on this island. The Inner Circle wouldn't send us here if they thought we might be in any real danger, right?"

The second Jack finished saying those words, Allegra's expression suddenly changed. She was staring over Jack's shoulder, fixated on something with a confused, somewhat scared look on her face. Jack turned around to see Skerren running toward him at full bore. He lunged at Jack with one of his unbreakable swords, letting out a guttural snarl as he thrust the blade forward. Jack fell backward and dodged the blade. As he fell, he locked eyes with a Rüstov Left-Behind that had been creeping up behind him. Skerren's sword screeched its way into the creature's chest.

Allegra screamed when she saw the Left-Behind. Skerren knocked the creature to the ground and pulled his sword out of its chest. He stood on the Left-Behind's stomach and immediately thrust the blade back into its torso. It was a good thing Skerren's skills were as sharp as his swords, because there were more Rüstov to deal with. At least three more by Jack's count. Very quickly, Jack started rethinking his doubts about the rumored Left-Behind squads in Empire City and on Wrekzaw Isle in general.

Jack's mind jumped back to the last time he had faced off against a Rüstov, when he had fought Revile. Jack prayed Revile wouldn't show up next. He had barely gotten away with his life that day, back when he didn't have any control over the way his powers kicked in. Just as he thought about that, any machinery that was even halfway working on Wrekzaw Isle started springing to life. His powers were firing up on their own again. Jack didn't know what to do. He wasn't ready to handle this kind of action by himself. He watched as Skerren pulled the sword back from the fallen Rüstov's midsection, spinning it in his hand as he drew out the other blade. Skerren shifted his weight, pivoting to swing both swords into another Rüstov Para-Soldier. With a single fluid motion, Skerren cut the Left-Behind into three pieces. It was the second Rüstov he'd dispatched in as many minutes. Before Skerren could turn his attention to the two that were left, one of them fetched him a blow that sent him reeling.

With Skerren down, the iron giant that had hit him stepped out of the darkness and turned its attention to

Jack and Allegra. Jack's stomach sank. It was just like when he had seen Revile back at St. Barnaby's. The creature was a rusted, Frankenstein-esque robot with exposed wiring, gears, and mummified skin. A scrap metal Robo-Zombie. A junkyard heap come to life.

The lead Left-Behind screamed a blaring static-filled cry and raised a fist toward the two children. Jack heard something snap into place on its wrist. By the time Jack realized the Rüstov had a gun, it was almost too late.

"Down!" he yelled, trying to push Allegra out of the way.

Allegra liquefied and Jack fell right through her. The barrel of the Rüstov's wrist cannon spun like a Gatling gun, and a combination of laser pulse blasts and bullets flew through the air. They hit the exact spot where Jack had been standing just seconds before. The blasts ripped harmlessly through Allegra's fluid form. She screamed just the same.

Jack scurried behind a rock, dodging sparks that were shooting out of broken machinery. All around, Wrekzaw Isle was trying to switch itself on, thanks to him. Random wheels turned, indicator lights flashed, and circuit boards shorted out and blew fuses. Everywhere in sight, Jack's powers were active, but he wasn't in control. He wasn't using anything on Wrekzaw Isle to his advantage. If Jack wanted to live through this, that would have to change.

Jack peered over the rock to see what was going on. One of the Rüstov soldiers was standing near the remains of a worn-out engine that was trying to run. Jack focused on that engine. There was a fan belt on it that was struggling to turn. Jack thought about that belt turning faster and faster until the engine finally blew. The explosion knocked the Rüstov forward into the channel of flaming oil. Seconds later, the creature emerged screaming and completely engulfed in flames. It ran wildly before exploding all over the battlefield.

There was only one Rüstov left. This one looked stronger than the others. It was bigger and had less rust and decay. It was firing plasma blasts at Allegra, but she defaulted into total liquid form and slinked off to a safe distance. Stendeval had told her that if a Valorian woman could banish all fear from her mind, she could become indestructible. *So much for that,* Jack thought as Allegra solidified and immediately grabbed for her beacon. There was nothing there. That's when Jack realized he was wearing it. Allegra's beacon had caught on his neck when he had fallen through her.

The two beacons hung heavy around Jack's neck. It was a lot easier to swear off using them when there weren't any Rüstov Left-Behinds around. As Jack debated whether or not to push the buttons, the last Left-Behind skulked around the campsite, turning over wreckage and hunting for the children. Across the way, Skerren was coming around. Jack knew he was going to attack again as soon as he could stand. He tried to get his attention. "No . . . wait!" he mouthed silently.

Skerren saw Jack but paid him no mind. He ran at the Rüstov again, swords drawn. He had no fear—that much was obvious. Unfortunately, he didn't have much control, either. In his rage, Skerren threw any attempt at stealth out the window. The Rüstov saw him coming and turned with his gun ready. He was going to cut Skerren to ribbons.

Jack thought fast. He broke it down to the simplest terms possible. The one thing he could understand. The spinning barrel on the Rüstov's gun. If he could stop that wheel from turning . . .

Click! The gun on the Rüstov's wrist jammed and misfired before he could get a shot off. It blew apart in its hand, and Skerren was safe. He rolled behind the Rüstov and slashed at him with his swords. The Rüstov tried to hit him, but his gun hand was damaged, hanging on by wires and tubing. He swung it like a mace, but Skerren was too fast, dodging his blows and cutting away at the Left-Behind bit by bit. Jack ran over to Allegra to make sure she was okay.

"I can't find my beacon!" she yelled. "I can't find my beacon!" Jack shook her off and turned to Skerren, who had the Left-Behind on the defensive. Jack wasn't thinking about hitting his button anymore, and he certainly wasn't going to tell Allegra that he had hers around his neck. He was thinking about how they were going to finish this thing off.

That's when he heard what the Rüstov was saying. It was only static at first, like white noise from a TV with no cable. As the fight went on, Jack was able to make out more and more.

"*KSSSHH-CHHSHA* . . . You are not the one . . . *KSSSHH-CHHSHA* . . . Where is the infected? . . . *KSSSHAHHCHCHCHCH.*"

303

Jack froze. The infected? The Rüstov *were* after him!

The Left-Behind grabbed hold of Skerren's shirt with its damaged hand. With a blast the hand detached at the wrist and rocketed off into the sky, carrying Skerren with it. He crashed into a trash heap. From the sound alone, Jack knew it had to hurt.

"Skerren!" Allegra screamed. It was a bad move. The Rüstov turned and saw her. He jumped over and threw away the scrap heap that she and Jack were hiding behind. The Rüstov stood over them, staring down like grinning death. Allegra backed away and fell to the ground, stumbling. Jack stood his ground.

"Why are you looking for me?" he demanded. "What do you know about me?"

The Rüstov snatched Jack up by his shirt collar and lifted him into the air. That's when Wrekzaw Isle's lights brightened up again, and the Rüstov got a good look at Jack.

"*KSSCHHSHH* . . . You!" it said between static bursts.

The creature stopped dead in its tracks. It lowered Jack down gently and fell to one knee before him.

"My liege," it said to him.

Jack and Allegra were stunned as they watched the Rüstov kneel in a state of complete submission. It took a second to register that the fight had just come to a screeching halt, and they were going to be okay.

"Did you do that?" Allegra asked Jack.

"I . . . I don't know," he said. Was this his powers at work or was it something else? "What was that the Rüstov called me? Did you hear that too?"

Out of the corner of his eye, Jack saw something flying through the air. It was Skerren's sword spinning end over end.

The sword sliced off the Rüstov's right leg, just above the knee. The Left-Behind screamed in pain, now short both a hand and a leg. Skerren limped back in with the severed hand still locked onto his shirt. He moved in to strike the killing blow, but Jack stopped him.

"Don't," Jack said. "It surrendered."

Skerren looked at Jack like he had just said something funny. "Surrender?" he snorted, raising his sword up to strike. "No. No surrender."

"Skerren, it's over!" Jack said, stepping in front of Skerren and grabbing his wrist. Skerren's eyes lit up with barely contained rage. Jack didn't back down.

"Siding with your own kind, I see," Skerren said. "Others are going to hear about this," he warned Jack.

"I don't care if they do," Jack said. "You're not going near this thing. Not until I find out what it knows."

"What it knows?"

"About me," Jack clarified. "It recognized me."

Jack half expected Skerren to cut right through him to get at the Left-Behind, but he didn't. Much to Jack's surprise, Skerren took a step back.

"Fine," Skerren said. "We'll bring it back alive. We still have to make sure it doesn't go anywhere tonight." Skerren took up his sword and stabbed the Rüstov through its good leg, pinning it to the ground. The Rüstov writhed on the ground, helpless. "There. That should do it." Jack and Allegra were taken aback. Skerren returned to his watch, noting that for all they knew, there were dozens more of them out there.

Thankfully, no other Rüstov troubled the children that night. When the adults returned the next morning, the children had quite a tale to tell. So did Prime and Hovarth. Apparently, the Rüstov encounter was not part of their test. Just like Jazen had said, Left-Behinds generally tried to avoid Revile's grave. In addition, Jazen had been there to clear the area, and he fully expected them to be alone all night. Prime was very impressed with everyone's courage under fire and specifically told Allegra how proud he was of her for not activating her distress beacon. Allegra laughed nervously in response to the compliment. Prime gave everyone passing grades with extra praise for not killing the enemy when they didn't have to. Skerren was pretty sore that Prime wasn't suspicious of Jack for pushing to spare the Rüstov's life, but it was Hovarth's decision that really burned him up.

"Boy, you have surprised even me," Hovarth said after the children retold the story of their adventure on Wrekzaw Isle. "It seems there is a fire in your belly that not even the Rüstov can put out," he told Jack. "You have my vote."

"WHAT?" Skerren cried. He looked hurt and betrayed that his mentor—his *idol*—was siding with Jack. "You . . . you're not really voting for him . . . ," he stammered out in disbelief. "You can't!"

Hovarth didn't need to defend his decision to Skerren,

but he did anyway. "He passed the test," Hovarth said matter-of-factly. "What else can I do?"

"No!" Skerren said. "We hate the Rüstov!"

"And we pity the infected. We mourn them before they die, but perhaps . . . perhaps this one is different. I, too, would not have guessed it, but Jack has surpassed my expectations. He has proven himself in battle. If I chose not to honor his achievements, the true failing would be mine. To keep my honor, I must grant him my vote. I cannot justify anything less."

Skerren pointed a finger in Hovarth's face. "Don't talk to me about justice," he said. "We both know how you've dealt with Rüstov in the past. Maybe you've forgotten, but I haven't—not ever!"

Skerren didn't wait for Hovarth's reply. He just stormed out of the garrison. Jack expected Hovarth to grab Skerren back by the ear and roar at him for his insolence, but he didn't. He just breathed a heavy sigh and let him go. Jack couldn't believe Skerren would talk so disrespectfully to his king, but he wasn't going to waste time trying to figure out what went on in Skerren's head.

Not when there was someone else there whose thoughts were so much more interesting.

This Left-Behind that Jack had helped capture . . . it knew him somehow. It recognized him. That meant it knew more about him than just about anyone else in the Imagine Nation, and Jack intended to find out exactly what that was.

CHAPTER

12

The One That Got Away

As the Left-Behind was being locked away in the Valorian garrison's quarantined detention block, Jack was already trying to find out the story behind his newfound status as "Rüstov royalty." The Left-Behind had knelt before him and called him "my liege." What the heck was that all about, anyway?

Prime expected it was because Jack had no tech-decay or rust. "A very fortunate case of mistaken identity," he called it. That was the only explanation. "Why else would a Rüstov cut short an attack just shy of the killing blow, and then kneel down before its target?"

Jack didn't follow.

"When a Rüstov parasite takes hold of a host body, the Rüstov eye is just the first mark to appear," Prime told him. "Over time the infection spreads through the body and the signs multiply. Veins turn into circuits, blood turns into oil . . . the skin mummifies, flaking away to reveal rusted metal bones. You may be infected, but you exhibit none of those features. That's what saved you. The Left-Behind, no doubt a mid-level Para-Soldier, was mistakenly humbled before your fresh-faced nobility."

Prime explained that in Rüstov society, only the social elite enjoyed hosts as fresh as Jack appeared to be. Rüstov Para-Soldiers had to push their bodies until the bones turned to dust before they were allowed new hosts, and even then they only got cast-offs from the upper class. The nobles, on the other hand, took fresh hosts from the body farms every day. The Rüstov emperor—the Magus— expected his fellow aristocrats to look presentable, and the penalties for defiling his court with decaying host bodies were severe. The Magus himself went through several hosts a day, casting off bodies at the first sign of the slightest imperfection. The mere hint of a single circuit rising up below soft skin tissue was enough to turn a fresh host body into an imperial hand-me-down.

Jazen agreed that Prime's theory made good sense, but he still didn't like that the Left-Behind was there to begin with. Jazen had cleared the area before he had left. If there had been a Rüstov within twenty miles, it should have showed up on his scan. "Somebody sent that Left-Behind after these kids," Jazen concluded. "Maybe after Jack, specifically. This is the second time a Rüstov has attacked him. Somebody told them where he'd be, and when he'd be alone."

Hovarth's eyes narrowed. "You don't mean to suggest . . . a traitor?"

"Isn't that what we've been saying all along?" a voice called out from the door. The voice belonged to Speed-razor, who was there with a superstrong Peacemaker called Flex to collect the prisoner. Left-Behinds had to be held in the most secure facilities possible, and that meant an electrocell in a secret undisclosed location. Probably one of the Peacemaker bases, Jack thought.

"I want to know where you're taking this thing," Jack

told the Peacemakers as they took the Left-Behind into custody. "I helped catch it. I deserve a chance to talk to it and find out if it knows anything about me."

"Take it up with Circleman Smart," Flex told Jack as he dragged the one-legged Left-Behind out the door. Jack intended to do just that.

A few days passed before Smart finally agreed to let Jack question the captured Left-Behind. Smart claimed he needed time to set up a full array of translators to record every word that passed between Jack and the creature. Jack wasn't concerned about any of that. He didn't have anything to hide—he just wanted to get in there and ask his questions. Now that he knew he could talk to machines—*really talk to machines*—it was time to see just what this Rüstov knew about him and his past.

Smart got word to Jazen that the creature was being held in the SmartTower subbasement, and Jack was invited to come interview the Rüstov prisoner. However, another round of Smart's annoying tests came first, and when they were done, Jack could tell that something was very wrong. When Smart's experiments were complete, Jack found himself alone in the lab. Usually, Smart didn't trust Jack enough to leave him alone. Jack rode the elevator down to the SmartPrison subbasement and found Stendeval, Smart, and Chi together outside an empty electrocell. Smart was pacing the room, disgusted. "And to think people have the gall to suggest my Peacemakers are no longer necessary!" he said.

"Jonas, you are jumping to conclusions," Stendeval told him.

"Am I?" Smart fired back. "This location was classified. It's impossible to think the creature didn't have help escaping. There are traitors among us, Stendeval!" Smart looked at Jack as he entered. "Speak of the devil," he said.

"What happened?" Jack asked.

"Oh, very good," Smart said. "As if you don't already know."

Jack looked to Stendeval and Chi for an answer. "What's going on?"

"A group of Left-Behinds crossed into the city this morning to free their captured brother," Chi explained. He motioned to the empty cell. "They succeeded."

"Wait, they were actually here?" Jack asked. "In SmartTower? This isn't just another possible sighting?"

"Obviously not!" Smart said, motioning to the empty electrocell. "You expect us to believe you didn't aid them in any way?" he asked Jack. "Where were you one hundred thirty-seven minutes and forty-nine seconds ago?"

Jack rolled his eyes. "This thing escapes from *your* prison on one leg, and you're looking at *me*?" Jack asked. There was apparently nothing that Smart wouldn't try to blame on him, he thought. As if Smart didn't know exactly where he was at all times, anyway. SmartTower tracked Jack's every move, scanning for his voiceprint, fingerprints, and retinas. On top of that, Jack had just spent the last three hours frozen in carbonite as part of Smart's latest random experiment. The first time Smart had tried to freeze him, Jack had short-circuited the machine, blowing out the coolant tubes and shooting aerosol carbonite everywhere. However, it had become customary for Smart to have backup machines at the ready for Jack's tests. The second time around, Jack had been able to endure the freezing without incident. He was getting better at reining in his emotions and keeping his powers under control.

"Jack's alibi seems solid, Jonas," Stendeval remarked.

"Frozen solid," Chi added with a wry grin. Stendeval

chuckled; Smart did not. He wanted Jack arrested.

"Jack didn't have to be physically present to aid in the breakout," Smart said. "He could have used his powers. He could have terminated the security measures and opened the cell doors for the Rüstov just by thinking about it. He's part of this—I'm sure of it! I'm the smartest man in the world! Why are you both so intent on ignoring me?

"Come now, Jonas," Stendeval began. "Jack isn't going to be arrested. The School of Thought testing cannot be interrupted. You know that as well as I. Unless you have proof of a crime, you'll simply have to be satisfied with the relentless battery of tests you are putting Jack through."

"Go ahead," Smart said through gritted teeth. "Make excuses for him. You've done little else since you returned. The fact remains, the creature was secure in its cell before this boy got here. This *city* was secure before this boy got here, for that matter! He arrives, and suddenly we have Rüstov Left-Behinds coming out of the woodwork. Gangs of Left-Behinds are spotted in the city, and our students are attacked at Revile's grave—a place, by the way, where Revile no longer even resides!"

"I thought you didn't believe me about Revile," Jack said.

"Yes, Jonas," Stendeval added with an air of suspicion. "I'm curious . . . do you believe Revile is alive? Or do you just care that *other* people believe it?"

Smart's lips curled up into an annoyed smirk. "Perhaps you've forgotten," Smart countered. "But I have a machine that can see into the future. And I have seen, in my TimeScope, Revile alive in Empire City."

"Where?" Jack exclaimed. "When?!! Doing what?"

Smart's smug expression faded. "I . . . can't say," he said. "Images in the TimeScope are not always crystal clear."

"Well, let's look again!" Jack said. "While we're at it, let's find out where that Left-Behind is going to be next. We can see if we're going to recapture it, or if it's going to come after me again."

"No, Jack," Stendeval said. "Please, put that thought out of your head. Do not seek out a time machine to tell you your future."

Jack looked at Stendeval. "Why not?"

"The future is always in flux," Stendeval said. "Hence the static generally found on Jonas's TimeScreen images."

"To which I might add, tampering with the time-space continuum upsets the natural order of things," Chi said. "It creates imbalance in the universe. That balance can be very difficult to restore. I would not advise the use of that machine under any circumstances."

Smart bristled at Chi's opinion of his greatest invention. "I don't know about unforeseen consequences or imbalance in the universe," he interjected. "However, I will admit that knowledge of the future is not a burden I would trust on the shoulders of a boy like Jack."

"For once we are in total agreement," Stendeval said. "We will find the Rüstov another way. Please, Jack, forget that machine exists. Life happens in the present. I suggest you follow the advice of one of your American presidents, a good and honest man from the state of Illinois who once told me, 'The best way to predict your future is to create it.'"

Reluctantly, Jack agreed. Resigned to leave the future to itself, he turned his thoughts back to the past. Once again, Jack asked Stendeval for hints, clues, or anything he could share about his past. With the Left-Behind gone, Jack was still no closer to finding out who he was and where he came from, how and when he was infected, or why and how he ended up hidden away from the Imagine Nation at St. Barnaby's. "When will I know?" he asked Stendeval. "You said I'd find out who I was before the time of testing was complete, but now it looks like this Left-Behind is another dead end. I still don't know anything new." Stendeval answered by calling for a virtue Jack possessed in increasingly short supply: patience.

Over the next few days, Jack did his best to do as Stendeval asked. He didn't have much choice in the matter. After the Left-Behind's breakout at SmartTower, it was an undeniable fact that Rüstov Para-Soldiers were skulking around Empire City in greater numbers than anyone had seen in years. Even Jazen had to admit, these were no mere rumors. The whole city was on high alert. People were worried that it was all just the start of something bigger, and a lot of them blamed Jack for what was going on. They didn't like the fact that he was training with the Inner Circle. For all they knew, he was the pointman for another invasion. Jazen was taking no chances. He told Jack he had to stay tucked away in the Ivory Tower until things calmed down. Every night the

Inner Circle and countless others scoured the city for Jack's fugitive Left-Behind. Every night Jack waited in vain for news of the Left-Behind's recapture.

In the meantime, Jack did his best to keep himself busy by practicing his powers with Jazen and Virtua. Despite the commonly held belief that teaching Jack was dangerous, and rising concern about the rate at which his powers were growing, Jazen and Virtua put their faith in what they knew of Jack, rather than what others feared about him.

Jack worked with Jazen to master thought communication with machines. He stayed up nights reading every book he could get his hands on, and spent his days diving through cyberspace with Virtua. There was a sensory deprivation tank in the Ivory Tower's data center, and Virtua was happy to guide Jack through every cybersite he cared to see.

While he was in C-Space, Jack got a break from the same four walls of Jazen's apartment. He literally devoured new information about any and all kinds of science and engineering, be it alien, Mecha-based, or otherwise. He was picking up things much faster with the help of the machines. He started talking to every machine he met and absorbing data like it was being uploaded straight into his brain. Jack found that as long as the machine in question was friendly, it was happy to do as he asked and also teach him all it could. Actually speaking with a bi-org was just as novel and exciting for the machine in question as it was for Jack. Well, most of the time, anyway. It all depended on a given machine's attitude and personality. Jack still had to hit the books if he wanted to learn how to control every kind of machine that was out there.

Unfortunately, there was only one machine out there that Jack was interested in: the fugitive Left-Behind. Jack was in his room reading with the holo-screen TV running in the background when there was finally a break in the case. It was late at night, and he was just starting to nod off when the TV volume kicked up to its highest level all on its own. A special newsbreak was interrupting the broadcast.

"Jazen, you better get up here!" Jack called out.

Jazen raced upstairs. "What's going on?" he asked. Jack only pointed to his holo-screen. There wasn't much to see yet, just a "Breaking News" graphic over a crowd of people and a crime scene. The footage showed yellow holo-tape, flashing police lights, and a lot of concerned faces. The news anchor was describing the scene as the cameras rolled:

"All right, this is live footage we're taking directly from SmartCams on the scene in Karateka, where early reports indicate that a fugitive Left-Behind engaged one or more heroes in a deadly superfight this very evening. We're being told that the superfight claimed the life of at least one of the combatants involved."

Jack and Jazen traded uneasy looks. They quickly turned back to the screen as the SmartCam floated up over the crowd to get a bird's-eye view of the situation. "Empire City Police aren't releasing any details yet, but we're trying to get a better angle for you here," the anchor continued. "Let's see if we can't figure out what's going on. . . ."

Jack leaned forward, waiting for the SmartCam to draw focus on the crime scene from above. If anyone had to get hurt, he really hoped it was the Left-Behind.

"I can't look," the anchor's cohost said as the camera moved into position. "I can't!"

Jack knew just how she felt. He held his breath, waiting for the news to come.

"Oh no," Jazen said once the SmartCam finally panned down to reveal the aftermath of the battle. Jack's heart sank as the camera zoomed in on a dead body sprawled out on the street. The telltale black supersuit and Smart-Corp logo identified the body as a Peacemaker.

CHAPTER

13

Karateka Knights

The SmartNews anchorman continued his report as the SmartCam footage rolled on. "I'm afraid this looks like Cyberai, the bionic ninja Peacemaker who was based in Karateka," he said solemnly. "This is terrible, just terrible."

Jack couldn't argue with that. He could see Cyberai was beaten up pretty bad. His supersuit was cut up and torn, and sparks were flying out of his hip and from one of his state-of-the-art robotic arms.

"I'm not sure, it's hard to tell from this angle, but it

looks like . . ." The news anchor paused. "Is he missing one of his cybernetic legs?"

Jazen turned to Jack. "Your Left-Behind was missing a leg," he said.

"Looks like he found a new one," Jack replied.

The anchor kept talking while Empire City police officers closed off the scene and pushed the SmartCams away. "One has to wonder," the anchor's polished voice began, "just how much of this increased Rüstov activity has to do with the infected child that Circleman Smart has been warning us about? And how much longer does the Inner Circle plan to ignore those warnings? It's certainly a fair question at this point. Is this boy involved? Is this the work of young Jack Bla—"

Jazen shut off the screen, but it was too late. Jack heard all he needed to hear. He was running his hands through his hair with a worried look. "This isn't good," he told Jazen. "This isn't just more bad press, Jazen, this is serious. Smart's really going to start calling for my head now, and people are getting tired of waiting."

"No one's coming anywhere near your head," Jazen said. "They'd have to come through me and Blue first."

Before Jack could say anything more, a call came in on the apartment videophone. Jack looked around as a computerized voice announced the caller's identity: "INCOMING CALL FROM . . . BLUE. INCOMING CALL FROM . . . BLUE."

"Speak of the devil," Jazen said. He answered the call, and a holographic image of Blue driving in his HoverCar appeared in the room.

"You guys watching the news?" Blue asked.

"We just shut it off," Jazen replied.

"Just now?" Blue asked. "Then you didn't see me take Cyberai's body, I guess."

"What?" Jack and Jazen exclaimed together. They leaned forward, looking at the holo-image of Blue driving in his car. The figure of someone or something in the passenger seat was just out of the frame.

"Blue, what did you do?" Jazen said. "Is that—"

"You heard me," Blue said. "I've got Cyberai's body. I'm taking it back to police headquarters. I need you to meet me there."

"Wait a minute, slow down," Jazen said. "What do you mean you've got Cyberai's body? Isn't that contaminating the crime scene?"

"Hey," Blue said. "Do I tell you how to do your job? The right way to sneak somebody into the Imagine Nation, or how to—"

"Yes," Jazen cut in. "Yes, actually you do! Now, what do you need me for?"

Blue's holo-image swerved through traffic as he thought about how to explain himself. "This is the first real lead we've had on the escaped Left-Behind in days, Jazen. I'm not gonna let the Peacemakers pull rank on me and just take it away. I need you to come down here, plug into Cyberai's systems, and tell me the last thing he saw. We don't have a lotta time here. You gotta meet me at the station, and I mean now."

Jazen grimaced. "Won't the Peacemakers be coming for the body?"

"That's why you gotta leave now," Blue said. "Look, if we catch the Rüstov because of this, no one's going to care how we did it."

Jazen started nodding, and Jack answered for the both of them. "We'll be there, Blue," he said excitedly.

"Whoa," Jazen replied, spinning around to look at Jack. "We're not going anywhere. I can't risk anything happening to you, Jack. You're staying here."

Jack glared at Jazen. "No way," he said.

Jazen returned Jack's determined gaze. "Jack, work with me here," he said. "You know it's not safe for you out there right now. You just said so yourself."

"That's why I need to go with you!" Jack argued. "That way, people can see I helped recapture the Left-Behind."

"Are you kidding?" Jazen said. "I don't want you going anywhere near any Left-Behinds!"

"I have powers," Jack protested. "I'll be fine."

"You're just learning your powers."

"That's not fair," Jack said.

"Hey!" Blue chimed in. "I'm a cop in a city where corporate mercs outrank me. *That's* unfair! C'mon, Jack, we all gotta deal with stuff we don't like."

"Not you," Jack said. "You're breaking the rules right now."

Blue looked flustered for a second. "I'm bending the rules," he said.

"Like Jazen bent the rules to bring me here in the first place?" Jack asked.

Jazen let out an exasperated sigh. "Jack, sometimes

you *have* to bend the rules," he said. "I'm the first to admit that. But only at certain times, and this isn't one of those times."

"How do you know the difference?" Jack asked.

"You just know," Jazen replied.

Jack shook his head. "Jazen, I can't stay cooped up in this apartment another night!"

"I know this is tough to swallow, partner," Blue said. "Jazen and I both know it's hard on you. Especially since the Inner Circle lets that Skerren kid hunt the Rüstov with them, but it's not the same thing with him. I mean, there are people out there who think you're responsible for all this Rüstov business! We gotta be more careful when it comes to . . ." Blue looked up to see Jazen motioning to him to stop talking. "What? What'd I say?"

Jazen was just shaking his head in frustration. "Nothing. Forget it. I'll see you in twenty minutes," Jazen said, and ended the call. Blue's image blinked out. "You big blue knucklehead," Jazen muttered to himself. He looked back over to Jack, who was justifiably upset.

"Skerren gets to go hunting for the Left-Behind with the Inner Circle?" Jack asked. "And you knew about it?"

"We'll talk about this later, Jack," Jazen said, fishing around in his pockets for his HoverCar keys. "I promise, we'll talk about it. And I'm sorry. I'm sorry I didn't tell you about Skerren. But right now I have to go. You heard Blue; he needs my help. With any luck, we'll sort this all out tonight. The best thing you can do is just stay here, and try to get some rest. Okay? Jack?"

Jack stared back at Jazen with hard eyes. "Whatever," he said. Jack climbed onto his bed and lay down on top of the covers, facing the window. In the reflection he saw Jazen take a step toward him but stop halfway. Instead, he turned around with a sad look and left.

As soon as Jack heard the door click, he sprang out of bed. There was no way he could sleep knowing that Skerren was out there tracking down the Rüstov and he was stuck indoors. Despite the lateness of the hour, the only thing Jack was tired of was waiting for someone else to catch the Left-Behind without him. He was going to get his answers from that Left-Behind, one way or the other.

Jack quickly struck up a conversation with the Empire City VideoPhone network and asked for Allegra's line in Galaxis. The VideoPhone network was a friendly program, happy to connect him and keep the line private and secure. Allegra was fast asleep when Jack called, and pretty surprised to hear from him so late at night. She was even more surprised when he asked her to meet him out somewhere that night. Allegra might not have agreed if she hadn't been half asleep, but she told Jack she'd meet him halfway between Galaxis and Hightown, in SeasonStill Park. Two minutes later, Jack was riding the elevator down to the lobby.

Jack was feeling pretty good about himself, having managed to ditch the SmartCams for the first time on his way out of the apartment. They weren't friendly contraptions that would do whatever Jack wanted, but he understood their video functions well enough to *make* them record and play back a loop of him watching TV for the next few hours. His studying was definitely paying off. Like Stendeval had said, knowledge was power. Jack got to the park ahead of Allegra and strolled in under no video surveillance whatsoever. He waited by the lagoon in Summershore Stretch, where the weather would be warmest, even in the middle of the night. A short while later, Allegra flew into the park on an open AirSkimmer, a vehicle that looked something like a flying metal raft. Jack called out to her, and she spotted him down on the boardwalk. She brought the AirSkimmer down and parked it in hover mode, tying it off on a nearby bench.

"Hey," Allegra said, taking a seat.

"Hey," Jack replied, joining her on the bench. "Thanks for coming. I knew I could count on you."

"Really?" Allegra asked. "I guess that makes one of us," she said, settling into a nook where two branches met above her. She looked around the park fretfully. "I wasn't so sure about this."

"Did you have trouble sneaking out?" Jack asked.

Allegra shook her head. "I live at the Valorian garrison—I didn't have to sneak out. They love that I'm not afraid to go to the park at two a.m., with an escaped Left-Behind running around the city."

"Right," Jack said, noting the sarcasm in Allegra's voice when she said the "not afraid" part. He remembered the Valorian credo she had recited back on Wrekzaw Isle, that a true daughter of Valor knows no fear. "I'm sorry to bring you into this with the Left-Behind still out there," he said. "But the truth is, I wouldn't have called if they'd already caught it."

"What's going on, Jack? You said you needed help. What is this? What are we doing here?"

Jack took a deep breath. He was about to ask for a lot more than what Allegra had had in mind when she had gotten out of bed. He might as well just spit it out. "I need you to help me go after the Rüstov Left-Behind," he said. "The one from Wrekzaw Isle. The one that got away."

Allegra's face rippled, but she kept herself together. "Why . . . why would you want to do that?"

"It's complicated," Jack replied. "The short version is, I think it knows me. Or at least knows something about me. I have to find out what that is. It's the only way to end all this. We can bring it in together. We did it once already, didn't we?"

"No, we only *sort of* did," Allegra said. "Skerren did most of the fighting, and the Left-Behind just got confused about what to do with you. I mean, really, Jack—" Allegra exhaled heavily, not at all comfortable with the idea of joining this caper. "I dealt with this thing on Wrekzaw Isle once already. That was enough for me."

Jack put up a finger. "Hold that thought," he said. Jack reached into his pocket and took out the distress beacon Allegra had lost back on Wrekzaw Isle. He held it out by its chain. "I think this belongs to you."

Allegra stared at the beacon, caught completely by surprise.

"*You* had it?"

Jack nodded. "It kind of got stuck on my neck when I fell through you," he explained with a shrug. "I think that ended up being a good thing, though, right?" Allegra didn't answer. She was transfixed by the beacon as she took it from Jack's hands. "You need to do this, Allegra," he told her.

Allegra tensed up and stared at Jack with apprehensive eyes. "You're not going to say anything about this to Prime, are you?" she asked.

Jack scrunched up his eyebrows. "No, I'm giving this back to you," he explained. "I would have given it back even sooner, but I didn't want anyone to see."

Allegra relaxed her posture. "Oh. Okay. Sorry, it's just . . . the only reason I didn't hit this button on Wrekzaw Isle was because I couldn't find it. You know that. That's the only reason I passed that test," she added, shaking her head. "When Prime told me he was proud of me, it was probably the greatest feeling I've had since I got here. I don't want him to find out that I'm still afraid."

"Come with me tonight," Jack said. "Help me catch the Rüstov and there won't be anything for Prime to find out. You're brave enough. You are. You came here tonight, didn't you?"

"I don't know . . ."

"You can do it," Jack said. "You need to do this for *yourself*. Forget about Prime for a minute. Tonight you can prove to yourself that you're not afraid. And I can finally find out who I am."

"Why does that matter so much?" Allegra asked. "Is that worth maybe getting killed for?"

"It matters," Jack said. "You don't understand." He paused, thinking back a moment to his time at St. Barnaby's. "I've wanted to know that stuff my whole life. You don't know what that's like. You were lucky. Well, not really *lucky* . . . that's obviously not the right word, but at least you know who you are. You know what happened to your family and how you ended up here. I want the same thing. I know my family is probably gone. I do know that. I just want to know for sure, and I think this Rüstov can help me find out."

Allegra groaned. Jack could see she didn't want to do this. "I can understand where you're coming from. And, of course, I owe you for what you did on Wrekzaw Isle, and for keeping your mouth shut about it, but . . ." Allegra paused a moment, then let out a resigned groan. "Promise me I won't regret this," she said.

"You're in?" Jack asked eagerly.

"Where would we look first?" Allegra asked. "*If* I were in, that is."

"If you were in?" Jack smiled. "I'd start in Karateka."

Jack and Allegra flew into downtown Karateka on Allegra's AirSkimmer, which was just big enough to hold the two of them and maybe one more, Jack hoped, if they did manage to catch the Left-Behind. Allegra wanted to know just how they were supposed to find this Left-Behind when every hero in Empire City couldn't. Jack replied that Skerren wasn't the only one who spent all his free time training. "I talk to machines, remember?" he said. "I can use my powers to track it."

On the way in, Jack told Allegra everything he knew about Cyberai's untimely demise. As he spoke, Allegra flew past floating NewsNets and she saw Cyberai's grisly fate for herself. The sight of it gave them both the chills, but they pressed on.

"Do you think you can control it this time?" Allegra asked, brimming with nervous energy. "The Left-Behind, I mean?"

"I don't think I'll have to," Jack said. "I can trick it. The Left-Behind thinks I'm royalty. It thinks I'm some upper-class Rüstov with a fresh host. We can use that. Turn left here."

Jack's first trip into Karateka made him think of the incredibly busy and overwhelming megacities found in most science fiction movies. Shiny new HoverCars and LaserBikes fired down MagLev highways at breakneck speed. AirSpeeders, Skimmers, and Skiffs raced around the borough's lively skyline. It was a lot like Machina and Galaxis in that regard. However, instead of taking on a clean robotic style or exotic alien design, Karateka's towers were fitted with a retro-Asian look.

All the buildings in Karateka were designed to mimic

the castles and temples known to traditional Japanese and Chinese architecture. On every building multiple tiers of curving roofs brandished sharp peaks and endpoints at multiple levels. Rectangular shapes of steel and glass were stacked together like boxes covered with ornate ridge-topped lids. For every sleek vertical skyscraper there was another jagged rectangular one, each styled after the temples of old.

A gentle rain fell and the wet streets became mirrors that reflected the multicolored lights of a million bright advertisements. Dynamic Asian letters were illuminated everywhere with giant characters written from top to bottom on long, vertical flashing signs, some of them spanning entire buildings. It was like flying through a giant jukebox.

Allegra followed Jack's directions around the city and swerved in between mammoth skyscrapers and flashing lights on the AirSkimmer. They weren't far from where Cyberai's body had been found. With any luck, the Left-Behind wouldn't be too far off.

"That way," Jack said, pointing, and Allegra turned the AirSkimmer to follow his fingers. Jack's connection to the Rüstov and his ability to talk to machines made him the perfect tracker. At first, the flashing signs showed him the way. They told Jack what they had seen of the Rüstov, and he repeated it for Allegra. As they picked up the trail, Jack began to feel the pull of the Rüstov, and he started directing things on his own.

Allegra slowed down as they passed a cluster of Smart-Corp high-rises. "The Left-Behind came through here," Jack said. "I bet the Rüstov's fight with Cyberai started somewhere nearby." Sure enough, as they passed between the buildings, they saw battle debris on windowsills and ledges, as well as laser-sword burns and fist-size impressions on building exteriors.

Jack watched the SmartCorp signs cycle between different languages, including English and some Asian languages he didn't recognize. SmartCorp really was everywhere. Something about the company's presence in every single borough felt wrong to Jack. Here in Karateka, Smart had ninja Peacemakers and entire blocks of office space and real estate. . . . Jack wondered aloud if there was any place in Empire City that Smart's fingers didn't touch.

"Just Cognito," Allegra answered. "Prime says Cognito will always belong to Stendeval."

Jack thought about the supervillains and rival ninja clans he always saw Chi fighting against in his old *ZenClan Warrior* comic books. "I hope Chi has the same grip on Karateka," he said as they followed the Left-Behind's trail into a dark corner of the borough. "This place is starting to look a little sketchy." As Jack and Allegra moved away from the brightly lit business district, the lights began to fade and the shadows began to loom large.

Jack and Allegra descended into what was undeniably the seedy underbelly of Karateka. Allegra said it made sense that the Left-Behind would hide out in a place like this. It was a dark, scary corner of town, lower to the ground, with smaller buildings and narrow alleyways for streets. Dilapidated walk-ups and boarded-up tenements were crammed in on top of each other. The streetlights were either busted and flickering or burned out altogether. The glow from Chinese lanterns strung to fire escapes and draped across the crooked streets provided the only dim light.

Allegra sped up a little as they coasted over the empty rooftops, clearly hoping the trail would lead out of these streets as soon as possible. Everything looked deserted, but it all felt wrong to Jack, like there was something dark and sinister lurking beneath the skin of these alleys. Allegra was jumpy. They both tried to stay alert, ready for whatever it was that they couldn't yet see. Jack didn't like being there either, but knew the Rüstov was close.

They kept moving, taking note of the graffiti marking some of the walls they passed by. They couldn't read it all, but a number of the symbols were clear. "This isn't good," Jack said, running his hand along a wall where a few of the markings were written in English. "ShadowClan," he read with dread in his voice. "I think . . . Allegra, I think this is Ronin territory."

"Ronin territory?" Allegra asked. "What's a Ronin?"

The sound of breaking glass shattered the night silence. Allegra stepped hard on the brakes as Jack pointed up ahead.

"They are."

The moonlight revealed the eerie limber forms of Ronin assassins on the rooftops ahead. Jack's stomach dropped when the Ronin's undead, cloudy eyes locked with his.

"Uh-oh," Jack said. "Not good."

"Not good is right," Allegra said.

The Ronin stepped toward them. Jack and Allegra could now run, or they could fight. Jack knew from his comics that there were no other options at this point. The Ronin were ruthless killers that would carve up Jack and Allegra just for setting foot in their territory uninvited. The Ronin said nothing as they inched forward toward the children. It was the exact situation Jack hoped to never find himself in.

"I hate these guys," Jack said. "I always hated these guys."

"All right, there's only a few of them," Allegra said. "Maybe we can . . ."

As if on cue, dozens upon dozens of Ronin crawled out of the shadows like spiders, emerging on all sides. The more directions Jack looked, the more Ronin he saw. They were clinging to fire escapes, perching on windowsills, and crawling on walls. They came out of nowhere and occupied everywhere.

"Allegra, let's get out of here," Jack said.

"You think?"

Allegra tried to back away, but they had nowhere to go. They were completely surrounded. Jack never imagined so many creatures could follow them without making a single sound. One by one, the Ronin all drew out three-pronged sai blades. Jack knew they meant to use them. Jack and Allegra tried talking to the Ronin, but it was no use. These creatures weren't much for conversation. Jack and Allegra braced themselves for what came next.

A trio of Ronin leaped forth to attack and were instantly cut down by a barrage of arrows and ninja stars.

Jack and Allegra spun around in surprise and saw a most welcome sight. A legion of ZenClan ninjas fell out of the sky, coming down on the Ronin from every possible angle. They moved in a unified wave, quickly forming a protective wall around the children. Jack breathed a sigh of relief when he saw Skerren and Chi among their number. It seemed he'd managed to join the Rüstov hunting party after all.

The Rüstov hunt, however, was momentarily put on hold as the Ronin counter-attacked in a dizzying blitz. The outer ring of Chi's ninjas broke out in every possible direction to meet the Ronin in battle. Chi flipped into the center of the protective circle around Jack and Allegra.

"Are you two unharmed?" he asked.

"We're fine," Jack answered.

"Yeah, now we are!" Allegra added.

Chi's cadre of silent warriors moved against the Ronin with the fearless agility that comes only with years of intense martial arts training. Their attack became a sort of acrobatic dance in the air. A dance of death. It was a breathtaking sight, watching the ZenClan fighters fearlessly go at the Ronin. The children were witnessing the art of the ninja at its best. Flawless technique. Graceful execution. Deadly perfection.

"What's going on?" Allegra asked Chi, not *quite* screaming. "Why are they attacking us?"

"We are here without permission," Chi said, plunging a fist of blue fire through the midsection of an advancing Ronin. "And we are not welcome." Black sand poured from the gaping wound in the Ronin's chest left by Chi's blow. The villain fell, but several more Ronin were slipping through the line of defense. Chi's ninjas were good, but the Ronin were too many. The ninjas needed help.

"Jack, focus on the Left-Behind," Chi said.

Jack blinked. "What? What about—"

"We'll last as long as we have to. *You* will have the time

344

you need." Chi dispatched two more Ronin with a series of kicks strong enough to topple an elephant. He looked to Skerren. "Our enemy is neither alive nor dead. Hold nothing back." Skerren bared his teeth in a vicious smile and dove headlong into the fray. He didn't need to be told twice. Before Jack could blink, Skerren was already slicing Ronin into sand piles with his unbreakable swords. Allegra did not join the battle so quickly, but she didn't liquefy either. Chi kicked a Ronin from her path, mere seconds before it struck her.

"Allegra, you are needed," he told her. He said nothing more. He just looked her in the eye and held up his arm. He flattened his fingers, extending them all the way straight. His hand was poised like an ax ready to chop. Allegra nodded, raised her arm to meet his, and it formed into a machete blade. The edge did not quiver. "The ninja's path is steady and balanced," he said to her. "We strike without fear or anger. Now, with me . . . FIGHT!"

Chi sprang forth at the Ronin. Allegra followed him into battle. She morphed her second arm to match her first and swung away. The black sand began to fly.

With everyone fighting the Ronin except Jack, it was

time for him to do his part. Amid the chaos, Jack reached out with his mind, listening for the Rüstov. The sound wasn't far off. It was like tuning in a weak-signaled radio station. Jack just had to filter out the static. The Left-Behind was nearby . . . and it was talking to someone.

"KSSSSCCHHHH . . . Report. Where is the child? The infected? You have failed?"

Jack's heart jumped. There were more Rüstov here than just the one that got away. And from the sound of it, they were all after him.

Jack jumped down from the AirSkimmer and looked around. The buildings here were close enough to one another for him to jump from one rooftop to the next without any trouble. He followed the voices away from the battle. They led him to the darkest of Ronin streets, where even the lanterns were burned out. He reached out with his senses to try and tune in the Rüstov's location. He was close. He could feel it.

He ran farther out into the darkness and reached the edge of a roof where a much taller building butted up against the ledge. An old, empty fire escape was clinging to the building's side. Jack reached up and started to climb. The rusty metal ladders creaked as he made his way up and looked over the top. On the far side of the roof, underneath a MagLev highway overpass, he saw them. Five Rüstov Left-Behinds—*five of them!*—all talking to one another, all in different states of decay. Jack recognized "his" Left-Behind among them. The fugitive, the one from Wrekzaw Isle. It was the one with the least rust and the highest rank. Its shiny new leg gleamed in the moonlight. Jack crawled onto the roof to get a better look.

"We did not fail," Jack heard one of them say. "The mission intel failed us. The child was not where our agent said he would be."

"Impossible," Jack's Rüstov replied. "Our agent would not lie to us. Our agent *could* not lie to us."

Jack got that cold feeling in his stomach again. He didn't like what he was hearing. Their agent? Another Collaborator? He also didn't like that there were five Left-Behinds on the roof. That was four more than he expected, and none of them seemed to think he was Rüstov royalty anymore. He decided to go back and get the others.

As Jack backed away toward the fire escape, he heard a sound from behind. He turned just as a Ronin's blade was about to descend on him. When the blade reached its highest point, Jack watched as at least a dozen arrows struck the Ronin's back, dropping him where he stood. The Ronin fell like a one-hundred-pound sandbag right on top of Jack. The Left-Behinds looked up in surprise. Chi's ninjas had saved Jack's life, but also had given away his position. "The child!" one of the Left-Behinds exclaimed, taking a step toward Jack. "He's come to us!"

"Stand fast," the head Left-Behind said to them, pointing across the rooftops. "Their numbers are too great," it added, eyeing the dozens of ninjas that were now running toward them, having finished off most of the Ronin assassins. "Fall back. Scatter and regroup at Location 12. Follow Omega Protocols if captured."

The Left-Behinds split up and ran off, all in different directions. Climbing out from under the fallen Ronin fighter, Jack was grossed out by the black sand all over him. He frantically beat the sand out of his clothes and struggled to untangle himself from the lifeless white suit. By the time he got clear of it, most of the Left-Behinds were already out of sight. One, however, was still within reach. Jack summoned his powers and asked it to stop where it was. Not surprisingly, it had no interest in complying with that request. That was fine, Jack thought. It was headed for the MagLev road. He waited until it was underneath the overpass and, with a simple thought, Jack reversed the polarity of the road. The forces of magnetic attraction pulled the Left-Behind's metal frame up to the underside of the highway and held him there. He couldn't have been locked down any tighter if he were tied with a thousand chains.

"Gotcha!" Jack said.

Jack started running across the roof toward the helpless Rüstov. Chi's ninjas followed. They were still a building or two behind Jack, but as he reached the MagLev overpass, Jack heard the hum of the AirSkimmer above him. He looked up to see Skerren driving it along an erratic, swerving path to reach the Left-Behind at the same time he did. Skerren dismounted on the roof next to Jack, and the two boys stared up at the trapped enemy.

"You caught it," Skerren said, somewhat surprised.

"Yeah," Jack replied. "It's not the same one as before, though. There were more of them here tonight. Five of them."

"Five?" Skerren repeated, looking up at the Rüstov. It wasn't struggling to free itself. The Left-Behind didn't seem to be paying him or Jack any real attention at all. It was grunting something to itself in Rüstov-speak. "Can you understand it?" Skerren asked. "What's that it's saying?"

"I don't know," Jack said. "I'm trying, but it's weird. It almost feels like half of it is turned off, and the other half is just . . . counting down."

Jack drew in a sharp breath, suddenly realizing what was going to happen. He prayed he wasn't too late and dove headlong into Skerren, taking them both over the side of the roof as the Left-Behind exploded. The blast carried with it enough force to blow the MagLev road apart and take out the roof of the building Jack and Skerren had just been standing on. They were in the air for only a brief second when the shockwave rocked them from behind. Smoke and dust from the explosion blinded Jack instantly. He held on to Skerren as tight as he could to keep them from being separated. Completely disoriented and falling through the air, he reached for help from anywhere. It was fight-or-flight instinct, not a conscious thought. Jack heard a loud hum and took a harsh blow to his entire body as he and Skerren both hit hard against a flat surface. It hurt, but Jack knew it should have hurt more. As the smoke cleared, the surface beneath Jack and Skerren started to rise up in the air. Jack and Skerren had been caught by the AirSkimmer. Jack had pulled it in with his powers just in time.

"You . . . you saved me," Skerren said, rubbing his head. He had a dazed look in his eyes.

"Yeah," Jack responded as the AirSkimmer brought them back to safe ground. "I'm just as surprised as you are."

Chi and the others raced over to the blast site, relieved to see the boys were both all right. When it was all over, the ninjas escorted the children safely out of the dark alleys and back to the ZenClan dojo. Jazen and Hovarth were there waiting for them when they arrived. Hovarth was glad to hear about Skerren's part in the recent battle, but Jazen was less than pleased about Jack's involvement. He was understandably upset with Jack for putting himself in such danger. Seated at the edge of Chi's stone garden, Jazen told Jack and Allegra just how lucky they were. "What would you have done if Chi hadn't been there tonight? You two would have had to face the Ronin alone."

Jack apologized to Jazen and admitted that it was all his idea. He was the one who had convinced Allegra to go, and said it wasn't her fault. He also told everyone what he'd seen and heard that night in Karateka. He said that the Rüstov were coming after him, and, to make matters worse, they had friends inside Empire City. "Someone was working with the Rüstov tonight," Jack said. "I heard them talking about an agent."

"Another Collaborator?" Allegra asked.

Jack shrugged. "Maybe," he said. "Or maybe we got the wrong guy last time."

"What do they want with you, Jack?" she asked.

Jack shook his head. He didn't know. Jack didn't know any of that because he didn't know anything about himself. Not the way the Rüstov sure seemed to. Why was it the only people who knew anything about him were the ones who wanted to hurt him?

Chi, on the other hand, said he knew everything he needed to know about Jack. About all the children, in fact. He told the students they had all shown skill, bravery, and selflessness that night. By working together toward a common goal, they had displayed teamwork, the asset he valued the most. With their actions they had earned not only his respect but his vote as well.

"If many can move as one, they can move mountains," Chi told the children. "But all concerned must understand this basic truth. They must share the same goal. The same direction, focus, and discipline. It is not about the individual. We are stronger together." Chi waved his hand out over the railing of the stone garden. "Look there," he said. "What do you see?"

In the garden, tiny pebbles covered every inch of the ground, all raked in tight, neat rows. A small number of larger stones, half buried in moss-covered patches, were scattered about. The pebbles were raked in perfect circles around the dry moss islands like ripples in a gravelly pond. Chi explained that the placement of every single rock was intentionally designed to produce a calming, Zen-like atmosphere. "The pebble is no more and no less important than the boulder," Chi said. "They work together to form the beauty of this garden. Like individual brushstrokes in a masterpiece, together they become something greater than their solitary selves. In battle it is no different." He looked at Jack and Skerren. "Regardless of your differences . . . in battle you are brothers. You are family."

"I don't *have* any family," Skerren said. He turned to Jack. "Don't go thinking we're brothers. I'm not even sure what you were really doing out there tonight."

Jack was shocked. "You still don't trust me after all this?" he asked. "I saved your life."

"Sure," Skerren said. "This time. What about next time? What if the next time I need you for something, you have a Rüstov mark on your eye?" Skerren shook his head. "It doesn't matter if I trust you or not. You're infected. *You* can't even trust you. The parasite could be pulling your strings right now and you wouldn't even know it. That's how it is with the Rüstov."

"You're not being fair," Allegra said to Skerren.

"Fair's got nothing to do with it," Skerren replied. "You think he's your friend, Allegra, but you can't be sure. Even *he* can't be sure which side he's on. He doesn't know a thing about himself!"

"That's the whole point!" Jack said. "That's exactly

why we were out there tonight. Look, Skerren, I get it. You hate the Rüstov, that's fine. But I don't know what you want me to do about it. I can't help what I am."

For a moment, Skerren actually seemed to look at Jack like a real person. "I know it's not your fault," he said, "but the Rüstov don't just want you. They've already got you. You're worth something to them and they've got a hook in you already. That's all there is to it. No matter what anyone says, you're already lost."

"Skerren," Allegra began, "why do you have to be like that?" Skerren was already on his way to the door. He didn't slow down and he didn't look back.

"Do not worry, Jack," Chi said, resting a hand on Jack's shoulder. "Families fight all the time. What matters is what they do when they need each other. When it counts. You were there for Skerren tonight. I believe the time will come when he makes the same decision. The universe is a balanced place. The more you give, the more you receive in the end."

"I don't even think I care anymore," Jack said. "I mean, if he can't get over his issues after a night like this, what's it gonna take? I'm just so sick of his attitude."

Allegra nodded. "I don't get why he's so angry all the time," she said. "He's good at everything. He's got his power totally mastered, all this stuff comes easy for him . . . what's his problem?"

Hovarth looked sadly at the gate Skerren had left by. "I wouldn't say Skerren has it all so well," he said. "Skerren walks a road just as hard as anyone's."

"What do you mean?" Jack asked.

"Well," the mighty king began, "I've known Skerren since he was a baby. His father was my blood brother in combat. He and his wife were my closest friends. I've never known happier, prouder parents. They loved Skerren and doted on him. And then one day that all ended. Rüstov Left-Behinds, in hiding since the invasion, emerged in search of new hosts, made their way into Varagog, and infected Skerren's parents.

"They turned before the boy's very eyes," Hovarth said. "It took only seconds. Taken over by Rüstov parasites, his parents tried to kill him. He had to fight them off, his own parents, just to stay alive. He couldn't have been more than seven or eight years old at the time. Just a boy. Skerren doesn't hate you, Jack. He hates what is in you. He hates the Rüstov, and with good reason. You think him a bully or a mean child, but in many ways he is not a child at all. He survived his parents, but his childhood died years ago. Since then, he has focused only on his training. And his anger."

Jack and Allegra were quiet.

"Did you know any of that?" Jack asked Allegra.

"No," Allegra said mournfully.

Jack didn't know what to say. Skerren's story was horrible. Really, it was much worse than his own. Life at St. Barnaby's was nothing compared to what Skerren had gone through. Jack always thought Skerren was a jerk, but nothing was ever as simple as it seemed. Skerren wasn't bad—he just had had to grow up too fast. Jack, like most orphans, knew exactly what that was like.

"I'm afraid this is by no means a unique tale," Hovarth said. "Nearly everyone in Empire City has a story like this to tell, some dating back to the invasion, and others, like Skerren's, that are more recent. Everyone here has a bad memory about the Rüstov, and that's all they can think of when they see you. They ask why you live with the infection when their loved ones died. Why is your life spared when theirs were lost? Sheds some light on why people look at you the way they do, eh? What they see is their pain. No doubt, Skerren sees his parents."

Suddenly, Jack saw both Skerren and Hovarth in a whole new light. "Do you see that too?" he asked Hovarth. "Skerren's parents, I mean? Your best friends?"

"They were already lost, Jack," Hovarth replied. "Once the Rüstov take root in someone, that person is gone." He reflected on that a moment, then added, "Except for you, it seems. When I voted against you in the sphere and said that sooner or later you would turn, I meant it. However, when I became Circleman of Varagog, like my father before me, I gave my word to uphold the will of the Inner Circle. It was the will of the Circle that you be tested for the School of Thought, so I gave you a chance. I gave you a chance because of Stendeval. I may not always agree with him, but I do respect him. Jonas Smart might be the smartest man in Empire City, but Stendeval is the wisest."

"What happened to Skerren's parents?" Allegra asked. "Did Skerren have to kill them to get away?"

"No," Hovarth said gravely. "I'm afraid that burden fell to me."

For the first time, Jack saw himself through everyone else's eyes. He began to realize just how badly everyone was wronged by the Rüstov. Suddenly, the harm that the Rüstov had done to the people of Empire City had a real face on it. Oddly enough, that face was Skerren's.

When Jack got back to the Ivory Tower, the evening took yet another unexpected turn. He and Jazen came home to find that while they were out, their apartment had been broken into and ransacked. Inside, the place was a wreck. Someone had turned the furniture over, rifled through the drawers, and kicked in the bedroom doors. A strong wind blew in from a window that had been smashed, and Anti-Gravity platforms hung down at uneven angles, blowing back and forth in the breeze. Jazen scanned the apartment for intruders before he let Jack follow him in. Once they were both inside, they sifted through the mess in stunned silence.

"I guess now I'm glad you snuck out tonight," Jazen finally said to Jack, trying to make light of the situation.

Jack wasn't laughing. He was well aware of what the break-in meant for him. "The Rüstov . . . ," he said, thinking back to what he had heard on the rooftops, just hours before. "Jazen, the Rüstov said I wasn't where their agent said I would be tonight. I was supposed to be here!"

"I know," Jazen admitted. "That crossed my mind, too."

"You don't think . . . ," Jack began, puzzling over a scary thought. "Jazen, what if this whole thing with Cyberai tonight was all just to get you out of the apartment?"

"No," Jazen said, shaking his head. "I only left the apartment because of Blue. That's a coincidence. No way it's more than that."

"Who else knows I live here?" Jack asked.

"Everybody," Jazen said. "Everybody knows, thanks to Smart's NewsNets."

"Smart," Jack said, putting up a finger, telling Jazen to hold that thought. He looked around the apartment. The mention of Smart's name triggered something in the room. Something connected to Smart that was trying to get Jack's attention. It was weird, but he could feel it there, just beyond his reach. Jack rushed into his room and began searching through the debris.

"What are you looking for?" Jazen asked.

Jack didn't answer him. He didn't know the answer, and he was too worked up to focus properly. After several moments Jack cleared his mind and really concentrated. When he was completely calm, the signal came in clearly. The noise came from something speaking to him, something that he hadn't looked at since his first night in Empire City. Jack walked over to the table next to his bed and picked up his birth certificate.

Jack held up the SmartPaper file. Its letters were scrambled into gibberish. Smart had said it was because the file was infected by the Rüstov virus. That was what had caused him to sever the file from his mainframe. Now that Jack knew how to talk to the file, he got a different story. When he closed his mind and looked into the file, he found no trace of the Rüstov virus whatsoever. Jack's birth certificate wasn't corrupted. It was encrypted.

The file had been permanently sealed by Jonas Smart.

14

The Enemy Within

Jack stomped around, muttered to himself, and waved his hands in the air like a nut. After several moments of watching the apartment lights surge on and off and listening to a great deal of words not regularly found in his vocabulary, Jazen finally got Jack to settle down and tell him what was going on.

"He's been lying to me since day one!" Jack yelled. "From the second I got here! I don't believe this!"

"What? Who has?"

"Well, maybe I *do* believe it, but still . . . it's not infected,

Jazen!" Jack said, holding up his birth certificate. "Smart lied to me! My file's not infected!"

"Not infected?" Jazen repeated. "Let me see that."

Jack handed Jazen the SmartPaper file. Jazen examined it, trying to see what Jack saw. "It certainly *looks* infected," Jazen said. "It looks like the data on it was broken and fried by the Rüstov virus, like Smart said."

"It's not infected!" Jack said. "There's a voice coming from the file—I can hear it!" Jack told Jazen what the file had told him. Jack swore he had heard a weak voice, faintly crying out in a barely audible tone. It was being muted by an encryption code that kept repeating the same message over and over:

Confidential. Eyes only, Jonas Smart.

"He knows who I am!" Jack said. "This whole time, he's known all about me. My real name, my family . . . they might still be out there!" Jack looked outside at the SmartCams. They were tapping at the Ivory Tower loft's window, just as they did every night. "All this time he knew I wasn't some Rüstov spy, and he still had his SmartCams follow me around like I was some kind of criminal. He ran all those stupid tests, freezing me,

shocking me . . . he even wanted to have me dissected!
The whole time, he knew that everything he was saying
about me was a lie."

"Jack, are you sure about this?" Jazen asked. "You have
to be sure."

"Absolutely," Jack said. "One hundred percent."

Jazen gripped the SmartPaper tightly. "That dirty son
of a . . ." Jack could literally see the wheels turning inside
Jazen's head. "He's been playing us this whole time," Jazen
said. Jazen couldn't talk to the file the way Jack could,
but he didn't need to. He put his hand to his forehead.
He looked upset with himself. "How could I have missed
this?" he said.

Jack didn't understand him yet. "What do you mean?"
he asked. "Missed what?"

"I don't believe it," Jazen said, still running with his
same train of thought. "I thought bringing you here would
loosen Smart's grip on this city, but he's been working
this from the very beginning." Jazen paused, still thinking.
"He gets so much power by keeping people afraid . . . I just
gave him everything he needed to stir up everybody's fears
again." Jazen looked to Jack like he had finally put the last

piece of a puzzle in its place. "I never did believe Silico did it," he said.

"Silico?" Jack squinted at Jazen. "What are you saying?"

Jazen's face turned deadly serious. "I'm saying, Jack, I think Silico was framed. I think Jonas Smart is the Great Collaborator."

Jack leaned forward with his mouth agape. He was speechless.

"It all makes sense," Jazen said. "You don't know what it was like here after the invasion, Jack. Suddenly, Jonas Smart was able to get away with anything. As long as he said it was to protect us against the Rüstov, he had free reign. He set up the Peacemakers as his own private army of supers. He set up the SmartCam surveillance program. Fear and paranoia ran rampant, and people stood by while the Peacemakers basically ruled Machina with an iron fist."

"Okay," Jack said. "But what does that have to do with me?"

"Think about it," Jazen said. "Don't you think someone as brilliant as Smart, someone who hates the Rüstov as much as he claims to, should be happy to meet someone like you? Someone who is fighting a Rüstov infection and winning?"

Jack nodded. He had to admit, he'd wondered about that once or twice himself.

"If the truth about you is something harmless, or maybe even something positive, that's no good for Smart," Jazen said. "But as long as you're a mystery, you're a potential Rüstov threat. A mysterious infected child talking about Revile coming back from the dead? It's almost too perfect. He's the one who benefits from all this. Why else would he be lying about you?"

"But would he really work with the Rüstov, though?" Jack asked. "Would he actually hand me over to them?"

"He had all the information he needed," Jazen said. "He knew where and when you'd be alone on Wrekzaw Isle, he obviously knew where the Left-Behind was being held, and tonight you made his SmartCams think you were here watching TV. If you went missing, he could have spun that any way he wanted. It'd be just like after the invasion."

"You really think it was him back then?" Jack asked. "You think he'd help them kick off an entire invasion?"

"Maybe," Jazen surmised. "He's always ten steps ahead.

If he liked our odds, or thought it was better for him in the long run, he'd go through with it. Smart wouldn't look at it the same way we do, Jack. If he calculated all the probabilities with his machines and *they* thought we would win, he wouldn't see the invasion as a tragedy at all. He'd see it as an opportunity."

"He'd just look at the logic of it all," Jack said, becoming convinced. "The invasion did happen right after Smart had his heart removed . . ."

"And SmartCorp must have acquired half of Empire City since then," Jazen said. "We have to tell the others. We have to at least look into this. We'll call for an emergency meeting of the Inner Cir—"

"No," Jack interrupted. "We have to do this. Just us. Tonight."

Jazen looked at Jack. "Tonight? What are you talking about?"

"There's more to this, Jazen. Something between me and the Rüstov. This might be my last chance to find out what that is, and I'm not going to lose this one too," Jack said. "Every time I think I'm going to get answers about my past, I get nothing. When you brought me here, you said all the answers I wanted were at the Hall of Records. When we got there, they said my file was ruined. When Stendeval came back, he said he knew stuff about me too. Stuff going back to the invasion. Then he wouldn't say anything either. Have patience, he said! Then the Left-Behind got away from us twice! They're all dead ends. I'm out of patience. Smart owes me answers and they're in his computer right now. I'm not accusing him of anything until I have proof."

"Jack, the file in your hand is proof."

"I can't read the file," Jack countered. "I tried, and the encryption code won't even let me copy it. What's the Inner Circle going to do, make Smart decode it? He'll delete it at the first chance he gets and call it a computer glitch or something. He only let me keep this because he didn't know I'd be able to talk to it. I'm not letting him near this thing."

Jazen reluctantly agreed that Jack had a point. If the file wasn't already severed from Smart's mainframe, he would have deleted it long before now. Jack was right—they couldn't risk Smart finding out what they knew. Jazen wanted to talk to Stendeval about this, but they had no way to reach him. Cognito was filled with hideouts, not homes. It wasn't like they could go knock on Stendeval's door. His door would have moved at least ten different times since they saw it last.

"What exactly are you suggesting we do?" Jazen asked. "I know you want answers, but the file's severed from the mainframe, and Smart's the only one who has access rights. For you to read it, the file has to think you're him. You'd have to feed it back into his personal computer."

Jack nodded slowly at Jazen. "Exactly."

Jazen suddenly looked like all the power had drained from his batteries. He peered out the window at the rapier peak of SmartTower. It was shining brightly in the moonlight. "Oh, no," he said. "Jack, no."

"You said sometimes you have to bend the rules," Jack reminded him.

"There's bending the rules and then there's destroying the rules," Jazen said. "This isn't like sneaking out of the apartment, Jack. You're talking about SmartTower. They've got security. Your voiceprint, your fingerprints, and even your retinas. You won't even get past the front door."

"I'm not planning on using the front door," Jack said. He told Jazen what he had in mind. It was a simple plan. It took guts, superpowers, and a partner in crime who just happened to be an android. Luckily, Jack had all three.

"If we get caught, it's going to be bad," Jazen warned. "Bad for us both. Everyone's going to say Smart was right about you. We could blow our only chance at this."

"Then I guess we better not get caught," Jack said.

A short while later, Jazen slid open the window on the 437th floor of the Ivory Tower. Jack felt a rush in every fiber of his being. From here on out, all safeties were off. He had learned a lot studying for the School of Thought, but the time for tests and homework ended at the window's edge. This time, Jack would be dealing with the real thing.

Jazen stepped out as far as he could go without jumping. Wind rushed into the loft, but that was all. The Smart-Cams stayed where they were. As far as Smart's inventions went, the SmartCams really weren't overly complex. They were just a bunch of flying cameras. Jack thought it was even easier to trick them the second time around. With the

SmartCams out of the way, Jack made some final preparations and climbed onto Jazen's back. "I'm not even sure I
can make a jump this far," Jazen said.

"The hydraulics in your legs told me you can clear this
easy," Jack said.

Jazen shrugged. "If you say -zzt-zzt-zzt- so." He turned
around and gave Jack a worried look, a bit surprised that
the boy was still causing him to have glitches.

"Did I do that?" Jack asked, thinking maybe he was a
little overexcited.

"Are you sure you want to do this?" Jazen asked.

"I'm ready," Jack replied, trying to convince himself as
much as he was trying to convince Jazen.

"If I miss this jump, this is going to be the shortest
secret mission ever," Jazen told him.

"One second," Jack told him. He spoke to the Smart-
Tower security cameras, getting everything ready. It was now
or never. "Okay!" Jack yelled before he could change his
mind.

"Hold on!" Jazen yelled.

With a rush of wind they were hurtling through the air
toward SmartTower.

Jack and Jazen smashed through a window on the 422nd floor with a huge crash. Jazen landed in a solid three-point crouch. Jack was latched on to his back, his arms wrapped around tighter than the sleeves of a straightjacket. He stepped down, relieved to be back on solid ground. Broken glass crunched beneath his sneakers as alarms screamed all around them. Now came the tricky part.

Although Jack had sent the tower security cameras to static before he and Jazen hit the window, he could do nothing to keep the crash quiet. He figured they had maybe a minute tops before tower security had someone up there to check it out. Turned out it was even less, because the someone who showed up happened to be Speedrazor.

Jack didn't even see him coming until he was right on top of them, but Jazen's mechanized eyes picked up the speedster easily. Jazen turned, stuck his metal arm out in the air, and clotheslined the Peacemaker at a hundred miles per hour. Speedrazor dropped like a stone. Jack thought it was awesome.

After Speedrazor hit the ground, a radio button on his uniform started squawking. A voice asked for a situation report. Jazen tapped the button to reply and answered the call. "Area secure. Just some collateral damage from a superfight," Jazen said in a perfect voiceprint match for Speedrazor. "Looks like Laser Girl hit our window again. Send up a maintenance crew to clean up the broken glass. Speedrazor out."

Jazen slung the Peacemaker's unconscious body over his shoulder and Jack gave him a thumbs-up. To avoid being picked up on the radar, Jack sent his thoughts directly to Jazen's mechanical mind using his powers. *Looks like Speedrazor falls into the seventy-two percent of attacks you can handle*, Jack thought.

I'd be lying if I said I didn't enjoy that, Jazen thought back.

Once they were inside, the rest of tower security actually wasn't that hard to circumvent. Jack tricked the building's ret-scanners and fingerprint-sensitive surfaces using only a blindfold and a pair of gloves. Jazen didn't have retinas or fingerprints himself, so he was safe from detection as long as all the security cameras were looping videos of empty hallways—and thanks to Jack, they were.

Blindfolded, Jack found his way to Smart's lab by reaching out with his mind to the tower's directional signs and maps. Telling people how to get places was the primary function of those programs, so Jack was able to get them to work for him just by asking nicely. When they got to the lab door, Jazen pried open Speedrazor's eyes for the ret-scanner.

"Peacemaker Speedrazor," the scanner said in a very pleasant voice. "Access granted." Speedrazor started to come around when he heard his name, but Jazen gave him another punch that ensured he was out for a good long time.

As the doors opened, Jack felt that rush again. He was moments away from finding out everything he always wanted to know. He had to keep his emotions in check. He couldn't let his powers flare up and make the lights start flickering. Any power surge was sure to alert security. Keeping the SmartCams back at the Ivory Tower under wraps took concentration too. He couldn't lose focus and let them tell everyone that he and Jazen had left the apartment. Jack walked to Smart's personal computer in the darkness, trying to keep cool. All those crazy endurance tests he had suffered through in this lab might've been good for something after all, because he managed to stifle any involuntary effects of his power.

Jack stood at Smart's desk and took out his birth certificate. All the hard work and study was about to pay off. He was about to feed the file into the computer screen when a voice startled him.

"I wasn't aware we had a test scheduled this evening," an all-too-familiar voice called out in the darkness, stopping Jack's heart.

"No," Jack whispered.

With the finish line only one step away, it was over. He took off his blindfold and turned around to see the tall, grim figure of Jonas Smart. In his hand was a shiny silver ray gun.

"Hello, Jack," Smart continued in his frozen acid voice. "It seems the part of you that I've been warning everyone about has come to the fore at last." It was Smart at his self-righteous best, and Jack could tell he was enjoying himself. "I knew I was right about you," he said. "Both of you. Nobody wanted to listen to me because of Stendeval, but I knew." He leaned down to check on Speedrazor, whom Jazen had left by the door. "I suppose I should be thanking you. This little break-in of yours has given me everything I need to make the

Peacemakers permanent fixtures in Empire City."

"That's what it's all about, isn't it, Jonas?" Jazen said. "Power. That's right, Jack and I know all about you, too."

"Spare me the bluster, Emissary Knight," Smart replied. "It's obvious what's going on here."

He smiled, squeezed the trigger, and fired a shot directly into Jazen's midsection.

"Jazen!" Jack screamed as his friend slid backward across the floor. Jazen groaned in pain, clutching at his stomach. Thankfully, he was only stunned.

"You, Emissary Knight, are either a Mecha Collaborator or you are currently under the control of this Rüstov-infected boy," Smart continued. "Either way, you can rest assured that this time, I *will* have you dismantled. And Jack . . ." Smart grinned a sickening grin. "You're finally going to see my dissection table after all."

Smart motioned with the gun for Jack to get away from the computer. Jack stared daggers back at Smart, but he did as he was told. Smart had him exactly where he wanted him.

"What have you got there?" Smart asked, grabbing away Jack's birth certificate. "Trying to steal my files?"

"It's my file!" Jack shot back. "The one you lied about!"

Smart's eyebrows perked up when he heard that. He seemed impressed as he looked over the "corrupted" file. "Figured that out, did you?" he said, brandishing the birth certificate that held Jack's real name. "Well, you can't blame me for wanting to keep the people of this city vigilant against the Rüstov. The less people know about you, the better. They have me to tell them what they need to know." Smart fed the file into one of his computer screens and keyed in a command. An image of Jack's scrambled birth certificate was projected into the air. "Computer, delete file," Smart commanded with all the sympathy of a jagged rock.

"NO!" Jack yelled. The file turned red and started blinking, fading away a little more with each blink. Jack tried to stop the computer, but nothing happened. He tried to take control of Smart's gun, but he couldn't even talk to it. Something was wrong.

His powers were gone!

Smart grinned again. "Power nullifiers," he said. "Specifically tuned to you. I have them stationed throughout the tower. They send out a signal that prevents you from accessing those extraordinary abilities of yours."

Jack's birth certificate blinked its last few blinks and then vanished. Jack felt his heart break. His name. His family. All of it was gone, and he was literally powerless to stop it. "Why?" he asked Smart in disbelief. "How did you . . ."

Smart laughed as Jack tried to figure out where his powers had gone. "What did you think all those extra tests I ran on you were for?" he asked. "I pushed you to the limits of your endurance, recorded your stress levels, and tracked your power output at every stage. I isolated your thoughtprint, the actual energy signature you emit when using your power. So far, tower security has only seen what you wanted them to see, but I've been tracking you from the moment you crashed through my window."

"Why didn't you trip the alarms, then?" Jazen asked with a grunt as he rose to his feet. "Why didn't you call the Inner Circle? You're hiding something."

"That's far enough, Emissary Knight," Smart said, turning his gun back to bear on Jazen. Jazen stopped where he was. "To answer your question, I terminated security measures for the lab after you entered. I wanted this moment for myself." Smart shrugged. "I had to see what you were up to, didn't I? Now I know."

"I told you," Jazen said. "We know about you, too. We know that you're the Great Collaborator. The real one."

Smart's eyes widened. "The Great Collaborator?" he exclaimed. "Are you mad?" Now it was Smart's turn to stare in disbelief. He looked at Jazen like he was crazy. "I *caught* the Great Collaborator," he said. "Silico was a Mecha, just like you! I caught him shutting down the city's defense grid. He let the Rüstov into Empire City!"

"You framed Silico," Jazen said. "He didn't have any motive to work with the Rüstov. No Mecha does. You're the only one who benefited from the invasion. You're the one who got to play king and run this city with your fear and division, and you lied about Jack to make sure things stayed that way!"

"I lied about Jack because when people aren't scared, they relax!" Smart yelled. "I don't want the people of this city relaxed, I want them vigilant! If there's a price to be paid for the security of the Imagine Nation, then it has to be paid. If it means a little boy doesn't get to find out who his parents are, then so be it!"

"Nice try," Jazen said. "I'm not buying it. Someone's working for the other side here. The Rüstov have an agent that's been moving against Jack since he got to Empire City, and I can't think of anyone who's got more against him than you do."

"How dare you!" Smart bellowed. "I've kept this city safe! I don't have to stand for this—I know the truth!"

The way Smart yelled at Jazen made Jack start to think that either he was a really good liar, or maybe he *was* telling the truth. He looked so unbelievably offended that his loyalties were being called into question. Jack wondered if it was possible that they were wrong about him.

"Here!" Smart said, using his pocket holo-computer to bring up a screen for all to see. "We'll see who the Collaborator is here. Someone in this room is transmitting! *Someone* is sending a message in Rüstov-speak right now, and it's certainly not me. What do you have to say for yourself now?"

"What?" Jack said. He was totally confused. "Jazen, what's going on?"

Jazen looked just as shocked as Jack did. He walked up to the holo-screen and stared at it. It was a schematic of the room, with a readout tracking Wi-Fi transmissions that were being sent out into the air. "No," he said, obviously devastated by what he was seeing. He put his hand over his mouth and looked over at Jack with horror in his eyes.

"Jack, I'm sorry, it's . . ." Jazen choked on the words, barely able to get them out. "It's me."

Before Jack could reply, the massive round window in Smart's lab exploded inward and the team of Rüstov Left-Behinds crashed into the room, guns blazing.

CHAPTER

15

The Awful Truth

Jack ducked for cover as broken glass whipped across the room. The Rüstov took control of the lab in seconds. They had the element of surprise and moved with ruthless efficiency. Jack and the others never stood a chance. Smart turned to fire on the intruders and grazed one of them with his ray gun, but not before another one hit him with some kind of electrovolt weapon. Smart screamed and dropped to the ground in an unconscious heap. Jazen rushed at the invaders as they came in, but the lead Left-Behind just raised a hand in his direction with his palm up.

"Freeze," the Rüstov said, and Jazen's systems locked up, stopping him in place.

"Uh!" Jazen grunted as he ground to a halt. Quickly realizing what was happening to him, he shouted to Jack. "I can't move, Jack! Get out of here!"

Jack backpedaled a few steps, completely lost.

"Run, Jack!" Jazen screamed again, more urgently. "Hide!"

Jack got it together and bolted just as one of the four Left-Behinds dove for him. Jack's attacker just missed him, and as it clawed at his feet from the ground, Jack ran back into the shadows of the lab. He was desperate to get out of there, or at the very least, to lose his pursuers somewhere among Smart's many experiments. He was also frightened beyond measure. He was trapped there alone without his powers, and Jazen was locked up like a statue.

What was going on with Jazen? Jack didn't know what was happening, but everything he thought he knew before he had broken into SmartTower was clearly wrong. It was a terrible feeling. It terrified Jack. Despite all the things that made Jack extraordinary, he was still just a boy of twelve, and all young boys get scared from time to time. Even the brave ones.

As Jack ducked behind a lab desk filled with machines he could no longer talk to, he heard his Left-Behind speaking to the others. "Fan out," the Rüstov ordered. "Find the boy."

The three Para-Soldiers struck out after Jack. They split up in favor of a three-pronged approach and stalked Jack across the lab slowly, simultaneously moving up the left, right, and center of the room. Jack's Left-Behind, the one that was currently using Cyberai's leg, stayed back at the window with Jazen. Jack could see what they were doing. They wanted to flush him out.

"What have you done to me?" Jazen asked the Left-Behind. "What is this?"

The Rüstov moved toward Jazen, its rusty scrap-metal gears scraping against each other as they turned. It looked Jazen up and down. "You are infected," it said in English. Across the lab, Jack's ears perked up in his hiding space.

"That's impossible," Jack heard Jazen say. "I'm an android. Your virus doesn't affect me."

The Rüstov grunted. "Yours is not the organic virus

lying dormant in the boy," it replied. "Perhaps you have experienced an unusually high amount of system errors recently? More glitches? Yours is a computer virus. What you see, we see. What you hear, we hear. We slave your systems to our will. We have many weapons."

"Spyware," Jazen said through gritted teeth. "You scum."

Jack drew in a deep breath as a Left-Behind crept by the lab desk he was hiding behind. It didn't see him because it kept moving. Jack shuddered as he exhaled, and backtracked to an area of lab that the Left-Behind had already covered. It was funny—as he went, he couldn't shake the memory of hiding from Mrs. Theedwheck back in the St. Barnaby's library. If he got caught this time, he was going to get a lot more than a yardstick thwacking. He had to get out of there. He crawled across the floor as slowly and quietly as he could, inching his way toward one of the lab exits. As he crept through the lab, he could hear Jazen and the head Left-Behind talking, even see them through an opening between two equipment racks. One of the Rüstov soldiers searching for Jack was between him and the exit. He stopped where he was, to keep safely hidden.

"How long?" Jazen asked. "When was I infected? Why me?"

The Rüstov looked at him with scorn. "You think you are unique. You think that somehow you matter. Rüstov scouts have been coming to this galaxy for years, preparing this planet for the Empire."

"What are you saying?" Jazen asked. "There are others? How many?"

The Rüstov bared its rotten teeth in a sick kind of smile. "Did you think the Rüstov Armada would simply go away after the first invasion failed?" the creature asked. "The war is not over. Our tactics are stealth. Patience. That is how we first entered your world so long ago. By infecting a Mecha like you. By forcing him to shut down your defenses."

Jazen glared at the Rüstov, simmering with rage. "His name was Silico," he said, defiant.

"Your names mean nothing to us," the Rüstov told Jazen. "We are the most advanced species in the universe. Renewable technology. Infinite life. Deadly purpose. That is what the Rüstov Armada represents. You are food and tools, nothing more."

The more Jack listened to the Rüstov talk to Jazen, the angrier he got. He had his own ideas about what the Rüstov Armada represented, and the Rüstov weren't going to get away with this. He wasn't going to let them. The three Left-Behinds searching for Jack were now far enough away for him to make it out, but he couldn't go through with it. He had heard what the Rüstov had just said, and he couldn't let it go. Silico *was* the Great Collaborator, but not the way everyone thought. He had been acting against his will twelve years ago, and Jazen was in the same boat now. Jazen was infected. Jack knew what that felt like better than anyone in the world. There was no way he was going to abandon his friend.

But what could Jack do without his powers? Jack looked around quickly, taking stock of his environment and trying to find anything he could use to his advantage. The three Rüstov had reached the far end of the lab. Having cleared the rest of the room, they were now coming back toward him. If he stayed where he was, he would be cornered, but that didn't have to mean he was trapped. Not here, it didn't. Something in the lab caught Jack's eye. He got an idea, and reached out to flip on a familiar machine the old-fashioned way. With his fingers.

The Left-Behinds were quick to react to the sudden activity on the opposite side of the lab. Their leader motioned to the others to head toward the running machine. As one of the decaying Left-Behinds closed in on Jack's position, Jack got a good look at the "most advanced species in the universe." Its drying skin was cracking to reveal oily bones and metal. Its rusty iron frame shed dirty orange-brown flakes as it walked. Jack would be doing this thing a favor, he thought. He hit a switch and ran as frozen carbonite poured forth from an overhead storage tank, completely covering the oncoming Left-Behind. This wasn't the aerosol stuff that Smart had frozen Jack with a few days earlier. This was pure and undiluted. The Left-Behind screeched in pain as its temperature dropped a hundred degrees below absolute zero, and every inch of its body crystallized and froze. Jack threw a piece of lab equipment at the creature and it shattered like glass, sprinkling across the floor in a million pieces.

"Jack, what are you doing?" Jazen yelled. "Get out of here!"

"Not without you!" Jack shouted back.

The other two Left-Behind stalkers came around carefully and shut off the flow of carbonite, but Jack was long gone from the lab station by then. Angered by the loss of their comrade, the Rüstov started throwing Smart's experiments and inventions this way and that, searching more aggressively for Jack now. The head Left-Behind stormed into the lab's work area as well and joined the hunt. It was just what Jack was hoping for. Once the coast was clear, he sneaked back out into the open. He went not to Jazen but over to Smart, who was still out cold on the floor. "Don't worry!" he whispered while going through Smart's pockets, looking for something. "I've got an idea." Jack reached into Smart's inside pocket and pulled out his holo-computer. He held it up. "Here!" he said, thinking that if he could shut off the power nullifiers, he could call for help. He could save himself and Jazen. He'd even save Smart.

But when Jack looked up at Jazen, he saw that he was twitching again. Another glitch. Jack knew what that meant now. Jazen was transmitting. The Rüstov could see what he saw, and that meant . . .

"There you are!" the head Left-Behind said as it grabbed Jack up off the ground. Its two comrades that were still standing were there as well. They had him now.

"NO!" Jazen yelled, struggling to break free. He strained to the point that Jack thought he might blow a fuse, but no matter how hard he tried, he couldn't move.

"Now you see," the Rüstov said, gloating. "You cannot defeat us when your own bodies betray you. It was you who alerted us to his existence in the first place! It was your eyes that told us there was a child resisting infection in Empire City. Your eyes told us everything."

"Jack, I'm sorry," Jazen said. "I'm sorry, I never—" Jazen broke off, his eyes darting down toward the ground. It seemed he couldn't even look at Jack.

"It's not your fault, Jazen," Jack said. "You didn't know."

"We knew," the Rüstov said, taunting Jazen. "And we know that with this boy's help, the Rüstov Armada will rise again. We are the future." He held Jack up and looked him right in the face. "Apparently, so are you."

"Why?" Jack yelled. "Why me? What does this have to do with me?"

"The Magus wants you," the Rüstov said to him. "That is all you need to know. The Magus will not be denied."

"Oh, he'll be denied," Jazen said, trying with all of his might to break free of the Rüstov's control. "He'll be denied!" At this point, Jack noticed that Jazen was able to wiggle his little finger. It was something the Left-Behinds didn't pick up on. At least not in time to do anything. Jazen let out a mighty roar as he broke free of the Rüstov's control and rushed them. The Left-Behind holding Jack backed away just in time, but Jazen grabbed hold of the other two and pushed them back. "They underestimate us, Jack!" he yelled at them. "We're stronger than they think!"

With indomitable willpower Jazen kept going. Jack watched him drive the two Rüstov back to the edge of the broken window and out over the side. He didn't let go of them for a second.

"JAZEN!" Jack screamed as his best friend tumbled out of the biggest, tallest window in SmartTower. In that instant, everything slowed down. Jack couldn't believe what he was seeing. He didn't want to. Even the Left-Behind seemed overwhelmed by what it saw. It stared out the window, dumbfounded. After a few moments it regained its bearings and dragged Jack off to the elevator, shaking the whole way. It pulled Jack inside, looking much less confident than it had moments ago. It hit the button for the roof deck.

Throughout the elevator ride, Jack remained disconnected from his powers. The elevator was rising. He needed to do something fast, but his mind was elsewhere, stuck on Jazen, and then on something the Left-Behind had said to him. There was something that didn't fit.

The Left-Behind had said that Jazen had told the Rüstov about Jack. It had said they didn't know about him or his infection until after they had hacked Jazen's systems. But Jazen hadn't known about Jack's infection until the Hall of Records. It didn't make any sense. *Someone* had known about Jack before then. The Rüstov had to have known, because they had come after him at St. Barnaby's! If this Rüstov didn't know about the one who came after him back at the orphanage . . . well, who did?

The elevator doors opened and Jack saw Smart's corporate HyperJet. Still blocked from his powers, Jack had no way of stopping the Left-Behind from forcing him into the ship and blasting out of there. The Rüstov dragged him out onto the roof.

The sloping spire of the tower peak curved up into the sky. It was still dark when Jack and the Left-Behind arrived on the roof, not yet morning. The flash of light that broke across the horizon was not the rising sun, but a laser blast that connected directly with the Rüstov's head, vaporizing it instantly. The Left-Behind dropped to its knees and fell forward, dead.

Jack looked up in the direction the blast had come from. There on the roof, hovering in the sky across from Jack, was the very Rüstov he was just wondering about. The one from the orphanage.

Revile the Undying.

CHAPTER 16

Deadly Reunion

Jack looked down at the Left-Behind's body. Sparks shot out of the spot where its head had been. The shiny new leg it had stolen from Cyberai twitched with lifeless spasms. The rest of it was completely still. It was dead, but Jack was not relieved at all. His situation had gone from worse to apocalyptic.

Revile slowly lowered himself to the roof. He touched down across from Jack, not ten feet away, and walked toward him with the slow, deliberate approach of the grim reaper. Jack was still exceedingly aware that his powers were not working. He didn't try to run.

"You're Revile," Jack said as the end drew nearer, step by step.

Revile nodded.

Jack got a strange satisfaction out of being right about that. No one had believed him about it, but he was right. He knew that it was Revile who had tried to kill him back in the marshlands outside the orphanage. Now he was back to finish the job. "You're here to kill me, aren't you?" Jack asked.

"Yes."

Jack gave a resigned sigh. Sometimes it really stunk to be right.

"I thought the Rüstov wanted me alive," he said. "For the Magus."

"That . . . is why you must die," Revile said, "so that I will never live." Jack cocked his head slightly. *So that he will never what?* Revile reached up to his faceplate, gripping it behind the jaw line on each side. Short bursts of air escaped as he depressurized his mask. Revile removed the faceplate and Jack finally had the answer to the question that had been gnawing at him in the elevator.

Behind Revile's mask, Jack saw his own face staring back at him. The skin was pale, nearly gray, and a black mark ran all the way around his right eye. Another line started at the inside corner of Revile's eye and ran down his cheek. It was Jack's own mirror image. The face was just a few years older, and the resemblance was uncanny. Despite Revile's adult size and imposing figure, his true face was that of a teenager, and there was no denying it was Jack's.

"Now do you understand?" Revile asked. His voice without the mask was normal. Human.

Jack shivered at the implications of what he was seeing. "You're . . . me?" Jack said.

Revile nodded. "And you are me," he said.

Revile let the words hang in the air. Jack didn't need convincing. The truth was written all over the nearly identical face that stared back at him from across the roof.

Jack and Revile looked at each other for a moment without saying a word. They studied each other's differences, knowing they were the same person. One was the other's tomorrow, and the other was the one's yesterday.

One was a six-foot patchwork collection of scrap metal in the shape of a person, and the other was an innocent twelve-year-old boy.

"So long ago," Revile said to Jack. He looked so sad. "This is where it began," he said, motioning to the empty roof. "Here. This moment. This is the place in time where you died and I was born."

"That's why they tried to take me?" Jack asked. "To turn me into you?"

"That's why they *took* me," Revile said, his voice cracking a bit when trying to talk about Jack. "There," he said, pointing to the getaway ship. "The Left-Behind. That ship." He shook his head. "I couldn't stop it."

"This doesn't make any sense," Jack said. "You were there at the invasion. I was just a baby then. How can I be you?"

"I was present at the invasion with the same mission I have today—to end this," Revile said. He twitched as if unable to completely control himself. "To end *us*," he repeated clearly. "Listen to me now. You have a right to know why.

"Everything the Left-Behind told you was true. The

Rüstov *do* win the war. They win because of you, because of us. Because of our ability to resist infection. Our powers made us the perfect specimen for a Rüstov supersoldier experiment, a host body that would never burn out. When I was twelve years old, as you are now, that Left-Behind took me to Rüst, the Rüstov throneworld. There they turned me into what I was destined to become: Revile, the unstoppable regenerating warrior of the Rüstov. Just as you are in control of the parasite now, when I became Revile, the parasite finally took me over. You may think me just a few years older than you, but it is only because the Rüstov's regenerative technology has stopped my aging. I am much older than I appear. I have killed thousands. I have ruined worlds, wiped out alien races, and subjugated entire planets. Earth was but the first."

Jack couldn't believe what he was hearing.

"It took years, but I eventually broke free of the Rüstov, just as Jazen did. But by then it was too late. There was so much blood on my hands . . . I could no longer stand it. There was only one way to make things right. You remember, Smart told us he believed time travel to be possible. That if someone were to dive through the hole he cut in reality for his TimeScope to look through, they could do more than see through time. They could physically travel through it. Smart had no proof that his theory was right, but I . . . I was willing to take the chance. And it worked. I went back to the Battle of Empire City. It was too late to save myself, but it wasn't too late to save the world from me."

"You came back to kill yourself?" Jack asked.

"My plan was to kill the infant version of myself during the chaos of the invasion," the future Jack said. "I was blown apart, I don't know how many times, but I did not waver. I was sure no one would be able to stand up to me, but Legend . . . Legend did. He and Stendeval, they separated me from the baby. From you. My target was hidden from me, somewhere in Empire City. My only chance to make sure I completed my mission was to annihilate the entire city. The Omega Protocol. That's when Legend flew me into the mothership's engine."

"The Legendary Sacrifice," Jack said.

"The sacrifice I intended was just as noble," Revile said. "I was trying to save everyone. They didn't understand. It took me years to regenerate after that, but as always, I lived, festering in the grave on Wrekzaw Isle. I survived in the barest informational form—little more than a program running through the dead circuits of the mothership's wreck. I couldn't sense your presence anywhere in the Imagine Nation . . . I lost track of you, and I was foolish enough to hope. For twelve years I laid dormant on Wrekzaw Isle. Then one day it was like a veil was lifted. I saw you. I felt your power, our power, glowing half a world away. I knew then my mission was not yet complete."

"When I was at St. Barnaby's," Jack said. "That's when you came to kill me. When I blew you up."

"You thought you defeated me." Revile shook his head. "After you caused that explosion, I hid. I was going to kill you there in the swamp, but . . . I couldn't do it. It wasn't like dealing with the baby. Looking at your eyes, I saw the boy I was. I hesitated. I decided to wait. To give you a chance. That chance has led us here. I hoped that if I killed the Left-Behind who abducted us, I could finish this without spilling any more innocent blood. But I have failed again. If it had worked, I would have vanished from the timestream. Obviously, I am still here. The Rüstov will not be denied. Eventually, they

will take you. It has to end. We have to end it here."
Revile put his mask back on, hiding away the last vestige
of his humanity.

"I'm sorry," he said. "For both of us."

"Wait!" Jack said as Revile started pressurizing his
mask. "You don't have to do this. We can work together!
Can't we? Maybe now that I know about this, there's
something we can do!"

Revile sealed his mask and primed his wrist cannons.

"You can't escape it," he said. "If you could, I would
not be here. Understand this, Jack . . . It has already happened. You are already me. I am still you. Powerful forces
conspire against you. There is no escape. You cannot fight
the future."

Jack heard Revile's wrist cannon power up with a whirr.

"It will be a hero's death—a death we can be proud
of," Revile said, raising his arm to Jack's face. The wrist
cannon was fully charged and inches from Jack's nose.
There was nowhere to run. Jack braced himself for the
inevitable. Twelve years ago, Legend had stopped Revile
from completing his mission, but right there on the roof,
there was no one left but Jack.

CHAPTER

17

Superfight

A plasma blast fired out into the early-morning quiet. It came not from Revile's wrist cannon but blazing across the sky, originating behind the SmartTower spire. It blindsided Revile and sent him sliding back across the roof. Before Jack even knew what was happening, a dozen more blasts pounded Revile, driving him right up to the roof's edge and then skidding over the side. Jack looked up. In the predawn light he saw the rapidly approaching Peacemakers side by side with the Inner Circle.

The rescue team landed on the roof next to Jack. The

Peacemakers were made up of Surge, Battlecry, Harrier, Flex, and Stormfront, all of the members of the Peacemaker alpha squad except Speedrazor. The Inner Circle was represented by Stendeval, Prime, Virtua, Chi, and Hovarth, all of the Circlemen except Smart. They swooped in over the tower roof next to Jack. The fliers hovered in place under their own power, and the others jumped down to the roof from AirSpeeders and AirSkimmers.

"Where did you come from?" Jack asked. "How did you know I was here?"

"Emissary Knight sent out a distress signal," Prime replied. "The Peacemakers picked it up. He said the Rüstov were attacking SmartTower."

"His transmission cut off midsentence," Surge said to Jack. "It sounded like there was a crash of some kind. Is he here?"

Jack shook his head gravely. "No," he said. He knew full well what that crash had to be.

"Peacemakers, detain the boy," Surge ordered. "He may be a part of this. Go inside and find Circleman Smart."

The Peacemakers that were closest to Jack took a step toward him, but Hovarth blocked their way, placing his giant battle-ax out in their path. "Hold," he said. He wasn't looking at them. He was looking up.

"Hovarth is correct," Stendeval added, looking up as well. "It would appear that our combined forces have more pressing matters to attend to."

Surge gasped when he saw what the others were looking at. Battlecry squinted in disbelief at the rusty metal figure rising up over the edge of the tower roof. There was a glowing red circle in the center of his chest. "Is that who I think it is?"

Chi nodded. "Revile."

"That can't be," Harrier said, extending her wings and backing up a few feet into the sky. "It can't . . . Revile's dead."

"You are free to tell him that," Stendeval said calmly. "Jack did warn us otherwise." Revile stared the group down from across the roof. Mainly, he stared at Jack. He didn't try to reason with the Inner Circle and explain the righteousness of his cause. He didn't try to justify what he felt was his right, perhaps even his duty, to do. Revile said absolutely nothing, but to Jack, his intentions could not be more clear. All the heroes in Empire City would not be enough to deter Revile. There would be no escape for Jack this time. Revile's metal frame was riddled with holes from Prime's plasma blasts, Surge's energy attacks, Battlecry's sonic booms, and Harrier's explosive shells. They all should have been lethal wounds, but Jack and the others watched as Revile's circuits grew out and wove together, filling in the gaps and making him whole again. Harrier was wrong about Revile. The fact was, he just didn't know how to die.

"I think we have to teach this one the error of his ways," Hovarth said. "The dead should stay dead."

Surge searched for his voice, but nothing came. His unit had been created to fight the Rüstov, but he never imagined he would face Revile. This was more than he and his men bargained for. "We have to work together," Chi told everyone. The Peacemakers all mumbled out distracted responses in the affirmative.

"Get behind us, Jack," Virtua said as the Inner Circle took defensive positions around him. Jack did as he was told, feeling pangs of guilt for the Inner Circle, and even the Peacemakers, as they prepared to put themselves in harm's way. They didn't know it, but they were protecting him from himself. Jack wondered what they would do if they knew the truth about him. Would they still protect him? Jack wasn't even sure if protecting him was the right thing to do. Not after what he had just found out about his future. Jack's entire life, all he ever wanted was to know who he really was. Now he knew. He had learned more about himself than he ever thought possible, and oh, how he wished he could unlearn all of it.

Revile flexed ominously in the sky, fully prepared for battle. Jack looked around, trying to spot Smart's nullifiers. Maybe if he could disable them, he'd be able to do something. Unfortunately, he had no idea what the nullifiers looked like. He was totally powerless.

Surge found his voice. "Peacemakers, ready," he said. The Peacemakers held their position as Surge looked to Stendeval. Stendeval, in turn, looked to Prime. They would move on his word. Stendeval may have been the most powerful member of the Inner Circle, but Jack realized that, because it was still several minutes before the dawn, Stendeval's daily power bank was at its lowest level and would not be recharged until the sun again rose over the Imagine Nation. He'd have to use any power he had left sparingly until after sunrise, assuming they lived that long. Prime steeled himself and raised fists that glowed with power. He was more than ready for this fight. "For Valor," he said to himself quietly, then shouted out the call to arms:

"CIRCLEMEN, STRIKE!"

Superfights were common occurrences in Empire City, but this was no minor skirmish between random super powers. This was Revile. This was the Inner Circle and SmartCorp's toughest Peacemakers. The combined super-human firepower of everyone involved in this fight was enough to bring Mount Nevertop crashing to the ground.

Jack watched as Prime unleashed wave after wave of devastating plasma blasts. He saw biokinetic energy pour out of Surge's hands, eyes, and mouth as he unloaded his power cells in a blinding display of lethal force. Chi harnessed the sum total of his being into blue fireballs that he pushed through outstretched palms at Revile. Some of the attacks connected with Revile, but most areas damaged by the shots regenerated quickly. As for the rest of the offensive, Revile was fast enough to dodge it. He was incredibly quick and agile for something so big and clunky. He had the advantage of flight over the majority of combatants, and he knew how to use it. As they opened fire on him, he immediately launched an aerial counter-attack, flying over the roof and strafing the heroes with rapid-fire pulse blasts. His wrist cannons opened up again and again as the plasma blasts came out, closing up tightly in between each shot. Stendeval spent some of his precious energy casting a protective shell over Jack.

Battlecry was shouting out sound waves with all the air in his lungs when Revile scored a direct hit on his regulating apparatus. His sonics went from tightly focused bursts to all-encompassing shockwaves that took out the AirSkimmers, broke every window for miles, and brought everyone on the roof to their knees. Pressing his advantage, Revile dive-bombed into the center of the roof as his enemies struggled to find their footing. He hit with such impact that Jack flew into the air, landing a few feet away from the protective enclosure of the Circlemen. Between that and the sonic boom, Jack felt like he had gotten run over by a rhino. With the Circlemen and Peacemakers down for the moment, Revile again went after Jack.

Hovarth was the first hero to rise. He threw his battle-ax and wildly missed Revile. Then, as Revile grabbed Jack, the ax's arc curved like a boomerang and spun back to return to Hovarth. The ax cleaved Revile's left arm from his body at the shoulder. Continuing on its path, the ax spun back into Hovarth's hand and he caught it by the handle. Revile screamed a horrible curse in the Rüstov tongue. The ax had taken off a sizable portion of his torso, but he still managed to throw Jack off the roof with his one good arm.

Jack screamed, flailing helplessly in the air. Prime became a blue and silver blur and shot into the air after him. Hovarth thundered toward Revile. The giant warrior king of Varagog hit the undying Rüstov soldier like a freight train, knocking him to the ground. He pulled his knife from his belt and stabbed down on the red circle in Revile's chest. The knife shattered without so much as scratching its target, and the damage that Hovarth had been able to inflict with his ax was rapidly being undone as Revile's severed arm reattached itself to his body. As Hovarth held Revile down, the arm clawed its way over to the broken AirSkimmer and started using its pieces to rebuild itself. Soon the arm was reformed and returned to Revile with one important difference. While regenerating the appendage, Revile had opted to transform it into a fusion cannon. He pointed it at Hovarth's chest and fired.

Hovarth was blasted directly back into Flex, who grew three times his size to absorb the impact but still went crashing back into the SmartTower spire with Hovarth. Together the huge men cracked the spire at its base.

Prime flew back to the roof with Jack in his arms. He slowed down just enough to drop him off with Virtua before tackling Revile up into the sky. Harrier, the other superpowered flier, circled Prime and Revile as they struggled back and forth, trading blows in the air. Harrier's bionic eyes allowed her to take clean shots at Revile with all the guns in her arsenal. With her cybernetically enhanced marksmanship, there was no need to worry about accidentally hitting Prime. Unfortunately, her bullets had no effect on Revile.

Surge shouted into his radio, calling for the Peacemaker beta team, the Peacemaker gamma team, and anyone he could raise. "We need reinforcements!" he hollered. "Repeat, we are under heavy fire at SmartTower! All available Peacemaker teams report in immediately!"

Virtua was way ahead of him. She had called for reinforcements the second the fight had started, reaching out through cyberspace for the Valorian garrison in Galaxis, Chi's dojo in Karateka, and her own data center in Machina. Jack had watched her send info-light data packets out into the city, hologram distress calls that would seek out any able-bodied hero willing to stand and fight. Jack could only hope that any help they found would get there in time to make a difference. Across the roof, Chi helped Hovarth and Flex get up. "Revile is not shooting to kill," Virtua said.

"No, not at us," Stendeval replied, waving off several more plasma blasts that would have killed Jack instantly. Revile snapped off potshots at Jack every single time he could get clear of his attackers, even if it was only for a second. With Revile's intentions clear, Stendeval acted quickly. He raised his hands, and red energy particles began to spiral out in the air. When the particles finished swirling, Blue, Allegra, and Skerren were all standing there on the roof. Blue paused for just a moment before joining in on the fight, and Skerren even less than that. Allegra ran to Jack.

In the middle of all the chaos, Jack watched the roof-deck elevator open, revealing an injured Jonas Smart. Jack saw Smart's eyes flash open at the sight of Revile and the superfight in progress on his roof.

The battle was going badly for the heroes. Reinforcements began to arrive in good measure, but Revile took them on one and all. Platoons of Valorian Guards, legions of ninjas, and random heroes from across the city—like Laser Girl, Midknight, Discman, and more—did what they could, but it was like shoveling sand against the tide. Revile cut them down like a woodsman clearing a forest. Attacking en masse, the heroes bravely returned fire, but every time they knocked Revile down, he got back up. They couldn't say the same.

Revile activated a sonic disrupter that scrambled Virtua's holo projection, and fired a concussion blast that knocked out Stendeval, canceling Jack's strongest protector out of the equation. Smart looked across the roof and locked eyes with Jack. From the look on his face, Jack could see he was assuming the worst. No surprises there. Smart pulled out his gun and staggered toward Jack, doing his best to dodge flying bullets, reeling supers, and even wild lightning that Stormfront had called down into the fray. Revile threw a Valorian Guardsman into Stormfront, and a stray thunderbolt slapped Smart across the roof with a force that rattled his teeth. Ninjas swarmed Revile next, riddling him with Chinese stars and deftly turning his plasma blasts back at him with carefully angled ricochets off their katana blades.

In the far corner of all this mayhem, Blue covered Jack and said they had to get him out of there. Allegra wanted to know what this was all about. "What's happening? Jack, are you all right?" she asked. In light of what Jack had just learned about his future, he didn't even know how to begin answering her. Whatever the case, it was plain to see that he and "all right" weren't even in the same zip code.

Smart found a safe spot behind some broken equipment on the roof. He propped himself up against the wreckage, struggling for every inch. He had lost his gun when he got hit by Stormfront's lightning, but a more strategic weapon was standing just a few feet away.

"Skerren, it's him!" Smart shouted. "It's Jack! He brought the Rüstov here! He brought Revile!"

Smart's accusations hit Jack like icicles stabbing his body. Smart was more right than he knew. Skerren looked back and forth between Jack and Smart, then fixed his eyes on Jack. Skerren's expression hardened.

"No!" Jack stammered. "Skerren, you don't understand!"

"It's the parasite inside him!" Smart railed. "It's finally taken him over! You have to stop him, Skerren. You know what has to be done!"

Meanwhile, Revile was getting blasted to bits by the Valorian Guard and regenerating as fast as he could. The Guardsmen were keeping him at bay, but even in several pieces, Revile was still a clever and dangerous foe. He rebuilt himself using materials from the already damaged SmartTower spire. Once Revile had taken enough steel from its base, the spire first creaked, then cracked. Thirty tons of iron and glass crashed down, headed straight for Jack.

"Look out!" Blue shouted, and rushed in to brace the broken spire. Flex and Hovarth joined in before it crushed him. In the shadow of the spire, Smart was still yelling that this was all because of Jack.

"It's true, isn't it?" Skerren said, approaching Jack. "He's here because of you?"

"No," Jack said, backing away. But as he looked at the

violence all around him, he had to admit that one way or another, he really was at the root of it all. "Well, yes." He nodded. "He is, but—"

Skerren reached for his swords but hesitated for a moment.

"Kill him, Skerren!" Smart raged from across the roof. "You have to kill him now!"

Skerren closed his eyes and swung his swords down at Jack as hard as he could. Jack had no defense. Maybe it was better this way, he thought. Maybe Revile was right. If he died here, then Revile would never come to be. Jack braced himself for a blow that never came.

Skerren's blades were stopped cold by something they couldn't cut, something that couldn't be broken. Jack watched as Skerren's swords rebounded off the silvery barrier of Allegra's stretched form. Skerren met his match in the form of a fearless Valorian girl, and his blades went flying across the roof. Skerren shook his arms in pain. "You!" he said, opening his eyes. He looked stunned. To tell the truth, so did Allegra. There it was, the hallmark of every true Valorian: unbridled, unflinching courage. All it took to bring it out was a friend in need.

Blue reached out with his one free hand and grabbed Skerren off the ground. Skerren struggled and shouted, but he wasn't breaking Blue's grip, and he certainly wasn't getting at his swords. Meanwhile, Revile unloaded another round of plasma blasts at Jack.

"You have to get out of here!" Allegra shouted to Jack.

Revile fired his fusion cannon again, knocking Flex into Skerren and Blue, taking them both out and leaving Hovarth to hold the spire by himself. More Peacemakers were arriving, but instead of helping Hovarth with the spire, they attended to Smart, who was still reeling from superelectric shocks. Smart waved the Peacemakers off and told them to go get Jack, claiming he was the one behind all this. Through all of it, Jack just stood there in a daze.

"Jack, snap out of it!" Allegra yelled at him. "They're after you! You have to go!"

"Go where?" Jack said. "He'll just follow me!" Jack knew he couldn't get away from Revile, no matter what he did. Besides, Revile was fighting every hero in Empire City and winning. If Jack wasn't safe from him with every hero in the city, he wouldn't be safe anywhere. Unless . . .

There was a chance. Jack saw it floating past the edge of the island. It was a slim chance. Maybe his only chance, but there *was* something he could do. Jack's survival instincts kicked back in, and he looked around the roof deck until he spotted Smart's HyperJet. The ship was a thing of beauty. Its design was simplicity itself, one smooth and flowing piece of metal. It's long, sleek frame flattened out and narrowed into a needle-sharp point at the ship's nose. Its shiny steel exterior was pristine, reflecting the battle all around on its hull better than any mirror could ever hope to. It looked like a sword with wings. From the second Jack had laid eyes on it, he could tell it was built for speed.

Jack looked up at Allegra and the advancing Peacemaker troops. It was going to be close, and even if everything went exactly right, he couldn't be sure this plan was going to work. But he was going to find out. This wasn't over yet.

"GO!" Allegra screamed again, placing herself between the Peacemakers and Jack. Jack ran. Revile saw him break for the ship. He fired relentlessly at Jack, which, combined with Allegra's running interference, held the Peacemakers back long enough for him to get inside. He jumped into the captain's chair and buckled in. Looking around the cabin, Jack saw that the ship's interior was every bit as smooth as its exterior. The dashboard in front of him was a flat silver surface without a single button or switch to speak of.

"Activate tangital control panel?" Jack guessed.

Lights started flickering rapidly in the cockpit as Hard-Light Holo flight controls materialized all around Jack. Suddenly, he had at his fingertips more meters, gauges, buttons, and switches than he could ever hope to operate or understand. He looked down at the throttle. He was going to have to get this thing off the ground the same way any completely untrained pilot would. By trial and error.

Looking through the windshield, Jack saw Hovarth holding the thirty-ton tower spire by himself. Hovarth somehow got leverage on the spire and threw it with all his might. It coursed through the air like a javelin, all the way past the city limits, and out into the sea. My turn, Jack told himself. He could do this. He didn't need his powers. He knew things; he'd studied hard. He started flipping switches until he got the power on, then gently pulled back on the throttle to bring the HyperJet up into the air. It rose up slowly in vertical lift-off mode. Jack was a little out of control, but he was airborne. He got rocked around the sky by clueless Peacemakers before Revile started picking them off with plasma blasts that were meant for him. Revile was being kept busy by the other heroes, getting swamped by attacks from every angle. For a second, Jack thought the supers might be able to buy him enough time to pull this stunt off, but Revile hit the red circle on his chest and a full-force laser blast poured out from its center, hammering his enemies with a powerful ray beam.

When the blast was over, every hero had fallen down. Revile drifted in the air for a moment, looking woozy. He was about to take off toward Jack when Stendeval raised a weary fist in the air and used what must have been the last drops of power for the day. He reduced Revile's body into several thousand metal pieces, none of them bigger than a marble. For the first time since the battle had begun, there was quiet.

As Revile went to work on reassembling himself, Jack

frantically searched the cabin of the ship for the main thrusters. As soon as he found them, he slammed down on the accelerator and punched the engine. With a roar his ship took off in a wild and untamed path, zigging and zagging through the sky toward Wrekzaw Isle. Seconds later, he crashed directly into it.

CHAPTER

18

The Last Stand

In all his life, Jack had never been so happy that he remembered to buckle up for safety. They say any landing you can walk away from is a good one, but Jack didn't walk away from this one—he ran. He sprinted away from his broken ship as fast as he could. For one thing, he was afraid it was going to blow up like things always did in the comic books and movies, and for another, the crash site would be the first place Revile would look for him. Jack knew he'd have to face Revile eventually, but his plan had very specific parameters about where he was going to do it. He had one chance on this island, and it was only in one place. Jack had to do this thing perfectly if it was going to work at all.

As he ran across the uneven terrain of junk that was Wrekzaw Isle, Jack felt his powers flooding back into his body. Thank goodness, he thought. The farther away he got from SmartTower and its nullifiers, the more he started to feel like himself again. It was amazing. In such a short time, Jack had gotten so used to his powers that when they had been taken away, he had felt like he was lost in the dark. He managed to live through the super-fight without them, but not without a lot of help. Now he was on his own, but with his powers coming back, he was feeling better about it. He was feeling like his plan might have a shot after all.

It was such a different sensation being on Wrekzaw Isle now as opposed to the first time he was there. Now he could hear everything on the island. Pieces of machinery that still worked were alive with energy that he could feel. Rüstov Left-Behinds that had tunneled into the landscape were crawling out to the surface. Jack could hear a local Rüstov hive buzzing with chatter about the crash and about him, and there were no Circlemen to clear the area before he landed this time.

Arms reached out of shrapnel heaps and grabbed at him. Faces opened up in the ground beneath his feet and called out his location to the others. Jack kept running from them. He ran for the place where he had spent the night the last time he was here. The mothership's engine. Revile's grave. When Jack finally got there, he found the place had a terrible new significance for him. This place didn't just belong to Revile. It was his now too.

"My former, future grave," Jack said to himself as he looked at the engine. He shook his head. It was a scary thought, and one that was better left alone. He had to focus. He needed to get ready. This was going to take at least a few minutes to do, and it was likely that was all the time he had. He talked to the machines in the area and found what was still working and what was willing to help. He got lucky with a few hydraulic lifts and some loading-bay docking arms that were nearby and functional. Among other things, he had them start spreading some of the area's debris around the site. He was setting the stage. He had to get this place ready before it was time to face the final curtain.

Once everything was prepared, Jack sat down and relaxed for a minute. He was surprised to find himself so steady and calm. Maybe it was because he knew the storm was coming, no matter what, and there was no sense in worrying about it now. He'd already done everything he could to prepare.

It wasn't long before Revile came soaring over the island's orange terrain of rusted metal, red rock shrapnel, and dust. He landed in the clearing near Jack, who stood out in the open with his hands held high.

Revile approached Jack fully aware that Jack's powers were no longer being blocked, but without any fear. That much was clear to Jack. Revile knew the extent of Jack's abilities. Of course he did. Jack's very high power level probably registered on Revile's scanners, but that wouldn't worry him. Revile was a machine, yet he knew his systems were too complex for Jack to understand and take control of. He looked around for any reinforcements that might be coming.

"If you're waiting for help to arrive and ambush me, it isn't going to happen," Revile said. "I have the entire area scanned."

"That's fine," Jack told Revile quite truthfully. "I'm not expecting anyone. This is just between us."

Revile agreed. "That is how it should have been from the start," he said. "The fight at SmartTower was regrettable. It's time to finish this."

"You don't have to do this," Jack said in the toughest voice he could muster. "Think about it," Jack said. "We can change things. We're changing things right now, can't you see that? We can make sure I never become you."

Revile looked at Jack sideways. He almost laughed. "That's entirely the point. My only reason for being is to ensure that I never will be," he said. "I thought you understood that."

Jack shook his head. "You don't have to kill me to make that happen. This . . . right here and now . . . this never happened to you. Things are already different. You changed the past. We changed the past!"

"But we haven't changed the future," Revile said. "Otherwise, I would not still be here. The simple fact that I exist means the Rüstov will eventually claim you. It is only a matter of time."

"We could work together," Jack said. "Together we could

stop it. You have to admit there's a chance. Isn't there?"

"There is," Revile said as he primed his wrist cannons. "Me."

Jack's heart sank.

"I take no pleasure in this," Revile told Jack. "I take no pleasure in anything. Thank me, Jack Blank. I do this now so that you will not have to one day stand in my place and do it yourself. I gave you a chance. You know that I did. I tried everything I could."

Jack nodded. "So did I," he said, sullen. He'd hoped that there was enough of him still left in Revile to get through to, that there was some measure of humanity left to appeal to. Now he could see there was not. Revile was completely lost. *He* was completely lost. Jack could understand Revile's reasoning. He just couldn't accept it. Revile raised his plasma cannons to fire on Jack. As the Rüstov supersoldier prepared to open fire, Jack told him that he was sorry.

Revile fired, intending to unload two full clips of plasma ammo into Jack. Instead of firing, however, both of Revile's arms blew apart as the very deadly and extremely unstable plasma backfired in each mounted cannon. Explosions erupted at Revile's extremities and ratcheted all the way up to his shoulders, blowing them to pieces. Sparks and flames flew as both limbs disappeared like a string of fire-crackers being torn apart. Revile's gun barrels had been jammed . . . by Jack.

Revile screamed out a cry that came as much from shock as it did from pain. When he was through, he took stock of his devastated torso and stared at Jack with his mouth agape. He found himself in the very unique position of having underestimated himself.

"I don't take any pleasure in this either," Jack said.

"How?" Revile asked. "How did you . . ."

"Sometimes you have to think small to think big," Jack said, recalling Stendeval's words of advice. "I didn't know enough about plasma blasts to stop your guns from shooting, but I know enough to close the lid on a gun barrel. You probably should have thought of that one. We learned that kind of control back in our first lesson with Stendeval."

"You're only delaying the inevitable," Revile said.

"Yeah, about that . . . ," Jack said to Revile. He wasn't finished yet. He spoke to the loading-bay docking system, and huge grappling hooks sprang to life from the scrap heap and clamped down on Revile. He writhed, helpless in their grasp. They would be able to hold Revile only until his arms rebuilt themselves, but that was all the time Jack would need. By the time that happened, the Infinite Warp Core engine would be ready to fire.

As if on cue, the ground began to rumble. Scrap metal, garbage, and the other debris that Jack had used to cover up the crater in the center of the clearing started to rattle and shake itself loose. The tremors revealed the main thruster shaft of the Rüstov mothership engine.

"The last time I was here, I used the machines on this island to fight the Rüstov," Jack said. "But I forgot that this whole island is a machine . . . a spaceship. I guess sometimes it helps to think big, too." Jack shrugged. "I've been talking to that engine since I crashed. I just asked it to help me. You know it thinks I'm Rüstov royalty?"

Revile roared at Jack, struggling against the clamps that gripped him. His arms were only about 40 percent complete. That wasn't going to be enough.

"I gave you a chance," Jack said. "I really hoped I wouldn't have to do this."

"What you are doing is dooming this Earth to me! To you! This will not end here," Revile said to Jack. "I am the future. I am tomorrow! This is not over!"

Jack shielded his eyes as the engine's hum built up in the background. "It is for today."

The island lurched as the engine fired. The sky went white as the brightest and hottest flames Jack ever saw poured out of the crater. The ground shifted beneath Jack's feet, propelled by the massive warp engine. He fell backward and rolled down the ridge. When he got up, he saw that once again, Revile was being consumed by the only flames hot enough to destroy him. Jack's future self was dying before his very eyes. The fires melted the docking arms around Revile instantly. Revile was melting a little bit slower than that, but he wasn't growing back.

"This is not over!" Revile shouted again, now in real pain. "They will never stop coming after you, Jack. Even these fires will not stop me forever! I will rebuild, I will return, I will . . ."

The last echoes of Revile's tirade melted away like a dying computer crashing, and then there was nothing left. Nothing but the roar of nuclear flames on a desolate rock in the middle of the sea.

Jack asked the engine to lower the flames to a slow burn. He was afraid to shut them off all the way, but he couldn't let them keep pushing Wrekzaw Isle around like this. Too much more would have shaken the island apart. The flames died down like a stovetop flame turning from high heat down to simmer. Jack double-checked with the shipwrecked systems, and the engine confirmed that the island would stabilize at this level of output. At minimum power Wrekzaw Isle wasn't going anywhere except in a slow orbit around the Imagine Nation.

Jack stared at the low flames deep inside the island's thrusters, at the spot where he, the hopelessly infected Rüstov spawn, had just killed Revile. Where he had just killed himself. It was quiet. It was over. And it was also just beginning.

Jack fell to his knees, turning over what had just happened in his head. It was a lot to deal with. Maybe too much for a twelve-year-old boy. Jack should have felt relieved, but instead he felt worse. The doubts he had pushed away during the battle came flooding back. Jack told himself that he hadn't had a choice. It was either him or Revile. Him now or him from the future.

Jack had given Revile a chance, but he hadn't taken it. Jack had done what he'd had to do. So, what did that mean? He had done what he'd had to do to survive, but again, he wasn't so sure he had done the right thing. Suddenly, he was wondering if he really had just damned himself to a future as Revile that would one day end right back here in this spot. Years from now, would he travel back in time, only to end up at this island on the receiving end of those flames?

As Jack pondered these questions, he found he wasn't alone. The sun was up, and red energy particles were swirling in the air around him. One of them drifted past Jack's face and faded away. He looked up and saw that the Inner Circle, and all of the other heroes from SmartTower who could still stand, had gathered on the scrap-metal ridge over Revile's grave. Stendeval floated in the center of the group. They were staring at Jack, completely speechless. Jonas Smart looked especially flabbergasted.

Jack stared back at them, his face drained of expression. They'd seen him with Revile. They'd seen him kill

Revile. But how long had they been there? How much had they heard?

Skerren jumped down from the ridge and walked toward Jack, sword in hand. Jack backed away from him and stumbled to the ground. Skerren approached briskly and stopped a few feet away from Jack. None of the others made any effort to stop him. Not even Allegra. Not this time. That sealed it, Jack thought. They had seen everything.

Skerren looked over at the slow burn of Revile's grave and then back to Jack. "It's over," he said. Skerren sheathed his blade and knelt down next to Jack. He didn't say anything. He reached out, put his arms around Jack, and helped him to his feet. "Come on, brother," Skerren said. "Let's go home."

CHAPTER

19

The Future Is Now

After using his powers to heal all the heroes' battle wounds, Stendeval flew everyone back to Empire City. He probably could have teleported everyone back just as easily, but if he had, Jack would have missed something that was a completely new experience for him, something much better than flying.

As Jack and the others passed over the six boroughs of the city, they found the entire city awake and cheering. He and the heroes were greeted by jubilant crowds out on their rooftops, down in the streets, and up in the skies.

The crowds cheered for all the heroes who had dared to fight Revile, but mostly they cheered for Jack, the one who had saved the day.

Jack was about to ask someone if they were really cheering for him when he saw the floating NewsNets telling his story in the sky all around him. Apparently, Stendeval and the others weren't the only ones who had followed Jack to Wrekzaw Isle. This time around, the SmartCams had made the trip as well. They had arrived at the same time the heroes had, and had sent high-definition images of Jack's deeds back to everyone in Empire City. As far as the Imagine Nation was concerned, Jack was officially a hero.

That was all very nice, and Jack appreciated the sentiment, but despite the cheers and congratulations, he didn't feel like much of a hero. In truth, he felt depressed and a little scared about what might be coming next. The future that Revile warned him about was horrifying, and nobody in Empire City realized that they were cheering Jack for defeating the worst villain ever . . . himself. What if Revile was right? What if it wasn't over? From the first day Jack had shown up in Empire City, people had worried that he was a Rüstov agent, and Jack had sworn up and down that it wasn't true. Now that the people had finally come around and believed he was not working for the Rüstov, he'd discovered that, in a way, he was.

The terrible guilt that Jack felt was compounded by the sight of Jazen's body as Stendeval lowered the group down at the base of SmartTower. A crowd was gathered at the scene when Jack and the others arrived. The people there moved aside to give Jack room as he marched stiffly toward the body of his best friend.

The MagLev road was dented where Jazen and the Left-Behinds had hit it. Jazen lay faceup on the ground, completely motionless with open eyes. He almost looked to Jack like he had a satisfied, proud look on his face. In the end, he had been stronger than the Rüstov. He had given everything he had to save Jack. Jack's eyes welled up at the thought of it. He knelt down beside his friend and took his hand. He reached out with his powers, trying to talk to Jazen, but there was nothing there. Jack held an empty shell.

A heavy hand came to rest on Jack's shoulder. It was Blue. Jack didn't even notice him crouching down next to him. "What happened?" Blue asked, reaching out to lay his other hand on Jazen's chest. Jack knew Blue would miss Jazen Knight every bit as much as he would.

"Jazen and I, we . . . ," Jack started to say but stopped himself. He swallowed hard, thinking about just how much he was going to share with everybody. He turned around and saw the Inner Circle, the Peacemakers, and all of Empire City hanging on his every word. SmartCams hovered over Jack, ready to broadcast his story across the city. "I thought I might be able to find out something about my past in Circleman Smart's files," Jack said. "I convinced Jazen to help me break into SmartTower, but we got caught." Jack looked up toward Jonas Smart. "The Rüstov attacked us right after that. We never saw them coming. Jazen gave his life to save me from them."

Murmurs ran through the crowd as people spoke quietly among themselves of Jazen's noble sacrifice. Virtua pressed her fingers to her lips, then reached out to lay the kiss on Jazen's forehead. With great sadness her hand continued down to close Jazen's eyes. Smart's eyes narrowed as Jack gave everyone his somewhat censored version of the events in Smart's lab.

"In the battle," Hovarth began, "why weren't you using your powers against the Rüstov?"

"I couldn't," Jack said. "Circleman Smart had power nullifiers set up in the tower. He turned them on after he caught us in his lab."

The Inner Circle turned to Smart with disapproving looks.

"And Revile?" Prime asked. "What did Revile want with you?"

"He wanted to kill me," Jack said quite honestly.

"Why?"

Jack shook his head. "I don't know," he lied.

Jack noticed that throughout his entire explanation, Stendeval had not said one word. He had merely stared down at Jack, listening quietly. Smart was about to say something, but a voice in the crowd spoke first.

"They wanted to kill him because he beat their virus!" a man in the crowd shouted out. "He's immune!"

"He's a hero!" another voice declared.

As the crowd began to once again cheer the boy who had killed Revile, Smart appeared to decide against whatever it was he was planning to say. He didn't seem happy about it either. His lips were scrunched up so tightly that he looked as if he'd just bitten into an onion. As the crowd's enthusiasm grew, people started edging in toward Jack to shake his hand and pat him on the back. He was getting overwhelmed when Stendeval stepped forward to give him some room.

"Please, all of you, this boy has had enough excitement for one morning," Stendeval said to the crowd. "But I think perhaps not enough for one *day*," he allowed. Stendeval gathered Skerren and Allegra near Jack and addressed the crowd directly. "I've seen enough from all of these children to make my decision on whether or not they belong in the School of Thought. Today the Inner Circle will settle the matter once and for all," he declared. "That is, if there are no objections," he added, deferring to his fellow Circle-men. The Inner Circle was, of course, in total agreement. Stendeval nodded. "There you have it," he told the crowd of people, as well as the people watching at home. "This day at sunset, at the sphere in Hero Square, the Inner Circle will meet to vote on the School of Thought candidates. We invite you all to attend the ceremony." The citizens of Empire City applauded, and Stendeval leaned down toward the children. "In the meantime, I suggest the three of you go home and get some rest."

Jack couldn't deny that he was completely worn-out. He exchanged hurried good-byes with Skerren and Allegra, arranging to meet up with them later. He walked across the street to the Ivory Tower, and when he reached the door, he noticed the SmartCams still following close behind him. "I don't think so," he said as he went inside. The SmartCams stopped in midair like they'd hit a wall.

Jack was almost to the elevators when Smart called out after him. "Jack," he said calmly. Jack turned around to see Smart standing alone in the Ivory Tower lobby. "A word," he said.

Jack stared at Smart from across the empty lobby. They were alone. He approached Smart cautiously. "What do you want?" he asked.

Smart studied him for a moment before speaking. "I noticed you didn't say anything to the others about your birth certificate," Smart observed, rubbing his chin slowly. "Your 'corrupted' file. Why not?"

Jack just shrugged. "It doesn't matter," he replied. "You deleted the file. We both know I can't prove anything."

Jack put his hands up. "What's the point?" he said. He started to walk off, but Smart grabbed him by the wrist.

"There's more to it than that, Jack," Smart said, his voice suddenly turning more threatening. "I was there with you when the Rüstov came through my window. Jazen Knight called them. You left that part out too."

The corner of Jack's lips turned up ever so slightly. He met Smart's gaze and didn't look away. "Now you're the one with no proof," he said, pulling his arm free. "Jazen called for *help*. He was broadcasting a distress signal. Even your Peacemakers got the call. Your machine must've got it wrong."

"My instruments don't lie," Smart said. "People do. What aren't you telling me?"

Jack thought about the Rüstov computer virus and what a threat to the Imagine Nation it represented. How there could literally be hundreds of Mechas out there who were under the Rüstov's control, innocent Mechas who didn't even know they were infected. Something definitely had to be done about it—that much was certain. But what would Smart do with that information? What would he do to Jazen's memory? To the lives of Virtua and her people?

"I don't know what you're talking about," Jack told him. He was lying and Smart knew it, but there wasn't a thing the Circleman could do about it. Jack was a hero now, and Smart didn't have a shred of proof that said otherwise.

"You thought I was the Great Collaborator, and now you know better," Smart said contemptuously. He shook his head. "*You* actually suspected *me*! The irony would be amusing if it weren't such an insult. Everything I do, I do to protect this city!"

"You don't get it," Jack said. "Making sure all these people are afraid of the Rüstov doesn't make the city stronger. It only makes *you* stronger. You've got the right idea. It's just too bad your heart's in the wrong place."

Jack turned around and started walking back toward the elevators. "I know your name, Jack," Smart called after him.

Jack stopped dead in his tracks. He didn't turn around. He didn't want to give Smart the satisfaction. He could practically hear the man's creepy grin getting wider, and that was bad enough already.

"That's right," Smart said, walking up slowly behind Jack. "You think I didn't read that file before I deleted it? I read it the day you came here, before I ever sealed it in the first place. Tell me what really happened back in my lab tonight, Jack." Smart leaned down over Jack's ear. "Tell me what happened, and I'll tell you who you are."

Jack turned around and looked Smart dead in the eye.

"I don't need to know that anymore," he said with conviction. "And I definitely don't need to hear it from you."

Jack got in the elevator and rode upstairs.

When Jack got back upstairs, he found that he couldn't bear to stay in Jazen's former apartment for very long. The place was still a wreck from when the Rüstov turned it upside-down, and everything in the loft reminded Jack of Jazen. The kitchen was the worst. Jack knew that if Jazen were still alive, he would have already been in there whipping up Flopflips, Floovberries, warp-speed milkshakes, and anything else he could think of to raise Jack's spirits. Jack's stomach growled for reassurances that he knew weren't coming, and it made him miss his friend even more. He got out of there almost as soon as he had come in.

Jack ended up spending the day walking around the city. He didn't get any rest in, but he really couldn't have slept if he had tried. His brain was too wired. He had a lot on his mind and he was having a hard time with all of it. He wound up in SeasonStill Park and circled through the seasons, just walking and thinking. For a guy whom all of Empire City was calling the greatest hero since Legend, he was having a pretty bad day. In all fairness, it wasn't every day you got your best friend killed because he went along with you on some harebrained scheme. It also wasn't every day you found out that you were going to grow up to be a mass-murdering supersoldier who would be forced to fight alongside your greatest enemies and kill everybody that you cared about. It certainly wasn't every day you had to save your own life by setting your future self on fire while he swore to come back and kill you the first chance he got.

It might have been easier if Jack could talk about the whole Revile situation with someone, but he couldn't tell anyone about it. Especially not now. People kept coming up to him in the park and telling him how amazed they were by what he'd done. They were in awe of him. They all said they were sorry for jumping to the wrong conclusions about him. What was he supposed to say? *Don't be! Turns out you were right! One day I'm going to turn into a Rüstov supersoldier and destroy the entire planet!* Obviously, Jack didn't tell them that, but just smiling politely and accepting people's praise made him feel phony. The more people congratulated Jack, the worse he felt. Every time it happened throughout the day, Jack thought that he would rather be anywhere else, even back at St. Barnaby's. No matter where he spent that day, he couldn't find peace. Nothing felt right. There just wasn't any place there for him.

When Jack arrived at Hero Square that evening, he found it even more packed and louder than it had been on Rededication Day. Once again, the crowd parted like the Red Sea as Jack approached, but this time the atmosphere was one of deference and respect rather than fear and anger. The crowd didn't quiet down this time either. It roared. Jack had no escort this time, nor would he need one. The slayer of Revile did not require such things.

Outside the sphere, Skerren, Allegra, and Blue were waiting for Jack. Blue could tell that Jack was depressed. Knowing nothing of Jack's connection to Revile, Blue naturally assumed that Jack's mood was entirely due to Jazen's death.

"I was just thinking that Jazen would have walked me here today," Jack admitted. "If he were still here, I mean. I got him killed, Blue."

"What happened to Jazen wasn't your fault," Blue told him. "That was the Rüstov's doing, not yours. And I know Jazen. If he had to do it all over again, he would do it in a heartbeat, no matter how it turned out. He was a hero, and he died making a difference. Don't forget what he told you, Jack. Making a difference is what being a hero is all about."

"Blue's right," Allegra said. "And you made the difference against Revile. You have to admit some good did come out of all this."

"Exactly," Blue said. "It looks like Jazen was right about bringing you here too. I think everyone here finally sees that," he added, motioning to the crowd. Again, Jack didn't quite agree, but he couldn't talk about the reasons why. Not here. Not with Blue or anyone else for that matter.

"It's true, Jack," Skerren said, perhaps sensing Jack's

skepticism. "I can see it now too, and I have to apologize for the way I acted toward you before. I hope . . . I hope you can understand. It was never personal."

Jack appreciated the thought, but really, it was the last thing in the world he was worried about at the moment. "I'm over it," he told Skerren. "Seriously. If I had gone through what you did, I probably would've hated the sight of me too."

Skerren looked confused.

"Hovarth told us what happened to your parents," Allegra said to him.

Skerren looked away. "Hovarth shouldn't have said anything about that."

"I'm glad he did," Jack said. "I'm sorry for what happened to you. We both are. Looks like the Rüstov turned all three of us into orphans."

"I guess so," Skerren said.

Lightening the mood a little, Allegra apologized to Skerren as well, telling him she was sorry she had had to use her powers on him and basically kick his butt. Skerren turned quickly. "You didn't *kick my butt*," he said, getting all defensive. "What are you talking about?"

"I seem to remember going all indestructible on you when you tried to kill Jack," Allegra said.

"Kill Jack? My heart wasn't in that!" Skerren protested. "That's why my blades didn't cut. Smart had me all worked up, but I knew something was wrong. I knew."

"Sure you did," Allegra said.

"I did!" Skerren said. "Let's try again if you're so *not afraid*. I bet I could cut you this time."

Allegra laughed a little at that. "I don't think so!"

Jack allowed himself to laugh a little too, despite his mood. With Allegra toughening up and Skerren loosening up, it felt like everyone was finally getting along. The way they were arguing, they almost sounded like friends.

As the sun began to set in the distance, Jack saw a platoon of Valorian Guardsmen flying in from Wrekzaw Isle. As far as everyone was concerned, Revile had been thoroughly vanquished by Jack, but prudence demanded that the Inner Circle make sure things stayed that way. Revile had been dead before. During the day, the Inner Circle dug into the burning wreckage as deeply as they safely could, but found no traces of Revile. It was decided that for safety's sake, the Infinite Warp Core engine would continue to fire in a slow, controlled burn, and a Valorian Guard post would be established on Wrekzaw Isle at Revile's grave. The Guards stationed at the mothership would be on watch twenty-four hours a day, keeping the fires burning to make sure Revile never reemerged from the flames. Blue said that Prime's men would want to debrief Jack on his encounter with Revile, and would be glad to hear anything he could tell them about the Infinite Warp Core engine. Jack said that was all fine. He just needed some time. He wasn't up to going back to Wrekzaw Isle just yet.

"What was it like?" Skerren asked Jack. "Facing Revile all by yourself?"

Jack swallowed up every feeling he could about Revile before answering. "It wasn't what I expected," he said finally. His words hung there in silence as a cold wind blew in from the ocean. An icy sea spray from the falls coated the square, spritzing everyone.

"The Imagine Nation is headed south," Blue said, shielding his face from the mist. "Looks like stormy weather ahead."

"Yeah," Jack nodded. "Yeah, I think you're right."

"We'd better go inside," Allegra said, motioning toward the sphere. "It's time."

Blue agreed and ushered the three children up the staircase below the sphere. They rose up into its base on the pedestal's floating platform and passed into the liquid metal sphere. As before, the sphere ran over Jack's skin like thick metal syrup. The children disappeared inside.

Inside, the sphere was as big and empty as it had been the first time Jack was there with Jazen. This time, the members of the Inner Circle were all there waiting when Jack and the others arrived. Jack stood in the same place as before, in the pit below their elevated round table.

The Circlemen welcomed the children into the sphere and explained what was about to take place. They would each now cast their votes for the record, officially endorsing or rejecting each child's nomination to the School of Thought. The ceremony would be followed by a great festival, an event that the people in the square were already assembled and ready for. Chi announced that it was time for the voting to begin.

"A formality," Hovarth said with a wave of his hand. "Most of us have already made our decisions known.

As for the rest," he added, eyeing Stendeval and Smart, "these children stood their ground against Revile. This boy defeated the monster himself! I should think they've more than passed our tests, no?"

"Yes, Jonas," Virtua said in a clever tone. "Before you vote, I feel obligated to remind you that voting against the boy who defeated Revile in full view of the entire city might be interpreted by some as the act of a Rüstov sympathizer. I'd hate to see you being investigated by your own Peacemakers, but if you were to cast such a vote, the people might demand it. Of course, that is just my opinion. By all means, vote your conscience."

Smart looked at Virtua like he'd just eaten two onions and then washed them down with a tall glass of turnip juice. She was enjoying the moment immensely. "Thank you, Virtua," Smart said sarcastically. "I am well aware of the city's newfound appreciation for young Jack. I assure you, I will not stand in the way of his education," he forced himself to say.

"You did say that if Jack passed all your tests and you deemed him safe, he'd have your vote," Skerren said to Smart.

"I remember," Allegra added. "I was there too."

Smart squirmed while the other Circlemen stared at him, waiting for an official, affirmative statement on Jack's status. "The boy has my vote," Smart finally said, looking away from everyone, especially Jack.

Skerren and Allegra flashed victorious smiles at Jack. He humored them with a halfhearted smile of his own. He appreciated their support, but it still felt wrong.

"In that case, I believe the only vote left in question belongs to Stendeval," Chi announced to the group. All eyes turned to Stendeval, who was sitting quietly in his chair with his hands folded before him. "Are you ready with your decision?" Chi asked him.

"I am," Stendeval said as he rose from his seat and floated down to join Skerren, Allegra, and Jack at the lower level of the sphere. "Hovarth is quite right—these children have been tested more than enough. When we first met in Cognito, I told them that I would not test them—life would. I don't think anyone here will disagree with me when I say that life decided to present them with greater a challenge than any of us ever imagined. For my part, I am now sure, more than ever, that these children are our future. I will welcome them into this school with open arms and go as far into that future with them as fate will allow. In the end, however, the decision to make that journey is theirs as much as it is mine."

Stendeval reached out his hand toward Allegra, as if presenting her to the Circle. "Allegra of Galaxis," he said, addressing his peers. "Born into bondage in a Rüstov body farm. Raised in fear on a refugee ship hiding in the shadow of the Rüstov Armada. She found, within herself, the courage that Valorians are named for. On the roof of SmartTower she called upon unshakable courage and indestructible strength. She did it to save the life of a friend. This is what heroes are made of. Allegra, I hereby grant you a seat in the School of Thought, with all the privileges and rights that honor conveys. Do you accept?"

Allegra said yes before Stendeval even finished asking the question, and then a few times more for good measure. The Circle applauded her and her skin rippled with excitement.

Stendeval moved down the line. "Skerren of Varagog . . . ," he began, "whose parents were taken from him by the Rüstov before his very eyes. That experience has driven this boy every day of his life. It has driven him to be a stronger, better fighter and the master of his unique abilities. It has also driven him away from friendship, brotherhood, and happiness. Afraid to get too close to anyone, this boy's only friend has been his anger. But this morning on the rusted plains of Wrekzaw Isle he found the compassion a hero is measured by. He learned to put aside his anger and believe in others. Skerren, I hereby grant you a seat in the School of Thought, with all the privileges and rights that honor conveys. Do you accept?"

"I do," Skerren said solemnly. "With all my heart, I accept." Stendeval shook Skerren's hand and the Circle applauded again. This time, they continued their applause as Stendeval approached the last student in line: Jack Blank of New Jersey.

"Finally . . . we come to Jack," Stendeval said as the Inner Circle settled back down into their seats. "Jack, whose life we know so little about, has been tested more than anyone here today. In the School of Thought we seek to train students to be the greatest of heroes. To create a better tomorrow. Jack has already begun this by ridding us of the worst villain of all time. We called him Revile. That was *our* name for him. We know not how the creature thought of himself. For us, *Re* was taken from his constant regeneration whenever destroyed, and *vile* from the fact that he was the most foul and base villain we ever encountered. Put together, it is a fitting name for one who will be cursed throughout history as the most ruthless killing machine ever known. It is said that Revile claimed more lives for the Rüstov Armada than any soldier who ever fought in all the years of their infinite war. Our assembled might could not put a stop to his merciless onslaught, but Jack . . . Jack did what we could not. Just imagine what he will do tomorrow."

"Here, here!" Hovarth shouted, setting off a premature smattering of applause for Jack's accomplishments. It was to be expected. Jack was the hero of the day. Still, every word Stendeval had said about Revile was like a red-hot needle poking Jack in the gut. Especially the part about what Jack would do tomorrow.

"Jack Blank, I hereby grant you a seat in the School of Thought, with all the privileges and rights that honor conveys. Do you accept?"

Jack took longer than either of the others to answer

Stendeval's question. He looked at the smiling faces of the Circlemen and those of his fellow students. For their sake, he shook his head and told Stendeval no.

"I can't," he said. "I can't do this. I don't belong here."

Without another word, Jack jumped down through the liquid-metal base of the sphere and exited the room with a hurried, melancholy retreat.

The crowd cheered Jack again when they saw him emerge from the sphere, but it was the last thing Jack wanted to hear. He took one look at the crowd and walked in the other direction. Blue was surprised to see Jack come back out so quickly, not to mention all by himself.

"Jack? What is it? What's wrong?" he asked. Jack just waved him off and kept walking down the bridge that led out over the edge of the city. He walked past the Rededication Day headstone and all the way out to the very tip of Empire City and the Imagine Nation.

If anyone were to ask him where he thought he was going, he would have said he didn't know. He was walking toward a dead end that hung out over bottomless water-falls running down to the depths of the sea. He just went as far as he could go. As far as he could get away from people in general. He stopped at the end of the path in front of the giant monument to Legend. The blue flame that Chi had lit on Rededication Day was still burning in the statue's palm.

Jack stared up at the monument. This was a real hero, he thought. This was the man who twelve years ago had stopped Jack before he had killed everyone in the city. Twelve years ago, Legend had ended Jack's future life for the first time. Jack shook his head. There was no way around it. Legend was dead. He had been killed by Revile, killed by Jack's future self. That had to mean it was real. The future was hard to deny once you'd seen it face-to-face and it had tried to kill you.

Suddenly, red energy particles began to swirl about and Stendeval materialized, floating in the air with his legs folded. Jack didn't turn around to look at him. He just told Stendeval that he couldn't do it. He couldn't go back in there. Stendeval didn't argue. He nodded and lowered himself down to the ground. He stood beside Jack, staring up at the monument of Legend. "So, that's it?" Stendeval asked Jack. "You're leaving?"

Jack nodded. "Yup." He actually hadn't thought that far ahead, but it seemed like the thing to do.

"I see," Stendeval said, disappointed. "Just like that? I can't change your mind? I thought you wanted to stay and find out who you are."

Jack let out a gruntlike laugh, like Stendeval didn't know what he was saying. "I already know who I am," Jack said. "I don't need you to tell me that anymore."

"I see," Stendeval said, nodding. "However, I don't recall ever saying that I was going to tell you who you were. I believe I told you to have patience," he said. "I seem to remember saying that one day *you* would tell *me* the answer to that question."

Jack remembered. "Right. Whatever. The point is, now I know."

"So? Tell me, then. Who are you?"

"I . . . it's complicated," Jack stammered. "I just know I don't belong here. I'm not meant to be here."

"There's nowhere you can be that isn't where you're meant to be. A young English songwriter once told me that."

"Well, he was wrong," Jack said bitterly.

Stendeval shrugged. "Most people would disagree. That songwriter and his friends became quite popular. They did very well for themselves."

Jack wasn't paying attention to Stendeval. He already had his mind made up. "I don't belong here," he said angrily. "Your school is a place for heroes. A better tomorrow, you said. I'm not going to be a hero."

"Really?" Stendeval asked. "You know this for a fact?"

"Actually, I do."

"How interesting," Stendeval replied, rubbing his chin. "Well, if that is what you think, then you are probably correct. It is your decision, after all. But I'm going to let you in on a little secret, Jack. There's an entire city behind me that thinks you're a hero right now."

Jack looked back at the crowd that filled Hero Square. He was not moved by it. "They've been wrong before too," he said. "You really want to know what I am? What I'm going to be?" Stendeval waited. Jack tried to tell him, but he just couldn't seem to spit it out just yet. "I'm . . . I'm exactly what you were describing in there. I'm a villain! The worst villain ever!"

"You know, a wise Mecha once told me that 'hero' and 'villain' are words that get overused sometimes. That some so-called villains are just people who are misunderstood."

"I know what Jazen said, and there's no misunderstanding with me. I killed thousands of people. More than that, even! Way more! Everyone here! The whole Earth!"

Stendeval looked at Jack like he was speaking in tongues. "You did?" he asked, confused. He looked out at the gorgeous sunset lighting the sky against the open sea. The whole Earth seemed just fine for the moment. "When did you do all that?"

Jack rolled his eyes at Stendeval. "I didn't do it yet . . . I'm *going* to do it."

Stendeval pondered Jack's answer with a very serious look on his face. He thought about it long and hard before finally asking, "Why?"

All the questions were getting Jack frustrated. "I don't *want* to do it," he said. "I don't have a choice. It's what my future is. Revile told me. I told me." Jack decided it was time to come clean and say it. It would feel good to say it. "I'm him!" he told Stendeval. "Revile! I grow up to be him."

Stendeval pursed his lips and looked at Jack. "I know," he said.

Jack stared at Stendeval like he had thirteen and a half heads. "*You know?*"

Stendeval just shrugged. "I know," he said nonchalantly. "That is to say . . . I know that Revile is one *possible* future for you."

"Possible!" Jack shook his head. "I saw it. I talked to it. He was here, Stendeval. I met the future. It was me. It had my face! And what do you mean, you know? How could you know?"

"It began during the Battle of Empire City," Stendeval said, "and if you calm down, I will tell you about it." Jack took a deep breath. His patience was just as short as it ever was, but he held his tongue and let Stendeval speak. Stendeval waited until Jack was fully ready to listen, and then continued.

"Twelve years ago, the Rüstov attacked," Stendeval said, "and Legend and I were right where we belonged—in the thick of the fight, alongside the other heroes of the day, doing our part to turn back the Rüstov invaders. The battle raged on nearly an entire day before we started to gain back any ground against our attackers, but we never gave up. We were just turning the tide when the Rüstov brought out their supersoldier. At least that's what we thought he was at the time. Chance alone placed us in Revile's path when he came hurtling through the sky, tossing Empire City's defenders aside like they weren't even there. He was invincible in battle and unwavering in his focus. Amid the chaos, through the wreckage and the rubble, I saw his target. A lone crying baby lying helpless on a street corner. You."

Stendeval shrugged. "What this creature wanted with an innocent baby, we had no idea, but naturally, Legend and I intervened. As the strongest of Empire City's heroes, it was our duty to take on the strongest of our enemies and protect the weakest of our people. But once we engaged Revile, we found we were too evenly matched. No matter how much damage we inflicted upon him, he regenerated. No matter how many times he knocked us back, we would not relent. In the end, he tried to reason with us. He knew me, and told me I would one day know him as Jack Blank. He told us what had happened to him and what he intended to do. He told us that the baby was him, and that he was here to kill it. That he had come back in time to prevent a dire future and we had to—*had to*—let him go through with it."

"Why didn't you?" Jack asked Stendeval, somewhat miffed.

Stendeval laughed at Jack's question. "You were a baby. You never hurt anyone. How could we stand by and let that happen to you?" Stendeval shook his head. "We couldn't do that. Legend told me to get you out of there. That he would hold off Revile. I didn't like leaving friends in danger, but I was low on power from the battle. I had only enough energy left to escape with the baby. With you, Jack. I was the one who hid you in that orphanage in New Jersey. I hid you far away where no one would ever look. And I stayed out there, watching over you."

"At St. Barnaby's?" Jack asked. "Where were you?"

"I was never far," Stendeval said. "Who do you think donated all those comic books to St. Barnaby's in the first place? I used my powers to keep you hidden from any prying eyes until the time was right for you to come home. I knew that Empire City wouldn't be safe for an infected child after the invasion . . . so I kept you hidden and wrote

Circleman Chi to expect us back in twelve years' time."

Jack was baffled by Stendeval's tale, as well as his actions. "Why?" he asked. "Why bring me back? Why now?"

"Because the time for me to make decisions for you is now past. You are old enough to decide your own future. You are old enough to learn how to protect yourself. It is up to you to decide if you will become Revile or something else. You can choose your own path. I stopped hiding you at age twelve and wrote to Emissary Jazen Knight, telling him where to look for you. Now here we are."

"Jazen," Jack said, remembering the rest of the problem. "You don't know about Jazen! The Rüstov were using him against me and he didn't even know it. They have another virus. A computer virus that lets them control the Mechas. That's how they got to Silico back during the invasion. He didn't know what he was doing either!"

"Another virus?" Stendeval repeated, leaning in toward Jack with a concerned look.

"The Rüstov aren't through with us," Jack told Stendeval. "They're coming back, and when they do, they're going to use the Mechas against us to get here. Innocent Mechas who don't even know they're infected."

Stendeval took a moment to think about what Jack was telling him. He looked surprised, but he didn't appear to doubt Jack's word for a moment.

"This is very serious, Jack," Stendeval said, still turning the matter over in his head. "It seems to me we're going to have a need for a hero who can talk to machines. Someone who can find out which Mechas are infected and help cure them. Someone who has experience in resisting the Rüstov infection."

"I can't cure anyone," Jack said. "I can't save anyone. Jazen was my best friend and I couldn't save him!"

"All the more reason for you to stay here and train in our school," Stendeval replied.

"No way," Jack said. "The more I learn, the stronger Revile is going to be one day," he warned Stendeval. "I've already learned too much."

"And now it is time for the greatest test of your life to begin," Stendeval replied. "I meant what I said back in the sphere, Jack. Our combined might could not stop Revile, but you can. As for becoming him . . ." Stendeval waved his hands. "You're thinking about this all wrong. Do you remember our first lesson? Do you remember what I asked you up on the Cloud Cliffs?"

Jack thought back to that first day at Mount Nevertop. He remembered being afraid to walk on the floating stones, then finding out that he already was. "You asked me if I had known the road ahead, would I have walked the same path," Jack said.

"Exactly," Stendeval said. "I ask you once again. You have seen the road ahead. You know where it leads. Will you still choose to walk it?"

Jack thought about that for a minute. "No," he said.

"But now you know you could," Stendeval replied. "That is all. Jack, just because you know something can happen doesn't mean that it must happen. It is good that you learned Revile's true identity. It is. You must be aware of all possibilities before you, but Revile's past is not necessarily your future. As I told you on Mount Nevertop, the path you choose to follow is your own. You are stronger than the Rüstov, Jack."

"Today, maybe," Jack said. "What about tomorrow?"

"Tomorrow will be what you want it to be. I do believe the Rüstov will bring war back to Earth, and you may very well be the key to its outcome, but it doesn't have to be in the way they think. You must prepare to overcome that which is the worst in you—this dire future of yours. It is a great burden, of that there is no question, but the future is not written. It lies in the choices you make. Our future is ours to decide. Always."

"You really believe that?" Jack asked. "Even with everything we've seen?"

"I know it," Stendeval replied, steadfast in his opinion.

Jack couldn't believe what he was hearing. As usual, life in the Imagine Nation never ceased to amaze him. "You really want me to stay here?" Jack asked. "Really?"

"Where else would you want to go?" Stendeval replied. "You came here to find a home. You came here to find your family. Look around you. You have both. This is your home. Those people over there . . . they are your family." Jack looked down the path and saw the others waiting for him underneath the sphere. Blue, Allegra, Skerren . . . they all hung back watching Jack and Stendeval with concerned eyes. "Of course I want you to stay, Jack, but the choice still has to be yours. You have to decide those things for yourself. A better tomorrow is always possible, but as we say in the Imagine Nation, you must believe in it to get there."

Jack held back tears. Stendeval knelt down and put a hand on his shoulder.

"For all its wonders, Jack," Stendeval began, "this is not a perfect world. A perfect world would be easy. A paradise that requires no further input from us. That is not the Imagine Nation. Imagination is ever changing and never static. It is always in motion and in constant flux. Imagination is like the future—uncertain. If this place . . . if the Imagine Nation is to be a perfect home for you, then you must make it so. Do you understand what I'm trying to tell you?"

Jack looked down at an inscription written on a pedestal at the foot of the monument. The words were familiar to him. They read:

Never underestimate the power you have over what happens today. Never forget the power today has over tomorrow.—Legend

"I think I do," Jack said.

"By your actions today, you have already met Jazen Knight's definition of a hero," Stendeval said, looking down at Jack. "Your actions *tomorrow* will decide if that continues to be the case. So, tell me again who you really are. Tell me for today and tell me for tomorrow."

Jack wiped his tears away and took a deep breath. "I'm Jack Blank," he said. "I'm not Revile, I'm not a Rüstov . . . and I'm not going to be either," he continued with conviction. "I'm going to be whatever I want."

"And what is that?" Stendeval asked.

"I want to be a hero," Jack answered. "A real hero. Like Jazen."

Stendeval smiled.

"Well, then, young hero, it seems to me that you have quite a future in store for yourself after all. There is much work to be done before you get there." He reached out his hand to Jack. "Let us begin."

ACKNOWLEDGMENTS

Fourteen years ago I sat on a picnic blanket with my wife and told her all about this great idea I had called the Imagine Nation. For two full hours I gave her a long and incoherent, yet painfully detailed description of this story. By the time I was done, my car had a parking ticket, and the only person who had any idea what I was talking about was me. But she listened to every word, told me it sounded great, and said I should write it. If that's not love, I don't know what is.

This story has changed in a million different ways since that day, and I have to say it's a relief to finally get it out of my head and down on paper once and for all. I don't have to memorize the details and tell them—or more accurately, ramble on about them—to anyone ever again.

It's all neatly packaged together in the collective pages of this book, which you would not be holding if not for some truly fantastic people, whom I would like to thank here:

Emil K. Hemsey and Joe Buoye, who read the very first draft of this book and told me straight up what needed fixing. This story is a better one because of them.

Superagent Chris Richman, who read that draft and then helped me take it to the next level, a feat he followed up by helping me achieve my lifelong dream of getting published.

My editor, Liesa Abrams, whose passion and excitement for this story was evident from the start and made her an absolute joy to work with.

My mom and dad, whose love and care in raising me gave me every opportunity in the world and made everything I have possible.

And finally, my beautiful wife, Rebecca, who believed in me from day one, and my son, Jack, who inspired me before he even got here, and whose arrival kicked off the greatest adventure of my life.

From the bottom of my heart, thank you all so very much.